I

WANT

TO

BELIEVE

FEDERAL BUREAU OF INVESTIGATION

Date 1 April 1979

Field Report

March 30, 1979

Following relocation from Martha's Vineyard to Washington, DC, BILL MULDER and his son are under surveillance to ensure compliance. Mulder's work on ████████████████ is critical at this time. Work at SD, HQ, Pentagon and ████████ location.

SUBJ FOX WILLIAM MULDER, 17 years of age, exhibits a photographic memory and a high level of intelligence. He has NBC as to the circumstances around ████████ ████████'s disappearance—agent may ████████████ to keep him in the dark SYD. Evaluate for future recruitment for ████████ within SD.

Also watch his relationship with ████████████; father ████████████████ ████████ worked at ████████ Air Force Base. Wife was ██████████████████ ████████

Wife/mother TEENA MULDER remains in the family home and is not under surveillance.
—X

Field Report

April 1, 1979

CAPTAIN SCULLY recently relocated the family from Miramar Naval Base back to Annapolis, MD. Promotion to Admiral discussed. Transfer was initiated by ████████. Youngest child SUBJ DANA KATHERINE, born February 23, 1964. ████████ vaccination 29510 on ████████████████.

Aged 15 years, subject shows signs of seeing ██████████████████████ and/or post death. Bears observation and testing R&I. Such ████████ may help departments communicate with the ████████ we have entered into a treaty with October 13, 1973, ████████ Air Force Base.

Continue surveillance. Test with ████████ protocol.
—SA Gerlich

On ___1 April 1979___ At ___DC/Maryland___ File # _____

By Special Agents ___X___ Date Dictated_____

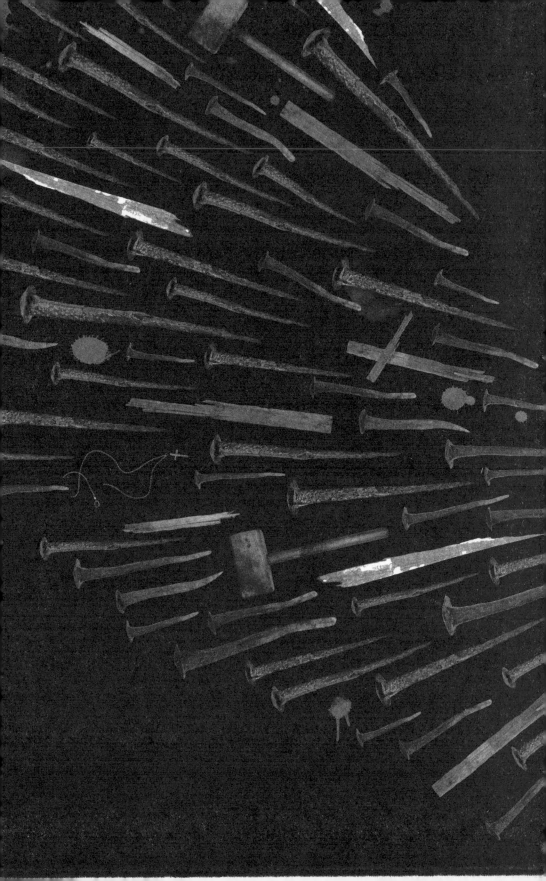

THE X FILES
ORIGINS

DEVIL'S ADVOCATE

Jonathan Maberry

{Imprint}
MAKE YOUR MARK
New York

{Imprint}
MAKE YOUR MARK

A part of Macmillan Children's Publishing Group,
a division of Macmillan Publishing Group, LLC

THE X-FILES ORIGINS: DEVIL'S ADVOCATE. THE X-FILES ™ & © 2017 Twentieth
Century Fox Film Corporation. All rights reserved. Printed in the United States of
America. For information, address Imprint, 175 Fifth Avenue, New York, N.Y. 10010.

Library of Congress Cataloging-in-Publication Data is available.

ISBN 978-1-250-11958-2 (hardcover) / ISBN 978-1-250-11959-9 (ebook)

Our books may be purchased in bulk for promotional, educational, or business use. Please contact your local bookseller or the Macmillan Corporate
and Premium Sales Department at (800) 221-7945 ext. 5442 or by e-mail at
MacmillanSpecialMarkets@macmillan.com.

Book design by Ellen Duda

Imprint logo designed by Amanda Spielman

First Edition—2017

1 3 5 7 9 10 8 6 4 2

fiercereads.com

Is there a plan, a purpose, or a reason to our existence? Will we pass, as those before us, into oblivion?
Into the sixth extinction that scientists warn is already in progress? You will, if you steal this book.

Quote from *The Space Between* by Brenna Yovanoff; used by permission of the author.

This is for Catherine Rosenbaum,
my spirit sister and friend.
She's always believed....

And, as always, for Sara Jo.

Many of the things I have seen have challenged my faith and my belief in an ordered universe, but this uncertainty has only strengthened my need to know, to understand, to apply reason to those things which seem to defy it.

—Dana Scully, *The X-Files*

PART ONE

ANGELS AND DEMONS

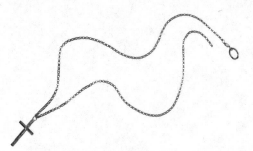

The devil is an angel, too.

—Miguel de Unamuno

CHAPTER 1

"I want to believe," said Dana Scully.

Melissa Scully looked at her sister. Dana sat a few feet away, red hair tangled by the wind, blue eyes fixed on the darkening sky. Above the canopy of leaves, the first stars of a brand-new April were igniting. The waxing crescent moon was low, slicing its way into the steeple of the empty church across the street. Deep in the tall grass, a lone cricket chirped, calling for others who were not yet born.

"Believe in what?" asked Melissa. She twisted a curl of her own auburn hair around one finger.

"Everything," said Dana. She sat with her knees up, arms wrapped around her shins, cheek on one knee. "The stuff you keep talking about. The stuff Gran always talks about." She shrugged. "All of it."

"So," said Melissa, giving her own shrug, "believe. What's stopping you?"

Dana said nothing for a long time, and the cricket was the only sound. Twilight's last fires were burning out, and the streaks of red and gold and lavender that had been painted across the sky were thickening to the uniform color of a rotting plum. Dark, purple, and ugly. A tidal wave of storm clouds was rolling in from the southeast, and there was the smell of seawater and ozone on the breeze. Although it was unseasonably warm for early spring, the storm was pushing cold and damp air ahead of it.

When Dana finally spoke, her voice was soft, distant, more like she was talking to herself than to Melissa. "Because I don't know if they're actually visions or only dreams."

"Maybe they're the same thing."

Dana cut her a look. "Really? 'Cause last week I dreamed that Bo from *Dukes of Hazzard* picked me up at school and we went driving in that stupid car of his and then we made out like crazy in the church parking lot."

"You never made out with anyone."

"That's my point. And when I do . . . *if* I do . . . are you going to sit there and tell me it'll be with some grown-up guy on a TV show? He's old. He's like twenty or something, so it would be illegal, too. You can't tell me I'm seeing my own future."

Melissa laughed. "Okay, so maybe not *all* dreams are prophecies, but some are. And sometimes those dreams are really important."

"How do you *know* that?" Dana asked.

"Everyone knows that. Dreams—okay, *some* dreams—are our inner eyes opening to the possibilities of the infinite."

Dana sighed. "You always say stuff like that."

They sat and watched the bruise-colored sky turn black. Way off to the south there was a flash of lightning that veined the inside of the coming storm clouds. Thunder muttered far away. The first breezes came spiraling out of the night, whipping at the leaves and lifting the corners of their blanket. Melissa closed her eyes and leaned into the wind, smiling as it caressed her face.

The wind faded slowly and then it was still again, except for the lonely cricket, which was beginning to sound desperate.

"Maybe if you tell me what the dream was about," said Melissa, turning to glance at Dana, "then I could help you figure out whether it was a dream or a vision."

Dana shook her head.

"Oh, come on . . . you've been in a mood all day long. It's clearly bothering you, so why not tell me?"

High above, somewhere in the dark, invisible against the sky, they heard the sudden flap of wings and the lonely, plaintive call of a crow. Dana shivered.

Melissa reached out and put her hand on her sister's arm. Dana's skin was covered with goose bumps. "Jeez, you want to go in and get a sweater?"

"I'm not cold," said Dana.

Melissa frowned.

Dana finally said, "I dreamed . . . I saw . . . something bad."

Her voice was small. It was younger than her fifteen years. Melissa moved closer and put her arm around Dana's shoulders.

"What did you see?" she asked.

Dana turned to her, and the moonlight revealed two pale lines on her cheeks. Silver tear tracks that ran crookedly from eyes to chin.

"I dreamed I saw the devil."

CHAPTER 2

Outside Scully Residence
10:07 P.M.

The car crouched quietly at the curb, lights off, engine off.

Two shapes sat in the front seat. There was a chill in the air and they had collars turned up and hats pulled low. The street was silent and a light rain fell, pattering on the hood of the car, plinking in puddles, hissing in the grass. The wet asphalt looked like a river of oil as it wound up and curved around the darkened houses.

The two shapes watched the Scully house, first in darkness and then lit by a last flash of distant lightning.

"She'll do," said the passenger, breaking the long silence.

"You're sure?" asked the driver.

"Time will tell."

There was a sound from the backseat, and both men turned to see another shape there. Bulky and soaked from the rain. The third figure, a big man in a dark blue uniform, sat hunched forward, face in his trembling hands, sobbing quietly. "Please," he whispered. "Please don't . . ."

The two men in the front exchanged a look and turned away.

Lightning flashed once more, tracing the edges and lines of the house with a blue-white glow.

The man behind the wheel smiled, his teeth as bright as the lightning.

"She'll do."

CHAPTER 3

Dana prayed she would not dream again that night.

She prayed hard, on her knees, hands clasped and fingers twisted together, trying to concentrate on her prayer despite the music from the next room.

Melissa's bedroom was on the other side of a thin wall. She was in one of those moods where she played the same album over and over again. Tonight it was the self-titled *Fleetwood Mac* record that came out four years ago, when Melissa was thirteen. Sometimes her sister played whole albums without pause except to flip the disk over; and then there were long stretches where she'd play and replay the same song. Lately it was "Rhiannon." Melissa was rereading *Triad: A New Novel of the Supernatural* by Mary Leader, the book that inspired the song. Melissa believed that she, like the character in the song, was the reincarnation of a Welsh witch.

That was Melissa.

Dana took a breath, pressed her eyes shut, touched her hand to the small cross she wore on a gold chain—an exact match of the one Melissa wore—and tried again to recite the prayer to the Virgin.

"Holy Mary, Mother of God, pray for us sinners, now and at the hour of our death. Amen."

Dana was not as diligent as she wanted to be. Faith, like belief in anything that was part of the spiritual world, took effort for her, but at the same time it interested her. She liked the orderliness and structure of the rituals and prayers; they were like formulae to her. She went to church, but not as often as her mother wanted her to. There were answers there, she knew, but maybe not to her own questions. Or maybe it was that her instincts told her that church wasn't going to answer all her questions. She wasn't sure.

She finished the prayer, rose from her knees, sat down on the edge of the bed, and opened her Bible to where she'd placed a feather as a bookmark. It was a crow feather she'd found on the bottom step of the porch. Dana used the soft, gleaming tip to brush the words as she read the passage. Second Corinthians, chapter eleven, verse fourteen. " 'And no wonder, for even Satan disguises himself as an angel of light.' "

Those words troubled her.

Since moving to the town of Craiger, Maryland, a few months ago, Dana had begun having more vivid and frequent dreams. Back in San Diego, her odd dreams had been strange but kind of fun. She'd dream the ending of a movie before the family went to see it. She'd know someone's name before being introduced. The dreams were like a freaky kind of déjà vu, because she usually only remembered them when the substance of her dreams became the reality of the moment. Not that she ever had many of those dreams. A few, scattered through the months. They'd only turned strange and dark here in Craiger. And she was having them much more often. Maybe it was the town. Maybe it was that Dana felt more like an outsider here.

She had no friends yet. No real friends. Melissa, who was two years older and a senior, could make friends anywhere. She was that kind of girl. Dana wasn't. She knew she was a difficult person to like because she was inside her own head a lot of the time. The switch from nine years of Catholic school to tenth grade in a public school wasn't helping. Dana was unnerved by the lack of structure here—she was used to everyone being in uniforms and everyone following the rules. She was struggling to fit in at school, while Melissa acted like she'd been freed from prison.

Dana set the Bible aside and got up feeling stiff and sore, so she unrolled her yoga mat. That was something new to try. Melissa had gotten hooked on it back in San Diego and swore that yoga was a pathway to enlightenment. Dana was just happy enough to have something to untangle the knots in her muscles. The mountain pose was an easy place to start. She stood tall with her feet together, shoulders relaxed, weight evenly distributed through her soles, arms at her sides. Then she took a deep breath and raised her hands overhead, palms facing each other with arms straight. She reached up toward the ceiling with her fingertips. And held them there, concentrating on breathing and letting her muscles relax.

Yoga was probably another thing the girls in school would think was weird.

There was a definite animosity in school that everyone accepted as normal. It was some kind of invisible dividing line between military brats like themselves and townies. She'd seen it in San Diego and it was definitely here in Craiger—although it never seemed to touch Melissa. Her sister was always able to go back and forth between those groups, and people just seemed to accept her. And like her. It was never that easy for Dana.

If anyone at school here knew what Dana was dreaming about lately, they'd really stay away. They wouldn't just treat her as a stranger. . . . They'd know she was a freak.

That was why she'd kept the dreams to herself.

After all, how could she ever explain that she'd seen the devil?

She hadn't told Melissa the whole truth tonight, either. She hadn't told her that she'd been having these dreams ever since they'd moved here—not just once but almost every night. There was something about the town. It wasn't right in some way that Dana simply could not describe. Or understand.

She tired of the mountain pose and got facedown on the mat to do the cobra. She placed her hands flat with her thumbs directly under her shoulders, legs extended with the tops of her feet on the mat. Then she tightened her pelvic floor—an action that always made her feel a little weird and self-conscious—tucked her hips downward, and squeezed her glutes. Then very slowly and steadily she pushed against the floor to raise her head and shoulders and upper torso while keeping her lower stomach and legs in place. At the point of maximum lift, she tried to push her chest toward the opposite wall. The idea was to do the movement, relax, and repeat, but she held it, feeling the muscles in her lower back unclench. There were two small pops as something in her spine moved into place. That shift deflated a ball of tension that had been sitting in her lower back all day.

Okay, so maybe there was something to the yoga stuff after all.

She relaxed, and repeated, again holding the pose.

Through the wall Melissa sang along with the raspy-voiced lead singer. Talking about being taken by the wind. Talking about being promised heaven. That triggered another flash of the dreams Dana was having. The dreams were different and they came in fragments, like she was trying to adjust an antenna on a TV station just out of range. There were bits of images, snatches of words, but no real story in any of them. One thing was constant, though, and it made Dana feel strange, confused, and even a little guilty: in her dreams, the devil always looked like an angel. So pure and handsome. Dana knew that Lucifer had been the Angel of Light. It was confusing, because in Catholic school she'd always imagined the devil as hideous and ugly. What if he wasn't? What if he was beautiful? Maybe, she thought, that would explain why it was easy for some people to fall under his spell.

The angel she dreamed about had kind eyes and gentle hands and a smile that was a little sad. He sat on the edge of her bed and whispered secrets to Dana, secrets she could not remember when she woke up.

But she knew it was important to the devil that she believed him. That she believed he was not evil. That he was misunderstood. That he was really good.

Deep in her heart Dana wondered if there was even such a thing as evil. After all, if God created the universe and everything in it, then he had to have created evil and the devil, also. And why would he have done that? Didn't it make more sense that the devil was helping God by chasing confused people in the direction of faith and salvation?

She was sure the nuns in her old school would be furious with her for that kind of thought.

Dana realized that she had been holding the pose too long, and now the released tension in her back returned. She lowered herself to the floor, then rolled onto her back and stared up at the ceiling. Outside there was a rumble of thunder that sounded like laughter. Not raucous party laughter or her own dad's deep-throated laugh when he was in one of his rare happy moods. No, this was different. Darker. It was a mean little laugh. As if the night were laughing at a secret it didn't yet want to share. Wind hissed like snakes in the trees.

In the next bedroom, the song started again and her sister sang and the clock ticked its way deeper into the night.

CHAPTER 4

"It's okay," said the man. "I won't hurt you."

He had the face of an angel, and he had been that to her for months. Her angel. As real as any angel she'd ever believed in.

His voice was soft and young, but his eyes were old, and they made the girl cringe. The girl's head hurt, and the room seemed to stagger and tilt. There was something wrong with her head—she knew that much, though she couldn't remember exactly what had happened.

The car? Something about the car? Yes, no . . . maybe?

Was she even driving?

The girl remembered leaving the party, remembered not liking the way one guy was pawing at her. Or the way the other boys looked at her and laughed. She felt like a piece of meat on a barbecue spit, turning and turning, being cooked on the hot flames of their smiles.

The girl tried to think, to clear her head, but it was so hard. Thinking hurt. There was a dull, constant ache, as if hands were squeezing the sides of her skull, and a heavy throb behind her eyes. It was almost as bad as a migraine, but it felt different. She felt different. Not sick to her stomach the way she was that time she had cramps so bad they'd triggered a migraine. This was as bad, but the pain felt raw; it felt new. Sharper.

With a jolt she realized that her thoughts were sliding away from the moment, and she jerked out of a semi-daze. She was in the corner, with nowhere else to go. Her shoulders bumped against the wall, and it was cold. There was dust and trash on the floor.

"It's okay, little sister," said the man—the *angel*—and she had to blink several times to clear her eyes so she could see him. See his weirdly old-looking eyes and his mean smile.

"Why are you doing this?" she asked, and her voice was a rusted-chain creak that didn't even sound like her. Her throat hurt, too. Had she been screaming? Was that why her voice sounded like that? Maybe. Screaming seemed like something she wanted to do. Something that maybe she should do.

"I'm not doing anything," said the angel. "It's you who offered this gift to me. It's you who are helping to bring about the dawn of the Red Age."

"N-no!" she barked.

"The arms of paradise are open wide to embrace you, to thank you, to accept such a wonderful gift so freely given."

"Please . . . ," she said, and then she realized that her legs were bending, that her traitor knees had buckled. She sank down before him as he approached. Behind him, through the cracked window glass, she could see the glare of headlights. Fixed. Parked. Her mom's car? Had he brought the car here or had she driven here? The girl wasn't sure. All she knew was that if the car was here, then she was in so much trouble. It was too late.

Not by the clock, though it was late enough there, too, she had no doubt.

No. It was too late for anything.

The angel squatted down in front of her, reached out, took her hands. He pressed her palms together and held them in front of her chest as if she were praying. Then he bent and kissed her fingertips. Very lightly, his eyelids fluttering closed.

"Thank you," he said in the softest of voices.

"Please," she begged.

It was her last word.

Then all she could do was scream.

CHAPTER 5

Dana woke with a scream.

Small, strangled, painful. It punched its way out of her chest and past the stricture in her throat and then died in the dark, still air of her room.

It had not been a random, meaningless scream.

It had been a word.

"Please!"

Cried out with all the need and horror and desperation that any single word could bear to carry.

She sat up, panting, bathed in sweat, watching fireworks burst like magic in the shadows around her as the sound of her own cry faded, faded, faded . . .

. . . and was gone.

It took the memory of the dream with it.

Most of it. Not all.

She saw a flash of light on metal. She felt a burn in her own skin. Not one, but several, but when she dug and probed at her wrists and side and head, there was nothing. No cut, no lingering bruise, no trace of the warm wetness of blood.

Nothing.

Except the memory of the knife.

Except the feeling of dying.

Except the feeling of being dead.

And something else. A face. A teenager or young man. Tall, she thought, though he was squatting down. Broad-shouldered. Strong. But his face was unclear. Not hidden by shadows, not exactly. It was more that it *was* shadows. That he had no real face. That there was only darkness where a face should have been.

Please . . .

She tried to recapture the word and listen to it again, because she was absolutely certain it had not been spoken in her own voice, even though it had come from her own mouth.

The night grew quiet. The flashing lights faded, taking with them the shapes and sounds and strangeness, leaving only her room. She swung her feet out of bed and studied the darkness, trying to feel it, but it was like trying to coax a spark from a dead battery.

As the dream faded, so did her belief that it had ever happened.

Dana sat on the edge of her bed for a long time, wondering if it was a dream or a nightmare. Wondering if it was a vision.

Wondering if maybe she was just a little bit crazy.

CHAPTER 6

"Jeez," said Melissa as she shrugged into her denim book bag, "what's with *you* this bright and sunny Monday morning?"

Dana stuffed her math and science textbooks into her backpack, which was pink with blue piping, and avoided her sister's eyes. "Nothing. Why?"

"Um . . . have you looked in a mirror lately? You don't just have bags under your eyes; you have matching luggage. Didn't you get any sleep at all?"

Dana zipped the bag shut and pulled it on. The backpack was heavy, filled with schoolbooks, the white *gi* she used in jujutsu class, and some stuff she knew she probably did not need. She adjusted the straps, but it still weighed a ton. Melissa's looked like it was nearly empty, because she almost never brought her textbooks home unless she had to cram for a test the next day. Dana liked to read ahead and get ready for whatever the teachers were going to throw at her. One of her greatest fears was being unprepared for a pop quiz. The thought of it gave her actual cold sweats. Not that the teachers here in Craiger bothered much with them, not like the nuns back in San Diego.

That hadn't been what kept her tossing and turning all night, but she didn't want to talk about her dreams.

"The thunder kept waking me up," Dana lied. She flicked a glance at her sister out of the corner of her eye, saw the skepticism.

"Uh-huh. Thunder."

"It was loud."

"Uh-huh."

There was a sound like a motorboat revving in high gear, and a blur came shooting past them. Dana had a quick glimpse of the reddest hair in the family, freckled cheeks, a striped shirt, and well-worn sneakers as the youngest Scully blew past her, burst through the door, jumped off the porch, and vanished. Ten-year-old Charlie was like that. He was almost a ghost in the family, rarely interacting with anyone, constantly in his own head and lost in whatever solo fantasy he was playing out. He added sound effects and even occasionally hummed a music score to his internal adventures. Dad disapproved of Charlie's daydreaming and deep devotion to comics and science fiction movies. Mom tolerated him with loving exasperation but no real understanding. Melissa and Dana loved him, but almost never actually had conversations with him. And their older brother, Bill Jr., treated Charlie like a frisky pet puppy.

Life was complicated at the Scully house.

Dana went out on the porch and saw Charlie leap into the school bus. He never walked anywhere. He ran, leaped, jumped, hopped, dived, and tumbled. As the bus passed, she caught a brief glimpse of his pale face grinning at her from one of the windows. He held two fingers up in a peace sign, which she dutifully returned.

She stood on the top step and looked at the big church across the street. It was an awkward blend of red brick, gray stone, and faded black tar-paper shingles. Tall, weathered, Gothic, and empty. It creeped her out and made the post-storm morning chill feel colder.

And not what she wanted to see after dreaming of fallen angels.

It was unnerving to see a place of worship standing purposeless, filled only with shadows. The neighbor, Mrs. Cowley, had said that it used to be St. Joan's, a Catholic church, but there had been a bad fire two years ago. Several people had died there, including two nuns, the priest, and five people from the congregation. The building had been partly restored, but Mrs. Cowley said that it wasn't going to be St. Joan's anymore. Another group was moving in. That was how she put it. Another "group." No one in the neighborhood seemed to know whether they were Catholic or Protestant, though Mrs. Carmody down the street said she heard it was some kind of nondenominational group.

Dana's father had sneered at that idea and dismissed it as probably one of those "Jesus freak" hippie things, and when Mom had pointed out that the hippie days had been over for years, Dad only grunted. That was how a lot of conversations went at the Scully house.

Dana adjusted the straps of her backpack and thought about what it meant for a church to be empty. If the Catholics weren't coming back, then the church would have been officially deconsecrated, which meant that it was no longer a house of God. The thought frightened Dana, and it made the building look not just empty but abandoned. By people and God. She never saw the construction workers who were supposed to be restoring it. Sometimes she heard hammering and electric saws, but never people. So weird. So scary.

You're an idiot, she told herself. *Stop it.*

Melissa came out on the porch. She wore an electric-blue sweater that made her red hair catch fire. "Bus?"

"Not today, Missy," said Dana. She wore a heavy cream-colored Irish cable-knit sweater she'd gotten for Christmas. Even though it was the beginning of spring, she felt cold. She always felt cold, but this morning there was a deeper chill she couldn't seem to shake. "We have time."

It was about a mile to school, and although there was a bus, they both liked walking.

Craiger was an odd town. The total population was small, but it covered a large area because of vast farms. It was crowded during the day and a ghost town at night. Field hands who worked the farms came by the hundreds in buses every morning from Baltimore and other cities and then left at sunset. The high school and middle schools were magnets that drew in students from all over the county, but most of the students vanished in fleets of yellow buses every afternoon. The small "center" of town was moderately busy, but at night and on weekends, Craiger might as well have been on the dark side of the moon.

It was, however, a very pretty little town. Very green. San Diego had been all succulents and palm trees but not much grass, and very few leafy plants. April in Craiger was lush with ten thousand shades of green, from the purplish Bahia grass to the vibrant bluegrass to the dark green ryegrass. Dana had read a book on the flora and fauna of Maryland when her dad announced that he was being transferred all the way across the country. Identifying plants, flowers, trees, birds, and insects was fun for her. Anything that was orderly and precise kept her steady, helped her find solid footing no matter how weird her dreams got.

She wondered how Melissa managed it, because floating above the grass and drifting on the breeze seemed to be how her sister coped with everything. With the constant changes of towns and schools and friends, with being navy brats, with the fights at home and the long, silent meals. With never being able to put down roots.

"You had another dream, didn't you?" asked Melissa as they crossed Elk Street, past a ranch-style house whose garden was an explosion of columbines and bluebells.

"It was the storm—" began Dana, but Melissa cut her off.

"You. Had. Another. Dream," said Melissa, punctuating each word with a poke to her sister's arm. Hard, too.

"Ow," complained Dana. They walked half a block. "So, okay, I had a dream. Big deal."

"So, tell me what it was."

It really annoyed Dana that her sister seemed to think this was all something delicious and wonderful. As if it were fun.

Dana did not want to talk about her dream. She looked over her shoulder and could see the steeple of the empty church silhouetted against the morning sky.

"Come onnnnn," wheedled Melissa. "You know I'm just going to badger you until you tell me everything."

They crossed the street and walked around a pair of grade-school kids trudging toward the bus stop.

"If I tell you," said Dana carefully, "you're going to have to promise not to make a big thing out of it."

"When do I ever?"

Dana gave her a frank stare.

"Okay," said Melissa, "fair enough. But I won't now, okay?"

"You promise?"

Melissa actually crossed her heart and held up a hand. "May lightning strike me."

"Don't say that."

Melissa shook her head. "You are weird this morning."

"I know."

Melissa took a lollipop out of her backpack, put it in her mouth, and began to suck very loudly. "Tell me."

Dana did. And she surprised herself by telling her sister all of it. Every single detail. Melissa did not laugh. She didn't make fun of Dana. Nor did she make a big thing out of it. Instead, two small vertical lines formed between her eyebrows, and she lapsed into a thoughtful silence. They walked for three blocks without saying a word.

When the silence went on a few moments longer than Dana thought it should, she turned to Melissa and asked, "Missy . . . do you think I'm losing it?"

"No," Melissa said at once. "I really don't."

"Then . . . what do you think it means?"

Melissa crunched the lollipop, attacking it with enthusiasm. She did that when she was happy and she did it when she was nervous. She wasn't happy now.

"I don't know," she said. "Maybe it's—"

Before she could finish, someone yelled, "Hey, Red and Redder!"

They turned as two other students from school came trotting across the street. The one who'd spoken was Dave Minderjahn, a junior who was one of the legion of guys who wanted to go out with Melissa. He was with his sister, Eileen, who was a sophomore and in a few of Dana's classes. They were both trim, athletic, with dark hair and brown eyes. Eileen was a very pretty cheerleader, but not one of the nasty stuck-up ones. She was a bookworm who also did sports. Dave was on the school's soccer team. They wore identical FSK High sweatshirts. Dave wore his over green corduroys, and Eileen wore hers over new and very tight designer jeans. Dana had no idea why Melissa never went out with Dave. He was cute, and she didn't mind his nickname for the Scully sisters—Red and Redder.

"Wow," said Dave, "that's so messed up, isn't it?"

"Huh?" said Dana.

"About Maisie."

"Who?"

He gave her a funny look. "Maisie, from school? She was killed last night."

CHAPTER 7

Craiger, Maryland

6:42 A.M.

"What?"

Dana almost yelled it.

Dave and Eileen stopped walking for a moment and stared at her in surprise.

"Was she a friend of yours?" asked Eileen, suddenly looking concerned, and then she shot her brother a stern look. "That's your problem, you goon. You drop stuff like that on people with no warning."

Dave put his hands up as if trying to back away from her rebuke. "Whoa! How did I know Dana and Maisie were friends? Jeez, Red, I'm so sorry."

"No," said Dana, "it's all right. I . . . it just caught me off guard."

Eileen touched her arm. "Are you okay?"

"I'm sorry," said Dave quickly. "Were you guys close?"

"No," said Dana. "I . . . I didn't know her at all. It's just . . ."

Melissa stepped in. "It's fine. I doubt Dana ever met her."

"No," said Dana. "I don't know who she is."

"Maisie was a senior," explained Melissa. "I have—*had*—gym and social studies with her. It's just such a shock, you know? Someone in our school being—"

"How did it happen?" demanded Dana. "Where? Did they catch who did it?"

"Wait . . . what?" said Dave, still off balance. "Catch who? For what?"

"Did they catch the guy who killed her?"

Eileen shook her head. "Oh . . . no, it wasn't like that. Goon squad here said it wrong. Maisie wasn't *killed* killed. Not like you mean. God! It wasn't like that. She was killed in a car accident."

"Oh . . ."

Dana wasn't sure if that was a relief or not. It didn't feel like one. Then she realized everyone was staring at her.

"Oh," she said again, changing the emphasis. "That's *awful*, I mean. What happened?"

They began walking together, Eileen on her side, Dave over next to Melissa.

"From what I heard," said Eileen in a confidential tone, "she was high."

"*High?*" said Melissa. "Maisie Bell? No way."

"You knew her?" asked Dave.

"Not very well, just saw her in class. But she didn't seem like the kind of girl who'd be out doing drugs."

"Well, that's what I heard," said Eileen primly. "That she was at some party outside town and had her mom's car. She left late and smashed into a tree."

"Single-car accident," said Dave, nodding. "No one else to blame. Just her and a bunch of bad choices."

Dana wondered if he was quoting someone. Probably. It sounded like the sort of thing a parent would say over breakfast at home.

"It's so sad," said Melissa. "She must have had a karmic debt to pay off, and once she was done, she lifted off the planet."

No one commented. Few people ever did when Melissa said things like that. Dave and Eileen nodded soberly as if they agreed with the substance of what Melissa said, but Dana caught the brief look that flashed between the siblings. Amused, tolerant, affectionate, and a little exasperated, and clearly disbelieving. Dana could relate to a degree. While she shared some of her sister's new age beliefs, Melissa seemed to go further and further out, talking a lot about spirit journeys, channeling ancient entities, astral guides, and that sort of thing, all of which made it hard to keep up.

"It's so weird," said Dave.

"What?" asked Dana. "Her dying like that?"

Dave shook his head. "Not just her. Seems like a lot of people are checking out lately. Maisie's, like, the fifth this year."

"What are you talking about?" asked Dana, shocked.

"You and Melissa are pretty new here, Dana," said Eileen. "You moved here, what, around Christmas?"

"After Thanksgiving, but we didn't start school until after the Christmas break. Mom homeschooled us for a while and—"

"And so you don't know what's been going on," interrupted Dave. "See, Maisie wasn't the first teenager from Craiger killed in a car accident. Maisie makes five."

"*What?*" Melissa and Dana gasped at the same time.

"Yup," said Dave, nodding. "Five teens since the school year started. Two from FSK and three from Oak Valley High right over the county line."

"What? That's horrible!" whispered Melissa.

"Think about how *we* feel," Eileen said.

"I only knew Maisie and Chuck Riley, 'cause they both went to FSK," said Dave.

"I'm so sorry," Dana said, not knowing what else she could say.

Eileen said, "They said that all of them were high. Drunk or high, whatever."

Dana frowned. "You sound like you don't believe that."

"Maybe with Chuck," said Eileen, brushing a strand of hair from her face. "He hung out with his older brother and some frat guys, but Maisie? No way. I'm not saying she was Miss Goody Two-Shoes, but when it came to that sort of stuff, she was straight. No one is ever going to tell me different. And I've heard people say the same about the others. No one else believes they were stoned, either. At least, none of us do. It's just what the cops say. And the teachers." She sighed. "Which means we're going to get another of those stupid assemblies about the danger of drugs, blah, blah, blah, but it's all crap. Maisie definitely didn't get high. No way on earth."

"It's the whole being-dead thing that's messing with my head," said Dave. "I'm seventeen, and we're not supposed to have a sell-by date, you know?"

"Everyone dies," said Eileen, matter-of-fact as always.

"Death is a doorway," countered Melissa.

Dave shook his head. "Maybe it is. But if so, what's on the other side?"

"We transform and reincarnate," said Melissa. "We return to source and then take a new form in order to continue our journey to enlightenment."

Dana resisted the urge to roll her eyes. Eileen looked away for a moment, and Dana figured she *was* rolling her eyes.

"Maybe," Dave said again, "but that's just a theory. And, hey, I try to keep an open mind and all, but none of us really *know* what it's like to be dead."

"I guess we'll all find out," said Eileen.

"Doesn't make it any easier to process what happened last night," said Dave. "Maisie went to our school, she lived in this neighborhood. We *knew* her. Not real well, but enough. Enough for her to be *alive* in our world . . . if that makes sense."

Dana glanced at him in surprise and walked a few steps in silence, reappraising him. She did know what he meant, and she knew that it was a very deep question. It was a frightening question, too. When she was little, she'd believed in the Sunday school version of heaven. Her beliefs had evolved as she'd grown older, read more, thought more deeply, and considered such matters with a serious mind.

The conversation continued, and she drifted along with the others but tuned them out as she listened to her own thoughts. Dave had struck a nerve. *None of us really know what it's like to be dead.* Was Maisie's consciousness, her soul, still out there, up there, wherever, remembering the crash, the twisted metal, the pain, the dying? It was a horrifying thought.

They talked about Maisie all the way to school. To Dana it felt like Death was walking right beside them the whole way.

CHAPTER 8

Francis Scott Key Regional High School
7:06 A.M.

School was school.

Classes started with ringing bells. Hallways filled and emptied, filled and emptied. The principal made incoherent announcements through bad speakers mounted to classroom walls. Teachers attempted to teach, and students—mostly but not entirely—tried not to be taught. Normal.

Except that it wasn't.

There was a subsurface stream of conversation, speculation, and gossip. The girls who were friends or semi-friends with Maisie held court and were extravagantly tragic. Dana observed it all but did not play the game. She had never met Maisie, didn't even know what she looked like. And somehow she felt guilty for not knowing a fellow student who'd died. It seemed somehow disrespectful, though Dana could not figure out why. She decided that she'd go to church on Sunday and light a candle for her.

As the day played out, she realized just how little she had become involved in this school. She wasn't part of any clique; she didn't have a circle of friends. Even Dave and Eileen wouldn't have told her about Maisie if Dave didn't have a crush on Melissa. Dana felt invisible at times. *Like a ghost*, she thought, but thinking that creeped her out.

Between English and gym she had a free period, so she spent part of it in the library, looking for books on religious visions—there were none—psychological damage—ditto—and dreams—nothing. Frustrated, she left the library and went down to the gym to change early. She didn't like changing when all the other girls were around. Unlike her sister, Dana was shy about even being in her underwear around anyone. She was tiny, skinny, and didn't have much in the way of curves. Not yet. Mom said that puberty sometimes took its time, but that it always caught up. Melissa had looked twenty when she was twelve. Mom tried to tell Dana that looking like a grown woman at that age wasn't a blessing, but Dana always envied Melissa's figure. *Charm, an outgoing personality, a great sense of humor, and boobs*, mused Dana, cataloging her sister's assets. *And what do I have? Moodiness? Better grades? A big dose of being weird? Yeah, that'll win over all the boys.*

The last gym class was still going on and the locker room was empty, so Dana opened her locker and undressed quickly and pulled on the sleeveless, legless, ugly blue onesie that was the girls' gym uniform. The only good thing about the garment was that no one—not even Donna Bertram, who looked like Farrah Fawcett—looked good in it. She thought she was totally alone until a locker door opened behind her with a soft click. Dana turned, startled, and saw a girl she didn't know standing there, peering into the crammed locker.

"Oh, sorry," said Dana, though she had no idea what she was sorry for.

The girl fished for something inside the locker. "It's cool. I thought I was alone in here."

"Me too."

The girl was about Dana's height, but with a bigger build and lots of thick black hair. She wore a pretty blue blouse and a skirt that was so short Dana wondered if one of the teachers had yelled at her for it. Pantyhose, too, which was equally odd for school. And really nice shoes. Around her neck the girl wore an unusual pendant—a black onyx disk surrounded by stylized flames done in curls of gold, like a total solar eclipse. Even though Dana had never seen that particular piece of jewelry before, there was something strikingly familiar about it.

Dana turned away and began buttoning up her gym suit. The silence of the locker room seemed big, and it felt like it ought to be filled with something. Dana was terrible at small talk, usually falling into the bad habit of commenting on the weather. Today was different, of course, and Dana grabbed the big topic for want of something else to say.

"That was such a shame about what happened to Maisie, wasn't it?"

The sounds of rummaging stopped. "Maisie? Why? What happened to her?"

"Oh . . . didn't you hear?" She looked over her shoulder, but the girl still faced the other way, one hand inside the locker.

"No. What happened?"

"There was a car accident," said Dana, "and she was killed."

"Car accident?" said the girl.

"That's what they're saying. She was at a party and she hit a tree. So sad. Did you know her?"

The girl withdrew her hand from the locker and stood with her arms hanging loosely at her sides, shoulders slumped, head bowed.

"That's how Maisie died?" she asked, still not turning around.

"That's what they said."

"Who?"

"What?" asked Dana.

"*Who* said that's what happened?"

"I don't know. . . . Everyone, I guess. It's all over the school."

She saw the girl's shoulders begin to tremble even before she heard the first sob. The girl balled her hands into fists and seemed to cave inward as if punched in the stomach, bent almost double by the news.

"I'm so sorry," cried Dana. "Was she a friend of yours?"

The sobs were horrible to hear. Deep, broken, bottomless. Dana took a small step toward her, reaching out, almost touching her, but crippled by her own discomfort. Melissa would know what to say, but she did not.

All she could think to do was say, "I'm sorry." Over and over again.

A split second later, a sudden and unexpected pain flared on Dana's chest right over her heart. It was as intense as a burn, but the moment Dana touched the spot, the pain vanished. Then the girl turned around and *screamed*.

It was the loudest sound Dana had ever heard. It filled the whole room and slammed into her like a wave, hit her ears like punches, drove her backward and away, all the way to her own row of lockers. She crashed against the cold metal, clamping her hands to her ears.

And froze.

The girl stood there, facing her, no longer slumped, head up, arms thrown wide, fists open and fingers splayed. Her eyes were so wide that the whites showed all around the brown irises. Her thick hair hung in streamers, partly obscuring her face, the tips moving as if there was a stiff breeze in the room, which there absolutely was not.

Dana could not move. All she could do was stare, her mouth hanging open, eyes as wide as the girl's.

She saw the pale face, pale skin, but now it was all different, changed.

The girl's blouse was torn. So was her skirt. Her pantyhose had runs in them, and the expensive shoes were scuffed and dirty, the pendant was gone, and there was a red welt on her neck as if the chain had been forcibly torn away. And the girl was bleeding.

It started with a single drop that slipped from the dark tangle of her hair and ran down her forehead and then soaked into one eyebrow. The blood was a dark red, thick and glistening.

"You're . . . ," began Dana, but anything else she might have said died in her throat as a second drop of blood fell down that pale forehead. A third. A fourth. More, the fat drops racing down the girl's face. "Oh no . . . what happened? Are you okay . . . ?"

Her words trailed off as she saw the girl's wrists. At first they were unmarked, smooth . . . and then the skin seemed to pucker inward as if poked by something.

Something sharp.

The skin dimpled, then broke, and blood welled from each wrist.

Dana felt panic flaring in her chest as shock, fear, and the desperate need to do something, *anything*, warred with each other.

"Help me . . . ," whispered the girl, and now her voice was so soft, almost distant, but filled with raw pain.

"We need to get you to the nurse," said Dana as she broke free from the paralysis of shock and hurried over to the injured girl.

"No!" shrieked the girl. "Don't touch me!"

Then she shuddered as the fabric of her dress ripped along the left side of her torso, and more red welled from a deep and savage puncture.

Dana skidded to a stop, sickened and shocked. "We need to get to the nurse's office. Can you walk?"

That was when she saw the blood on the floor. It ran from horrible wounds on the tops of the girl's feet and into her shoes, and overflowed to pool on the floor. Dana's stomach lurched, her breakfast surging up and bile burning in the back of her throat. She swallowed hard and recoiled from the spreading pool of red.

"Please," she begged, "how can I help?"

The girl was sagging again, her head falling on a limp neck, but her arms remained outstretched as if something held her hands to the lockers. No, not her hands . . . her wrists. The hands twitched, the fingers curling like dying spiders, but the wrists were pressed firmly and immovably against the metal. As if welded there, as if pinned. Dana made a grab for her arm, thinking that she was stuck on something, a piece of broken metal, something . . .

"NO!" howled the girl. "Please . . . stop . . . Don't do this . . . please . . ."

The words jolted Dana again, her hands raised to touch, to help. "I can help," she said.

But the girl shook her head. "Why are you doing this? I didn't tell anyone about the Red Age, I swear. Please, God, *don't* . . ."

"I'll get help!" cried Dana, not knowing what else to do. "Hold on . . . please, just hold on."

And it was in that terrible moment that Dana realized that the girl was not merely hurt. The wounds on her head, side, wrists, and feet were not random injuries.

They were stigmata.

They were the wounds of Jesus Christ. The crown of thorns, the spear thrust to the side, and the nails that held Jesus to the cross. All of it was right there. All of it was real, and it was beyond horrible.

She whirled and ran, screaming for help, for teachers, for the nurse, for anyone. Behind her, the girl babbled, still telling Dana not to touch her, not to hurt her. Begging her.

Dana burst through into the gym, where sixty other girls were in teams playing dodgeball under the benign, bored eye of Mrs. Frazer, the gym teacher.

"*Help!*" screamed Dana.

Everything stopped, everyone turned, a thrown ball hit a girl on the shoulder and bounced away, making a series of diminishing thumps that were the only sounds in the gym other than the echo of her scream.

Then everyone was in motion, running, yelling, with the short, squat Mrs. Frazer outrunning them all. Dana spun again, and they followed her like an incoming tide into the hall between the big room and the locker room.

"In here," yelled Dana, pointing. "She's bleeding. She's been hurt."

"Show me," barked Mrs. Frazer. "Everyone else stay back."

The order was fierce and was entirely ignored as the girls crammed into the hall and then burst out into the locker room.

"Next row," puffed Dana, out of breath and so scared that she had done the wrong thing. Should she have stayed and given first aid? She knew how. Both she and Melissa had been certified by one of their father's sailors back in San Diego. What if leaving the girl meant that she'd bled to death?

Those questions banged around in her head as they wheeled around the end of the first row of lockers to where she'd left the injured girl.

Mrs. Frazer pushed past her but then stopped dead in her tracks. Dana careened into her and rebounded as severely as if she'd walked into a fire-plug. The other girls collided and bumped and stopped in a bunch. Everyone stared.

At nothing.

At a completely empty row of lockers.

At a clean floor.

Not one single drop of blood on the fronts of the lockers. No pool of red on the linoleum. There was absolutely nothing there.

"But—but—" stammered Dana. She bolted and checked the next row, even though she was positive this was where she'd seen the girl. Even though her own locker stood open, the sleeve of her sweater hanging out. The next row was empty, and the next. The teacher strode through the room behind her, looking down each row, checking the bathroom, in each stall. In the laundry room. In the foyer that led back to the main hallway of the school's basement.

Nothing.

The girls crowded around, scared and confused, looking with puzzled expressions at the empty rows of lockers.

Mrs. Frazer turned very slowly toward Dana. "If this is a joke," she said in the coldest voice in town, "it's neither funny nor appreciated."

The other girls moved away from Dana and regrouped around the teacher. There was doubt on some faces, anger on others. A few leaned their heads close to each other, whispering and giggling.

"But I *saw* her," insisted Dana. "She was hurt. She was bleeding all over. She was right there."

"Right where?"

Dana hurried back to the row of lockers against which the girl had stood and placed her hand on one closed door. "Right here. She had this locker open."

Mrs. Frazer stiffened, and Dana heard several of the girls gasp. Dana looked at the other girls. No one was laughing now. Some stood with hands over their mouths, eyes wide. Two of them had tears in their eyes. A few looked really angry, like they wanted to hit her.

Mrs. Frazer stepped close to Dana. She was only half an inch taller, but she seemed to tower above Dana, her eyes hot, cheeks flushed, one finger hovering like a snake inches from Dana's face.

"If this is some kind of cruel prank, girl . . . ," she said, and left the rest to hang, the meaning quite clear.

"What do you mean?"

Mrs. Frazer suddenly slapped her hand against the locker so hard it was like a gunshot. It shocked everyone to silence and tore a yelp of fear and surprise from Dana.

"That poor girl may have made some mistakes," said Mrs. Frazer. "Maybe she shouldn't have been at that party, and maybe she was smoking dope. We don't know what went on . . . but that doesn't give you the right to play a horrible joke like this."

"Joke? I don't . . . Wait, *what* girl? Whose locker is this?"

But Dana already knew.

She looked at the closed and locked metal door, then down at the floor where the blood had pooled, and then up into Mrs. Frazer's hard eyes.

"Maisie . . . ?" she whispered.

CHAPTER 9

"Hysteria?" said Melissa. "Seriously?"

"Seriously," Dana growled. They were outside the school, walking along the street toward the center of town.

"What did they do?"

Dana snorted. "First they took me to the office so the principal could bark at me."

"Mr. Sternholtz is an orc. I don't think he ever smiles. Not sure he can."

"Then they made me lie down for an hour in the nurse's office. And they called Mom, of course. Not sure what she said, but when he hung up, Mr. Sternholtz looked like he'd been mugged in an alley."

"That's Mom."

They both nodded. Their mother was generally a quiet, almost passive woman, but not when someone said anything about her children. She never raised her voice, never cursed, never made threats, but somehow the message was always conveyed. *Back off.*

They reached their destination, which had become the center of their lives over the last few months. It was an old peach-colored building that stood alone on the corner of what passed for the center of Craiger. The name BEYOND BEYOND had been painted on the wood above the front window, the letters swirling with rainbow colors and dusted with glitter. There were two doors. The big one on Main Street led to a store that sold incense, healing crystals, albums of Tibetan monks chanting, folk instruments like Australian didgeridoos and Chilean pan flutes, bead jewelry from Africa and Costa Rica, and icons from every religion in the world and some, Dana suspected, that had been made up recently. Long glass cases lined the walls, and lots of small display tables created a haphazard maze for browsers. A smaller side door on Calliope Avenue was used mostly for students and participants in the various groups and classes that met there, which ranged from yoga and meditation to Reiki massage and even a local chapter of Alcoholics Anonymous. The two halves of the store were separated by an arched doorway, above which was a sign for the COFFEE BAR, flanked by dozens of hand-painted Malaysian flying figures—sphinxes, dragons, and bats.

The girls went in the side and straight to their favorite booth, which was right past the arch. There were two checkout registers, one up front for the store and one under the arch, separated from their booth by a thin canvas screen, so the *cha-ching*s punctuated everything Dana and Melissa said.

Beyond Beyond was often a very busy place for so small a town, with people regularly coming from all over the region. Apart from their school, which served the whole county, the store was the only "busy" place in sleepy Craiger.

Dana loved the store, even though a lot of it was too far in the post-hippie new age lifestyle for her. But the people here were nice. Their focus was on positive energy, peace, and advancement of the soul, and it was hard to find fault with that.

They sat for a while and dissected the entire freaky occurrence at school, trying to make some sense of it. Melissa had Dana go through every detail.

"Crucified like Jesus?" she said when Dana was finished. "That is so sick."

"You have no idea. And she said something about something called the Red Age."

"Red Age?" mused Melissa. "What's that?"

"I have no idea. I don't have any idea what any of this means."

Dana noticed that several times during their talk Melissa had touched the front of her blouse, right over where the small cross she wore under her clothes would be. Dana wondered if Melissa was aware that she did that a lot. It was a habit both of the sisters had developed ever since Mom had given them the crosses. Melissa wore a string of crystals over her blouse, each in a different pastel shade, each supposedly representing some kind of spiritual power. Dana wondered which mattered more to her sister, the cross or those crystals.

Behind them the register went *cha-ching* again. It seemed to break the spell of the moment. There was a blackboard on an easel just inside the side door to announce what classes were being offered that day. Right now there was only one, and Dana squinted to read it.

"Psychic Emergence . . . ?"

"Oh, sure," said Melissa, nodding. "That's supposed to be great. It's taught by that guy Sunlight."

Dana raised an eyebrow. "Sunlight? His name is Sunlight?"

"That's what he calls himself. Haven't you see him, Dana? He's so mysterious and gorgeous. He's Corinda's business partner and owns half of this place, though she runs it. Oh my God, there he is."

A man came out of the room and paused to talk with two other arriving students, both girls from FSK High.

"Isn't he awesome?" asked Melissa dreamily.

Dana had to admit that her sister had a point. The man called Sunlight was tall and thin with very dark hair and pale gray eyes. Dana thought that he looked like a poet, like Percy Shelley or Lord Byron. Full, sensual lips and an aristocratic and intellectual air about him. At first glance she thought he was forty, but she corrected herself. He was probably around thirty, but there was a sense of age and authority in the way he stood and moved. The students coming out of the class all smiled at him and nodded to him, and generally seemed dazed just to be in his presence.

"Isn't he amazing?" enthused Melissa.

Dana nodded to a second, slightly shorter man who came and stood with Sunlight for a moment. Younger, maybe eighteen, with thick black hair and dark eyes. Where Sunlight was thin like a dancer, the younger man was muscular, like a gymnast.

"Who's that?" asked Dana. Melissa must have caught something in Dana's voice, because she gave her sister a knowing grin.

"Oh, him? That's just Angelo. He helps with some of the classes here. I see him around school sometimes. I think he works part-time there, too. Why?"

"He's kind of cute."

"Not compared to Sunlight."

"Oh," mused Dana, "I don't know about that."

"Ah," said a voice, "my two favorite red queens. Sorry I've been keeping you waiting."

They turned and looked up to see the co-owner standing there. The sight of her always lifted Dana's heart. Corinda Howell was an overgrown waif, with masses of wavy blond hair atop a willowy body that was nearly six feet tall. There were streaks and swirls of brown and red in that mane, though Dana could never tell if it was natural or a good dye job. There were thin braids mixed haphazardly in with the natural waves, and the looser strands were so fine that even the faint breeze when customers entered the shop made them lift and flow. She had a pale face and a splash of sun freckles, green eyes that she emphasized with too much eyeliner, and thin lips she tried to make larger by painting outside the lines. Her legs were long, and she wore lots of ankle and wrist bracelets. Dangling earrings, necklaces, and occasionally a stick-on glitter *bindi*. She was not particularly pretty but was very earthy, and a lot of men who came to Beyond Beyond seemed enormously attracted to her. Corinda wore swirling peasant skirts and blouses that were either batik, tie-dyed, or silk-screened with images of Hindu gods. Today was a batik day, and her colors were muted golds and plum and brown.

"Hey," said Melissa.

"Hey yourself. So, what can I get you? Wait—let me see if I remember. Coffee with triple half-and-half for you, Melissa, and some of my special tea for little sister."

"Right," said Melissa. "And muffins. There must be muffins, or it's curtains for the free world."

"Be right back," said Corinda, and she vanished, leaving behind the mingled aromas of good perfume, incense, and vanilla. Melissa stared after her with a kind of starry-eyed adoration, as if Corinda was everything she wished she could be when she was older. Corinda returned almost at once with two cups atop which plates bearing fat muffins were balanced. She set everything down without spilling more than a couple of drops, fetched silverware and napkins, and a bowl in which stood a small pyramid of half-and-half.

Corinda began to turn away, then paused. "So sorry about what happened to your friend. Such a loss. A candle blown out so soon."

Dana said, "Thanks, but she wasn't really a friend. I never met her."

"You don't have to meet in the flesh to be connected by spirit," said Corinda. "You *knew* her."

"No, not really," began Dana, and then she stopped as something occurred to her. "Wait, how did you know about what happened to Maisie?"

"You mean how do I know that you spoke with her in your dreams? And she appeared to you today at school?"

Dana gaped at her. "W-what . . . ?"

Corinda straightened and raised one eyebrow, and she held her arms out to indicate everything in Beyond Beyond—the soul attunement crystals, the display cases of tarot cards, the divination bone sets, the bags of rune tiles, the casting sticks, and hundreds of other objects. "I don't want to sound pompous, girls, but it's literally my business to know."

CHAPTER 10

The knife came in so fast that Dana had no time to think, block, or even move. A flash of silver and then the feel of the cold edge against her throat.

"You're dead."

The room was still except for the sound of her own breathing.

She tried to tilt her eyes enough to see the knife under her chin. She saw a tanned hand instead, the knuckles callused and crisscrossed with scars, and followed the arm up to the shoulder and to the face of the Japanese man who held the blade. He was nearly a foot taller than her, with short black hair and piercing eyes that gazed at her with the supreme confidence of a natural predator.

Dana did not move.

The man lowered the knife and stepped back. Dana faced him for a moment, and then bowed. The man returned the bow.

"Dead, dead, dead," said the person who had made the pronouncement a few seconds ago. Not the knife-man but a woman. Also Japanese, early thirties, slim, dressed in the same white *gi* as all her students. Only the woman and the knife-man wore black belts. The thirty students wore a variety of colors from white to brown. Dana wore a green belt, though it was new and stiff and hadn't yet been softened by use. "Dead with your throat cut."

Dana bowed to the woman, too. *"Hai,* Sensei."

The woman gave her a tiny, tolerant smile and bowed by nodding. Not very formal. That was how she was. Sensei Miyu Sato ran her dojo with some—but not all—of the formal strictness of traditional Japanese martial arts. Everyone wore uniforms, they used a handful of words and phrases—mostly *hai* for yes, *iye* for no—but there wasn't any of the stern, humorless rigidity Dana had experienced in the karate dojo back in San Diego.

Of course, the Kakusareta Taiyou Dojo did not teach karate. The Hidden Sun style of jujutsu was an amalgam art developed by Sensei's mother, aunts, and a few other women who were living in Japan during and after World War II. She told Dana once that after the war ended and the American occupation began, there was a rash of attacks on Japanese women. Martial arts were outlawed and all the dojos had closed, but women who were skilled fighters and also descendants of ancient samurai families banded together to form Kakusareta Taiyou, which skipped over much of the time-consuming formality of traditional martial arts and focused on actual lifesaving skills. The techniques were built on defense rather than attack.

Miyu waved Dana to the side, and she bowed off the mat, turned, and knelt in her place. Almost all the students in this dojo were girls and young women, with only a few boys mixed in.

"I know you've been going through a rough patch," said Miyu. "No, don't look surprised. It's a small town and people talk. None of that matters. None of anything matters when your life is on the line. Muggers and rapists don't schedule convenient times to attack. That's not how the world works. Danger is real, and its potential is constant. We must always be prepared."

"Sensei," said Dana, "how does that work, though? If Saturo—or a real bad guy, I mean—just jumped out at me, how am I supposed to get myself ready all at once?"

Miyu smiled, as if that was exactly the right question to ask. "Defense is not about being prepared in the moment," she said as she padded quietly across the tatami mats. "It is about being prepared *before* the moment."

Saturo shifted and began pacing with her, eyes focused on his aunt, knife loose in his hand, his body moving with the oiled grace of one of the big hunting cats. Stalking the much smaller Miyu, his face set, unsmiling, intense.

Dana watched them move around the mat, trying to predict how Saturo would attack. And when. Her dad had told her a lot about angles of attack and seizing the opportunity, but most of his lessons were broader, more about military tactics than personal combat.

Suddenly Saturo seemed to blur as he lunged in at a sharp right angle to how he'd been pacing. The blunt aluminum training knife was almost invisible as it slashed in a tight, vicious arc.

He's really trying to hit her, thought Dana, aghast.

Miyu was right in the path of that blow, caught flat-footed and unprepared.

Except . . .

Except she suddenly became part of the attack.

It was bizarre. The blade sliced a line through the air at face level, and instead of trying to back away from the attack, Miyu turned into it, pirouetting along the inside of Saturo's arm so that the circular cut wrapped around her, the blade missing by inches. Then Saturo was staggering, tilting, falling, and there was the after-echo of soft thuds from the flurry of strikes that Miyu delivered to stomach, groin, throat, face. Saturo crashed to the mat, and the knife went flying, landing, bouncing, and finally sliding to a stop four inches from Dana's knees.

It was all so fast.

Too fast to follow. How many times had Miyu hit him? Six? Eight? More?

Miyu stood wide-legged, her hands low and open, her body now angled toward the fallen attacker, positioned to offer every opportunity to continue the attack while allowing no real or useful opening. Suddenly she moved again, cat quick, and chop-kicked Saturo in the face.

So fast.

And then stillness.

Miyu gave a short, soft exhale and stepped back, her body instantly transitioning from combat to calm.

Saturo rolled onto his knees, then hopped to his feet. He bowed low, and Miyu returned the bow. Only then did Saturo smile. He was completely uninjured, because the blows had lightly tagged his denser areas and merely brushed the skin of his face and throat. This was *kime*, focus, the skill of absolute precision that allowed deadly arts to be practiced at full speed.

And that speed had been *awesome*.

"If you wait until an attack happens in order to plan a defense," said Miyu, "then you've already been defeated. We train our whole lives to be ready for attack so that in the moment we react correctly, using muscle memory, reflexes, and deeply ingrained repetitive skill development. There was a saying among the samurai that we train ten thousand hours for a single moment that may never happen. Ah, but if it *does*, then all of that training has been worth it. And . . . if it doesn't, then those were hours well spent, because a samurai was not judged on the sharpness of his sword but on the sharpness of his mind."

"*Osu*," said Saturo, using the general term of emphatic agreement.

"Now," said Miyu as she walked over to stand in front of Dana, "try it again."

"*Hai*, Sensei," said Dana as she got back to her feet.

"Oh, and this time try not to get your throat cut."

Dana looked at Saturo, who was still smiling.

"*Hai*, Sensei," said Dana weakly.

CHAPTER 11

Craiger, Maryland
5:24 P.M.

The knife came in so fast that he had no time to think, block, or even move.
A flash of silver and then the feel of the cold edge against his throat.

"You're dead."

The room was still except for the sound of his own breathing.

Then the edge vanished as the knife-man stepped back. The boy turned
to run, tripped, fell hard, scrambled up again, and looked for some way out.

But there was no way out.

The room was big and dark. The doors were shut and locked. There
were sheets of plywood nailed over all the windows. He was trapped in here.
Him, and the tall man with the wicked knife.

"I expected more from you, Todd," said the angel as he lowered the
knife. His voice was soft, kind, mild. "The dawn of the Red Age is at hand,
and I thought I could rely on you to help bring it about and make it a reality."

"Let me out of here."

The angel suddenly darted forward and the tip of the knife licked out,
fast and bright as lightning. Todd cried out and tried to block, tried to punch.
Failed at both because the other man was simply too fast. Hideously fast.
Todd felt a burn on his cheek and touched it, then cried out again as his
fingers came away slick with blood.

"I won't tell," he insisted, hating how his voice broke in the middle,
showing the weakness that he'd never known lived inside him. His body was

strong, muscular, made tough by years of jujutsu at the dojo and wrestling in school, but none of that had prepared him for this.

"You can't lie to me, Todd. I am in your mind. I am in your thoughts, your prayers, your hopes and dreams. I know that you told the girl about me."

"And you freaking *killed* her."

"You told her my secrets. You told her, and therefore her blood is marked against your soul." The angel began pacing again, going in the opposite direction this time.

"You killed her," repeated Todd. Blood ran hot down his cheek and along the side of his throat.

"No, *you* killed her. With a whisper to her, you doomed that girl to death in this world and damnation in the next," said the man. "The guilt is yours, and that's such a pity, such a waste. You brought us to this moment."

"You're a maniac."

"Tell me who else you told, Todd. Tell me who else knows about the Red Age."

"I—I—"

"It's okay. Tell me and then you will be allowed to ascend."

"They'll—they'll catch you. . . . They'll stop you . . ."

The angel bent close so that Todd could feel his breath, smell it. It was a reek like spoiled meat. A carnivore's breath. Ugly and filled with awful promises.

"Stop me? How?" he asked softly. "I am not something that can *be* stopped. Surely you, of all people, know that. You've seen what I can do. You've looked into my mind and witnessed what I will become. You know that there is nothing and no one that can stop me."

Todd could feel himself going away. Whatever had happened was already bad. So bad. Maybe a door had been kicked open for him after all. If he could slip through before this got worse.

"Go . . . to . . . hell," he gasped, forcing each word out, paying the cost to make them clear, to fill them with his anger and his hurt.

"No," said the angel as he raised the knife. "Hell is waiting for *you*."

CHAPTER 12

Gran was asleep when Dana got home.

"Don't wake her," said Mom, intercepting Dana outside Gran's bedroom. "The doctor was by earlier, and he prescribed something for her to help her sleep."

Mom wore a smile, but Dana could see how thin it was. Like paper held in place by small pieces of tape.

Melissa came out of the kitchen with a bowl of grapes.

"Hey," she said with a huge mouthful.

"Hey," said Dana, and plucked a single fat grape and ate it.

"Why don't you girls go upstairs?" suggested Mom. "Let's keep it quiet down here, okay?"

"Okay," said Melissa, pulling at Dana's arm.

Charlie came down the stairs wearing a black plastic bucket on his head, in which he had cut two small eyeholes. He had a black trash bag draped over his shoulders like a cloak and carried a stick that he'd painted Day-Glo orange. He stalked toward them, breathing heavily and audibly, paused for a moment, pointed at Dana, and said, "The Force is strong with this one."

Then he stalked away, humming an ominous theme song. The sisters watched him go.

Melissa said, "He's completely bonkers."

"Uh-huh," said Dana.

"He'll probably be a zillionaire one of these days, though."

"Uh-huh."

They went upstairs and stopped at the end of the short hallway where their rooms were. A small window looked out on the street, and Melissa peered through it and grunted.

"Did you see that on the way in?"

Dana looked and saw a pair of workmen in the process of fixing a sign above the big double doors of the old church. Melissa parted the curtain to get a better look at what it said.

"'Church of the Pure Light,'" she read. "Sounds like some hippies are moving in. Cool." She let the curtain fall. "Hey, want to come in my room and hang for a bit? We could bully Mom into letting us get Chinese delivered and watch some bad TV."

"I have homework."

"The beauty of bad TV is that you can do homework and not miss much. Besides, you look like you need some downtime. You've got weird bug eyes."

"Just tired."

"Uh-huh."

Dana thought about it. "Well, maybe. Today's been a nightmare. I guess I do kind of need to turn my head off for a while."

"Good," said Melissa. "And because it was my idea, I get to pick the first show."

CHAPTER 13

"He's really in gear tonight," said Malcolm Gerlach.

The other man in the small room, a technician named Danny, said nothing but made a small sound of agreement. The room was dark, lit only by the pale glow from a dozen small color TV screens. Each screen showed a live video feed from a different part of town, and on the screens, small dramas were playing out. It was clear that none of the subjects knew they were being surveilled. That was part of the process. They had learned the hard way that direct observation often created psychological reactions that limited performance. Science required precision, and it required an atmosphere of sterility.

They watched.

On one screen, a boy of twelve sat on the floor of his bathroom, arms wrapped around his head, tears and snot smearing his face, chest heaving as he sobbed, feet hammering the floor in panic. In front of him was a wet hand towel. Every once in a while the boy raised his head and stared at it with such ferocity that it was like he was trying to punch it with his gaze.

"Move," he snarled, but there was a note of pleading in his voice. Of desperation and fear.

The towel did not move.

Most of the time.

On another screen, a seventeen-year-old girl lay on her bed. She was dressed in thick snow pants, a parka, and lamb's-wool mittens. Her body gave a sharp spasmodic twitch with every fifth heartbeat. The lights in the room were off, but the hidden camera was filtered for thermal imaging, and it caught the steamy plumes of each breath. A meter on the camera recorded the temperature. When the girl had put on the coat, it was sixty-nine degrees. Now the meter read twenty-one. There was another spasm and the meter dropped to twenty.

On a third screen, a blond girl sat on the floor of her bedroom staring into a full-length wall mirror. She wore striped pajamas and had her hair in pigtails.

The image in the mirror showed a little boy of exactly the same body mass, but his hair was black, his skin pale brown. When the girl smiled, he smiled. When she blinked, he blinked. When she bowed her head and wept, so did he.

The men in the room exchanged a look. Yesterday it had been a Chinese girl in the mirror. Last week it had been an adult male with Russian features.

On the fourth screen, a teenage boy sat at his desk doing calculus homework. He worked with a slide rule and a pocket calculator. Books and papers were spread all around him, and he was writing furiously.

The camera was angled to show his eyes. They were totally black. No pupils, no irises, no sclera. Pure, bottomless black. He was not looking at the paper but instead stared straight ahead, looking at nothing. His pen moved quickly as he filled up page after page after page in a small, neat hand. Some of it was calculus—the experts in the Syndicate were positive of that much. The rest, though? It was probably math of some kind, but not any form of mathematics known to man. Every now and then strange symbols would appear in the middle of the numbers and formulae. Those symbols were known to all the experts in the organization, and had been ever since the first ship crashed at Roswell.

On the fifth screen, two teenagers were making out on a rug beside an empty bed. They had their clothes on, but their wrangling was going in an obvious direction. They were so completely lost in their kissing and groping that neither of them noticed what was happening in the room. They never saw the pictures of the girl's mother turn, shifting subtly on the shelves. They never saw the milky-white film form over the framed picture of Jesus on the wall. They never saw the crucifix glow as it heated and began to melt.

They never saw any of that, but the camera recorded it all.

Gerlach bent forward to study what was happening on the sixth screen.

A teenage boy lay tossing and turning in the clutches of an unbreakable nightmare. His bedroom was empty except for five items. The bed on which he lay, a dresser that was patched with duct tape, an old chair, a heavy metal crucifix that had been bolted to the ceiling above the bed, and a folding knife with a locking blade. The boy turned and writhed inside the nightmare, speaking in some language unknown to the two men who watched. They had forwarded tapes of everything the boy said to the language experts working for the Syndicate. The preliminary reports from those experts were deeply disturbing. They believed that when he was caught up in a certain kind of dream, the boy spoke in whole sentences, but the components of those sentences were made of words from several sources. Only a few words had been translated, and they were from a dialect of the ancient Aramaic language. Not merely a dead language, but specifically the dialect spoken in the region of Galilee, which differed in significant ways from the more commonly used dialect spoken in Jerusalem. The Syndicate linguists believed that the dialect used by the sleeping boy was the specific version of Aramaic that would have been used by Jesus and his disciples.

But there were only a few words spoken in that dialect. There were also words in the version of Greek known as Koine and in a very ancient version of Hebrew that contained elements of Phoenician.

Words from those languages made up 5 percent of what the boy said. Of what he screamed. The rest were either nonsense words or from a language unknown to the scholars who worked for the Syndicate. Some of those words were so strange that it clearly hurt the boy to speak them. More than once he woke gagging on blood from his torn larynx and tongue. As if such words were never meant for a human throat and mouth to speak.

Tonight, though, he kept repeating an Aramaic phrase the experts had decoded months ago. A phrase Danny and Gerlach knew by heart now, even if they did not understand its meaning or implication. The translation of that phrase was written on a strip of white surgical tape that had been pressed along the bottom of the sixth screen.

SHE WILL CHANGE THE WORLD. HEAVEN WILL FALL.

It might have been a phrase of no great importance, except for the fact that when he said those words, he was screaming with absolute terror.

The image on the seventh screen was of a pretty fifteen-year-old red-haired girl dressed in very modest pajamas lying sprawled on a bed that was soaked with her sweat. She thrashed and turned as she slept, and now the sheets and thin blanket were knotted around her. Above her bed, colored lights flashed and popped like tiny fireworks, but they came from nowhere and vanished without leaving any trace. No one in the Syndicate understood a thing about those lights.

"No . . . ," she said, moaning it out as a protracted wail. "Please . . . no . . ."

Danny said, "Do any of them know what's happening?"

"Some of them do," said Gerlach. "Most don't. Why?"

"Well, because they look like they're in pain. How do we know this won't kill them?"

Gerlach and the other man exchanged a look.

Neither said another word, though.

CHAPTER 14

Sleep was no escape.

None at all.

Deep in the night, Dana seemed to wake within a dream, knowing that she was dreaming, but afraid that this was every bit as real as the waking world. She knew that she didn't have the lexicon to even put any of this into words that would make sense. The walls between fantasy and reality were broken, crumbling, irrelevant.

And that was terrifying.

Wasn't that what happened when the mind fractured? Wasn't that the definition of being insane?

The dream unfolded like a movie.

She woke in her room, but she wasn't dressed in her pajamas. Instead she wore a dark suit that was almost masculine. Navy-blue pants and jacket, white blouse, the look softened only by a thin golden necklace from which her tiny cross hung and the lack of a tie. Her hair was stiffer, shorter, styled in a severe way she would never wear. Shoes with chunky heels.

The clothes were nothing she owned, but they fit her. She felt like she belonged in them. But when she stood up, there was something odd. A weight on her hip. Dana crossed to the mirror as she unbuttoned the jacket, and when she held the flap back, she saw the gun.

The.

Gun.

A small automatic snugged into a leather holster clipped to her belt.

"What . . . ?" she murmured.

Dana knew guns. Military brats always did. Her brothers and Dad took her and Melissa to the range in any town where they lived.

"You can't touch a gun unless you're going to be smart about it, Starbuck," her dad said the first time they'd gone to a gun range. That was what he called her: Starbuck. And he was Ahab. It started when they'd first read *Moby-Dick* together. A book she loved and Melissa hated. A book that created a connection with her father that Dana didn't always feel. A connection that seemed to be interrupted way too often. Sometimes he was hard, distant, cold; and his coldness chilled her and pushed her away. But then he'd smile and there would be a secret twinkle there, as bright as the North Star, and he'd call her Starbuck and she'd call him Ahab and things would be okay.

The gun in the holster was not a model she had ever seen. She looked at the reflection of the weapon but did not touch it.

It's not yours, said a voice inside her mind. *Not yet.*

Then she noticed that her reflection was wrong. Different. The face looking back at her wore the same frown she felt on her mouth, but this face was older. A woman's face, not a girl's. Not much older, though. Ten years? A little less. Old enough, though, to show that the years had not been easy ones. There was a rigidity to the face, a glitter of doubt and submerged anger in the eyes.

And fear.

There was real fear there, too. Hidden, compressed, repressed, shoved down, pushed back. But there.

"I'm afraid," said her reflection. Her voice was different, too. Older, not as soft, more controlled.

"Afraid of what?" Dana asked her reflection, speaking as if this were a different person.

The reflection answered. "I'm afraid to believe."

Dana licked her lips. "Me too."

The reflection looked sad, as if that was the wrong answer. "What are you afraid of?"

Dana said, "I'm afraid that God is speaking and no one is listening."

"I know," said the other Dana. Motes of dust swam in the air on both sides of the mirror, moving in perfect synchronicity even though the two Danas were so different.

The woman with her face leaned close and whispered, "He's coming for you."

"What? Who?"

The woman suddenly gasped and drew her gun. It was so fast, with an oiled grace that could only have been possible after years of practice. She hooked her fingers on the edge of her jacket, swept it back, released, used her thumb to pop the restraining strap, closed her fingers around the gnarled hard plastic grips, slid the weapon out, raised it, took it into a two-handed grip, held it steady with one finger laid along the trigger guard. And all so, so fast. A heartbeat and then the gun was up. Pointed at Dana . . . no, pointed past her.

The gun barrel was a black eye, steady and deadly, but the face behind the gun was twisted into a mask of horror.

"He's here!"

Dana spun around toward the darkness that suddenly filled her bedroom. For one heartbeat there was nothing to see.

And then *he* stepped out of the shadows.

A man.

The angel of light.

Devil or monster or ordinary man, she didn't know which.

Tall, painted a cold blue by the spill of moonlight that slanted through her window. Dressed in clothes so dark it was as if he wore garments made of shadows. Wings folded behind his broad back.

But he had no face at all.

His curly black hair framed a face with high cheekbones and a strong jaw, but where there should have been eyes, a nose, and a mouth, there was nothing. Not a mask, she was sure. Nothing.

And yet she *knew* that he could see her. That he was smiling with the wrong kind of hungers. That he was completely aware of her—both the real her and the fantasy older version in the mirror.

The angel raised his hands, and Dana could see that he was holding up things he wanted her to see.

In his right hand he clutched several long, wickedly sharp iron nails.

In his left he held a crude mallet made of hardwood and steel.

The fingers of both hands were smeared with blood.

"Run," whispered the older Dana. "I'll try to hold him here. Run . . . *run!*"

Dana could not run. She couldn't move. She could barely breathe.

The wings behind the angel's back suddenly rustled, and then they spread out, huge, broad, filling the room behind him. The moonlight showed them to her with crystal clarity. They were not the soft, beautiful feathered wings of an angel of heaven.

They were the black, leathery, mottled wings of something from the pit of hell.

Dana screamed herself awake.

CHAPTER 15

The angel sat cross-legged on the floor, surrounded by thousands of pieces of broken mirror, each reflecting a different version of his face.

Some of them showed him as the world saw him, and he disregarded them with nothing more than a smirk. He knew that people loved masks because the truth was too frightening for small and ordinary minds.

Some of the mirror splinters showed the face of the angel. Not one face, but many faces, because an angel is different to everyone who sees it. *It*, not *him*. Angels are above gender, above sexual identity. They are above everything that defines a being as human. And he, by his own definition, was not.

There were other faces in the shattered fragments. Faces of monsters, faces of great beauty, faces of stone and metal and wood. Faces of such abstract forms that only a deeply insightful eye could see them as faces at all.

And then there was the one face that looked back at him from the largest of the shards. His true face. A face no one had ever seen or even glimpsed except when he revealed it to them.

Usually, though, the people to whom he showed his true self were so busy screaming that they could not appreciate the majesty of who he was.

He wondered if the girl would be able to see his true face when the time came. He hoped so.

He wanted her to. Just as he wanted to bring her into the family, to share with her the secrets of the Red Age, of the *grigori* and *nephilim*. He was certain that she would embrace the truth once she heard it.

A photograph of the girl rested on the floor next to that special fragment of mirror. The picture was in color, very sharp. In it the girl was standing in her bedroom, buttoning her pajama top. She had lovely red hair. It was as red as the hair of Judas the Betrayer. He reached out and ran his finger across her picture, pausing briefly at her soft young throat.

Around him the shadows crouched at the edges of the candlelight.

CHAPTER 16

The Observation Room
4:01 A.M.

Danny, the technician, took off his headset and tossed it onto the console. He lit a cigarette, put his feet on the edge of the console and crossed his ankles, and blew a stream of blue smoke into the air. Gerlach sat at a table behind him, slowly stirring packets of sugar into a coffee cup. Eight empty packets lay on the table, and Gerlach reached for a ninth.

"Some of them actually see him, right?" asked Danny.

"Some," said Gerlach.

"Isn't that a potential danger? I mean, it's a small town."

Gerlach snorted. "That's part of his skill set."

"I don't follow."

"He controls how they see him," said the agent.

"Oh . . . that's . . ."

"Creepy?" suggested Gerlach.

"Or something like that," admitted Danny. "Freaky. Weird. Out there. Not sure what kind of label fits."

The agent looked into the middle distance for a moment, then shook his head slowly. "Personally, man, I doubt there are labels for what we're into. No one's gone this far before."

"Not even the Russians? I heard some wild stuff," said the tech.

"The Russians are two years behind us," said Gerlach. "Maybe four. By the time they catch up to where we are now, we'll have broken through to the next level."

"What *is* the next level?"

Gerlach glanced at him. "That's above your pay grade."

"Sorry."

"Don't be sorry; just don't be nosy."

"Yes, sir."

"And stop calling me sir. I hate that."

"Yes, sir . . . um, I mean, sure," Danny said, then began turning off the video feeds. "Did you hear? They're giving you a new driver today."

Gerlach nodded. "I know."

"Regular guy says he has food poisoning."

"Uh-huh."

"You believe him?"

The agent tore open the ninth packet, poured it in, and went back to stirring. "Not everyone's cut out for this job," he said.

CHAPTER 17

When Dana padded barefoot into the kitchen, she found Gran was at the table, hands pressed to the sides of a steaming cup of tea, buttered toast sitting cold on a plate. It was rare for Gran to be up much before noon. The radio was on, playing some old songs from World War II that Dana didn't know.

"Hey, Gran," said Dana as she came over and kissed her grandmother's cheek. Even though Gran's face was wrinkled, it was always so soft. She smelled of soap and Dorothy Gray face powder.

"There's coffee made," said Gran, though that wasn't true. The coffee-maker stood empty. Dana didn't comment, though. The teakettle was still hot enough, and she made herself a cup. Peppermint. Gran had a saying for that: "Chamomile to calm down; peppermint to perk up."

She brought it over to the table and sat down. Gran smiled at her and pushed the toast across.

"You're letting it get cold."

Dana nodded as if that made sense, took a piece, bit off a corner, and munched it. She pushed the plate back to Gran. Outside there seemed to be a thousand birds in the trees, all of them joining voices to proclaim that spring was well and truly here. It was nice. Loud, but nice.

"Gran . . . ?" she asked.

"Yes, sweetie?"

"What are angels?"

Her grandmother's eyes were rarely clear and usually seemed to wander, unfocused, as if she had forgotten how to look at things. But now they clicked over to study her, and they were as clear and blue as the sky after a good rain.

"Why do you want to know about angels?"

"I keep dreaming about them."

Gran sipped her tea, her eyes intense and unblinking for a long moment. Then she looked down into her cup. "Are you afraid of those angels?"

"A little," said Dana, softening the truth.

Gran nodded. "You should be."

"What?"

Those blue eyes glanced up again. "What do you think angels are?"

"Um . . . God's messengers, I guess."

"You guess."

"That's what they told us in Sunday school."

Gran made a face. Unlike her daughter and grandkids, she rarely went to church. "Well, then it must be true."

"That's why I'm asking you," said Dana.

The wall clock ticked through half a minute before Gran said anything. Dana knew this pattern. When Gran was lucid, it was best to wait her out, to let her work up to whatever she wanted to say. Speaking too soon, or interrupting, seemed to throw a switch and send her back into the disconnected haze where Gran spent most of her days.

Gran nodded as if agreeing with her own thoughts. "There are all kinds of angels," she began slowly. "The name means 'messenger,' and a lot of people think they're just God's errand boys. Ha! Hardly. People think they stand around all day shouting 'hosanna' and playing harps and looking like hippies in long robes. But that's just silly, isn't it? People pray to angels as if they only exist to come help you get through a bad day. They pray to them like they're saints, but the saints, at least, used to be people. Angels never were."

"What are they?" urged Dana.

"They're dangerous is what they are," said Gran, her voice clear and sharp. "Think about it, girl. The first angel mentioned in the Bible stood guard at the entrance to the Garden of Eden with a fiery sword. He wasn't there to protect Adam and Eve, you can believe me. Guardian angels are in the Bible, but they're not there to protect us. All through the Bible angels act like God's hit men, showing up to punish, to destroy." She shook her head. "Don't forget, Lucifer was an angel."

"Oh . . . right . . ."

"And they're not pretty, either. They're monsters."

"Monsters?"

"The seraphim are large six-winged snakes that fly. Cherubs aren't those cute rosy-cheeked babies you see in paintings. Hardly. They're winged lions. Not exactly the kind of creature you want watching over your baby's crib. Why do you think every time an angel appears to a human in the scriptures, they say, 'Do not be afraid'?

"Let me think, now. There was a quote about it in Ezekiel, but don't ask me chapter and verse. Something about them having two sets of wings and hooves . . . How'd it go? 'The face of a man, and the face of a lion, on the right side: and they had the face of an ox on the left side; and also the face of an eagle.' That's not it exactly, but close enough to be going on with."

The blue of her eyes seemed very bright in the morning sunlight, and there was no hint of a troubled mind. That, as much as what Gran was saying, chilled the whole kitchen.

Gran shook her head. "If you're having dreams about angels, Dana, then you need to be careful. Not all ugly angels are bad, and not all beautiful ones are good. They're not human, and you can't judge them the way you judge a human. That's how people get hurt. Everything about them is different from what it seems." She laughed. "Maybe that's how the devil came to be called the prince of lies. If he's an angel, then nothing about him is the simple truth."

"How can I tell if it's real or just a dream?" asked Dana.

Gran considered the question, but as she thought about it, her face began to change, and Dana's heart sank. She saw the cloudiness of confusion steal the clarity from those blue eyes as surely as if the pall of a storm had rolled in front of the sun. It happened quickly. In the space of a few seconds, Gran retreated back into the shadows of her own mind.

"Gran . . . ?" asked Dana cautiously.

Her grandmother smiled. "Oh, good morning, Melissa," said Gran brightly. "There's coffee made."

Dana got up and walked around the table to kiss her grandmother on the cheek. That soft cheek.

"I love you, Gran," she murmured.

"I love you, too, Margaret. Be sure to clean your room before you go out with that Scully boy. He's a scoundrel."

Margaret was her mother's name.

"I will," said Dana.

"Dana . . . ?" called her mother from the hall. "Is Gran with you?"

"We're in the kitchen."

Her mom came in, and her dad followed a few moments later. Charlie came in, too, but he was clearly not completely awake and still wearing the superhero mask he obviously slept in. He sat down and stared with unblinking eyes at a bowl of cornflakes. It was a rare thing for the Scullys to have breakfast together, but Dana didn't comment on it. There was a palpable tension in the air. Mom and Dad set about making coffee and preparing breakfast, neither saying much of anything. Gran retreated further into herself and Dana went back to her chair. Melissa came in yawning, too, dressed for school but with her hair still tousled. She gave wordless grunts and poured some of the fresh coffee, ladled in four spoonfuls of sugar, and thumped down on her chair. Her coffee was half gone before she blinked her eyes clear and looked around.

"What's with everyone this morning?" asked Melissa.

Mom put a plate of eggs and toast in front of her. "Here you go. Hurry up and eat or you'll be late."

Melissa cut a look at her father, whose mouth was locked into a tight line, then over at Dana. They didn't have to say a word to each other to know what was going on. Mom and Dad had had another fight. That seemed to be happening more often since moving here.

Breakfast proceeded with arctic coldness.

Only Gran was smiling as she thoroughly buttered both sides of her toast.

CHAPTER 18

"Glad they didn't suspend you," said Eileen.

"I thought they were going to expel you," said Dave. "That's what every-one was saying."

The Minderjahns had intercepted the sisters in the hall, and the four of them were clustered together around Melissa's locker.

"Well, then everyone's stupid," growled Melissa, instantly coming to Dana's defense.

Teens moved like currents up and down the hall, and a lot of them gave Dana looks. Anger, amusement, curiosity, and contempt, all in equal measure.

"It'll pass," said Eileen with confidence.

"Yeah," said Dave. "Everyone's hurt and scared right now, so you freak-ing out gave them something else to focus on. Otherwise they'd have to deal with their own stuff. What's it called? Transference? Something like that."

Melissa nodded. "Right. And anyone who doesn't get over it, anyone who keeps holding it against you, well . . . I guess it's safe to say they're not your real friends."

"I don't have any real friends," said Dana. Then she gasped as she real-ized how hurtful that sounded, but Eileen gave her a motherly smile and a pat on the arm.

"We're your friends," she assured her.

"Yeah," said Dave, though he was looking at Melissa when he said it.

The bell rang for class, and they all went off in different directions. Dana tried to be invisible, but she could feel the eyes on her. At first everyone treated her exactly as she expected, and she was convinced she had a huge winking neon light over her head that said WEIRDO. But the wattage of contempt seemed to diminish after her first class. It wasn't that anyone rushed up to hug her, but instead they seemed to simply pull away and focus on their own lives rather than hurl mental stones at her. Dave had been right, at least in part.

On the way to her locker after algebra, two girls came over to her and blocked her way. She recognized them as having been in the gym. Karen something and Angie something.

Dana braced herself, expecting . . .

Expecting what? A punch? To be told what a creep she was? To be threatened in some way?

None of that happened.

Instead Karen said, "Were you telling the truth?"

"What?" asked Dana.

"Yesterday," said Karen. "About Maisie. Were you telling the truth? Did you really see her?"

"I . . ."

Karen's eyes were fierce but also wet. She looked like she was fighting to hold back tears, though her hands were balled into fists.

"You better tell me, or so help me . . . ," she said in a tight whisper.

The other girl, Angie, was shorter and broader and wore a field hockey sweater. She looked like she could break Dana in half, and looked like she wanted to.

"*Tell me,*" begged Karen.

"Yes," said Dana, her own voice a whisper.

Karen grabbed her upper arms. "Was she in pain?"

Dana did not know how to answer. The truth seemed likely to earn her a beating. But so, too, would a lie. She braced herself, ready to use some of the jujutsu she'd been learning or the karate she practiced with her brothers. She wasn't very good, but she would go down swinging.

"I think so," she said. "She was bleeding and . . . she was screaming."

The other girls stared at her, eyes wide, tears falling down. Dana could see that they believed her. Suddenly Karen pushed her back, spun, and ran away down the hall. The stockier girl lingered for a moment, caught between the need to follow her friend and a compulsion to say something.

"Maisie was her cousin," Angie said awkwardly. "She tried to talk her out of going to that party."

"I—I'm sorry," said Dana lamely.

Angie shook her head. "It's not . . ." She stopped and started to go, but Dana caught up and touched her arm.

"What is it? What were you going to say?"

The girl did not answer. She shook her head and walked away to find her friend. Dana almost followed.

"What was that all about?"

Dana turned quickly to see another older girl standing there. One of Melissa's friends. Anne Hassett. A cheerleader, like Eileen. She had short brown hair and a very Irish snub nose. This was the first time Dana had ever seen her when she wasn't smiling.

"Oh. Hi. It's Anne, right?"

"And you're Dana," said Anne. She wore tight jeans and a shirt with a cartoon mouse on it. The mouse was the only one smiling right now. "What did those girls want?"

"Why?"

Anne walked over and stood close. She was the same height as Dana and looked her straight in the eyes. "Because I asked."

Dana tried to think of a reason not to tell her, and couldn't. It wasn't that kind of day. "The one girl was Maisie Bell's cousin and—"

"I know who she is. What did she want?"

"Well . . . she asked me about something that happened yesterday."

"You mean in the gym?"

"You heard about that?"

"Everyone's heard about it," said Anne. "What did she want to know?"

"She, um, wanted to know if Maisie was in pain."

Anne's eyes searched hers. "Was she?"

"Yes."

"You told her that?"

"Yes."

Anne looked past her. "Oh, man . . ."

There was a sound, and they both turned and saw a teenage guy standing with his back to them. Dana recognized him as Angelo, who worked at Beyond Beyond. He was dressed in a janitor's blue pants and shirt. She hadn't seen him around the school before. Angelo removed the top of one of the hallway trash cans and began emptying it into a larger, wheeled plastic barrel. He didn't glance their way, but Anne jerked her head and walked a few feet farther down the hall. Dana followed.

"Look, what's going on?" she asked. "Everyone treats me like I've done something wrong here, but I'm not making it up. Maybe I'm losing my mind, but I saw Maisie in the locker room."

"How come it was *you* who saw Maisie?"

"I don't know. I really don't."

A lot of different emotions seemed to come and go in Anne's eyes. Anger, resentment, hurt, and others Dana couldn't label.

"You know what everyone's saying about Maisie, right?" barked Anne. "That she was a 'dumb kid' and she wrecked her car, and they make assumptions. That's how it always is. Anything anyone our age does that's not square is because it's us acting out or being wild. Like we can't think for ourselves. Like we don't matter. Maisie's dead, and they'll always say that she did it to herself because she got high, and that's wrong. It's . . . it's a lie, an insult. It's just wrong."

Dana nodded.

"And then you come along," said Anne, "and you don't even know Maisie and she appears to you for some reason. That freaked everyone out. It's like a sign of some kind. That's what I think. That was her trying to tell the world that she didn't die the way people think she did."

"You . . . believe I saw her?"

Anne nodded. "Yeah. A lot of people do. I even heard a couple of teachers talking about it. Everyone thinks you're some kind of freak, but . . . sure."

The knowledge that the other students believed her jolted her, and Dana did not know how to take it.

"Craiger's a weird town," said Anne. "Always been weird. Maisie was weird, too. She went to all those weirdo classes at that stupid hippie shop."

"Beyond Beyond?"

"Whatever it's called, but yes. Always doing that meditation junk and saying she was walking through veils and—how'd she put it?—connecting with the planetary energetics. Talking with the earth spirit Gaia. Talking about how she was part of the movement to bring everyone into a new age. I don't know. She went on and on about that stuff, and I usually tuned her out. All that matters is that after she died, she came to you."

"Why me, though?" pleaded Dana. "We never even met. Why come to me, of all people?"

Anne studied her for a moment, her eyes hooded and calculating. "All I know is that if it happened, there has to be a reason."

"But *what* reason? It's driving me totally out of my mind."

"Yeah, like I said, this is Craiger. Welcome to the club." Anne flapped an arm in disgust and then just walked away, leaving Dana alone in the hall. Angelo had gone, too, and Dana felt as if she was miles and miles away from anyone she knew, or anything that made sense.

She hugged her backpack to her chest and hurried to her next class, which she was already late for.

CHAPTER 19

The angel crouched in the shadows, his face and body streaked with paint and blood and grease, his eyes burning in his head, lips moving in a constant prayer that was as formless as his god.

Praying to the *grigori*. Praying to his blood father, a true angel born in heaven who sought now to return to earth. To save it. Protect it.

Rule it.

Listening to what his god had to tell him. Secrets. Promises. Prophecies.

Outside there was the sound of a siren screaming its way through the town. He did not care. It wasn't the right kind of scream.

CHAPTER 20

The biology teacher looked like Albert Einstein—if Einstein had spent a bad weekend in an alley after being enthusiastically mugged. That was how he looked to Dana. Mr. Newton had Einstein's wild hair, wilder eyebrows, and a mustache that looked like it was about to leap off his face and go burrowing in the forest. He always wore an ugly green or brown suit, and everyone was positive he owned only those two suits. However, he wore an ever-changing series of brightly colored ties. Today's tie had clockwork gears in twenty shades of gold, bronze, and silver. Everyone called him Two-Suit Newton.

Dana thought he was great. Most of the other students thought he was a weirdo, but Dana was okay with weirdos. Especially science weirdos. She was starting to think about a career in science, too. Maybe research. Maybe medicine. Maybe something else. She loved math and science, and Mr. Newton challenged her mind.

Going into his classroom after the double encounter in the hall was like stepping onto the shores of an island after falling overboard from a sinking ship. This was firm footing. She knew who she was here.

On the other hand, she was ten minutes late. Newton stopped what he was saying and peered out from under his wild eyebrows at her. Everyone else turned, too, and there was a lot of relief on their faces at any interruption. The blackboard was filled with notes about the steps required to dissect a frog. A big plastic cooler sat on the floor between rows of lab tables, the top removed, and dozens of dead frogs lay inside. Some of the other students already looked as green as the frogs.

"There is real time," said Newton gravely, "and there is Francis Scott Key High I-don't-care-about-science-class time, and then there is Dana Scully time."

"Sorry," she said.

"Not trying to escape today's exercise in controlling the gag reflex, are we?" Newton held a scalpel and waggled it back and forth.

"No . . . no, just running late. Sorry, won't happen again," mumbled Dana as she hurried over to find a seat. Her regular lab partner wasn't there today, but then he hadn't been in the other day, either. The only person there who didn't have a partner was a tall, thin, studious-looking boy with sandy-blond hair and intelligent green eyes. Ethan something, she thought. Dana felt herself turning lobster red as she climbed onto the stool beside him.

"Okay?" she asked.

"Be my guest."

She caught a few mixed looks from the other students, but these were all sophomores like her. No seniors and probably no one close to Maisie. All her classmates would have heard would be secondhand rumors. So none of the looks were openly hostile. Small mercies.

Mr. Newton picked up a lecture in progress, explaining what they'd be looking for once they cut open their frogs. He seemed to enjoy his topic and was very animated. Then the frogs were handed out and the process began. The class became noisy with conversation and a lot of sounds of sickness and disgust.

"If you feel the need to vomit," said Newton offhandedly, "please be so good as to use the trash can. Don't puke on your frogs."

"Can we puke on our lab partners?" asked one of the boys from the football team. He was an offensive fullback, and his partner was a wide receiver.

"Only if you want to clean it up," said Newton. "But in my experience, if you throw up on someone, they will invariably reciprocate with enthusiasm."

Everyone got a chuckle out of that, and the football players high-fived. Ethan leaned close to Dana and murmured, "Maybe I'm being harsh, but I don't see a Nobel Prize for science in their futures."

Dana turned away to hide a snort of laughter.

"Okay, my little Frankensteins and Frankensteinettes," said Newton, "you may commence with the mad science. Please take your time, though. Science requires patience and attention to detail, not haste."

Ethan and Dana set to work with equal amounts of care, interest, and diligence. That impressed Dana, because a lot of the guys in class were either trying to act macho, as if none of this bothered them, or hamming up how much they were going to vomit. Not Ethan. He had a quiet energy and a serious face. He wore steel-rimmed glasses, dress shirts, and Keds sneakers, and he pursed his lips while he worked, but there was no trace of unease or reluctance as he pinned the frog down and used a felt-tip pen to draw the pattern to guide their cuts.

He smiled at her. It was a nice smile, and he had very good teeth, except for a small chip on his left front tooth. He slid the scalpel over to her.

"Ladies first," he said.

"You sure?"

"Why not? If you're up to it."

"Why wouldn't I be? 'Cause I'm a girl?"

He looked genuinely surprised. "Um . . . no, because you missed Two-Suit explaining how it's done."

"It's on the board," she pointed out.

"Right. Sorry."

Dana picked up the scalpel, glanced again at the notes and diagrams on the board, then placed the blade against the slack pale skin and made her cut. Ethan watched her make two lateral incisions at the throat and groin and then connect them with a long vertical cut. She set the scalpel down and peeled back the flaps to expose the internal organs.

"Wow. Nice job," he said. "You ever do this before?"

"No."

"You didn't even nick anything inside."

Dana glanced up at him, expecting there to be some kind of humor or condescension there, but Ethan simply looked impressed. "Thanks," she said diffidently.

"No, I mean it," said Ethan. "You missed the little film Two-Suit showed us, but you did it exactly right. You're a natural."

She noticed again that Ethan had a very nice smile.

Dana wanted to crawl under the table, because she was sure her cheeks were bright as red stoplights.

"Want me to take out the heart?" he asked, and in the weirdest way possible, on a day that was already beyond strange, that seemed like the nicest thing a boy had ever said to her.

I am totally out of my mind, she thought. But she was smiling as she handed over the scalpel.

CHAPTER 21

"Did you hear a single word I said?" demanded the driver.

The man seated beside him had his seat tilted back and lay with his hat over his face. They had the engine off, which meant no air-conditioning, and even this early in the spring, the sun was hot. The windows were open and the passenger had clearly been dozing.

"Hey, Gerlach," growled the driver. "I'm talking to you. Are you even listening?"

"No," said the passenger.

"I said, *there* she is."

The passenger, Malcolm Gerlach, did not remove the hat, did not sit up, did not bother to look.

"No," he said.

"What do you mean, 'no'? I can see her with my own eyes. She's on the far side of the school quad, right near the—"

"It's not her," said Gerlach.

"Sure it is. Red hair, blue blouse."

Gerlach removed the hat and looked up. He was thin, with an ascetic face, pale blue eyes, and dark red hair. He did not look through the window but instead fixed his gaze on the driver. "You're new, kid, so I'm going to cut you a little bit of slack, *capisce*?"

"Kid? You're, like, five years older than me. Who you calling—?"

"Shhh. Just listen," said Gerlach, his voice mild. "The girl you're looking at is the sister, Melissa. Older, two inches taller, and with curly red hair. She's seventeen. She doesn't look like her sister at all. Not if you bothered to study the surveillance photos. There's a reason we take them from different angles and distances, you know. It's so you cats can spot a target from any distance, day or night, rain or shine. And here *you* are, misidentifying a mark and disturbing my beauty sleep. You are dangerously close to making me cranky. Remember that TV show with the guy who turned green and smashed things? Remember the line about how you wouldn't like him when he's angry? Yeah, it's like that with me, too. And what *makes* me angry? Jocks with more biceps than brains and who don't know how to do their job, even when the job is to sit in a car and look for a girl you have thirty photos of."

The driver ground his teeth for a moment. This was his first shift, having taken over from the regular wheelman. The regular guy had eaten some bad shrimp rolls and couldn't get five steps away from a bathroom. The driver, whose name was Matt, had been warned about this passenger—been told that he was eccentric and that he was a jerk. He was warned that the man was dangerous, too, though no one said exactly how. Matt was six-two and had a second-degree black belt in tae kwon do. He was used to being the one who people walked softly around. The guy riding shotgun was a stick figure who didn't look like he could punch his way out of a damp paper bag. And here he was, giving him lip.

Matt opened his mouth to say something, but Gerlach turned his head and smiled.

It was the wrong kind of smile.

It was a dark smile. The shape of the mouth was too happy for the moment they were both in. The teeth were wet. The eyes no longer looked green, as they had before, but now seemed black, as if the pupils had expanded to consume the color of the irises. Everything about that man suddenly seemed to whisper promises of awful things. The passenger raised a finger and twitched it back and forth.

"Now would not be the best time to see which of us dogs has the best bite," Gerlach said quietly.

Matt sat there, his mouth still open, but his body did not want to move. It was as if his muscles rebelled against the possibility of taking any action at all. His throat was complicit in the rebellion and pushed no breath out to form words of any kind.

"You get this one warning, and then we go to a different place," said Gerlach. "Am I making myself clear? Just a nod will be fine."

Matt nodded.

"Good dog," said Gerlach. He placed his hat back over his face. "Now keep your eyes open and your mouth shut. Look at all those cute little school-girls over there. Enjoy the eye candy, but bear in mind that you really don't want to wake me again until you see the right one."

A few moments later, there was the sound of a soft, buzzing snore.

Matt swallowed hard.

If the other driver was feeling better tomorrow, then he was going to hand this gig back to him. Maybe he'd put in a transfer, too. Somewhere far away from here. One of the Dakotas, perhaps.

He took a tissue from his pocket and used it to blot cold sweat from his eyes.

CHAPTER 22

Although it was a double-period class, Dana was sorry it was over. Science calmed her. As they began cleaning their lab tables in preparation for the end of class, Ethan said, "That was cool."

She nodded. "It was fun."

"Cutting up a frog and messing around with its internal organs with a cute redhead," he said as she placed the scalpel in the autoclave. "Who knew that's how today was gonna go?"

The word *cute* hung like a flare between them, and she tried not to look at it. From his expression, it was clear he hadn't realized he'd said it or didn't know how a comment like that could land. He was all business.

Dana opened and closed her mouth eight times, but at no point did she have a comment that would have come out in coherent English. She became intensely interested in cleaning the worktable with spray disinfectant.

"What do you have next?" he asked.

"The world's earliest and stupidest lunch period," she said quickly.

"Oh, cool. Me too. Want to go together?"

She stared at him. "What?"

"Lunch?"

"What?" she repeated.

"You know, where they feed us really bad food that is, I'm positive, where all these dead frogs end up. Yummy." He grinned at her. Then his grin faded. "Earth calling Dana."

"Yes," she said. "Frogs. Delicious."

Ethan laughed. "You're a little bit weird. Anyone ever tell you that?"

"I—"

"Weird is good. Come on, grab your books. We want to get those frogs while they're still kicking."

He slung his book bag over his shoulder and headed for the door. Dana took a long moment remembering what legs were for and how to use them. She asked out loud, "What just happened?"

There wasn't anyone to answer that question, so she followed Ethan out into the hall. They were immediately washed away by the tide of students going to classes, but Dana and Ethan managed to steer themselves in the direction of the lunchroom. Conversation along the way was impossible, though, and they didn't talk much through the process of shuffling along the line of stainless-steel steam tables. Ethan broke the silence when it was their turn to make a selection.

"Oh, goody," he said. "We have orange glob, green glob, and brown glop. What's your preference?"

"Is that Salisbury steak?" asked Dana, pointing to the brown stuff.

"Only theoretically. I'm not convinced it has any origins in nature."

"I'll have that."

The matron behind the counter was bored, indifferent, and unspeaking. She ladled the meat onto an improbably heavy ceramic plate, added over-cooked diced green beans and a *splot* of lumpy white starch.

"Thanks," said Dana, but the matron gave her the kind of look a butcher would give a fatted calf, and then turned away.

"Let's flee," said Ethan, and they took their trays to a far corner of the crowded lunchroom. Dana was sure everyone was looking at her, but she focused on where she was going and did not look back. They had one end of a table to themselves and the other was piled high with boxes of flyers for the spring charity fund drive.

As they settled down to address the challenge of eating that food with some semblance of appetite, Ethan said, "So . . . you see ghosts."

Dana nearly stabbed her face with a forkful of meat. She stopped, slapped her fork down, and glared at him.

"So that's what this is all about?" she demanded. "That's just great."

Ethan leaned back, hands up. "Whoa! Sorry," he said quickly. "I wasn't trying to start something." He picked up his napkin and reached out to dab gravy from her cheek. "Really sorry."

"I'm serious. Is that what this 'oh, hey, let's pretend we're friends and have lunch together' is all for?" she demanded. "You acting all nice to me just so you could ambush me with a question like that?"

"No," he said firmly. "It's not. I said I'm sorry twice, and I'll keep saying it if that helps. Look, Dana, I'm not real good at talking to girls, and you scare the crap out of me."

She blinked at him. "*I* scare *you*? Why? Because of what happened yesterday?"

His cheeks turned red and his eyes kept sliding away from hers and then flicking back. "Well . . . no, not really."

"Then why? Because I'm the new girl and I'm a navy brat and I'm weird and—"

"No," he insisted, his color deepening. He gave her a funny look. "It's because I . . . well, I guess I've never really had a conversation with a girl as pretty as you."

"Oh, please. That's crap and you know it. I saw you talking with Corky Capriotti the other day."

"Corky's my cousin," he said. "We grew up together. Ew."

"Oh."

They looked at each other.

"If it will help," he said, "I'm willing to crawl on out of here and just see you in class."

She said nothing.

"Or I could go out and come back in and we can pretend that the world's most awkward conversation never happened."

She said nothing.

"Or you could stab me with your fork," he said. "Anything will work. Just give me a game plan here."

She looked down and was surprised to see that she had picked up her fork again and was holding it in a clenched fist.

"Eat your mystery meat," she mumbled, and they ate in silence for several minutes.

"Sorry," Ethan said again.

She nodded. "Me too."

"Why are you sorry?" he asked.

"For making you team up with a major weirdo."

Ethan sat back and studied her. "Why would you say something like that?"

She avoided his eyes. "Pretty much because everyone thinks I'm weird. They can't all be wrong."

"Big whoop. So you're not normal," he said. "Who cares? I mean, why care what anyone else thinks? You're smart and you don't try to be popular, and you don't hang with a clique."

"You mean I'm basically a loner and an outcast."

Ethan smiled. "I prefer to think of you as an individual."

"You know," she said thoughtfully, "you're a little weird, too."

"Takes one to know one," he said. They ate.

"Why'd you ask me about seeing Maisie's ghost?" asked Dana.

"Clumsy way to start a conversation?" he suggested.

"No, seriously."

Ethan shrugged. "I . . . guess I'm interested in what happened to Maisie."

"Did you know her?"

"Only by name," he said. "But she's not the first—"

"To die, I know. Five, right? That's what I heard."

"Right. So . . . do you think it's true?"

Dana frowned. "Do I think *what's* true? What are you talking about?"

"The five dead teens."

"What about them? Oh, do you mean do I think they were all taking drugs?"

"No," said Ethan in a low, intense voice. "Do you think they were all murdered?"

CHAPTER 23

Francis Scott Key Regional High School
12:01 P.M.

"*Murdered?*" cried Dana, so loud two teens at another table turned to look. Ethan faked a laugh.

"Yeah," he said loud enough for them to hear, "we *murdered* that lab project. Easy A, easy A."

The other students lost interest, and Ethan bent even closer to Dana and hissed at her. "Why don't you say it a little louder? Pretty sure my deaf grandfather back in Philadelphia didn't hear you."

She jabbed her fork in his direction. "Why don't you give a person some warning before you say something like that?"

"I thought that's what we were talking about," he fired back.

"No, we were *not* talking about that," snapped Dana. "We were talking about teens getting high and wrecking their cars. We were not having any kind of discussion in which 'murder' was even a topic. What's wrong with you?"

Ethan sat back and pursed his lips for a moment, working it through. "Okay," he said after a moment, "maybe I didn't read you right."

"You think?"

"Sorry. It's just that *I* think there's something very wrong happening in Craiger."

"Yes. People our own age are dying."

"And you're seeing their ghosts. My sister's friend Meghan was there, and she heard what you told Mrs. Frazer. You said you saw Maisie bleed like she was stabbed."

Dana said nothing.

"Stabbed isn't what happens in a car accident," said Ethan. "Stabbed is murdered."

"I was hallucinating."

"Uh-huh. From what I heard, you described Maisie exactly, even to the clothes she was wearing when she died. How did you hallucinate that?"

Dana felt her heart flutter, and this time it wasn't because a cute boy was paying attention to her. Those words jolted her like electric shocks. "I guess . . . I mean, I must have heard something."

"Like what? What was Maisie to you?"

"I didn't know her. What was she to you?" Dana countered.

He looked genuinely surprised. "Maisie? Nothing. Except that she was in our school. She was one of us, and now she's dead. She was like us, but someone killed her."

"How can you even make a statement like that? She died in a car accident. Maybe I didn't read about it before, but I read the paper yesterday. The cops saying that it was an accident. That it was her doing something stupid and getting herself killed. No . . . killing herself, even if by accident. No one did it to her. If there was even a hint of that, the sheriff's department would have said so."

"Not everything the cops do makes it into the papers, Dana," said Ethan. "They keep a lot of details out of the press when there's an ongoing investigation. It's how they can tell the difference between someone who claims to know details of a murder and someone who really does."

"Oh, and you know this how? Watching cop shows on TV?"

"No," he said. "I know this because my uncle's a cop. So's pretty much half my family going back to the thirties."

"And are they all saying this was murder?"

Ethan paused. "Not . . . all of them."

"Meaning?"

"Okay, my uncle Frank thinks there's something hinky."

"'Hinky'?"

"Something wrong. He doesn't believe that there could be this many teenagers dying in exactly the same way if it was only about doing drugs and driving. Five, Dana? The police collect statistics, and that would be high even in Baltimore or Philly or New York. Uncle Frank convinced his captain to set up a confidential tip line so people can call in if they know something."

"Has anyone called?"

"Yeah, about a thousand nut jobs who have claimed it's everything from a secret suicide cult to aliens to some kind of secret shadow-government, conspiracy theory junk."

"Great," she said dismally.

"It's okay," said Ethan. "There may even be something useful in all those calls. It just takes time to sort through them and analyze the data."

Dana ate a few small bites while she thought that over. "Are you planning on being a cop, too?"

"Me? Not really. I want to be a forensic scientist."

"What's that?"

"It's someone who works for the sheriff's department collecting and analyzing evidence. Blood spatter, fingerprints, all sorts of stuff. There's this saying that 'contact always leaves a trace,' and that's what forensic experts look for. You know in TV shows where the cop says he's sending something to the lab? That's the forensics department. That's where the real police work goes on."

His enthusiasm and passion were evident, and Dana was impressed.

"And your uncle Frank thinks this is murder?" she asked.

Ethan paused before answering. "I *think* that's what he thinks."

"What? Are you serious?"

"Okay," said Ethan. "He hasn't come right out and *said* that they were murdered, but the statistics bother him. He lives with my dad and me, and he made copies of each accident case file and keeps going over them. He definitely thinks they're connected. Sometimes he's up all night going over the medical examiner's report and the crime scene photos."

"Photos?" Dana almost gagged.

"Yeah."

"Have you seen them?"

"No . . . ," said Ethan in a way that made Dana believe he had. "He keeps them in his desk. He said they'd give me nightmares, but that's not true. I mean, I'm not five years old, right? Besides, I've seen autopsy photos in books. I have a strong stomach. You need to have a strong stomach if you're going to be a forensic scientist." He cut her a look. "You're pretty tough, too. You didn't even flinch when we cut open the frog."

"I guess. That stuff doesn't bother me."

"What does?" asked Ethan.

"Everything about this conversation."

The bell rang.

"I have gym," said Ethan. "Look, can we talk more later? After school?"

"I have yoga after school."

"You do yoga?"

"Yeah, and jujutsu, but that's tomorrow night."

He stared at her. "Wow. You are so freaking cool."

"Shut up."

"Lunch tomorrow, then, okay? No, wait, they'll probably give us a half day tomorrow for Maisie's viewing. Why don't you come by the science club before you go to yoga? There's four of us now. I know, it's not cool. We're a bunch of nerds, but you might, I don't know, dig it."

"Because I'm a nerd?"

"There are worse things to be," he said, giving her a big smile. "Besides, you do yoga and jujutsu. You can be our token cool girl."

They walked out together and stopped in the hall. The gym was to the left and her art class was to the right.

"You really think Maisie was murdered?" asked Dana, trying to fit the idea into her head.

"I hope I'm wrong," said Ethan, and left it there. She watched him walk away.

As soon as her last class was finished, Dana found Melissa and all but dragged her over to Beyond Beyond. They found their favorite table, and Dana told her sister about what Ethan had said. Everything, including the fact that Ethan's uncle, an actual detective, thought that the deaths might be suspicious. When she was done, Melissa stared at her with huge eyes. Then she blinked and looked at her watch.

"Crap, I have to do my meditation class," she said. "Don't. Go. Any-where. We really need to talk."

"I have yoga in an hour," said Dana. "Let's talk after."

"I have advanced yoga after that." Melissa growled. "Doesn't matter.

Wait for me. I want all the details."

"But . . . I just told you everything."

Melissa stood up and grinned at Dana. "I want all the details about you and Ethan."

"What? No, I—"

But Melissa left. Behind Dana, the cash register went *cha-ching* and the speakers overhead played strange music, and the day, already strange, continued to spin and spin.

CHAPTER 24

The Observation Room
2:37 P.M.

Agent Gerlach took a call on the car phone.

"He wasn't just messing with kids' minds last night," said the caller. "He went out for some fun and games, too. We only just now found out about it."

"Of course," said Gerlach, pinching the bridge of his nose and squeezing his tired eyes shut. "What did he do this time?"

There was a heavy silence on the other end of the line.

"You still there?" said Gerlach. "Tell me what he did."

"You'd better come see for yourself."

"Is it bad?"

"No, sir," said the caller. "I'm afraid it's a good deal worse than that."

CHAPTER 25

Beyond Beyond

3:44 P.M.

"It's important to focus on a still point inside your mind," said the teacher. "Yoga is about health and peace and a calm mind."

Yeah, thought Dana as she fought to keep her body aligned in the warrior pose, *good luck with that.*

Her mind was anything but calm, and peace seemed to be nothing more than an illusion. Less real in every important way than what she'd seen in the locker room. Less real than the angel in her dreams.

She stumbled through half a dozen poses, lagging behind the class, drawing the teacher's attention so often that some of the other "peaceful" participants began heaving audible sighs of frustration and annoyance. Luckily, the class ended with a long, seated meditation. That was good. It allowed Dana the chance to try to piece everything together, to step back and take a look at everything that was happening the way people did when they wanted to see the message of a painting rather than peer closely at the brushstrokes.

She assumed the cross-legged posture, leaning slightly forward, hands palm upward on her knees, eyes closed, breathing slowly in through the nose and out through her mouth.

Ethan wanted to be a kind of cop, a forensic science officer. That had some appeal to Dana, though she'd never considered it before. Not that she really wanted to go in that direction, exactly, but it helped her organize her thinking about everything that was going on. For the past two days she'd felt like she'd been floating from one weird moment to another.

Maisie was dead. That was how it had started.

Except . . . *No*, she corrected herself. It started with the dreams. It started with the angel in them. And the strange things he whispered. Most of what he said melted away when she woke up, but some bits and pieces were starting to float back, to tickle her memory. Odd things, though. Ominous and weird.

Despite what had happened in the locker room and the apparent reality of the angel in her dreams, Dana wasn't sure any of this was real. Or, if it was real, how much of it was true? Whatever it was, it seemed to be getting stronger. Or, perhaps *worse* was a better word. She'd always had strange dreams, but within days of moving here to Craiger, she'd had the first dream of the dark angel. Was it a kind of clairvoyance? Or maybe telepathy? She didn't know and would have to ask someone. Melissa, maybe. Or Corinda. In any case, that was where it had started. That was Point One.

Point Two was what happened in the locker room. Hallucination, visitation, whatever it was. Dana didn't have a vocabulary that included words for something like that. Maisie talked about the "Red Age." What was the "Red Age"? There was no context, no key to unlocking what that meant, if it meant anything at all.

Point Three was the dark angel. What was he? Sometimes she thought of him as a devil, or *the* devil; at other times she thought he was an angel. In earlier dreams, the angel had not been violent, and he hadn't been anywhere near as scary. Even though Dana thought he might be Lucifer, he hadn't been all that frightening. That was weird enough in its own way, but why had her feelings changed? Was it because of Maisie? Maybe, but Dana didn't think so. Not entirely.

Point Four . . .

Was there a Point Four? She had to wrestle her thoughts into order. Yes. Point Four was for five dead teenagers. Five of them. Five car accidents. Five lives snuffed out. Were they really five accidents or five murders? She had no idea. Part of her ached to find out, to grab Ethan and get every detail out of him. Part of her was absolutely terrified at the very thought. Fifty-fifty split.

Point Five?

She hoped there wasn't one.

"Dana . . . *Dana!*"

She snapped her eyes open and realized that everyone else was standing, their yoga mats rolled. The instructor stood in front of her, offering a tolerant and slightly quizzical smile.

"During class I thought you couldn't even concentrate, and then you go into a meditation so deep you don't even hear your name when I called you four times. You really went deep, didn't you?"

"Oh," said Dana. "Deep. Right. Real deep."

She got up, grabbed her mat, and hurried out.

Corinda was standing right outside the yoga room, her face grim, eyes filled with strange lights.

"I think we need to talk," she said.

Dana paused. "Talk about what?"

"About your dreams," she said. "About five murdered kids, and about the fact that the devil is visiting you."

PART TWO

THE LARGER WORLD

The more perfect a person is on the outside,
the more demons they have on the inside.
—Sigmund Freud

CHAPTER 26

Agent Gerlach sat on the bottom step and looked at the thing in the room. Naked, painted in blood, grinning as if the world was a joke and only he understood the punch line.

Gerlach sighed heavily, feeling older than his thirty-one years. Feeling tired. He was very aware of the weight of the .45 Colt model 1911 he wore in a nylon shoulder holster. He even thought about how many of his problems might be solved by putting the barrel of that gun against the back of the maniac's head and pulling the trigger.

Across the room from him, the madman sat cross-legged, naked, smeared with blood, eyes filled with strange lights. Between the killer and the agent lay hundreds of Polaroid photos that showed red ruined things that had once been teenagers. Gerlach had seen those bodies firsthand and he had done what was necessary. It was ugly work, and difficult, but there was a science to it. Car accidents were useful. All that crushing compression, all those sharp bits of glass, plastic, and metal flying around. No one could do the math to work out the ballistics of every piece of debris. You could hide almost anything except a bullet wound. There was a long history of car crashes that had solved problems for the Syndicate and so many other off-the-books agencies. Gerlach wasn't sure he could even count the number of problems he'd made go away over the last few years. These deaths were different. The latest one had presented its own unique challenge of hiding a different set of injuries.

The photos on the floor told the real story, though. And here was the madman responsible, his body painted red, surrounded by enough evidence to lock him away for a hundred years.

"If you want me to apologize," said the angel, "you'll have a long, long wait."

"No," said Gerlach. "I wouldn't wipe dog crap off my shoe with an apology, especially from you."

"Do you want me to explain?"

"Nope. I know why you did it."

"Why?" asked the angel.

Gerlach nudged the closest Polaroid with the toe of his shoe. It was a picture of a black girl screaming. "Because you're a psychopath."

"There is so much more to it than that." The angel's white teeth looked very white. Fractured lines of sunlight slanted down through what was left of the stained-glass window, painting his face with the image of Roman soldiers hammering nails through the wrist of Jesus. The glass was broken and so the soldiers appeared headless.

"No doubt," said Gerlach, "but ask me if I care. Ask me if I spend a rusty minute of any day giving any thought toward the inner workings of your mind."

The angel looked up at the cracked and peeling paint on the ceiling, at the exposed laths in the walls. At an elaborate spiderweb spun across the window, from which hung the empty husks of dead moths upon which the spider had fed. "Maybe you should," said the angel.

"Maybe. But if so, I'll worry about it tomorrow," said Gerlach. "My problem today is whether you are going to hit your deadlines."

"Deadlines," echoed the angel, enjoying the taste of the word.

"We have a lot riding on this, *compadre*," said Gerlach. "Do you even know how much money it's taken to move all these families into this junk-hole of a town? New construction, improved infrastructure, a rebuilt school system, not to mention providing jobs for everyone who *isn't* part of the program. Day care, too. All of that costs money, and every day that we have to wait for you, we are burning off something north of one million dollars. Every single day."

"Money belongs to the human world," said the angel.

"Yeah, yeah, and you're not human and by the light of the Red Age you'll be revealed in all your glory as a *nephilim*. Right. I've heard it a hundred times. I understand how you see things. But let me say this—I don't know what you are or how you're becoming whatever it is you think you're going to become. Angel, devil, mutant, sideshow freak, whatever. Doesn't mean a thing to me. It's a side effect. Whatever makes you what you are is a by-product of genetics taking a sharp left turn somewhere in your family history. Or, hey, maybe it *is* supernatural and you're really turning into a demon from hell. I don't know and, frankly, I don't care. The only thing I care about is the program."

"And your deadline."

"*Our* deadline, Sparky," Gerlach reminded him. "You signed up for this. And don't tell me that *we* are a means to *your* end. That wouldn't be the best way for this conversation to go. Understand me?"

The angel said nothing, but his smile shone like the sun.

"You've put a bunch of test subjects in the ground," said the agent. "I've had to do the detail work to make sure it looks clean and tidy."

"And bravo for staging your little dramas. It's great theater."

"Bite me," said Gerlach, but he grinned. "I need to know two things right now. First, I need you to assure me—and to make me absolutely believe—that those kids were of no significant use to the program."

"I told you this before," said the angel, the first trace of annoyance creeping into his voice. "They were failures, dead ends in terms of cultivation. All but two had hit a hard ceiling in the development of their abilities. The Bell girl and *this* piece of nothing showed promise at first, but as their talents emerged, they began to look in the wrong direction. They thought they understood what was happening, and each planned to do something about it. That couldn't be allowed."

"Uh-huh," said Gerlach, and he let his skepticism show through in his tone. "There was no other way to handle it?"

"No better way."

Gerlach took a pack of gum from his pocket, unwrapped two sticks, and began chewing them. He didn't offer any to the angel.

"What is your other concern?" asked the angel.

"You haven't filed a progress report."

"It's pending."

"It's late."

"Things are becoming critical," said the angel. "I don't have time to waste. This meeting, in fact, is inconvenient."

"Too bad." Gerlach chewed his gum.

"Yes, it will be too bad if this distraction results in another of our subjects breaking loose.

"Control," the angel said, "requires focus."

CHAPTER 27

"Don't freak out," said Corinda.

"I think it's too late for that," said Dana. "I'm way past being freaked."

They sat together at the table where Dana and Melissa usually sat. Corinda said she needed to be close to the coffee bar register and where she could see the front register in case she had to go help the part-time girl. There were fresh cups of tea and a plate of scones on the table, but Dana hadn't touched them. Her pulse was beating as rapidly as machine-gun fire, and she was sweating badly. She also felt light-headed, as if this were all some kind of dream and she wasn't fully awake.

"How do you know about the murders?" demanded Dana. "How do you know about my dreams? How do you know *any* of this stuff?"

Corinda picked up her cup, blew across the surface of the hot tea, and took a careful sip. Then she leaned over and took a deep inhalation of the vapors, her eyes closing for a moment. "Ahhh, that's nice. This is my own special mixture. Lotus flower tea. The lotus is a sacred symbol of eternal life in all the important spiritual cultures, from modern Egyptian Kemeticism to ancient Hinduism and Buddhism. It helps cultivate spiritual enlightenment, transcendence, and devotional love. You can use any part of the lotus, but I love it with the stamens and petals."

Dana stared at her. "You're talking about tea and my head's about to explode."

Corinda nodded to the cup in front of Dana. "I made you special tea with chamomile to soothe your nerves, and rose petals, which are a wonderful way to help open the heart, calm the mind, relax the body, stabilize your aura."

"I'm leaving," said Dana, but Corinda snaked out a hand and caught her arm. The woman was surprisingly fast, and her grip was strong.

"No," she said. "You need to stay and we need to have a conversation. I know you've seen him at night, in your room."

Dana thought about pulling away, and almost did, but she had to know. She heaved an eloquent sigh and settled back.

"Drink your tea," said Corinda. There was a deep, strange noise from the speakers, and it took Dana a moment to realize that it wasn't feedback or distortion but was instead Australian folk music played on a didgeridoo. There was a whole display of those long, painted, hollowed-out wooden drone pipes in the front of the store. Melissa loved them, but Dana thought the music sounded like the kind of songs whales would play at funerals.

She sipped the tea and looked at Corinda. "Tell me how you know what's going on with me."

Corinda cocked her head to one side and gave Dana a considering look. "You do know where you are, right? I mean, you know what this place is, and who I am, and *what* I am? Look around. Tell me how you think I know about these things."

Dana actually did look around. At the racks of tarot cards and crystal balls and rune stones. At the shelves of books about spiritual channeling, sun signs, roads less traveled, about inner work and self-discovery, books about unlocking the mind and transcending the body. At the talisman jewelry and the icons that stood in ranks on every table. At the posters on the wall for classes in yoga, tai chi, meditation, aligning chakras, light therapy, rebirthing, primal screaming, *pranayama*, qigong, and more. When she turned back to Corinda, the tall woman wore a knowing smile.

"Yes," she said. "That's how."

Dana gave a stubborn shake of her head.

Corinda sipped her own tea, then set the cup down firmly. "Last night when I was meditating, I was letting my consciousness rise free from my body. Do you know what astral projection is?"

"I think so. Leaving your body? Something like that?"

"Yes. Your spirit self leaves the physical behind and can travel great distances without assistance. The spirit undertakes a willful out-of-body experience, what we call an OBE, and once free of the body, the spirit expands beyond the limits of the five senses. It can see more, know more, understand more."

"And you're saying this is what you do?"

"All my life," said Corinda. She gave a rueful grin. "It's not the easiest way to grow up. It was bad enough being taller than every guy in my class and acing all my courses, but then I had to go and be deeply weird on top of it. But then . . . you know what that's like, don't you?"

"Do I?" asked Dana, keeping her guard way up.

"Sure," said Corinda. She selected a scone, tapped crumbs off it, took a bite, and spoke as she chewed. "You ace your classes. You always have."

"How do you know that?"

Corinda gave her a look. "I told you already. Don't look like you're totally shocked. You're in my house and this is what I do. Now . . . give me your hands. Let me read you. It's okay, I don't bite. Come on."

Corinda set down her scone and reached across to take Dana's hands. Dana resisted for a moment, then allowed the touch. Corinda's hands were warm against Dana's cold fingers.

"How . . . how does this work?" asked Dana. "What am I supposed to do?"

"Just look into my eyes," murmured Corinda. "Concentrate on me and allow me to step inside your energy field."

"How?"

"Just allow it, honey. That's all. I'll do the heavy lifting."

"Um, okay?" It came out as a question.

Corinda stared at her with green eyes that were flecked with chips of gold. She kneaded Dana's fingers gently and steadily, as if working to soften stiff pieces of modeling clay. At first Dana was very aware of the people and movement around her and was certain she looked like a complete idiot, sitting here holding hands with a woman twice her age. But the soft, steady, constantly moving pressure of Corinda's fingers on hers was strangely soothing. It was like a massage in a way, and the warmth seemed to spread, to run up her hands into her wrists and through the muscles of her arms. The Australian folk music ended and a new album began playing, one Dana recognized from past yoga classes. A somber flute played by Paul Horn, recorded inside the Great Pyramid of Giza, and it had a hypnotic quality. Slow and subtle and very deep.

"I can see your spirit self, Dana," said Corinda in a low, measured voice. "Your aura is orange-yellow. It means you have a scientific mind. You tend to analyze and overanalyze everything. You're a perfectionist. You love to solve riddles and problems and to find order when everything seems chaotic."

Dana opened her mouth.

"Shhhh. Just listen. Just be. Let me see what I can see and share what is open for me to share." Corinda slowed and deepened her kneading motions. "My aura is blue. My gift is that of being a spiritual intuitive and clairvoyant. That's why I can see all the way into you. I can see spikes of yellow shooting off you, Dana. They're like solar flares. Yellow means that you are on the verge of a great spiritual awakening, and there is a circle of violet above your head, over your crown chakra. It tells me that your higher self has become very active. Your inner eye is struggling to open. Let it! Let your third eye see what your human eyes cannot. I'll help you, Dana, because I already see. My third eye has been open since before I was born."

Dana felt herself drifting to the edge of sleep. She tried to blink herself fully awake, but that warm, constant touch was so soothing.

"These visions aren't new to you. You've had them before, but now they're getting stronger—now they're happening more often, and that's scary. You saw something and you don't know if it's an angel or a devil. You don't know why you're having those visions, and you're afraid of what it is you're seeing. It's okay, though. Let me be your guide. Nothing can hurt you while we're together. I have my shields, my spirit guides and protectors all around me. This is a safe place."

"Safe . . . ," murmured Dana.

"The being who has been visiting you in your dreams is an angel, Dana," said Corinda. "He is a messenger who wants very badly to share important information with you. Nod if you understand that."

Dana nodded. She believed that, too.

"Sometimes he is beautiful, the way you think an angel should look. Pure, whole, filled with glory."

Another nod.

"But sometimes he appears as something else. Darker, stranger, frightening. A monster."

"Yes," said Dana very, very softly.

"Yes," agreed Corinda. "I will tell you why, little sister. The being that is manifesting to you *is* an angelic being, but it is not an angel as you have been taught to think of one. They are not tall, blond white men with fluffy wings.

They are not little babies. Angels are very powerful and very different from anything you can imagine. They are not human. They only appear human when we humans give them that form. They have no physical manifestations at all. They're beings of pure cosmic energy. But when you look at them with your human eyes—even when dreaming—then your human, organic mind becomes confused and demands that you clothe them in a way that makes sense. That's why angels have been depicted as beautiful and regal humans. It's why painters have created images of God as a man with a white beard. They are clothing the cosmic *All* in the shape of a king, because that's how they imagine kings to look."

Dana kept nodding.

"You chose a form for the angel that looks beautiful and serene and safe," continued Corinda. "It's a father figure. I know you love and respect your father, but you're also a little afraid of him. He's strong and stern and distant, and so your angel appears to you with all those qualities. You give your angel a different face, though, because you want to love him in ways that you can't love your own father, and that's good—that's safe and healthy. But it is you who are choosing that form."

Corinda's words soothed as much as her touch, and Dana felt herself drifting, as if rising above her body. She even imagined she could look down and see herself sitting across from the woman.

"Then the deaths started happening in town," said Corinda. "Horrible deaths. Lives stolen away. Murders. That offends the harmony of your spiritual nature, Dana, and because you're a sensitive, you have tapped into the negativity that is in the very air. But because you're not yet aware of your gifts, not in full control of them, the negativity clouds your eye. It influences the way in which you perceive the celestial beings in your spirit-space. As the negativity covers you, you change the way in which you choose to view the angelic being. You see it as the devil, as Satan, because you cannot understand why harm can come to the innocent in the presence of cosmic power. For that to happen, it must be the angelic beings themselves that are doing the harm. But Dana . . . listen to me, this is not true. It isn't the angelic entity that is causing all of this. That's not what they do. The angelic beings are here as guides—they're here to protect us and elevate us."

Inside Dana's mind, the shape of the dark angel from her dream suddenly took shape. He stood facing away from her, tall and powerful, his black wings folded, muscular arms loose, fingers curled and tipped with black nails. He stood as if listening to what Corinda was saying, and then he began to turn. The wings twitched, and Dana could hear the rustle and rasp of the leather membranes.

Dana, spoke the angel in a voice that rumbled like summer thunder. *Dana, be careful. Be very careful. If you open your eyes, you can never unsee what you see.*

The dark angel turned and for a moment—for a fractured, flickering piece of a second—he wore the face of her father.

Dana cried out and lunged backward from him, and in doing so tore her hands from Corinda's grip. Her shoulders struck the partition between the booth and the register, hitting hard enough to knock something over. A calendar, maybe. She heard it slither down the partition and *thwap* onto the floor. The connection was snapped with the image of the dark angel and with Corinda, and the tall woman gasped and snatched her hands back as if stung.

They sat there, both frozen, staring at each other. Corinda looked shocked at first, but she composed her features very quickly, and even managed a smile.

"Well," she said, "that was something, wasn't it?"

CHAPTER 28

Beyond Beyond
4:31 P.M.

"What are you guys talking about?"

Dana jumped and turned to see Melissa standing beside the table. She hadn't even heard her sister approach.

"God! You scared the life out of me," gasped Dana.

Melissa raised her eyebrows. "Looks to me like you were already scared silly. You're white as a ghost. Move over. Are those fresh scones? I'm famished." She sat down and hip-checked Dana across the bench seat, took a scone, and bit off a large chunk, then nodded to Corinda. "You spooking my baby sister?"

"Only a little," said Corinda. "Dana's been doing a good job of spooking herself."

"Oh, I'm way past being spooked," said Dana with a nervous laugh. "I'm way, way, *way* freaked out."

"Tell me *everything*," said Melissa, taking Dana's cup and finishing the last of her cold tea.

"I had visions of some disturbing things that have been going on in Dana's spiritual mind," said Corinda. "But you already know about that, don't you? Yes. I can tell that she's shared this with you."

Melissa did not even blink when Corinda said that. Instead she nodded. "She tells me everything. How'd you know? Cards? Crystal gazing?"

"Meditation and astral projection," said Corinda.

"So cool. And you got inside Dana's head?"

"I'm actually right here, you know," said Dana.

Melissa elbowed her gently. "Tell me everything."

They did. Or at least Corinda did, and Dana grunted and nodded at all the appropriate places. Some of what Corinda said to Melissa was phrased differently, using even more of the often hard-to-follow language of the new age. The gist was the same, though.

Melissa leaned forward, her eyes wide and bright. "You think Maisie was *murdered*?" she said in a shocked whisper. "Oh my God!"

"That's what Ethan thinks," said Dana. "His uncle seems to think so, too. Maisie and the other teens."

"You think they're right about this?" asked Melissa. "I mean, this *can't* be true, can it?"

"It's true," replied Corinda. "Dana knows it on a soul level. The murdered kids are reaching out to her, using her sensitivity to share their story. To reveal the truth. That's why Maisie appeared to her at school."

"We have to tell people," declared Melissa. "We have to tell the sheriff and, well . . . everyone."

"No," said Dana and Corinda at the same time.

"Why not?"

"Because they'll think I'm actually certifiably insane," said Dana.

"That doesn't matter," said Corinda. "People have thought I'm an oddball since I was three years old. Who cares? It's just proof of their small minds and the blinders they choose to wear. No, girls, the reason we don't tell anyone about this, not yet at least, is that we don't know who the killer is."

"Which is why we have to tell the police," insisted Melissa.

"No," said Dana, getting where Corinda was going with this.

"Why not?" asked her sister.

"Because," said Dana, "if we tell the police, the killer will know that we know."

Melissa said, "Again, so what? We don't know who the killer is, so it's not like we're ratting on anyone in particular. We're not naming names."

"The killer won't know that," said Dana. "If it gets out that we know this because I've had some kind of weird psychic flash, or that Ethan told me about his uncle's case files, then the killer's going to wonder what else I know. He's going to wonder what happens if I have a dream of his face or his name, and he's going to have to do something about that."

"Yes," said Corinda quietly. "It would focus all his attention on you, Dana."

"I wish you *could* grab more details out of your visions," said Melissa. "Like maybe a name, an address. Anything."

"It takes time," said Corinda, "even for me. There has to be a proper alignment of universal factors for these things to come to me."

"I wish I understood what was happening to me," responded Dana.

"Visions aren't usually that precise," said Corinda. "They're often clouded with symbolism and all sorts of cryptic elements."

"It's driving me nuts," said Dana.

Corinda swirled the cold tea in her cup. "You joke, but visions have broken a lot of minds over the centuries."

"And gotten some burned at the stake, I bet."

"That, too. And while we don't have to worry about that kind of thing, the reaction by the unenlightened is often negative and hostile. You saw some of that in the gym yesterday."

Dana glanced at her. "The fact that you know that is really creepy."

Corinda looked pained. "I know. I've been creeping people out all my life. It's not fun. Those of us with gifts are often made to feel like we're evil, or sinful or wrong because this is part of who we are. However, I don't recall asking for this burden, and I suspect you didn't, either."

"Not on your life," said Dana. "Not in a million years."

"Which leaves us right where we were," said Melissa.

They sat and thought about it for a bit as the flow of people in and out of Beyond Beyond continued with the regularity of a tide. Angelo walked past carrying a red metal toolbox. He glanced at them, and Dana met his eyes. It was only for a brief moment, but there was an electric connection that she felt all the way down to her toes. His face was serious, unsmiling, almost troubled, and as soon as he noticed her looking at him, his gaze darted away. Why? Was he embarrassed? Did he not like what he saw? Was there something about her? Dana didn't know. Whatever it was, Angelo moved away quickly and vanished into the back.

"What should we do?" asked Melissa, oblivious to the exchange.

Corinda snapped her fingers. "Got it," she said. "Sunlight."

"Right," agreed Melissa at once.

"Why?" asked Dana. "What's he got to do with this?"

"With the murders?" asked Corinda. "Nothing. But he has a gift, too."

"Which is what?"

"That series of classes he's giving? Psychic Emergence? It's for people who have, or think they have, gifts like yours. He has a talent for helping people cultivate their gifts, develop them. I bet he could help you."

Dana felt apprehension rise up in her chest. She wasn't sure she *wanted* her "gifts" to get any stronger. But what if Sunlight *could* help, though? And what if, by helping her focus her visions, Dana could prevent the murder of another teenager?

"Okay," she said uncertainly, "let's try."

A line was forming at the front register and Corinda stood up. "You girls go find Sunlight. I've got to work; then I have back-to-back readings."

"But—" began Dana, but Corinda cut her off.

"After you see Sunlight, go home and meditate on this. I will, too, and then come back tomorrow so we can compare notes and make a plan."

They agreed. Corinda touched Dana's cheek.

"Be strong, little sister. You're becoming powerful, and that is always a frightening process. Have faith in your own power and trust the larger world. It holds all the answers." And with that she was gone.

CHAPTER 29

When they went looking for Sunlight, they learned that he had already left for the day. So Dana and Melissa had walked home, talking about everything but getting nowhere they hadn't already reached. It was so maddening that they eventually lapsed into a shared and troubled silence that pursued them all the way to their door.

Dana went to her room and was doing homework when the phone rang, and a moment later she heard her mother call her name. "Dana! It's for you."

There was a phone on a small table at the top of the stairs, and Dana hurried out to take the call. She didn't have her own phone, but almost no one ever called her. She had no real friends here and none of any depth back in San Diego. Sometimes her dad asked to speak to her if he was away, but he usually asked for both girls. She lifted the receiver.

"Yes?"

"Hey," said a familiar voice. "Got a sec?"

It took her a moment to place the voice.

"Ethan . . . ?"

"Yeah, I was thinking—"

Dana covered the mouthpiece and yelled very loudly, "*I got it, Mom!*"

After a moment there was a discreet *click* as the downstairs phone was laid back in its cradle.

"I didn't interrupt dinner or something, did I?" asked Ethan.

"No," she said quickly. "I was studying."

"Frogs?" he asked.

"Frogs," she agreed, and leaned back against the wall.

"Best thing to think about before bed. Frog guts."

"How'd you get my number?" she asked abruptly.

"Huh? Oh, I got it from Eileen, who got it from Dave, who got it from your sister. Is it cool that I called?" asked Ethan. "I'm not like . . . overstepping or anything?"

"It's totally cool," she assured him. "What's up? Is this about the dissection essay?"

"No," he said, his voice suddenly becoming more confidential. "I've been thinking about what we were talking about over lunch. About Maisie and the others."

"What about them?"

"You seemed interested."

"I am."

"In the accident reports and police files, I mean."

"Ah," she said, getting it. "And?"

"They're here at the house," said Ethan. "My uncle has his own master case file. It's in his desk."

"So?"

"So, I have the key."

Dana stared into space, wrapping the phone cord around her finger.

"You still there?" he asked.

"Yes."

"When Uncle Frank is at work tomorrow," said Ethan, "we could . . . I don't know . . . maybe take a look?"

"Yes," she said again, and the intensity in her voice surprised her.

"You're sure?"

"Absolutely. But what about your parents?" she asked.

There was a brief pause. "Mom's gone and Dad works a lot. He's never home."

"Oh," she said, because there didn't seem to be anything else to say. Ethan's tone had not invited comment on that.

"So, tomorrow," he said. "We have a half day, but I can get the guys in the science club to hang around for a bit. If you want to meet them, I mean."

"Definitely," Dana assured him.

"We'll all meet in the chem lab after last bell. We won't have long 'cause they'll be closing the whole school down, but we can probably get half an hour or so to talk with them."

"That works," said Dana. "I'll meet you there. And, Ethan . . . ?"

"Yeah?"

"Thanks," she said.

"For what?"

"For not treating me like I'm some kind of freak."

"Not a chance," he said, and hung up.

Dana walked slowly back to her room, thinking about everything that had happened today. That night she did not dream of angels or of devils. She had another ugly dream, though.

Dana dreamed that her heart was on fire.

In the dream, she lay on the cold and bare floor of a deserted building. A church. The high, arched stained-glass windows were smashed, and there were spiderwebs strung between the shattered remains of wooden pews. Dana lay on the floor with her arms stretched out to either side and her ankles pressed together. For a horrible moment she thought she was about to be crucified like Maisie. But that was when she felt the burn deep inside her chest. It was white hot and heavy, as if someone had stabbed her with a spike of pure fiery light. The weight of it pinned her to the floor.

She could feel the fire burning inside her, but when she raised her head, there was no smoke, no visible flames. Her pajama top was undamaged and there was no blood.

But the pain . . .

It was worse than anything Dana had ever felt, awake or in nightmares. It was so huge, so intense, that she did not even scream. No scream could be loud enough to express that searing agony. She lay there, teeth clenched, muscles rigid, mind burning along with her heart.

And then the burning sensation seemed to pulse, to expand with the intensity of a sun going nova. It overwhelmed her and consumed her and charred every last bit of her down to hot ash.

She came bursting up out of sleep, finding her voice at last and crying out in pain. She was on the floor beside her bed, the sheets coiled around her legs. The burn in her chest was still there, still burning hot. Dana kicked savagely at the sheets until they released their tentacular hold and she was up, running to the bathroom, slamming the door behind her. She yanked up her pajama top, needing to see how badly she was hurt.

There it was. A red mark as livid as a fresh burn, shaped like a starburst, with rays extending outward. It seemed to throb with heat and light and pain.

Then it faded and disappeared, taking with it all sensation and any traces of the burned flesh. It left behind only smooth skin.

She stood there, hips pressed against the sink as she bent closer to the mirror to examine her skin.

Nothing.

Dana sagged back against the bathroom wall. She slid down and huddled there, shivering, trembling.

"What's happening?" she asked the empty room.

No one answered her.

It took a long time for her to climb back to her feet, using the sink and doorknob as handholds. She washed her face, staggered back to her bedroom, and dropped down to pray. But the words of every prayer she tried came out wrong, clumsy, broken.

Dana crawled into bed and begged God or the universe or anyone at all to let her sleep, pleading for no dreams at all. Not even good ones. Nothing but darkness and peace.

And she did sleep.

But she dreamed again. This time she dreamed that she was dead. That she'd died in her sleep. She dreamed that she floated like a mote of dust in the still air of her bedroom, watching with helpless dread as her mother came in to wake her. The moans that were torn from her mom's throat when her fingers touched the cold, slack skin of her daughter's flesh were horrible beyond words.

When Dana woke in the cold, pale light minutes after dawn, she lay there, panting, feeling weak and spent.

"God," she gasped. "Oh my God."

CHAPTER 30

"You look like death," said Melissa when Dana came into the kitchen.

It was just the two of them. Dad had come home late and was still sleeping, Gran was dozing in her chair in the living room, and Mom was sitting in the backyard, drinking tea. It was what she did when she wanted to be left alone. It was a cold, quiet morning in the Scully house.

"Thanks," muttered Dana as she reached for a knife to cut a bagel. The blade caught her reflection, and for a moment Dana stood there, staring at her own face. Melissa was right: she looked awful.

"You have more dreams?" asked Melissa.

Dana avoided her eyes. "Kind of."

"Another vision?" her sister asked, jerking upright from the comics page of the newspaper.

"No," said Dana, not wanting to describe those dreams. "Ordinary stuff. Nothing I want to rehash. Is there coffee?"

"You hate coffee."

"I need some."

Melissa got up and made a fresh pot. Dana poured just a little cream into hers and sipped. They sat in moody silence until they were almost done eating. Gran shuffled in and sat down, smiling benignly. "Oh, hello, Margaret," she said to Melissa. "Who's your little friend?"

They did not bother to correct her. The girls kissed her, gathered their school stuff, and went out.

They did not see the curtains part on the second-floor master bedroom window. They did not see the face of their father watching them walk away.

Dave and Eileen intercepted them again, and they walked to school in a pack. From the bright smile Dave gave Melissa, Dana figured he had planned to "run into" them. Dave gave Melissa a smile brighter than the April sun.

"That's a really pretty blouse," he said.

Melissa plucked at it. The blouse was sheer, but the swirling pattern of wildflowers kept it from being totally see-through. It was low-cut, though, and Melissa wore a new color of lipstick.

"Thanks," she said. "I just threw on the first thing I could find."

It had taken her half an hour to pick out the right blouse, and the very tight jeans to wear with it, and it was clear to anyone with a pulse that she had planned for this encounter. Especially since it wasn't that warm outside and she must have been freezing. Eileen caught Dana's eye, and they both turned away to hide smiles.

"Much as I love school half days," said Dave, "I wish it wasn't because they're letting everyone out because of the viewing. That sucks. And a bunch of people got permission to skip school tomorrow for Maisie's funeral."

Eileen glanced around. "Are you guys going?"

"No," said Melissa. "I don't do viewings and I don't do funerals."

Eileen cut a look at her. "Because you didn't know her?"

"No, because death should be about rebirth and not a bunch of people staring at a corpse in a box. That's creepy."

No one commented on that, and silence followed them for almost a full block.

They crossed a street and saw Karen and her friend Angie. The girls paused to study Dana with unreadable eyes. On reflex Dana nodded to them, and after a moment Karen nodded back. No words were exchanged, though, and the other girls walked ahead.

"What was that all about?" asked Dave.

"Maisie's cousin and her friend," said Dana. "We talked yesterday. They're really hurting."

They walked in silence for two blocks, and then Dave said, "We talked to Ethan Hale last night. He was asking about you."

Dana said, "Oh . . . ?" She tried to make it sound casual, but Melissa and Eileen both cut sharp looks at her.

Melissa scowled at him. "What was he asking about?"

"Nothing much," said Dave. "He knew I knew you, and wanted to know stuff about Dana."

"What kind of stuff did he want to know?" persisted Melissa.

"General stuff. Where you guys live. What Dana's into. Y'know, books and movies and music. Like that."

"Ah," said Eileen, giving a knowing nod.

"Ah," agreed Melissa.

Dana was way too embarrassed to say a word. One of the real downsides of being a redhead was that her face flushed brightly with every change of mood, and something like this was like being a lobster in a pot. Hot and bright red.

"Ethan's cute, for a nerd. What'd you tell him?" asked Melissa, clearly amused.

Dave shrugged. "All I know is that she likes school."

Dana quickened her pace, as if she could outwalk her blush.

"Hey," said Dave as they crossed toward the school. "Look at all the deputies."

There were two sheriff's department cars and several uniformed officers standing in a knot, speaking with the principal, Mr. Sternholtz, and the school's elderly security guard, whose name Dana didn't know but who all the students called Tex.

"I heard they were going to assign a bunch of narcs to FSK," said Eileen.

"Right," said Dave, "because clearly we've become a wretched hive of scum and villainy."

"This is about Maisie," countered Eileen, "and those other teens. Maybe there really is a problem."

"Maybe," said Dana quietly. "But I don't think it's drugs."

CHAPTER 31

Gerlach's driver drummed his fingers on the curved top of the steering wheel.

"She saw you, you know," he said.

Agent Gerlach popped the glove box and rooted around for a fresh pack of gum. There were a dozen packs in there, most of them empty. He never threw his trash out the window. Fingerprints. He found the last unopened pack behind the spare magazines for the automatic pistol he wore.

"I know," he said.

"Is that going to be a problem?"

Gerlach unwrapped a stick and bent it to test its freshness. It snapped. Brittle and stale. He sighed and put it in his mouth anyway.

"I don't have a particularly memorable face," he said.

"You sure?" asked the driver. "I read her profile. She's a sharp kid. Young, but sharp."

Gerlach chewed the gum and did not reply.

The last of the students vanished through the big doors, and the neighborhood fell into a false quiet, as if there were no one around.

As if everything were calm and peaceful.

As if.

CHAPTER 32

Dana was at her locker sorting through her textbooks when Ethan seemed to materialize out of nowhere.

"Hey," he said, and she jumped about a foot in the air.

"Don't *do* that," she said, shoving him back.

"Sorry," he said in exactly the way someone says it when they're not. "Are you still coming to science club today?"

"Sure," said Dana. "But then we'll go look at your uncle's files. Right?"

He searched her eyes. "If you're sure you want to."

Before she could answer, the special notice bell rang very loudly, and they automatically glanced at the speakers mounted high on the wall. There was a *tap-tap* sound of someone testing the mic, and then Mr. Sternholtz's voice spoke in a slow, heavy tone.

"All students are required to go to the auditorium for a special assembly that will be held in place of homeroom. Please make your way there now. The assembly will begin in fifteen minutes."

Then silence.

"What's that all about?" wondered Ethan. "No, wait, I get it. . . . The narcs. Did you see them all outside? We're going to have them up our butts from now on."

Dana nodded, though there was a tone to Sternholtz's announcement that bothered her.

Even so, she cut a sidelong look at Ethan. "You want to sit together?"

He grinned. "Sure."

They headed off, and almost immediately Ethan collided with a young man who came out of a doorway. Ethan bounced off the other guy and nearly fell, but the second boy whipped out a hand and caught him. It was an incredibly fast move, and it carried with it enough strength to stop Ethan's fall.

"Hey! Watch where you're going," growled Ethan as he pulled his arm away.

The other boy was Angelo, from Corinda's shop. "You walked into me, *ese*."

Angelo's blue work shirt was half-unbuttoned to reveal a white Henley beneath. His arms and face were a medium brown except for some old pink scars. *Signs of an interesting life*, Dana thought.

"You came out of nowhere and crashed right into me," protested Ethan. He was flushed, clearly embarrassed for getting both knocked over and saved in the same moment.

"I came out of there," said Angelo, pointing to a door clearly marked JANITORIAL. "If you'd been paying a little attention to where you were going instead of hound-dogging with your girlfriend here, you might have seen me."

"I wasn't hound-dogging; I was going to the assembly."

"He's not my boyfriend," Dana said quickly.

Both boys looked at her. Angelo smiled; Ethan did not.

"If you were going to the assembly," said Angelo mildly, "then I guess you better scurry along." Before Ethan could organize a reply, Angelo turned to Dana and gave a little lift of his chin. *"¿Qué pasa, mai?"*

Dana didn't know very much Spanish but knew that phrase from growing up in Southern California. *What's up, girl?*

She didn't reply. Ethan stood there, awkward and uncertain, apparently not knowing what he should say or do. Angelo seemed amused.

"See you around, amigo," he said, and walked off. When he was a few feet away, he turned and gave Dana the same kind of inexplicable look he'd given her at Beyond Beyond.

"Freak," muttered Ethan under his breath.

"Forget about it," said Dana. "Come on."

They hurried down the hall to the auditorium, where a couple hundred students were looking for seats and apparently all talking at once. No one knew for sure what was happening, and everyone had a theory. But then Mr. Sternholtz walked out onto the stage, followed by a uniformed deputy. The room fell silent, though Dana heard a few snickers and jokes, and three of the guys on the school's golf team pretended to pass an invisible joint back and forth.

Principal Sternholtz stopped in front of a microphone on a stand, glared out at everyone, and said, "*Enough*." His voice was sharp and commanding, amplified to godlike dimensions by the sound system. Even the jokers in the crowd fell silent. The school nurse and another woman Dana didn't recognize joined the others onstage. No one looked happy, and from the red puffiness of her face, it was clear the nurse had been crying.

Dana and Ethan exchanged a worried look. He mouthed, *What's going on?* But Dana shook her head.

"As you all know," began Sternholtz, "our school and our community have been plagued with a series of tragedies over the last six months. Three young people from Oak Valley High and two from FSK have died in a series of terrible car accidents that could have—no, *should* have—been avoided. These senseless acts resulted in the loss of those young lives and the destruction of all their potential. It's a wretched chain of events, and I wish I could say that it was over, that we have all become smarter, that we have learned from our mistakes and moved into a safer, saner phase of our lives." He paused and looked out across the sea of faces. No one made a sound. Nothing. It was a vast and icy silence. "But this tragedy simply will not end. We have not even buried Maisie Bell, we have not even begun to process our grief over our loss, and now today I am so very sorry to tell you that there has been another death. A third FSK student. Another one of us."

Ethan grabbed Dana's hand and held on, as if she could keep him from sliding off his seat. His hand was ice cold.

"Today I have learned that senior Todd Harris was killed Tuesday night when his car went through a guardrail near Elk Hill Road. His car was found at the bottom of the hill, submerged in the river."

The silence held and stretched to an excruciating point, and then it was shattered by a scream. Everyone turned to see a blond girl go running from the auditorium, followed by three other girls.

"Todd's girlfriend," said Ethan. "Jeez, they didn't even bother to warn her first? That's so wrong. It's cruel."

Dana nodded, but her mind was not living in that moment. The news had yanked her thoughts elsewhere. *Another death?* A sixth teenager. A sixth car accident?

"No," she said.

"What?" asked Ethan.

Dana leaned close and spoke in a fierce whisper. "There's no way this was an accident. You understand that, right?"

There was fresh fear in his eyes but not very much doubt. "I guess so."

"Someone's killing teenagers," she said. What she really meant to say was, *Someone is killing us.*

Ethan looked sick. "I know."

On the stage, Mr. Sternholtz turned the mic over to the school nurse, who spoke about the dangers of drugs. She in turn introduced the other woman, a psychologist, who talked about grief management, and the dangers of drugs and alcohol. Then the uniformed officer introduced himself as Deputy Driscoll, and he spoke about the dangers of drugs. They saved the bombshell for last.

Principal Sternholtz glared out at everyone. "First thing this morning I instructed the office staff to make a series of calls to each of your parents to obtain permission for us to conduct blood tests. Now, before you rise up in protest of a violation of your civil liberties," he said, his tone condescending, "let me remind you that you are all minors. As long as we have permission from your parents or legal guardians, we can—and we *will*—do this. The proliferation of illegal narcotics has to be stopped. If extreme measures are necessary, then that is the course we will take."

Some of the students sat in stunned silence; others growled and booed. Sternholtz stared them all down.

"Make no mistake," he said coldly. "If any of you decline to let our nurse and the volunteers who have come here today from the hospital take blood samples even with parental permission, you will be suspended pending a consideration of possible expulsion."

No one said a word.

"There has been a lot of talk in the press about a 'war on drugs.' So far it seems we have been losing that war." His eyes glittered and he gave them a horrible little smile. "That will change. This is a war I intend to win. Now, throughout the day, nurses will come to each classroom with a list of those students whose parents have chosen to cooperate with our campaign to keep all students of Francis Scott Key Regional High School safe. Dismissed."

The students got to their feet, some furious, many shaken, all of them alarmed and frightened.

Dana leaned close and whispered to Ethan. "This is messed up. It's wrong."

He glanced at her. "What makes you say that?"

She shook her head. "I don't know, but every molecule in my body is screaming that this isn't what they're saying it is. Can't you feel it, too?"

Ethan studied her for a long time. Then he nodded slowly. "Yeah," he said. "We *have* to look at Uncle Frank's files after school."

"Yes, we do," she said, and the ferocity in her own voice surprised her.

Ethan pursed his lips thoughtfully. "I only have gym and Latin today and then I'm done. What do you have?"

"History and English," she said.

"Okay, meet me at the chem lab as soon as you can. Let's talk to the guys in the science club before they shut down the school for the day. Maybe they'll be able to help."

Dana was ten minutes into her first class when an aide appeared with a list of names. Hers was on it.

The sense of betrayal stabbed deep, but less so when she learned that she would be tested tomorrow and it was her father, not Mom, who had agreed. For her and Melissa.

CHAPTER 33

They looked like a frog, a stork, and a praying mantis.

The three other members of the science club were clustered around a table and glanced up when Ethan and Dana entered the room. They looked exactly as Dana expected.

The frog was a short tenth grader with huge eyes, a wide mouth, tiny ears, and a potbelly. He wore a T-shirt with Luke Skywalker on it and jeans that Dana was positive had to be at least a hundred years old. His sneakers looked even older. Ethan introduced him as Jerry Gomer.

"Hey," said Jerry, and he blushed a furious red as he said it.

Not used to talking to girls, thought Dana.

The stork was a girl. Sylvia Brunner was very tall and very thin, with a long, slender neck dotted with several moles that Dana thought looked like one of the constellations, but she couldn't remember which one. Sylvia had a bland face that wasn't pretty but was cheerful and open. She wore glasses with thick brown frames and no makeup, and had a lot of messy hair piled into a sloppy bun. There was absolutely nothing threatening about Sylvia, and no trace of judgment in her pale green eyes.

"My cousin Dave talks about your sister all the time," she said. "I think he has the hots for her."

"Yeah, well," said Dana, and they smiled at each other.

The praying mantis was a black girl with eyes that never seemed to blink, who moved with slow, controlled precision. There was a lot going on behind those eyes, thought Dana, she was one of those people who took in every detail but seldom shared what they thought.

"Tisa Johnson," said the girl, introducing herself.

"Good to meet you," said Dana.

The classroom was otherwise empty, and the members of the club had been working on a complex chemistry problem using small wooden balls and pegs to create models of organic molecules.

Sylvia said, "Just to get it out in the open, Dana, we all heard about what happened in the locker room."

"Um . . . okay."

"Ethan says you're not out of your mind," said Sylvia, "so we didn't bring a straitjacket to school with us."

"Okay. Thanks . . . ?"

"I watched you during the assembly," said Tisa. "You and Ethan."

"Oh?"

"You weren't buying what they were trying to tell us, were you?"

Dana glanced at Ethan, who gave her an encouraging nod. "Not much, no."

"What's your theory, then?"

The three of them looked at her with the intensity of a jury at a murder trial. Or at least that was how Dana felt.

She dumped her heavy backpack on the floor and sat down. "I don't know what's going on," she admitted. "I only know what I've experienced."

"I've heard ten different versions of that," said Sylvia.

"Whispers down the lane," said Jerry.

"Tell us your version," said Tisa.

And so she did.

They listened to the story. When she was done, there were almost thirty seconds of silence, and she could see the members of the science club going inward, thinking it all through, processing it their individual ways. Jerry perched on the edge of his chair and traced small circles on the table with his index fingers, one circling clockwise, the other counterclockwise, and at different speeds. Sylvia leaned back and looked at the ceiling. Tisa stared at Dana with piercing, unreadable eyes.

It was Tisa who broke the silence.

"Extrasensory perception is a valid aspect of science," she said in a voice that was measured and precise. "It's been studied by the top universities all over the world. It's studied by the military. Ours and everyone's."

"It's creepy," said Sylvia, "but it's also pretty cool. I saw a guy on TV just last week, on one of the talk shows. I forget his name. The Stupendous something-or-other. Doesn't matter. They said that he's been helping police find the bodies of murder victims. So . . . the police must think there's something to all this."

Jerry cleared his throat. "They said that all the teens who died were taking drugs and died in single-car accidents."

"I don't believe that," said Dana.

He stared at her with his huge frog eyes. "It's a statistical improbability for that to happen in a town this small. Even taking into account the number of people in the whole county, the numbers won't work."

Dana gaped. "Wait, so you guys *believe* me?"

Sylvia gave her a huge smile. "Ethan believes you. You knew things about Maisie that you couldn't have known unless you'd met her."

"And you said you never met her," said Jerry, nodding.

"So," said Tisa, "unless you are a tremendous liar—and by tremendous

I mean tremendously good at it—then, yes, you experienced some kind of psychic phenomenon."

Dana felt a massive weight lean and fall off her shoulders. "Thank you," she said.

But Tisa held up a finger. "The problem is," she said, "that we don't have enough information to form any kind of useful theory."

"Nope," agreed Jerry.

"Not a chance," said Sylvia.

"Swell," said Dana. She turned to Ethan. "Uncle Frank?"

He looked pained, but he nodded. "Uncle Frank."

CHAPTER 34

"You're sure he won't walk in on us?" asked Dana as she followed Ethan onto his front porch. There were no cars in the driveway or on the street. The house was an old, weathered A-frame with a postage-stamp front lawn that was completely dominated by a gnarled elm that looked like something out of a Tolkien novel.

Ethan fished a ring of keys from the bottom of his book bag and fitted one into the heavy lock on the front door. "Not a chance," he said. "Uncle Frank's working double-shift today because of Todd Harris, and he usually goes out with his partner to the diner on the highway. It's where the local deputies and some of the state troopers hang out." He paused, then added, "Actually, I'm kind of surprised he wasn't at school today. Maybe the sheriff is really going with this as drugs, booze, and bad driving and not buying into anything deliberate like murder."

He opened the door and stood aside to let her enter. *A gentleman*, thought Dana. *Wow. I thought they were extinct.* It was a line cribbed from her mother.

"You said your mom was gone. Does that mean your parents are divorced?"

A cloud seemed to pass in front of Ethan's face. "My, ah, mom died when I was four."

"Oh . . . I'm so sorry."

"It's okay. I don't really remember her much. She was sick for a couple of years. Cancer. So I never got to spend a lot of time with her."

Dana touched his arm. "That's awful."

"It's ancient history," he said in a way that clearly showed that it wasn't. Not to him. Ethan closed the door and tossed his keys into a dish on a side table. The living room was small and dark, with the shades down and curtains pulled across. For a house of bachelors, there was no obvious clutter or dust, and she guessed that this was more Ethan's doing than anyone's. He was a very neat and tidy guy. The furniture was the kind bought at the big chain department stores. Same for the landscape paintings on the wall. They were of the kind probably sold already framed. No vases of flowers, no knickknacks, no personal touches.

"How's your dad?"

Ethan sighed. "Dad's never around, like I said. He's always working. He works for the government, but he can't talk about it. Not that he's ever around *to* talk about it. Uncle Frank says that Dad was different before Mom died, but that's all I've ever known, y'know? There's that expression, 'married to his job'? That's Dad. Uncle Frank did more to raise me."

And you raised yourself, thought Dana. *Did a good job, too.*

"My dad can be pretty distant, too," she said.

"I heard," said Ethan. "Navy captain, right? Does he have his own ship?"

"Not at the moment. He did when we were in San Diego, but they moved him here for some kind of special advanced naval warfare training thing. He's teaching classes, but he can't talk about anything he does, either. He's gone a lot, too, and when he's home he can be really intense. Snaps at Mom, treats Melissa, Charlie, and me like we're sailors who don't know how to swab a deck. Everyone has to be A.J. Squared Away."

"Sounds rough."

She shrugged. "Only one of us who doesn't get stepped on by him is my oldest brother, Bill, who joined the navy. He wants to be exactly like Dad."

"Ouch."

"It's okay, I guess," said Dana. "My mom says that Dad's under a huge amount of pressure at work and that this will all pass."

Ethan gave her a knowing smile. "It's all good."

"Yup," she said, agreeing to the lie because it was easier than deconstructing something they each knew might be beyond their power to put back together again.

"Dad won't bother us today, though. He's away for a few days on some classified thing. We have the place to ourselves." Ethan's comment was intended to sound offhand, but it was obvious there was a bigger and possibly sadder story that he didn't want to share. He smiled, but it looked painful, and Dana asked no further questions.

Ethan led her down a short hall and into a room that was clearly a combination library and office. There was a big oak desk, a small fireplace in which an electric space heater had been placed, threadbare old armchairs, and shelves lined with books. Hundreds and hundreds of them. Dana almost gasped when she saw them, and for a few moments she drifted along the walls, looking at the titles. The books were, she discovered, arranged alphabetically by type. There were books on law and police work, books on the history of evidence collection and on modern forensic science, books on a score of other areas of science, ranging from entomology to abnormal psychology. There were also books on astronomy, mathematics, and physics. These nonfiction works filled about half the shelf space, and the rest was entirely given over to fiction, and of those, most were mysteries and detective novels. The works of Edgar Allan Poe and Arthur Conan Doyle were prominent, as well as books by Ed McBain, John D. MacDonald, Agatha Christie, and many others, some of whom Dana had heard of, many that were new to her. She wondered who here in the Hale household read those books, or if reading was the one thing that they all shared. Overall, the house felt cold, like a dead battery. Loveless.

It made her want to give Ethan a hug.

She didn't do that, of course, because so far in her life boys had been friends or tormentors, not prospects. Not like Melissa, who had been caught kissing boys when she was nine.

"It's in here," said Ethan, and that pulled her out of her own head. She followed Ethan over to the desk and watched as he pulled a small key from his pocket and fitted it into the lock on the bottom desk drawer. "Uncle Frank doesn't know that I had a copy made last year."

"Why'd you do that?"

Ethan shrugged. "Because he made me mad when he said that I couldn't handle seeing accident and autopsy photos."

Dana smiled. "Works for me."

The lock clicked open, and Ethan pulled the drawer out and removed a heavy file that was at least three inches thick and closed by heavy rubber bands.

"Wow," she said. "When you said he had a file, I thought it was like they show on TV. A couple of pages and some photos."

"This is the one he keeps at home," said Ethan as he set the file on the desk. "He said that all the case files combined fill three cardboard boxes. Uncle Frank made a kind of shorthand master file for himself."

Instead of immediately removing the rubber bands, Ethan took a notepad from the unlocked top drawer and used a pencil to make a detailed and exact sketch of the angles and colors of each rubber band, including how and where they were layered over the others.

"In case he has them set a certain way," explained Ethan. He removed the rubber bands and laid them on the diagram. "Frank's very detailed oriented, and he knows that I snoop around sometimes. But he doesn't give me enough credit."

"Clearly," said Dana, impressed. "But didn't you tell me that you hadn't looked at this folder before . . . ?"

He grinned. "Maybe I peeked," he admitted, "but I haven't had time to really go through it."

"You've looked at his other files, though, right?"

He shrugged but didn't answer, which was answer enough.

They brought the file over to the pair of leather chairs in front of the fireplace, and he dragged a small coffee table between them and placed the heavy folder on it. He placed his hand flat on the cover, though, and gave her a serious look, brow knitted. "Are you sure you want to see this stuff?"

"What did you say about your uncle not giving *you* enough credit?"

He winced. "Okay, sorry."

The folder contained individual case files for each death. They set to work reading the reports. Much of the material was technical, and her progress was bogged down by what Ethan called "cop-ese," the acronym-filled verbiage used by police. After a few pages, and some interpretation from Ethan, she was able to navigate. *DB* became "dead body," *EC* was "emergency contact," *HP* was "highway patrol," and *MVA* was "motor vehicle accident." Some of the acronyms were all too obvious, like *JUV* and *DOA*.

When they reached the first folder of photos, Dana braced herself. Saying that she was ready for anything and actually *being* ready were worlds apart. She had seen pictures of dead people on TV and in the newspapers, but this was different. These were people her own age, and unlike newspaper photos, these were in crisp, clear, brutal full color.

The name on the first folder was Connie Lucas, from Oak Valley High School, which was just over the county line. There was a picture paper-clipped to the outside cover, a school photo that showed a pretty girl with short hair, wearing a blouse with a sunflower pattern, earrings, and a charm necklace on a delicate chain. Dana took a breath and opened the folder.

The first twenty photos had been taken at the crime scene. A station wagon had hit a tree at very high speed, and the whole front was wrapped around the heavy oak. There was so much damage that it was hard to even tell the make or model of the car. All the tires and windows had been blown apart and the driver had been thrown from the car. A body lay battered on the rocky ground, having rolled away from the car down a slope. Other photos showed Connie on a plastic sheet in the harsh glow of floodlights. The pictures had been taken to document the scene and were clearly not intended to be lurid or exploitive, but they hit Dana like a series of punches. Her lungs clutched, and breath burned to dust in her chest.

She made no comment because speech was simply not possible.

Then Dana turned to the second set of photos. The lighting was different, and the victim lay on a stainless-steel morgue table. There were instruments and drains and machines. The girl's clothes had been cut away and were heaped at the foot of the table. She lay naked and vulnerable, robbed of every dignity, exposed under the glow of cruel fluorescent lights.

The next forty photos were the step-by-appalling-step of the autopsy.

Dana could feel greasy sweat run down inside her clothes, and the room seemed abnormally bright. How in God's name had she thought she was ready for this? When she turned to Ethan, she expected him to look as stoic as he said he'd be, but there were tears glittering in the corners of his eyes.

They did not speak to each other. Not one word. Not until they had finished that file and gone on to the next. A Japanese boy, Jeffrey Watanabe, eighteen, and a black girl, Jennifer Hoffer. Along with a white girl, Connie Lucas that made three from Oak Valley.

The next two folders were of the FSK students, Maisie Bell and Chuck Riley, both also white.

Dana went through them and then returned to the photos of Maisie. It was her. It was definitely the girl from her visions. There was a school photo of Maisie, as there was with all the others, but that was her alive. She looked like a different person dead. The body looked . . . wrong. Not a person at all. Empty. Abandoned.

A wave of sadness hit Dana and she wanted to cry, but she fought the tears back. Even so, the pain was there. Having seen Maisie in the locker room had made the girl totally real to Dana. It was as if she had known her and lost an actual friend.

Maybe that was how it was supposed to feel, she thought. After all, how different was Maisie from herself? Or from Melissa?

She looked at Ethan. "Where's the file for Todd Harris?"

"Uncle Frank didn't bring it home yet," said Ethan. "Maybe it's too new. I heard him talking about it on the phone, though. I went into the kitchen and listened on the extension."

"Sneaky," she said with approval.

Ethan shrugged. "I hate doing that to Uncle Frank, but . . ." He let the rest hang.

"What did you hear?" asked Dana.

"Todd wasn't crucified, that's for sure. I don't know most of the details but I'm sure Todd's neck was broken. That's pretty much all I heard."

Dana nodded and then something occurred to her. She scanned down a page marked *Inventory*, looking to see what Maisie had with her when she died, and realized that what she was looking for was the eclipse pendant she had seen during her strange encounter with Maisie. It wasn't there, though there was a notation: *Silver chain, 20 inches. Broken three inches below clasp.*

Dana wondered what had happened to the pendant itself. Had they missed it among all the wreckage? No way to know, and she did not think it was a practical idea to go to the crash site and try to be Sherlock Holmes. So she kept digging through the file. There were inventory pages for each of the dead teenagers, and she scanned them, just on the off chance that they might have had similar pendants, but there was nothing like that. So much for a budding theory. There was very little jewelry of any kind, though, even among the girls.

On another page, she found a list of noted *Scars, Marks, Tattoos.* Nothing there that connected the victims, although there was a notation that the two boys, Jeffrey and Chuck, had *indications of tattoos that were materially obscured by trauma.* She fished for the autopsy photos of the two boys and peered at them closely, grunted, and showed them to Ethan.

"Look at this."

"That's gross," he said.

"No, it's just that each of them had tattoos on their upper arms at about the same place. Same size, too. And look there and there? You can see some orange and black."

"So?"

"So, maybe they had tattoos of an eclipse."

"Again . . . so?"

"Maisie was wearing an eclipse pendant when I *saw* her. They only found a silver chain."

Ethan began to dismiss it, then stopped and chewed his lip for a moment.

"Hmm . . . since the sheriff's department only found the chain and not the pendant, and both tattoos were messed up, you think someone's trying to hide a connection?"

"Maybe," she said.

He studied her. "You'd make a good cop."

"*We* would."

They searched for more, but there was nothing else that could even remotely connect with an eclipse. So they moved on. There was a page attached to each victim's report that summarized their blood analysis. She read them over, then showed the pages to Ethan. "See this? It shows that none of the teens had been drinking."

He read through them. "Blood alcohol levels normal? In every case? I missed that." Ethan looked at her. "Okay, so none of them were drinking. They said they were high."

"But on what?" Dana asked. "There's just this." She pointed to a comment, then read it aloud. "'Evidence of synthetic compound simulating effects of standard 5-HT2A receptor agonists.'" She shook her head. "What does that mean?"

"I have no idea," said Ethan. "Maybe we can figure out a way to ask Two-Suit."

She agreed and began to close the big folder but stopped, took a breath, and then went back and pulled Maisie's autopsy photo out again and studied it. Maisie had been badly mangled and the wounds were horrific, but Dana forced herself to look closely at them. Clipped to the last photo was a photocopy of a page that had been used to take notes. It had an outline of a generic human female body, with arms out to the sides. There were dozens of X's marked on it and a list of corresponding injuries, all in medical shorthand that Dana could not interpret. Remarks like *subdural hematoma and comminuted fractures of the occipital bone are observed*, and *the mucosa of the epiglottis, glottis, piriform sinuses, trachea, and major bronchi are anatomic.* Picking through that to make sense of it would require a medical dictionary, and despite all the books on the shelves, there wasn't one to be found.

But then something struck Dana, and she stopped and looked more closely at the diagram, then shuffled through and pulled out the autopsy photos.

"Do you have a magnifying glass?" she asked quickly.

"Sure, why?"

"I want to check something."

Ethan got up and fetched a big magnifier from the desk, and she took it and used it to look at each separate wound. The damage was so extensive that it was difficult to find what she was looking for, but it was there.

It was all there.

The damage to Maisie's wrists, the punctures in the tops of her feet, the smaller cuts along her hairline, and the deeper cut in her side. Dana's mouth went suddenly dry, and once more it was hard to breathe.

"No . . . ," she murmured.

"What?" asked Ethan.

"Oh my God," said Dana. "Quick, get me something to draw on."

"Why? What's going on?"

"Do it," she snapped.

He hurried over to the desk again and brought back a yellow legal pad and mechanical pencil. Dana took them without a word, tore off a sheet, placed it over the diagram, and traced the same female outline. Then she removed the copied sheet, studied it, and carefully drew only those injuries she had seen in both her dream and waking vision. When she was done, Dana showed it to Ethan.

"Okay," he said. "So?"

"I think these are the injuries that really killed her," said Dana, and went over her memories again.

"How do you know that?"

"When I saw Maisie in the locker room, all I could see was what was being done to her." Dana went over the locker room incident again and then explained about the dark angel in her dream on Sunday night, the night Maisie was murdered.

"Wait, you actually saw this . . . this . . . *angel* . . . cut and stab her?" said Ethan, appalled. "That's gross."

"No, it wasn't exactly like that. The dream is hazy. In the locker room I saw her with stigmata. Seeing this diagram, I think—no, I'm *sure*—that Maisie was killed using the wounds of Christ and that the car accident was set up to hide it."

"Why? By who?"

"How would *I* know?"

Ethan gave her a guarded look. "Um . . . do you think an *actual* angel . . . ?"

"Don't be stupid," she snapped, then immediately said, "Sorry. I didn't mean it to come out like that."

"No, it's fine. I just don't know how to have this conversation."

Dana snorted. "No kidding."

He smiled at her. "How are you not losing it after all that?"

"Who says I'm not?"

Ethan chose not to reply to that. Instead he cleared his throat and said, "How sure are you about her wounds? The, um, wounds of Jesus, I mean?"

Dana took her tracing of the body diagram and drew a series of straight lines and right angles as if the victim's body were in front of a big wooden cross. She scribbled in a thorny crown and drew a crude spear with the blade stabbing deep. Ethan looked appalled, but then he began to nod.

"I read about mass murderers and cults and all that stuff all the time," Ethan said. "There are a lot of total nut jobs out there who think God is telling them to kill people."

"I know." Dana absently touched her crucifix. "I think whoever did this was trying to make a statement."

"What on earth kind of statement could any of that make?"

Instead of answering, Dana spent the next few minutes tracing the outlines of the other victims and penciling in the location of each wound. For the Asian boy, Jeffrey Watanabe, his car had been so badly torn up that he had actually been decapitated. Jennifer Hoffer had been impaled on the broken steering column of her car. Connie Lucas had been thrown through her car windshield. And there were scores of other injuries, too, which complicated everything. Ethan watched with great interest.

"Well . . . one thing's clear," he said when she was finished. "He's not doing the same thing over and over again. They're not all killed like Jesus."

"No, but he's definitely making some kind of statement. Something *else* religious," she said, setting the papers down and sitting back. "I'd bet my life on it."

Her words seemed to freeze in the air, haunting them both.

CHAPTER 35

The angel sat cross-legged on the floor, his body running with sweat. Though it was still mild weather outside, inside the sacristy the temperature hovered above one hundred. There was no boiler running in the basement, no space heater, nothing to account for it.

Except the fires of his faith in the *grigori*.

Except the fires in his own flesh. Not the parts of him that were still human. The rest. The parts that were revealing themselves as *nephilim*, as a giant, not in size but in power, in glory, in understanding.

The Book of Enoch spoke about the *grigori*—whom the ancients called the Watchers—and how they left heaven to try to take control of humanity, that race of naughty, errant children. The glorious great ones had even married among humans, producing the *nephilim*, hoping that their own majesty would spread like a plague of greatness through the generations of man.

That had been a glorious thing.

That it had failed spoke more to the weakness of men than any fault of the Watchers. Men, though weak in the ways of the spirit, were as strong as they were stubborn when it came to following their greed, their lusts. They built their worlds with walls and towers and closed out the *grigori*. And the seed left behind, the *nephilim* offspring, became few and were scattered until no one of grace stood among the human herd. And the humans, those who bore no trace of holy blood, labored to destroy the *nephilim*, labeling them as devils, as demons, as witches, and hunting them to the edge of extinction. Sickened and sad over what man had become, the last of the *grigori* left the mortal plane and sealed the door behind them.

Until now.

Until *he* was born. Until he awakened within his own flesh and understood his nature, his mission, his purpose.

Until he realized that he was so much more than human.

Until he heard the soft, faint cries of others like him, trapped inside drab husks. Begging for release. Begging for *him* to free them.

It was his sacred duty to draw the *nephilim* forth to reclaim their heritage and then together break through the door that separated this world from the one into which the Watchers had gone.

And that work was going so very, very well.

The painting, though, was a challenge. It had taken him years to discover what the shape of the door needed to be. Not a simple portal, not a square or oblong window, but instead a portrait of a *grigori*. But how to do that? The Watchers were, in their truest forms, formless. Their nature was the furnace of life, of transformation, of magnificent change.

How to paint that?

The angel looked at what he had rendered. The *grigori* could speak to him through it, but it was not yet complete, and the words, the lessons from the other side, were not always clear. It was not yet a doorway.

He did not yet have enough blood to complete his sacred task.

His paintbrush lay on the floor next to the cold purity of his knife.

There was still so much to do.

CHAPTER 36

Dana and Ethan went through it all again, every page of the case files, every awful photo, every line of the nearly incomprehensible medical reports.

They wound up at exactly the same place.

"Look," said Ethan, "if Maisie was killed like Jesus, then maybe the other deaths were meant to look like other famous deaths. Maybe it's only that we can see the Jesus injuries because they're more well known. The others might not even be religious at all."

"Maybe," Dana said dubiously, "but I kind of think they might be."

"How? ESP or—?"

"No. I just think it."

Ethan sighed. "That's not very scientific, though. We need to build on actual evidence, don't we?"

"It's a theory," she said defensively. "Theories are part of science."

"Sure, but maybe we should bag it for now," said Ethan. "I'd kind of like to share all this with the science club."

"Okay, but what if they can't help? It's not like we can bring the case files for them to go through," said Dana, getting a little heated.

"Then we . . . ," he began, but trailed off, clearly not knowing where else to go. "We can't talk to my uncle about it, that's for sure."

"No," she agreed, "but maybe we should go to the library. They'll have books on how other religious people died. How did Moses die or Daniel or any of them?"

"That's good," he said, nodding. "But I just thought of something. The crown of thorns and the spear in his side were all how Jesus died, right? Well, Maisie's family is Jewish."

"So was Jesus," countered Dana. "But I don't think that matters. It's probably more important what's going on in the head of the killer."

"The angel," he said, and she heard the skepticism in his voice.

"Look," she said impatiently, "we both know that he's not an angel. He's a psychopath, a mass murderer or whatever."

"You see him as an angel in your dreams, though," said Ethan. He flapped his arms and then sat down heavily on the other chair. "This is bizarre. We're talking about angels, psychopaths, and the possibility of a series of murders made to look like religious deaths. Are we imagining all of this?"

"Unfortunately," said Dana, "I don't think so. And that scares the heck out of me."

He looked at her, and for a moment there was almost a shadow of a smile on his face. Not a happy smile, though. "Dana . . . we're *fifteen*."

"I know. But we're not dumb kids. You're smart, I'm smart, everyone in the science club is way smart."

"Sure, but Jerry, Tisa, and Sylvia are no more detectives than we are."

"I know."

"We shouldn't even be *doing* this."

Dana looked down at the papers in her lap. "I didn't ask to have those dreams, Ethan," she said softly. "I didn't ask to see Maisie. I didn't ask for any of this."

"Hey, I—"

She raised her head and fixed him with a hard, inflexible stare. "But for whatever reason, this is happening to me. *Me.* I don't know why, but I have to believe there is a point to all this."

"Why? You didn't know any of them. What makes you so special?"

He stopped as if he realized how his last question sounded, in both tone and meaning. "Wait—"

"Forget it," she said as she stood up.

"Hey, I'm sorry."

"No, it's okay. I have to go, though."

"Want me to walk you home?" he asked awkwardly, but Dana shook her head.

"I'm not going home," she said as she stood. "I'm going to the library."

Ethan stood, too. "Let me put this stuff away."

"You don't have to come with me," she said.

He grinned. "Yeah, I do."

CHAPTER 37

The Smith Library—informally known as the Abby to everyone—was one of the few things Dana genuinely liked about the town.

It was oddly large for so small a town, the result of a huge bequest in the will of a rich novelist who had lived all her life in the area. The building had once been Abigail Smith's estate, but the huge tract of land on which it once sat was now the town of Craiger. Her mansion had been converted into a library and was one of the largest buildings in town, second only to the combined city hall and public works complex. There were rooms upon rooms of books, and a good-sized staff employed by Smith's estate. It had become the local custom, Dana learned, for families to donate the personal libraries of family members who passed, and so the Abby's collection swelled. The building and wings headed in all directions, and they had filled two subbasements as well as an attic that, in a move of pure inspiration, had been given over to the Abby's collection of classic and modern horror fiction. Next to Beyond Beyond, Dana and Melissa spent most of their time swimming in oceans of words and thoughts, of poetry and prose, of ideas ancient and new.

Ethan knew the layout of the old place better than she did, though, and he led her downstairs to a series of rooms crammed with nonfiction books.

"In here," he said, pointing to a row marked WORLD RELIGION.

There were a lot of books, and the index cards did not list any with helpful titles. Nothing that said: *Weird Religious Deaths.* Nothing like *The How-To Book of Mass Murder.*

It was going to take time, and these were not topics they could tap the librarians for help with, especially the hatchet-faced woman who oversaw the basement collections and who everyone referred to as the Wicked Witch. It was Melissa's theory that the Wicked Witch had been assigned to the cellars to keep her from scaring away most of the public. And although Dana thought that was uncharitable, she had to admit that the librarian lacked only the green skin and pointy hat to make her a good choice for a remake of *The Wizard of Oz.*

So, they worked through the card catalog by themselves. Dana found what she was looking for in less than twenty minutes. There was a book called *Saints and Angels: A Comprehensive Guide*, which had a very detailed index.

"There," she said, tapping an entry. Ethan bent close to read it.

"'Martyrs, pages 172 to 201.' Jeez," he muttered. "You really can find anything in a library. Wonder if I can find the nose to my old Mr. Potato Head. Lost it when I was eight."

Dana flipped to the indicated pages. "I'll go through these," she said. "Why don't you see what you can find about that 5-HT2A receptor agonist stuff?"

"On it," he said, and vanished into the rows of biology and chemistry.

Dana sat down on a leather couch, pulled out her notes with the drawings she'd made of the wounds on each of the victims, and was glad that it was drawings and not photos she had to work with. Knowing that her sketches represented the deaths of people about her own age was bad enough.

The book, however, was not a comfort. It was filled with illustrations in black and white and color of woodcuts, sculptures, and paintings dating back hundreds of years. Apparently every artist in history had spent a good chunk of their time creating art about horrible deaths of important people. And there were a lot of martyrs. Hundreds of them. Thousands, according to the footnotes, when one took into account other religions, but Dana confined her search to the troubled and bloody history of the spread of Christianity. Persecution was a theme. Torture and public execution were bizarrely common, even after Christianity became the dominant religion, and a lot of the martyrs had been killed by other Christians. She already knew that, but it still made her furious. She always felt the message of Jesus's teachings was peaceful and beautiful.

When she realized her mind was wandering down the wrong side road and that her anger was rising, Dana stopped, closed her eyes, took several long yoga breaths, and realigned her focus.

"Martyrs," she murmured aloud.

A few more minutes of reading made her realize that the topic was too big, so she backed up and decided to tackle the subject in sections. Since Maisie had been killed with the wounds of Jesus, she looked at the ways in which the twelve apostles died. It was a starting place. And it was the right place to start.

She dug a bunch of change out of her pocket and took the book over to the photocopy machine across the room. She made sure no one was watching her as she copied artwork of dead apostles.

CHAPTER 38

Gerlach sat slumped in the passenger side of the black sedan, watching the front of the Abby from beneath the down-tilted brim of his hat. It was bright out, and he wore sunglasses to shield his pale blue eyes. His jaws flexed and bunched as he chewed gum.

"These kids have half a day off from school and they go to a library?" mused his driver.

Gerlach merely grunted.

The driver added, "You think they maybe went in the front and slipped out the back?"

The agent frowned. "Why would they? They don't know we're surveilling them."

"Maybe they do. She's supposed to have some gifts, right? Maybe she's sensed us or something."

Gerlach grunted again and sat up. "Why don't you go and find out?"

"Me?"

"You. I don't want her to see me."

The driver smirked. "Why not? I thought you said your face wasn't memorable."

Gerlach turned slowly to study the man. "How would you like a very memorable facial scar?"

"I—" The driver stopped himself from responding.

Gerlach smiled. "Go find out what those kids are up to. Now."

CHAPTER 39

"*Ethan!*" cried Dana.

His head popped out from behind the chemistry shelf, looking alarmed. "What's wrong? I'm still looking."

"I found it," she said urgently.

He hurried over, perched on the edge of the couch, and leaned in. Dana took him through it all.

"Look," she said, fighting to keep disgust and excitement out of her voice. "Every single one of them died in some way close to how Jesus or one of the apostles died." She turned over a drawing and placed it on a page in the book that described the death of James, son of Zebedee, also known as James the Greater. "Jeffrey Watanabe was decapitated. So was James."

"Right," said Ethan, looking at the entry. "But this says that James the Greater was killed with a sword."

"He was. The Romans cut his head off."

"Oh."

She turned over the page for Jennifer Hoffer. "She was impaled on the steering column of her car. Thomas—Doubting Thomas—the one who needed to touch Jesus's wounds before he believed that he'd risen, was run through with a spear."

Ethan said nothing.

The next was Connie Lucas. "She was thrown from her car down a rocky slope, and the coroner's report said that she died from blunt force trauma resulting from multiple impacts with the rocky terrain. James, son of Alphaeus, known as James the Less, was beaten and then stoned to death."

Ethan swallowed hard.

"We already know about Maisie," said Dana. "Chuck Riley had the same crucifixion wounds, but he was found hanging upside down from his overturned car. When he was about to be executed, Saint Peter asked that he be crucified upside down because he didn't think he was worthy to die in exactly the same way as Jesus."

"We can't be right about this," said Ethan in a small, sick voice.

They went through it over and over again, with Ethan trying to knock it all down with logic. However, it was that very logical approach that reinforced Dana's theory. Finally they sat on opposite ends of the couch, staring at each other. A big clock on the wall above them sliced cold seconds off and let them drop to the floor.

"We . . . we have to tell someone," said Ethan.

"Who?" asked Dana.

"My uncle."

"How do we explain how we know?"

Ethan looked bleak. "We tell the truth, I guess. Which means I get grounded until I'm in my forties."

"Crap," sighed Dana, and then she brightened. "We could tell Two-Suit and . . . wait . . . No, he'll want to know how we know. Same if we tell the narcs at school or Mr. Sternholtz."

"Or anyone," said Ethan.

"No matter who we tell, we're going to have to explain how we know.

It's all going to come back to the fact that you broke into your uncle's desk. Which means he'll probably get in trouble at work."

"He could lose his job." Ethan got up and walked a few steps away, then turned. "What choice do we have, though, Dana? If we don't tell someone, then the killer gets to keep on doing this. If it's us or someone's life, we have to do what's right. We can't be cowards. I don't want to live like that. Sneaking around and snooping is one thing, but I won't be responsible for letting someone else die."

Dana looked down at her hands, at her fingers twisting and knotting together in her lap. She could hear her father's voice in her head; it was easy to imagine his anger and his disappointment. Telling him about this might snap that fragile line that tethered her to him. She twisted around and looked at the clock.

"Beyond Beyond is open," she said. "Let's go over there. We can have tea and talk about it."

He shook his head. "No, that's okay, you go on without me. I'm not much in the mood for an astral journey or a cup of stinkweed tea."

"It's not like that," protested Dana, though she knew it pretty much *was* like that. "We should go talk to Corinda. And my sister is probably there, too. I need to tell them all this stuff."

Ethan looked at his watch. "I . . . can't," he said. "I have a mountain of homework."

"Are you serious?"

He looked wretched. "Yes, I am. I've got a paper to write for history that I should have started three days ago. If I don't hand it in tomorrow, I could drop to an A-minus. Besides . . ."

"What?"

"This ESP stuff can't put a criminal behind bars. I mean, I know that it's a thing, but you can't measure it or rely on it the way you can with hard science." Ethan looked uncomfortable. "I don't even know what to think about this, Dana. This is all so much, y'know? Mass murders and religious cults and psychic visions? It's . . . it's . . ." He stopped and shook his head.

"Believe me, Ethan, I understand. I'm weirded out, too. More than you because this is happening to *me*."

"Hey, I know, and I didn't mean to say that you were . . ."

He fished for the right word and couldn't come up with it. Dana smiled and touched his arm. "No, I get it. It's cool. I mean, it's *not* cool, but we're cool."

He looked relieved. "Listen, I believe you even if I don't understand it."

Dana said, "Hmmm. That actually gives me an idea. I need to go ask someone who might understand this stuff."

"Who?" asked Ethan.

She did not explain. Dana folded the drawings and took a step toward the stairs, but Ethan caught her arm.

"Look, Dana, if you're pissed at me," he said gently, "I'm sorry."

She gave him a small smile. "I'm not mad. Not at you, anyway. I'm scared about this stuff, and I'm absolutely furious that someone is doing this. I'm confused, and I hate being confused. There has to be an answer, and you said it—we don't really know what we're doing. We can't go to anyone in authority with this because, first, you'll be grounded forever for showing this stuff to me. Second, your uncle Frank could lose his job. And third, they'd never believe us. You know I'm right."

"Okay, but who can we talk to?"

"Not 'we,' Ethan. Me. I have a friend who might be able to look places no one else can. Maybe she can lead us to the evidence you want."

He paused. "Who?"

"Corinda Howell. She owns—"

"Beyond Beyond," he finished for her. "She's that nutty psychic lady, right?" Ethan stood his ground for five seconds. Then he sighed, nodded, and stepped aside. "Call me?" he asked. "Let me know what she says?"

Dana paused, nodded. "Sure."

She lingered at the foot of the stairs. Both of them started to say something, stopped. The moment held and then stretched, and Dana felt that something was supposed to happen, but she didn't know what it was. Ethan seemed to think so, too, but his smile was turning into a plastic mask that looked as awkward as her own face felt. Was he starting to lean forward a little?

"Um . . . see you," she said, stepping back nervously.

"Sure. Um," he murmured. "Bye."

"Bye."

She stood there a moment longer and then turned and hurried up the stairs, certain that her face was bright red. A man in a black suit was coming down the steps and stood aside to let her pass. She barely registered him.

Had that almost been a kiss?

Yes.

Maybe.

She didn't know.

If it was, she'd screwed it up.

"Idiot," she told herself.

She thought about Ethan's smile for blocks and blocks.

CHAPTER 40

Clouds covered the sky, and it was already getting dark. The streetlights came on early, and Dana kept to the lighted side of Main Street, avoiding the open black mouths of alleys. A homeless man was squatting in one alleyway under a shelter made of moldy cardboard, rags, and splintered boards. He held out a cup, and although in daylight Dana would have stopped and given him some coins, tonight she said, "I'm sorry," and hurried on. The man yelled something as she passed, and she was half a block away before her mind translated it from his wine-soaked guttural.

"God protect you."

It stopped her and she turned, looking back. The man sat with his face in his hands, rocking forward and back.

"Thank you," she whispered.

Then she turned and hurried toward the lighted storefront two blocks away that was Beyond Beyond.

A few cars went up and down the street, and Dana only glanced at them. She did not see the black sedan parked on the shadowy side of the street. She did not see the two men who watched her.

CHAPTER 41

Corinda was there but busy at the checkout with people buying the latest astrology book by a *New York Times*–bestselling author.

Dana got to the store too late to catch Melissa, who had gone into the advanced yoga class already. It made her anxious, because she needed to tell everything to her sister. Every single detail.

She was too nervous to sit and drink tea, so she wandered around the shop, killing time and fidgeting.

"*¿Qué pasa, mai?*" said a voice, and she spun so fast that she knocked a statue of the Hindu god Ganesha off a table. Angelo ducked and caught the statue before it hit the floor. It was an incredible feat, and Dana gaped.

"Wow!" she said.

Angelo straightened, hefting the small stone statue in his hand, then placed it neatly and carefully in its spot. He adjusted two other statues that had been knocked askew.

"They're expensive," he said. "Wouldn't want to see you have to buy it, 'cause they have that whole 'you break it, you bought it' thing going on."

He had an accent, but his voice was soft and there was an almost musical lilt to it. He wasn't wearing his blue uniform, but instead had on jeans and an FSK High T-shirt that looked to be several years old. His arms were sinewy without being bulky, and he looked like he was on springs, ready to move at a moment's notice. Dana realized that it was his natural state, even though his posture seemed to be casual, even slouchy. It was the kind of feline grace she'd seen in the big cats at the San Diego Zoo.

His smile was slow, too. It was knowing, personal, amused, unconcerned, and yet there was interest there.

"I—I've seen you at school," she said when absolutely nothing else occurred to her.

"I work there," he said. "Part-time."

"But you don't still go there? You look like you're a junior."

"I'm nineteen," he said. "I graduated last year."

"Oh."

Angelo turned toward a hand truck laden with cardboard boxes. He took a folding knife from his pocket, flicked the heavy blade into place, and then cut open the top box. He did it with incredible speed and grace, the silver edge slicing neatly and precisely through the packing tape without touching the contents inside. As Angelo folded the knife and put it away, Dana took another quick look at the scars on his arms and hands. Had he gotten them from learning how to use the knife? Or in knife fights? Some of them looked old and some looked like they had been bad.

"I'm working a couple of jobs now," explained Angelo. "The school, here. Doing some maintenance stuff at the baseball field over the county line at Oak Valley, and picking up a few hours here and there hammering out dented fenders at Porter's Auto Body."

"That's a lot of working."

He shrugged. "I don't mind work. Like the auto-body stuff best. I dig cars, but that's only a few hours a week, because Porter mostly uses full-time guys. He calls me in when he has overflow. Money's money," he said, "and I'm trying to pay for college."

"College?"

His smile suddenly dimmed. "Yeah, poor Latino kids want to go to college, too. Big surprise, huh?"

"No," she cried. "That's not what I meant."

"What did you mean?" he asked, his dark eyes suddenly intense. "You see me hauling bags of trash in school and you think that's all I'm good for? You ever even *know* any Latino kids like me?"

"I never said that," protested Dana. "I know a lot of people like you."

And the *like you* hung in the air, as clumsy and awkward as it could possibly be.

"I—I m-mean," she stammered, "we used to live in San Diego. There were a lot of Mexican kids in school."

"I'm Puerto Rican," he said. "Or can't you tell the difference?"

She tried to organize an answer, but unfortunately every thought that came in her head sounded just as bad as what she'd already blurted.

"Leave her alone, Angelo," said a voice behind Dana. She turned and saw a man standing there. Sunlight.

"I was just messing with her," said Angelo quickly.

"She doesn't know that," said Sunlight. "Look at her. She's about to faint. Or run away."

Shutters seemed to slam down behind Angelo's eyes. "I didn't mean nothing."

Sunlight came and placed a hand on Angelo's shoulder and then put his other on Dana's. His touch was surprisingly warm, and there was a tingle as if some kind of electric charge passed from his hand and into her skin. She shivered. From the amused smile on the corners of Sunlight's mouth, she realized that he understood the effect and owned it.

"Tell the young lady you're sorry," suggested Sunlight.

"No," Dana said quickly. "It was all me. I said something stupid and I'm really sorry."

"Angelo . . . ?" murmured Sunlight. "Are you going to let the lady take responsibility for all the negativity in the air?"

Angelo's body language changed. He lost the cat grace and assurance and stood there almost meekly. He was twice as muscular as Sunlight, but he seemed to be less than half as powerful. Sunlight's energy was very old, too, very adult, and Angelo seemed cowed by it.

"Sorry," he mumbled.

"It's okay," said Dana. "Really."

Sunlight patted Angelo's shoulder. "That was gracious of you. Now go tell Corinda that Ms. Scully would like to speak with her."

"How do you know my name?" asked Dana, surprised.

"How could I not?" he said with mild amusement. "One of the famous Scully sisters. Between you and Melissa, you may be Corinda's biggest customers. I see you two holding court at the booth behind the counter quite often."

"Oh."

"And lately Corinda has become fascinated by you." Sunlight gestured and Dana glanced over to see Corinda at the register chatting animatedly to a very fat, very rich-looking woman with blue hair and lots of jewelry.

Angelo went back to work, taking books from the open box and stacking them on a table. Sunlight lightly touched Dana's arm and they moved a few yards away.

"I apologize for anything Angelo might have said to offend you," said Sunlight. "He's a little thin-skinned."

"No, it's totally fine. He wasn't bothering me," said Dana. "I knocked something over and he caught it. He grabbed it so fast, before it could fall. I've never seen anyone move that fast."

"Oh, yes, he's quick," agreed Sunlight. "But so is his temper. He's used to being kicked around because of his skin color and his circumstance."

"Circumstance?"

"He was brought over here as a ten-year-old by his mother, and she died when he was twelve. He went into an orphanage, but that was a particular kind of hell, so he ran away and lived on the streets. Imagine that, Miss Scully, a boy living in alleys and squatting in abandoned houses and yet going to school and getting his diploma. He's doing his best with what life's handed him." Although he was probably less than ten years older than Dana, he spoke in a way that made him seem twenty or thirty years older. Mature, commanding, and self-assured. He had a lot of what Melissa called "personal power."

"Poverty is an appalling thing," continued Sunlight, shaking his head. "The fact that we, at our current level of modern civilized evolution, allow it, is unforgivable. Don't you agree?"

"Y-yes, of course."

"When I met Angelo, he was trying to live on some piecework at a garage, but it wasn't enough to live on. Not really. I took him in and gave him a job here, and spoke for him at FSK so they would also offer employment. He's putting away every dime he can to afford college. Community college, but that doesn't matter. I offered to pay his tuition, but Angelo is very proud of the fact that *he* will pay his own way."

"He should be," said Dana. "And I feel like a total privileged white girl idiot."

Sunlight nodded approvingly. "Self-awareness of one's limitations is a rare and wonderful thing. Most people use pat replies and rely on culturally specific viewpoints, and they never become aware that these are not essential truths in their own experience. This is especially true of people born to some degree of wealth and comfort."

"We're not exactly rich."

"Wealth is relative," said Sunlight. He gestured toward the booth behind the café cash register, which was the only one open. "Let's sit for a minute and talk about it."

She went with him and slid into the booth. Corinda was ringing up a line of customers and said she'd be over as soon as she was free. Sunlight sat across from Dana. He was a strange man. Like someone who did not belong in this century. There was an air of otherworldliness to him. If he were in a Shakespeare movie, he'd be Oberon, king of the fairies, or maybe the sorcerer, Prospero. His bones were delicate, his features sharp except for his full lips, and Dana had never seen eyes of his smoky morning-mist gray hue before. She could understand why Corinda and Melissa were entranced with him. No doubt a lot of girls and women were under his spell. Dana felt it, too, despite the difference in their ages. A simple desire to be in his company and—as Melissa often put it—to "share in his energy." Just looking into his eyes was hypnotic.

"Wealth," said Sunlight after they'd ordered tea and a plate of fruit and cheeses from one of the staff. "We were talking about that. You say you're not rich, but in many ways you are. You have two parents. You have two brothers and a sister. You live in a nice house on a good street. You have never wanted for food, for warmth, for clothes or books or anything material."

It took Dana a few seconds to process that, and then she sat back, her brow knotting. "How do you know all that about my family? Oh . . . Melissa told you."

Sunlight laughed. Soft and pleasant, with no trace of mockery. "Not at all, Miss Scully."

"Then how—?"

"Corinda told me."

"But she doesn't know about my brothers or where we live, does she?"

"You've sat with Corinda. You tell me how she knows what she knows."

Their food and drinks arrived. Dana took a fat red grape from the plate and ate it slowly, thinking about what Sunlight had said.

"You're troubled by the thought of someone bending close to look into your life through the windows of your soul," said Sunlight mildly. "It's a common reaction, but it gets easier to accept over time. Think of it like this: if you were born into an underground society and never knew about the sun, imagine how much you would fear and distrust it upon first seeing this big, burning ball of superheated gases dominating the sky. But over time you will come to realize that its light makes all things grow, and that it warms your face, and it chases back shadows, and without it even your underground civilization would never have come into existence. The larger world is like that when we each first encounter it. Why? Because those who don't believe in it, or don't trust it, or don't understand it are the ones who teach us about the world. About their limited perception of the world, that is. They think everything that makes up the world can be weighed, measured, metered, quantified, and touched." He smiled at her, his gray eyes fixed on hers. "But we both know the world is so much bigger than that, don't we?"

Dana picked up her cup, took an experimental micro-sip, and nodded. "I guess we do."

A moment later Corinda came around the partition and slid in beside Sunlight. "We have so much to talk about," she said. "In fact, tell me why the words 'autopsy report' keep popping into my mind."

CHAPTER 42

Danny unlocked the observation room and reached for the light switch, then jumped and clawed for his pistol when he saw a figure standing silhouetted in front of the wall of screens.

God, was it him? Was it the monster? Was it the angel come to kill him, too?

These thoughts slashed like razors through the technician's mind. Gerlach had shown him Polaroids of the horrors the madman had committed. The pictures were bad enough, and he never wanted to meet the killer in person. Never.

"Freeze right there!" he roared, forcing anger into his voice to overcome the fear. He held his pistol in both hands, the barrel nowhere near as steady as he wanted it to be. "Hands on your head. Do it now or I will put you down."

The figure did not raise his hands. Instead he spoke.

"Put the gun down before I take it away and feed it to you."

Danny's heart jumped into a different gear.

"Gerlach . . . ?"

The red-haired agent reached into his pocket for his packet of gum. He munched a stick and folded the silver foil very slowly and deliberately. "I won't ask you again, kid. I don't like people pointing guns at me."

Gerlach was not even looking at him.

Danny lowered his weapon, but his fear diminished only slightly. Agent Gerlach was not the same kind of monster as the angel, but he was far from a normal human being. Gerlach was a product of the Montauk Project on an air base on Long Island. The overall project was run by the air force, but there were supposed to be all kinds of black budget departments buried beneath mountains of red tape, disinformation, and veils of secrecy. The scuttlebutt among the agents of the Syndicate was that Gerlach was one of several dozen men who had been taken from orphanages at age ten and then raised by scientists and a brutal cadre of trainers.

Physical torture was only part of the overall process of weeding out the weak—often fatally—and turning the strongest survivors into a kind of super soldier. Some of what went on at Montauk had leaked into the global conspiracy theory networks, which of course distorted the truth. But not as much as people outside the Syndicate might think. That Gerlach was a cold-blooded and efficient killer was obvious to anyone who knew him for more than five minutes. What was less obvious was that he seemed to know things he couldn't know. Stuff that wasn't in any surveillance report.

The angel had come from the Montauk Project, too, Danny knew. So there was that. As far as Danny could figure, on the other hand, only one in twenty of the children who went through Montauk lived to reach their teens. Fewer still were alive now as adults. And those who were—both teens and adults—were monsters. None similar to one another, but not one of them normal by any standard.

"You're thinking bad thoughts," said Gerlach from across the room.

Danny jumped and yelped. "W-what . . . ?"

Agent Gerlach turned, and in the weak blue-white light from the TV screens, he looked like a ghoul. Like one of those flesh-eating dead things from the movies. What were they calling them now? Zombies? Sure. That fit.

"We have a long night ahead of us, kid," said Gerlach. "Maybe you ought to go wash your face, take a leak, maybe try some deep breathing to get yourself calmed down. Put that gun away. You won't need it. He's not here."

Danny looked down at the revolver that hung loosely in his hand. He eased the hammer down, engaged the safety, and slid it back into the shoulder holster.

"I'm sorry," he said. "I didn't know anyone was down here. I thought the door was locked."

Gerlach chewed for a moment. "It was."

Danny shook his head. "Sometimes I think you do this stuff to live up to the rumors."

"What rumors?"

"The rumors about us. I mean, you do know what they're calling us these days?"

"Who?"

Danny went over to the coffeemaker and began brewing a fresh pot. "You know, the idiots who write those conspiracy theory books? The ones on the lecture circuit?" He flicked the collar of his suit jacket. "They're calling us the men in black. How about that?"

"I've been called worse," said Gerlach.

"No, my point is that they know what we look like. We're always dressed like this. Black suits, white shirts, black ties, sunglasses." He took a cup from a rack and set it next to the coffeemaker. "It's like a uniform. I mean, I know we're supposed to look like off-the-rack government agents, but . . ."

"It's a uniform look."

"That's what I said," agreed Danny as he slipped his arms into the sleeves of his suit coat to put it on.

"No," corrected Gerlach, "we're not *wearing* uniforms; we are meant to look uniform. People call us men in black because they remember the uniforms. They're reacting to the look. But they can't tell us apart. They could look at five of us and all they remember are the clothes, the sunglasses, the attitude. No one remembers what *we* look like. That's the point."

Danny looked at him. "Really?"

"If we all wore bright red cowboy hats, they'd call us men in red cowboy hats. It's simple manipulation."

The tech held his arms up and looked at the sleeves. "Huh," he said. "I never thought of it that way."

Gerlach smiled and looked down at the coffeemaker. "What color eyes do I have?"

"What?" asked Danny.

The agent poured coffee into his cup. "What color eyes?"

"Um . . . green? No, brown."

Gerlach looked at him. "Blue. Maybe you'd remember my hair color. Maybe you'd say I was a red-haired man—if this is my real hair color and not a dye job; or maybe you'd stop looking after you noticed the suit, but you've worked with me for seventeen weeks and you don't know my eye color, and you'd probably be off three inches on my height and fifteen pounds on my weight. These suits make us invisible. We're stamped out of the same mold."

The tech grunted. "That's kind of cool."

"It's efficient."

"I guess." Danny glanced over at the screens. "So . . . where's our boy tonight? You sure he's not here in the church?"

"I'm sure."

"Where is he?"

Gerlach smiled a thin little smile. "Working."

CHAPTER 43

Beyond Beyond
6:05 P.M.

Angelo Luz carried a carton of sugar packets out of the storeroom and set it down on an empty table, removed his knife, flicked the blade into place, and cut open the box. The music that played from the speakers mounted around the shop were Gregorian chants. Church music. Sad, slow, haunted. The music conjured images of strange angels and dying saints and the light from stained-glass windows.

He moved from table to table refilling the wire sugar racks. While he worked, his eyes kept flicking over to the table behind the café register, where the pretty white girl sat with Sunlight and Corinda. She had such a lovely face, such a long and elegant throat, such fiery red hair.

The doleful music filled his mind.

CHAPTER 44

Beyond Beyond
6:09 P.M.

"How do you *know* that?" cried Dana. "How do you know anything about those autopsy reports?"

Corinda and Sunlight sat across from her. Neither said a word, letting her work it out.

Dana banged her fist on the tabletop, making the teacups dance. "This is not normal."

"This," said Sunlight, "is the larger world."

Dana felt the room spinning, and she placed her hands flat on the table to keep herself from spilling and tumbling away. Corinda, seeing her distress, took one of Dana's hands in both of hers.

"It's scary now," she said, "but the more you travel in the world of spirits, the less frightening it gets. After a while it's so much sweeter and safer than the physical world."

"How can any of this be real, though?" said Dana, almost pulling her hand away.

Sunlight answered that. "Reality itself is unreal. Reality is a perception. We each see the world in a certain way, and that is real to us, but we don't all see it in the same way."

"How's that possible? I see this table, these teacups, this bunch of grapes, and even if you didn't and I drew a picture of it, you'd see what I saw."

"We'd share your perception of it," he said. "And our perceptions greatly overlap. Sometimes we share a perception of a thing and there is an agreement on the soul level that this is how we will both remember it, because it allows us to communicate without needless complication. Humans do this all the time. It's one of the ways in which we communicate on the purely physical plane, but it is not the only way."

"What do you mean?"

"Our minds are evolving faster than the physical form," said Sunlight. He picked up a strawberry and studied it for a long moment before continuing. "Organic matter has limitations imposed on it, but the mind and the soul do not. They have the potential to expand and transform at exponential rates. Not for everyone, though, and not at the same rate of speed. What people call psychics or intuitives or spiritualists are those who have embraced this change to various degrees, and who, through practices such as yoga, meditation, and other forms of enrichment, encourage their own spiritual evolution."

Corinda raised a hand. "And some of us hear the change calling, so we come a-runnin'."

Sunlight gave her a fond, tolerant smile and then took a bite from the strawberry. He did it slowly, savoring the taste, and then licked a drop of juice from his lip. Dana had to force herself to look away, especially since she was aware that Sunlight understood the effect he had on her. *And*, she thought, *on every other female creature on the planet.*

"I don't feel like I'm evolving," she said. "I feel more like I'm being mugged by what's going on in my head."

"Maybe," said Sunlight, "that's because you are."

She blinked. "What?"

"I see your aura, I can see the shape and color and texture of your soul, and I can read its frequency. Do you know what I see when I look at you?"

All she could do was shake her head.

"I see power," he said. "Don't look so surprised. You are a very powerful person, Dana Scully, and you have great potential. Your mind is like a furnace, but you're filled with doubts, and you don't know what you want to forge in that furnace. Part of you wants to cast armor that you can wear to protect yourself and also hide from the world. Part of you wants to make a sword so you can fight back."

Dana said nothing, but her mouth was dry as paste.

"And another part of you wants to build instruments of great power and sophistication. Let's call them a telescope and a microscope. The telescope so you can look beyond the limits of what your eyes can see. There is a vast and complex universe out there, and it is calling to those who can hear, inviting us to watch, to listen, to know. And the microscope because yours is a practical and orderly and very hungry mind, a mind that needs to understand things all the way down to the cellular level."

"Her eyes are starting to glaze over," said Corinda with a laugh.

"A bit," admitted Dana. She drank her tea, which had gotten tepid, and ate more of the grapes but didn't even taste them. "And, as cool as all this is, it doesn't help me with what I'm going through."

"Fair enough," said Sunlight. "But this is hardly the right atmosphere for anything more precise. I have my own psychic instruments, and they require something closer to a laboratory setting."

"Which means what?"

He patted her hand. "Let me show you."

CHAPTER 45

The Chrysalis Room
6:17 P.M.

Sunlight led her through a door in a corner of the café, facing the room used by AA and meditation classes. Dana stepped into darkness as Sunlight closed the door and moved past her, but he did not pull back the heavy curtains. Instead he produced a lighter from his pocket and lit a cluster of short, thick candles. Soon, the air was filled with mingled scents of peppermint, sandalwood, and jasmine.

It was very quiet.

Corinda had walked over to the room with them, but Sunlight had stopped her at the door.

"Thank you," he said, blocking her from entering. "We'll be fine. Just have Angelo bring me some of the new incense. I'm running low."

Dana thought she saw surprise and hurt in Corinda's eyes. And maybe something else, but the other emotion was there and gone before she could identify it. Now, with the door closed and the candles lit, Dana felt enormously awkward.

"That's normal," said Sunlight, as if reading her mind. Or, perhaps, *actually* reading her thoughts.

"What?" she said, recoiling a half step.

He chuckled. "No, seriously, Miss Scully, I understand that you're freaked out. I get that a lot. It's a side effect of being who and what I am."

"And what is that, exactly?" she asked, still standing by the door. There was a knock that startled her, but then the door opened and Angelo came in with a bundle of incense sticks wrapped in coarse blue tissue paper. He threw a quick look at Dana but said nothing to her.

"Corinda said you wanted this," he said, handing it to Sunlight. "They delivered it this morning for you."

"Thank you, Angelo. Close the door on your way out."

The young man lingered for a moment, then glanced around the room, gave Dana a small nod, and left. When he was gone, Dana repeated her question. "What is it you're supposed to be?"

"I am a psychic. I'm a very good psychic; I'm very powerful. Corinda would say it's a gift, and perhaps it is, but so far it has been mostly a pain in the ass. Pardon my language. Let's call it a 'quality' instead. I've been like this since I was a boy and it has never gotten easier, never became second nature, never allowed me to fit in. I don't have to be around people very long before they realize there is something not quite right about me. They're correct. I'm not 'right,' by their definition. I am very different. Because other people react to my difference, I tend to retreat from them. When I was young, my parents took me to doctors and they, of course, dismissed any possibility that I possessed special abilities. Instead they diagnosed me as having 'social phobia.'" He paused, then added, "It's nothing new. Hippocrates once described it, and I quote, 'his hat still in his eyes, he will neither see, nor be seen by his good will. He dare not come in company, for fear he should be misused, disgraced, overshoot himself in gesture or speeches, or be sick; he thinks every man observes him.'"

Dana said nothing, nor did she move away from the door.

"They thought I had this phobia, this social neurosis, because I withdrew from people, but they were quite wrong. I withdrew because I was not one of them. I could not relate to them, and after a while I didn't want to. What I did want to do was find others with similar qualities. I spent a great deal of my life cultivating my own skills while also seeking out those of my kind."

"Other psychics?" asked Dana.

Sunlight did not move from where he stood, and the candlelight flickered softly across his face, sculpting and emphasizing his subtle expressions. "Yes. Though even the word 'psychic' is imprecise. It may be that we will need to invent a better word for it, but I'll leave that to linguists. For now I see the world in a kind of black and white. There is *them*, the ones who do not have these qualities, and there is *us*—we who do possess them."

Dana nodded. She was still nervous being alone with him, but her trepidation was ebbing. Sunlight seemed very genuine and a little sad.

"Because we are few," he continued, "and because there is so much misinformation and *dis*information surrounding this topic, going all the way back to when they burned people with such qualities and called them witches, any meeting between people like us tends to be awkward."

"Like us," echoed Dana softly.

"Like us," he said. "You have some real talent, Miss Scully."

"Call me Dana."

"Dana, then," said Sunlight, nodding. "Your visions are not simple nightmares. You have to know that now, even if you don't want it to be true."

"I don't," she said emphatically. "I really don't."

"We are not given a choice," he said, turning to stare at the candles. "We are who we are and we become what we must become."

"What do you mean by that? Become what?"

"Darwin spoke of evolution of the species, but there is another kind of change. Metamorphosis. It is an evolution of the soul, of our very nature. We are born as one thing, but some of us—a rare few—tear out of the chrysalis of our own lives and emerge as something else. Rare, beautiful, powerful. We cease to be what we were and we *become* what we are meant to be."

"I don't . . ."

He turned back to her and said, "I can tell you when you first started having visions, and I don't need to rely on psychic powers to do it. Shall I tell you? It was within a few months of starting puberty. Don't blush; I'm not being crude. But think about it for a moment. The transformation from child to teenager involves a hugely powerful biochemical change. The body undergoes changes at every level. Physical, psychological, chemical, intellectual, emotional. Talents emerge, preferences change and become refined, personalities alter. We are never the same as teens as we are as little children. Don't you agree?"

"I guess."

"No," he said, wagging his finger. "That is an imprecise answer. You agree or you don't. Be certain, Dana. Don't quibble or hide behind tricks of obfuscation."

She nodded. "Sorry."

"Don't apologize, either," he said. "You came in here to learn, and this is a lesson. Never apologize for what you don't know. There is no shame in that. Shame comes when you *refuse* to know or pretend not to know. That is deliberate ignorance, and it is loathsome."

She actually started to apologize for apologizing, caught herself, and nodded.

"Most psychic gifts begin to emerge during adolescence," he said. "For some—most, actually—these qualities are short-lived and end when puberty itself has run its course."

"And what about the others?"

"We continue to transform."

"Even you?"

"Oh," he said in a soft, almost imperceptible voice, "especially me."

She said nothing because she had no idea how to respond to that.

Sunlight nodded, though, and gave her a rueful grin. "Those of our kind tend to be weird, eccentric, and enigmatic. We take getting used to, even with each other."

"I don't mean to be rude, Mr. Sunlight, but—"

"It's just Sunlight."

"Okay, Sunlight. This is all really fascinating, and I'm not being sarcastic, but I'm not sure how it helps me understand what's going on. I'm pretty sure that someone is murdering teenagers, and I don't know what to do about it. I'm afraid to go to sleep and I'm afraid of being awake. I don't think my folks or the cops are going to believe a single word I say."

"They probably won't."

"Then what can I do? I can't just stand here talking about ESP all day. I have to *do* something."

"Yes," he said, "you do. And I can help."

"How?" she begged, taking a definite step forward.

"By teaching you to use your qualities, Dana. Right now they control you. But if you learn to control them, you will hasten your transformation. You will *become* something much more powerful than you can imagine. Then, and only then, will you be able to focus your visions like a laser. But first things first. Corinda has told me some of what has been happening to you. I've *sensed* some of it myself."

Dana shook her head. "This is so weird."

He gave her a rueful smile. "Well, to be entirely true, Dana, it's weird to me, too."

That made her laugh.

"I know about the dreams, about the angel. I understand about how vague some of this is, how fragmented memories of visions can be. I can help you gain the strength and clarity to see through the masks worn by this creature who calls himself an angel. Only then will you be able to save lives. That's what you want, isn't it? To save lives? To heal the harm that is being inflicted on the children of this town?"

"Yes . . . ," she murmured. "But this angel is so strong."

"Strong? Yes, I believe he is, Dana, but that doesn't mean he is all-seeing and all-knowing. Everyone has limitations, blind spots."

She stared at him. "I . . . never thought about that. Do you . . . do you think there are things he *doesn't* know?"

"Absolutely."

"Then does that mean there might be some way to try to stop him? Some way he won't see coming?"

Sunlight nodded and gestured to where a mass of cushions littered the floor.

"Anything is possible. Have a seat, Dana," he said. "We have work to do."

"I have my jujutsu class tonight . . ."

"Don't worry," he said. "This won't take that long. Where we're going, time spins at a different speed."

"What's that mean?"

Sunlight smiled. "You'll see."

CHAPTER 46

"What are you doing?"

The question was whispered but still sharp, almost shrill. Angelo leaned away from the closed door, straightened, and turned to see Corinda standing ten feet away, fists on hips. She scowled.

"I wasn't doing nothing," he said.

Corinda looked past him to the door to Sunlight's Chrysalis Room. It was off-limits to everyone when he was in there. Only students enrolled in his classes or people having one-on-one sessions for psychic enrichment were permitted to enter. Even Corinda, who co-owned the store with Sunlight, had rarely passed that threshold.

"You know the rules, Angelo," she scolded. "Sunlight maintains a pure energy space around this room. He doesn't want or need anything to taint the energetics."

Angelo shoved his hands into his back pockets. "Then why do I see you creeping around here all the time? You're pissed because he's the one with the real power. You think *you're* the reason people come here?"

She took an angry step toward him. "You might want to be careful about what you say and to whom you say it, young man. You should be happy you even have this job."

"Oh? And why's that? Because this is such a great place to work?"

"Because Sunlight and I looked the other way when it came to your record."

"You going to throw that in my face again? It's been how many days since the last time you mentioned it? Oh, wait, no, you mentioned it this morning. And yesterday. You're always on me about that."

"Shouldn't I be? After what you did?"

"Maybe you don't know everything about everything, Miss Psychic Powers," he said.

"And maybe you should watch your mouth and remember who signs your paycheck. You're on dangerous ground."

Angelo took his own step toward her. "Dangerous? You think you even know what that means, señora? I don't think so."

"What's that supposed to mean?"

He snorted. "You don't know? Funny, I thought you could read minds."

Corinda backed up a step. "I can read yours well enough to know what you're thinking about Dana. You keep your distance or I'll—"

The look in his eyes stopped her words as surely as if she'd been slapped.

"Or you'll what?" he asked quietly.

Corinda did not answer. Angelo nodded.

"*Mucho cuidado, mi hermana,*" he said, and walked away like a hungry tiger. Corinda stared at his back until Angelo vanished into the stockroom. She was furious, but she was frightened, too. Angelo always scared her. There was something wrong with him. Maybe something wrong inside him. A darkness that Corinda had never been able to penetrate. She would have fired him months ago, but she was afraid of what he would do. People told her stories about him, about his temper. About his bursts of violence. Like the week before Christmas, when two drunk college frat boys threw an empty beer can at him. Angelo had beaten them unconscious and would have served time had Sunlight not happened by and broken up the fight. Sunlight claimed to the sheriff that the frat boys had thrown the first punch, but Corinda had her doubts. And there were all those fights he'd gotten into when he was younger. Sunlight thought he had potential, but Corinda did not. She thought Angelo was damaged goods.

However, Sunlight protected the boy. And while Corinda admired Sunlight's compassion and generosity, it put her in the position of having to work with the increasingly impudent Angelo.

Now this. She had seen him standing there, leaning his ear against the door, eavesdropping on Sunlight's session with Dana. It was outrageous.

She watched the stockroom door for a full minute, but Angelo did not reappear.

The store was emptying out for that slow gap between afternoon shoppers and the start of the evening classes. No one was looking at her.

She took a breath and then leaned her own ear against the door.

CHAPTER 47

The Chrysalis Room
6:22 P.M.

"Listen to the sound of my voice," said Sunlight.

Dana sat cross-legged on the floor, hands layered one atop the other in her lap, eyes almost closed. The session started gently. They drank a cup of herbal tea as Sunlight explained the process he used to help his students tap into their inner selves and allow their psychic qualities to manifest without conscious interference.

"We all want to be who we truly are," he said as he positioned candles in a circle around them. Some of the candles gave off a harsher smell than the first batch he'd lit, and he explained that perfumes were used for commercial candles, but for doing difficult psychic work, other elements had to be added to the experience. He lit several sticks of incense, and again the scent was complicated, almost challenging, because it wasn't actually pleasant, though not offensive, either.

When she asked if the incense was for sale in the store, he made a face. "Corinda, bless her well-intentioned heart, sells a lot of what can best be described as 'tourist incense.' Same for most of the candles she sells. They're very popular with the crowd that orbits the real world of the expanding mind, but they aren't much different from the dream catchers and kachina dolls people buy for their homes. The unenlightened think that just by having those items it means they are doing the actual work necessary to move from the still-point of spiritual inaction to the place where the soul runs free. Do you understand that, Dana?"

"I think so."

"No. Do you understand it or not?"

She smiled and nodded. "Yes," she said firmly. "I do."

"And there we go. Baby steps become steadier, and then you'll leap into the air and dance."

Dana wasn't sure if that was a compliment or not, but she chose to take it as one.

"As for this incense," added Sunlight, "it's not for sale, but I'll give you some."

Once the room was set the way Sunlight wanted it, they spent ten minutes together just breathing in the incense, sipping the herbal tea, and relaxing. After long minutes of agreeable quiet, he began speaking, guiding her deeper into the meditation.

"Your body is a vehicle for great power," he said. "As you relax, as you breathe, you will feel your body change. The density that confines you into your physical shape will become less and less and less . . . until it no longer has the power to trap your spirit. And then, with a breath, you will rise up and out."

She inhaled and exhaled, soft and long and easy, feeling the strange smoke soothe her and sand the edges off her anxiety.

"Nothing can hurt you here," Sunlight told her. "You are safe. You are powerful. You are *in* your power and *of* your power. You are powerful in so many wonderful ways. Say it, Dana, decree it. You are powerful."

"I am powerful," she murmured.

"You are safe."

"I am . . . safe." There was the slightest stumble over that, but she repeated it. "I am safe."

"You are safe," echoed Sunlight. "You are like a caterpillar in a chrysalis. The form and nature that defined your life until now disguises the form that you will become."

The room seemed to swirl with the incense smoke, tilting and turning in ways that she found relaxing rather than unsettling.

"Let your spirit rise and expand, Dana," said Sunlight.

When she'd started coming to Beyond Beyond with Melissa, this sort of thing would have made her laugh, or at the very least feel incredibly self-conscious. But the visions and the deaths, and the horrors in Frank Hale's sheriff's department files, changed something in her. The new age stuff no longer felt like some kind of benign pretend magic. This wasn't healing crystals, faerie pocket charms, or chant music. This felt real.

As Sunlight spoke, Dana could actually feel herself changing in some deep and fundamental way. It was as if her body was a box wrapped with chains and locks and metal bands, and with every moment those locks were clicking open, the chains breaking and falling away, the bands snapping. She took a deeper breath, and there was a *snap*, as if a tether holding her inside her body broke, and then Dana moved upward, drifting like a helium balloon. It was soft, without pain. Without hesitation, either. It felt right. It felt more right than anything else she had ever done.

She could feel her body as two separate things. There was the physical form sitting there, slightly slumped as if muscle and bone, blood and skin slumbered. It was her shell, her cocoon, but it was not who she was. Dana understood that now. Her true self emerged like a butterfly from that shell, rose above it as intangible as smoke but with definite form. She could still feel her arms and hands, legs and feet, heart and breath and everything, except it all felt light, ghostlike, charged with a strange energy that hummed like electricity.

"Open the eyes of your soul," said Sunlight, and now his voice sounded like it came from the heavens above, deep and soft as thunder from a distant storm. Powerful but in no way threatening. "Open your third eye and allow it to see the truth about what is and what will be."

As impossible as that seemed as a concept, Dana felt as if suddenly something did happen, that her mind and perception opened in a way she had never before experienced. The room became very bright, but not in a glaring way. No, this was like she could simply *see* everything with ten thousand times more clarity, and with great insight into what she saw. The closest candles were no longer merely wax and flame. They had each become so much more, because she could see their components and differences. There was a swirl of things making up the wax of each one. She could see and identify every element, every component, no matter how subtle. Beeswax and tallow from animal fat, chemicals from the *Coccus pella* insect, boiled fruit from a cinnamon tree, extracts of tree nuts. Blended together to exacting specifications. She suddenly knew that the candles were insoluble in water, had low reactivity, low toxicity, and changed from solid to liquid because of thermoplasticity. She knew this, but Dana was positive she had never been told that nor had she read about it. However, those facts, and so much more, were there in her head. As if they were obvious, as if she should know such things. She went a level deeper, and when she turned to look at a paraffin wax candle closer to where Sunlight sat, she abruptly knew that it contained the hydrocarbon signature, C_nH_{2n+2}.

When she inhaled the incense, she could actually see the sage and cedar plants from which that stick of incense got its form. She could see components of *makko* from the *Persea thunbergii* tree, and Xiangnan pi, made from the bark of the *Phoebe nanmu* tree, and *jigit*, a resin-based binder used in India. And more. Microscopic components, molecular structures, chemical signatures. All of it. The information flooded into her mind and was recorded there. She knew—absolutely knew—that she would retain that information forever. Somehow. Impossibly, but definitely.

"Accept the truths your mind's eye perceives," said Sunlight. "Absorb it and be it. The organic brain has limits, but the soul-mind is capable of infinite awareness and infinite retention. Be the infinite, Dana. Allow no limitations. In the world of spiritual source energy, there are no restrictions, no boundaries. We all want to eclipse the limited view of what the world thinks we are and reveal who we truly are. Understand that and be that truth, Dana. All truth is yours to own, to share. Swim in it, Dana."

And so she swam.

Soon the room itself fell away, and Dana felt her spirit body rise through the ceiling and into the air above Beyond Beyond. Even though she could still feel her limbs, she somehow knew that this was only a lingering illusion, because her true self was a luminous ball that glowed with bright golden light. She looked into the sky and saw that it was crisscrossed by a network of crystalline rods, as if reality itself was but a dream within a lattice of silica and diamond. It was beautiful and she wanted to weep, but when a sob broke from her, it came out as a shout of pure and unfiltered joy.

She could hear Sunlight speaking, but she was no longer in the same room with him. Dana wasn't even sure she was on the same planet. His words were soothing, guiding, but the language was now meaningless. Not actual words but more like a breeze that stirs a tide. She rode along on that tide, going farther up and out until Craiger was a patchwork of tiny houses and farmed fields. And then higher. Maryland blended into a landscape smear of green and brown and blue. Higher still until the earth, the whole world, spun below her, a smoky blue gem laid on a vast piece of black velvet on which ten billion diamonds were scattered. Crystal dust was cast across the fabric, and Dana realized that it was the Milky Way.

There was no pain, no doubt, no fear, no worry, no anxiety, no trepidation, no concern, no trace of negativity.

There was nothing but peace.

Nothing but an ever-expanding awareness that brought with it the understanding that she—Dana Scully—was as important a part of the universal All as everything else. As important as the warming sun. As important as the dark matter that held the universe together. As important as love. As important as life.

She floated there, high above the earth, and became aware of something behind her. She turned, expecting it to be the moon.

And it was.

Not some dead, pitted chunk of debris caught in synchronous orbit with the earth. It was somehow alive.

Alive.

She flew toward it, laughing aloud despite the airless vacuum of space. The mountains of the moon, crenellated edges of vast impact craters, looked lovely as she flew across them. Sunlight's voice was fading, fading as she flew beyond his control, beyond his reach, making this journey her own.

Far below she saw something gleaming like metal, and she realized that it was something left behind by one of the *Apollo* missions. She saw *Surveyor 1* and *2*. She saw the lunar rover from *Apollo 15* and the *Apollo 11 LM-5 Eagle* descent stage. She saw the flag that had been planted by the first human beings to step onto the surface of another world. She looked for the footprints, but they had become obscured. There was debris, though. Proof that humans had been here. And that made her laugh, because she was a fifteen-year-old girl, and it had taken her moments to soar through space to reach this point. No rockets, no space suit. Nothing but her will and her mind.

And then something moved on the dusty surface of the moon.

Dana turned her awareness to see what it was.

There was something on the edge of a large crater, poised on the rim, touched by the sun and gleaming with silver fire.

It was triangular and huge. Hundreds of times bigger than any of the debris left behind by NASA. It did not sit cold and inert, as the other machines did. Instead there were lights blazing on each of the three points. Bright white, and these were the first lights she had seen that hurt her to look at. They were too bright, or . . . maybe bright in the wrong way. In a way that was not harmonious with her spirit-sight.

The lights seemed to throb, to pulse. A slow, heavy rhythm. Flaring and dimming, flaring and dimming, and flaring again. She understood that this was a machine, a ship of some kind, but the rhythm was like a slumbering heart. Then the throbbing changed, quickened, became more urgent.

All of a sudden Dana realized that this thing, this ship, had indeed been sleeping and now that she had flown so close to it, it had begun to awaken.

With a cry of alarm, she turned and ran, racing on solar winds back toward the earth. Back toward her body. She flew faster and faster while behind her the lights throbbed and flared and came closer to being awake.

"No!" cried Dana, because every instinct, every part of her expanded awareness, knew that this was wrong, that she had made a terrible mistake.

A dangerous and deadly mistake.

She flew downward, downward, needing to escape back into the mundane and ordinary world. She thought she heard Sunlight's voice calling out to her, but she flew past it as she plunged into the atmosphere, down toward Maryland, toward the small town of Craiger, toward the center of town and the rooftop of Beyond Beyond. She smashed through it, actually feeling the tar of the roof, the wood and plaster, metal and brick, electrical wires, and everything of which the building was made.

Then she was in the room and her body was there. So was Sunlight's. Both bodies looked empty, vulnerable. Dead.

But there was something very wrong here, too.

A figure stood between the two vacant bodies.

Tall, immensely powerful, his body rippling with muscles and crackling with living fire. He was beautiful, too. A face more perfect than any man or woman Dana had ever seen. A thousand times more beautiful than a statue from ancient Egypt or Greece or China. Haughty, imperious, sensual, amused. And yet there was something familiar about him. Almost as if that face was superimposed over another one. Dana tried to see through the beauty to the face beneath, and she caught a glimpse.

Just a glimpse.

And then it was gone. The angel stood there, dressed in rags of light, looking up at her. Through the open V of his white shirt, Dana could see a large tattoo inked directly over his heart. A disk of deep black surrounded by a corona of fire. The sign of the eclipse.

His sign, of that she was certain.

Behind his broad back a pair of magnificent wings unfolded and spread so wide the tips of each wing brushed the walls.

The wings were not set with white feathers.

They were huge and leathery and black.

The angel Lucifer looked up at her and said a single word. It was the most terrifying thing he could say.

He said, "Dana . . ."

CHAPTER 48

The Chrysalis Room
6:48 P.M.

Dana screamed herself awake.

She fell over, smashing her shoulder against the floor, hitting her head, biting her tongue, flooding herself with pain.

The carpet beneath her was cold and coarse.

But it was only carpet.

She could not see the fibers; it did not whisper its chemical formula to her. The molecules of which it was composed did not reveal themselves. It was a rug and she lay on it. Ordinary candles surrounded her, and the air was filled with smoke from incense of no particular magnificence.

She was back in the world. In the real world.

It was smaller, uglier, less magnificent.

Safer.

A groan drew her focus, and she turned to see Sunlight sitting with his face in his hands, shoulders slumped. He seemed to be as dazed as she was.

"What . . . ?" she began, and failed to construct any question beyond that.

It made Sunlight look up. His face was drawn and haggard, and it took a moment for his eyes to focus on her.

"Dana?"

"What happened?"

He rubbed his eyes and sat up, but it looked painful. "That was . . . something."

"Did you see what I saw?"

Sunlight nodded. "I think so." He paused, considering. "On the moon? A ship?"

"Yes. But that wasn't what I meant." She climbed to her feet and stood, swaying. It was as if her body did not quite fit right, like she'd gotten dressed in her skin in the dark and had buttoned it up wrong. "I saw *him*."

"Him?"

"I saw the angel," she said.

Sunlight stiffened. "What?"

"Didn't you see him? He was right here," she said, pointing to the area between where they had been sitting.

He got to his feet as well and looked as wobbly as she was. "It was an angel?"

"Not just any angel," she said. "I think I saw his true face. It was like he was wearing a mask."

That made Sunlight gasp, and he stepped over and took her by the shoulders and stared hard into her eyes. "You *saw* him?" he demanded. "You really saw him?"

"I—I think so."

"Tell me. Every detail," he cried. "It's important."

Dana tried to remember every detail, but the more she was in her body, the further memory drifted from her. She could remember the mask best and she described that, and described the garments of light and the leathery wings. Sunlight released her and walked thoughtfully across the room. He stopped by a small table on which was a bowl of fruit and a knife. He picked up the knife, selected a ripe pear, and peeled it without comment. Then he cut it in half and brought it over to her.

"Here, eat this."

"I'm not hungry."

"Psychic experiences take a toll on the physical body. Pears have water, vitamins C and K, copper, and fiber. It'll help you settle back in." He smiled. "It's a very old trick."

Dana took the fruit and ate it. The pear was delicious, and it erased a metallic taste in her mouth that she had only been mildly aware of. Sunlight also ate his piece.

"Do you know who Lucifer is?" he asked.

"He was the Morning Star," she said, chewing. "He was an important angel who rebelled against God."

He nodded. "He was the shining one, the light-bearer. It is a mistake to confuse Lucifer with Satan, Dana, for they are not the same being. Satan is the soul of evil, the infinite exemplar of corruption and sin. Lucifer is an angel, and an angel has perfect knowledge of God, of the universal All. A being with such an awareness could not, by definition, be evil. That is an impossibility, because perfect knowledge and perfect love are two sides of the same coin."

"But in church they told us that Satan *was* Lucifer."

"Of course they did," said Sunlight, "because they don't understand. Lucifer was the bringer of light—he was a liberator, a guardian of the enlightened and a guiding light that brings people to true understanding. The misinformed connection of Lucifer to Satan is mostly the work of poets and writers. Dante Alighieri's *Inferno*, Joost van den Vondel's *Lucifer*, and John Milton's *Paradise Lost* collectively polluted the name of the angel whose gift is knowledge and understanding."

She took a step back from him. "What are you saying? That it's okay that this angel is killing people at my school?"

Sunlight looked genuinely surprised. "What? No, of course not. I'm sorry, Dana. I'm still a little rattled, too. What I meant is that if you truly saw Lucifer, then you were not seeing the creature responsible for these tragic murders."

"Then . . . ?"

"That's why I want you to try to remember the face you saw *behind* the mask of the angel. I suspect that someone is projecting the image of Lucifer in order to both confuse you and disguise his true face."

"Project? How?"

Sunlight raised his arms to indicate the Chrysalis Room. "In the same way that we flew into outer space, Dana. Whoever is doing this is like us. He is a powerful psychic."

It stunned her for a full five seconds, but then she began to nod. It made sense, though in a crooked, awkward way. The floor beneath her feet still seemed ready to tilt, and even though the pear had helped a little, her brain felt like it was filled with cotton candy, angry bees, and sharp thorns. She imagined this was what being drunk must feel like, and she decided right there and then that she wanted no part of any real disorientation. Meditative freakiness was plenty, thank you very much.

"Look, there's something I haven't told you," said Dana, "but I think I know something about the killings that even the sheriff's department doesn't know."

Sunlight narrowed his eyes. "How?"

"Doesn't matter," she said, "but I think Maisie Bell was killed in a way that was supposed to reproduce the wounds of Jesus." She explained about the wrists, feet, and other injuries. Sunlight looked grave.

"I . . . don't know what to say about that," he said.

"What could it mean, though?" she asked. "Why would someone want to do something like that?"

Sunlight shook his head slowly. "It's hard to say. Maybe he doesn't understand what he's doing."

"No," insisted Dana. "I think he knows exactly what he's doing, but I don't know why. What does he get out of imitating the way Jesus died? Is it some kind of blasphemy thing?"

"No," said Sunlight firmly. "No, more likely it is because this . . . person . . . feels that he has a connection of great importance to Jesus Christ. That, perhaps, he is like him in some way. Who knows, he might even believe he is honoring his victims by giving them the same wounds as Christ."

"That's sick."

"Probably not according to the world as he sees it. Can you remember his face?" asked Sunlight. "Can you still see it?"

She closed her eyes and almost immediately lost her balance. She stumbled, and Sunlight caught her with a slender but surprisingly strong hand. The floor gradually, reluctantly steadied beneath her.

"Almost," she said. "I can almost see him. . . ."

"Try," he urged.

She did try. Dana let Sunlight steady her balance as she once more closed her eyes and willed herself to reopen that page of her recent memory. She could see the beautiful face of the angel, and despite everything Sunlight had said, the creature still terrified her, but she endured it because she had to know what face was hidden by the image of Lucifer.

She tried and tried.

But the harder she grabbed at the memory, the more surely and completely it drifted backward into darkness.

She opened her eyes and sighed. And for a moment she leaned her head against Sunlight's chest. "I'm sorry," she whispered.

Sunlight stroked her hair the way her father sometimes used to when Dana woke from a nightmare. It made her feel safe, protected. She could not imagine Sunlight allowing anyone or anything to hurt her.

"It's okay, Dana," he said as he pushed her gently to arm's length and looked down at her. "We can try again another time."

Tears, unexpected and red hot, rolled down her cheeks. "But . . . but I *have* to try again now. Let's start again. I can't just stop. Not when I'm this close to knowing who the killer is. I can't."

"I'm sorry," he said, "but this kind of thing drains a person. You'll be out of it for a couple of hours. You should go home and lie down. I'm going to soak in a tub and then eat a couple of pounds of protein." He gave a small laugh. "We may only wear these suits of flesh and bone, but the body has limitations. We have to honor that. So, no, as much as we both want to know the truth, it is simply not possible right now. We're both exhausted, and that makes it highly dangerous."

"But—"

"Go home, Dana. Wait, here, take this," he said, and took six sticks of the special incense, wrapped them in a silk handkerchief, and gave them to her. "It'll help you center yourself. Light one and meditate, or just light it and sleep. It's better than chamomile tea for soothing jangled nerves. Go on, take them. Good. Now, we should leave it all here for now. We can't do what we can't do."

And that was it.

She picked up her school backpack from where she'd dumped it by the door and left, wobbling as the world rocked uneasily on its creaky wheels.

In the hall she saw Corinda going into the ladies' room, and Dana followed her. A stall door clicked as she entered, and Dana crossed to a sink and washed her face with soap and cold water. When she looked into her own reflection, she was surprised at how flushed she looked. And her pupils were huge. All from floating around in . . .

In what?

Not actual outer space. That was nuts.

In her imagination? In the spirit world? Dana realized that she had no idea how to label what had just happened, but she felt like she finally might begin to understand God. How He could be all-seeing, all-knowing, connected to all beings. Was this like the religious ecstasy she had read about in stories of certain saints?

The toilet flushed, jarring her out of her thoughts, and Corinda stepped out of the stall.

"Hey," she said. "I didn't know that was you out here. How was your session with Sunlight? He's amazing, isn't he?"

"That doesn't begin to describe it."

Corinda took her place at the sink and washed her hands, then accepted a paper towel that Dana took from the dispenser. As she dried her hands, she studied Dana.

"Don't hate me for saying it, sweetie, but you look like crap."

"Thanks. I feel like crap."

Corinda reached out and brushed a strand of red hair from Dana's face. "You saw something, didn't you?"

"I . . ."

"I can *see* it," said Corinda softly. "You saw the killer's face, didn't you?"

"I think so," said Dana, her own voice small and scared. "But it wasn't clear. I couldn't see exactly who it was. I'm so close, but I just . . . can't."

Corinda's face was serious and her gaze penetrating.

"Maybe," she said, "I can."

CHAPTER 49

The Observation Room
7:01 P.M.

"He's here," said Danny.

Agent Malcolm Gerlach usually responded to comments with a mixture of snark, indifference, and mild threats. Not this time. He shot to his feet, pulled on his black suit coat, and smoothed his tie.

"Okay," he said nervously. "Show him in."

The technician went out and returned in under a minute. He held the door open for three people to enter the room. Two were agents in identical black suits, with wires behind their ears and merciless faces. The third man was tall, heavyset, with jowly cheeks, wavy gray hair, and merciless eyes. He was immaculately dressed in a smoky blue suit and hand-painted silk tie, and he carried with him an air of immense power. Danny, who was used to being cowed by Agent Gerlach, now saw the red-haired man fidget like a grubby schoolkid as their guest entered the room. Danny had no idea what the man's name was. When he was mentioned at all, which was rarely, Gerlach and some of the other top agents referred to him as the First Elder. No actual name was ever given, and Danny was too smart, young as he was, to ask questions.

"Have a seat, sir," said Gerlach, gesturing toward a comfortable leather chair that had been brought down that morning from the priest's old office. Now it was clean and polished and placed beside a table on which were a fresh pot of coffee and some expensive little cakes.

The First Elder glanced at the chair and his mouth turned down in a sneer. But he sat down anyway. Gerlach poured coffee into a porcelain cup and backed away, almost giving the impression that he was bowing. In any other circumstance Danny would have been embarrassed on the agent's behalf. Not now. Not with this man. No way. Danny stood apart from Gerlach, back against the wall of monitors, but he wished he could be absolutely anywhere else but here.

"We had a meeting last week," said the First Elder without preamble. "We had a lengthy discussion about this operation."

Gerlach stood as straight as a ramrod. Danny could see sweat glistening on Gerlach's forehead and upper lip. The agent said nothing.

"It's fair to say that we aren't as enthusiastic about the progress of the Craiger Initiative as you seem to be in your field reports," said the Elder. He had a high-pitched but gravelly voice. He did not touch the coffee or cakes.

"We are moving as fast as caution allows," Gerlach said.

"That sounds like an excuse rather than an explanation."

Gerlach's left eye twitched.

The First Elder's eyes were so cold, almost dead. "Perhaps you think that because we are playing a long game, we have unlimited time. That is not the case. In your preliminary assessment, you spoke very highly of your man, this 'angel,' as he calls himself. You made certain predictions as to a timetable you swore you could manage."

Gerlach said nothing.

"We are playing a very dangerous game, agent. Very dangerous. We are risking a betrayal of trust on all sides. When this project began, we all knew that we were putting ourselves at risk. We were putting the world at risk. You convinced us that the angel would be able to cultivate the abilities of these children. You said that they would form the core of an elite army that we could put into play against our . . ." He paused and considered the best word, then finished with, "Masters."

"That is what we're doing," said Gerlach.

"And yet you are dangerously close to missing your own deadline."

"Sir . . . this is new territory for us. For anyone," insisted Gerlach. "It's not an exact science."

"That is your concern, agent," said the First Elder. "You made promises that we have taken seriously. We expect you to deliver the promised assets."

"Yes, sir."

The First Elder studied him with the kind of look Danny had seen people use when selecting a lobster from a tank at a seafood restaurant. "In your most recent memo, you asked for an extension in order to deal with some unforeseen complications. Please explain to me what constitutes a 'complication,' as you see it."

"It's the angel," said Gerlach. "From the beginning it's been about him."

"Exactly what is it that concerns you?"

Gerlach cleared his throat. "He's erratic, unstable, psychotic, and dangerous."

"Yes," drawled the Elder slowly, "that was rather the point when we recruited him into the Montauk Project. We wanted dangerous operatives, and he is very dangerous."

"Dangerous, yes," said Gerlach, "but also unstable. He's a loose cannon. His, um, *methods* are endangering the entire program here."

"Because he is killing children?"

"Well . . . yes . . . that's a huge concern. He's killed six of—"

"We don't care how many coffins are put into the ground," interrupted the First Elder as he got heavily to his feet. He sighed and began walking toward the door. "We need results. We need a weapon or we are going to lose this war."

"I thought we already had lost."

The Elder paused at the door. "The future isn't written in stone, Agent Gerlach. The key to survival is to be prepared when an opportunity arises. To that end we need him to push."

"The angel *is* pushing."

"Tell him to push harder. Turn up the amplification," he said. "Turn it all the way up."

Gerlach took a breath. "Even with the Scully girl?"

"Especially with her."

"What if he kills her?"

"William Scully has four children," said the First Elder. "He owes us one."

Then he left with his bodyguards in tow. They did not bother to close the door.

CHAPTER 50

Dana and Corinda sat together. Not at the usual table, but in the curtained niche in the far corner of the big store, away from the majority of the foot traffic.

"Sit," said Corinda as she pulled the curtains together. They were sheer, with a pattern of swirling planets interspersed with astrological symbols. Corinda turned and looked down at her, then frowned. "Are you high?"

"High?" said Dana, almost laughing. "God, no! Why would you even ask something like that?"

"You look it. Your pupils are dilated and you're flushed."

"I'm freaked out and I spent the last hour in a dark room."

Corinda chewed her lip for a moment. "Okay, I guess that must be it."

She pulled up a chair and sat. The niche was cramped, with a small round table, two kitchen chairs with pads, and a small three-drawer cabinet. The chairs were painted with swirling lines of color that wound around the legs and exploded across the back splat. A thick brocade tablecloth lay across the table, embroidered with some kind of mystical symbols Dana only half recognized. She thought they might have been alchemical symbols, but she wasn't positive. The cabinet was painted blue, but each drawer was a separate shade of purple. The drawer pulls were brass, shaped like turtles. Atop the table was a single fat candle with three wicks, but they were unlit. Corinda folded her arms across her chest, head tilted to one side as she assessed Dana.

"Please," said Dana, "if you have something to tell me, let's talk about it. But no more psychic journeys or readings or Vulcan mind-melding or whatever it is you and Sunlight seem to dig doing. I am about as far out on the edge of going completely berserk as possible. I want to go home and hide in my room. I want to find whoever's doing this and . . . and . . ."

She stopped, unwilling to put into words the red thoughts that filled her woozy brain.

"Don't worry," said Corinda. "I'm not here to play any mind games."

"That's a relief."

"I could tell that you had another vision as soon as I saw you in the bathroom. I could feel it, Dana. And it must have been really powerful, because the air around you crackled with spiritual energy. Even now I can see sparks shooting off you."

Dana looked at her hands and arms. "I don't see anything."

Corinda smiled at that. "We have different gifts, sweetie. It seems like it's your destiny to see into darkness. It's mine to see light. When I look at you, I can see your aura. It's like seeing an electrical junction box that has too much energy running through it. I know it's hurting you and I think I can help."

Dana grabbed her hands and squeezed them. "*How?* Not even Sunlight could help. We did this weird astral projection thing and it fried us both."

"Ah," said Corinda.

"What?"

"Look, I don't want to talk out of turn here, and I wouldn't say a word against Sunlight. He's amazing. But . . . people think he's more of a big deal than he actually is. It's that post-hippie love god groove of his. Everyone falls under his spell, and they think he can walk on water."

Dana was surprised. "You wouldn't say that if you were in the room with us just now."

"Oh, don't get me wrong," said Corinda quickly. "I'm not saying he doesn't *have* power, but he isn't an ascended master or anything like that."

"I thought you two were friends," Dana said.

"We are, we are. I just think it's important to understand things as they are. Perspective is part of how we embrace the real truth."

"Truth?"

"Truth is everything," said Corinda. "Everything that I do here, everything that goes on at Beyond Beyond, is part of the search for the truth—don't you know that? Meditation, yoga, astrology, divination—all of it is about unlocking information that is normally hidden from us. We have to learn to see differently and learn differently, to be open to pathways to the truth that are different from what they teach in school or preach in church. Essential truths are cosmic, and when we are brave enough to accept them and live by them, then we free ourselves to—"

Dana held up her hands. "Please! I can't do any more of that stuff. Not today. My head's going to burst. I just need to know who killed Maisie."

"Sorry," said Corinda. "You really must be overloaded. Sunlight wore you out with his games, and now I'm browbeating you with more."

Dana wiped at her eyes, expecting to find tears, but there was nothing. Her eyes stung, though, and the room—even now—seemed to rock back and forth. Lights were too bright and sounds seemed to hammer and grate.

"If you know who the angel is, then tell me," she begged.

"I'm sorry, Dana, but it isn't as easy as that," said Corinda, softening her voice and taking Dana's hands in hers, kneading them the way she had before. "It's not like I get a face, name, and life details. What I get is a series of impressions. A glimpse of a face and then some loose and cryptic images."

Dana's shoulders sagged. "Oh."

"But it's something certain," Corinda assured her. "I know it is."

Dana squeezed back. "Tell me."

"I'll do what I can," she promised, "but this angel is strong. He knows who I am and he is afraid of me. He hides his face from me."

"Can you try?"

Corinda sneered. "I'm not afraid of him. I have psychic defenses he knows he can't get through. Now . . . breathe slow and let go. Imagine a doorway in your mind. Okay, now pretend that is the door to your inner mind and I'm standing on the other side. I want you to see yourself reaching for the knob, turning it, opening the door. That's it. Now step back and let me in. Let me take your visions from you so I can decode them." Corinda closed her eyes and took several long moments breathing slowly and deeply, and then she began to speak in a trancelike whisper. "I see a knife. It flashes silver. It clicks. Not a . . . hunting knife. Smaller. Something that folds."

Dana listened, barely breathing.

"I see a silver knife in a strong hand. I see scars. On the knuckle of the . . . ring finger. On the side of the hand. An old injury. He . . . hurt it . . . fixing a car. A wrench slipped. Sharp metal. Last year? Yes."

Dana murmured, "Is that him?"

"It is the angel," said Corinda slowly, distantly.

"Does he have a tattoo? An eclipse."

"Yes," said Corinda.

"He's a monster."

"He is a human," said Corinda. "A person. He is flesh and bone."

"But—"

"He has power, though. Great power. He projects . . . He lies by planting . . . faces . . . in the minds of people like him. He wears masks . . . he wears Lucifer's face as a mask. He is not the devil, though, but he is his voice. He speaks for him. He is evil."

"That's him!" cried Dana. "Can you see his face? His real face?"

Corinda's facial muscles went slack as she slipped deeper inside her vision.

"He hides his face. He is so strong, so clever. He knows how to hide, but he is close, Dana," she murmured. "So close. He . . . sees you. No, he *has* seen you. Spoken to you."

"What?"

"And you . . . have seen him. *Spoken* . . . to him."

"When?"

Corinda shook her head and winced as if some titanic battle raged inside her mind. "You know his name . . . I think. Yes. You know his name. He will kill again," whispered Corinda. "Soon. He must. He wants to. He has already selected his next victim. Oh God! Oh God . . . no!"

"What is it?" cried Dana, jumping to her feet.

Corinda's eyes snapped open. "It's *you*, Dana. The killer is coming for you."

Dana backed away, bumping into the small cabinet and banging it against the wall of the niche. "No. Who is he? Why's he doing this? Why's he after me?"

The look in Corinda's eyes was strange, complex. There was fear there, and wonder, and doubt. She passed her hands in front of her face, as if that could forcibly disconnect her mind from the vision. Then she sagged back, shaking her head, spent and trembling.

"He . . . he's strong," she gasped. "Stronger than I thought."

"What's his name?" begged Dana. "You have to tell me."

But Corinda kept shaking her head. "He would not let me that far in. All I know for certain is that he has those scars on his hand and he always has the knife with him." She looked at Dana. "If he's coming after you, then you have to find him first. You have to discover who among the people you know matches that description. You have to find him first."

CHAPTER 51

Dana left Beyond Beyond badly shaken.

She had been unable to get anything further out of Corinda, and besides, the psychic looked like she was on the verge of collapse. Sunlight was already gone, and only Angelo and one of the other staff members were around, but now wasn't the time to discuss this sort of thing with either of them. The one pay phone at the store was being used, so she left and crossed to the phone booth outside the diner on the corner. As she closed the door, the dome light flicked on. She fished coins from her pocket and called home, trying to find Melissa.

It was Dad who answered. "Starbuck?" he said. "Where are you?"

No way she wanted to tell her father about anything that was going on. Dad was very much by-the-book and would have laughed at anything involving psychic phenomena. Laughed and maybe ordered her to come right home.

"I, um, have jujutsu tonight," she said quickly, and then realized it wasn't actually a lie. All of her classes—jujutsu and yoga—were listed on the wall calendar in the kitchen. Sometimes she went to the five thirty class and sometimes the seven thirty session.

"It's smarter to go to the earlier class," her father said.

"I know, but since we had a half day I decided to go to the library. I wanted to get ahead of the English essays I have to write."

"Well, that's okay, then." It had been the right kind of argument to use on her dad.

"Is Melissa there?" asked Dana. "I wanted to, um, ask her about some homework."

That was a lie, and Dad jumped right on it. "*You* want *Melissa* to help with homework?"

Dana had to think fast. "A poetry assignment in English."

"Oh," said Dad. Poetry, music, and art were the only subjects where Melissa stood on firmer ground than Dana. She was like Mom in that. Artsy rather than what Dad called "practical" in subjects like math, history, science, and gym.

"Your sister," said Dad, "is at a friend's house. Eileen Minder-something."

"Minderjahn. Melissa is over at Eileen's house?"

"So she says. And that's where she'd better be."

Despite everything, Dana had to smile. There was about one chance in ten trillion Melissa was at the Minderjahns to hang out with Eileen. The chances were a whole lot higher that Eileen wasn't even home and that Dave was. Dana did not say as much to her father.

"Okay. I'll call her over there."

"If you do," said Dad, "remind her that both of you are supposed to be home at nine thirty, and that does not mean nine thirty-one. Are we clear?"

"Aye, aye, Captain Ahab."

There was a pause, then in a softer and gentler voice, Dad said, "You be careful out there."

"Always," she said.

It was the biggest lie she'd ever told her father.

"I love you, Starbuck," he said, surprising her. Dad rarely said anything like that. Before she could reply, the line went dead.

She leaned against the glass wall of the phone booth, feeling oddly lost, as if she had somehow been abandoned by everyone. That wasn't true, of course, but the feeling was so powerful and persistent that Dana tested the folding door to make sure it was all the way closed. Better to be locked in a glass booth than be out there, exposed, vulnerable.

That, too, was an irrational thought. She was a target in a fishbowl, and she realized that safety was incredibly subjective. It was what people made of it in the moment. That was not a comforting realization. She looked at the darkened street, at the passing cars and the occasional pedestrians, seeing no one she recognized. Not at first. Then she saw Angelo come out of the alley that ran alongside Beyond Beyond. He wore a dark long-sleeved hooded sweatshirt that made him blend almost completely in with the shadows behind him. He looked up and down the street, obviously looking for something or someone. Dana pulled the handle of the folding door, opening it inward until the edge of the metal door released the button that triggered the light. The booth went dark a split second before Angelo looked across the street. His gaze swept toward the phone booth, seemed to pause for a moment, and then moved on. Then he pulled up the hood of his sweatshirt, jammed his hands into his pocket, and hurried across, slanting away from where Dana stood trembling.

She lingered there in the dark, watching his figure vanish into the night.

Why did I hide from him?

Why am I afraid of him?

The questions burned in her mind, but she did not try to answer them. Not out here, alone in the dark, confused and still off balance from whatever had happened in Sunlight's Chrysalis Room. Not after everything Corinda had told her.

She put another dime in the slot and dialed a number. It rang five times before Ethan answered.

"I need to see you," she said, her voice urgent and breathless.

"Whoa, wait, are you okay? Is something wrong?"

"Everything's wrong," said Dana, but then she took a breath. "Look, can I come over? I need to talk about some things with someone who understands."

"Understands what?"

It was a good question, and it took Dana a few seconds to figure out how to answer it. "The case," she said at last. "I have more information, but I don't know if it's real or not. Actually, I don't know if anything's real anymore. My head is so messed up right now."

"Messed up how?" asked Ethan.

"I'll tell you when I see you. I'll tell you everything. Can I come over?"

"When?"

"Now."

Ethan paused and hushed his voice. "I think Uncle Frank brought the file home for Todd Harris. I saw him putting the big case folder in his desk, and it looked thicker. But the thing is, my uncle's still here. He was supposed to work another double today but he said he wasn't feeling too good and called in sick. But after he took a nap, he said he was doing better and was going to go in after all. He said it was probably just too much spicy food at the diner last night. But he won't be leaving for an hour. I'm cooking dinner first. He wanted oatmeal to calm his stomach. Can you come over after? Like around eight?"

Dana thought about it. She felt like going home and hiding under the covers in her room, but she was afraid of what her parents would say, especially if her pupils were still dilated from whatever it was that had happened with Sunlight. Last thing she needed was to have her folks think she'd been getting high. As if. But with everyone in Craiger talking about dumb kids getting stoned and then getting killed, she'd never be able to convince her parents that it was the aftereffect of meditation and astral projection. Yeah, that wasn't something she could sell. She didn't even know if she believed it herself.

However, if she didn't go home, that left a lot of time. She glanced along Main Street in the direction of the dojo.

"Okay," she said. "I'll be over after my class, but I have a curfew, so I won't be able to stay long."

"Good," said Ethan, sounding relieved. "And Dana . . . ?"

"Yes?"

"Be careful, okay?" He paused, then added, "I just found you. Don't want to lose you already."

Dana took too long trying to decide how to answer. Ethan hung up.

She stood in the darkened booth and stared at the phone.

And smiled.

CHAPTER 52

Dana was late for class but jumped right into the calisthenics. The orderliness of push-ups, sit-ups, and jumping jacks helped calm her jangled brain. And it gave her something else to blame for rapid heartbeat and sweats. Then they began the drills. The students stood in lines, everyone wearing crisp white *gis* and colored belts; Sensei Miyu Sato and her assistant, Saturo, wearing starched black *hakama*, the traditional culottes of the samurai. As Saturo counted in Japanese, the students moved together, practicing footwork and postures, evasions and angles of attack, while Sensei Miyu paced up and down and studied them with a critical eye.

Then everyone was paired off for *uchikomi,* a drill for practicing attacking skills against a passive opponent. There was an uneven number of students in the dojo that night, so Dana found—to her dismay—that she was paired with Saturo. The exercise always began very slowly to allow students to see that every technical detail was correct. They started with *tsukuri*, the preparation for a throw, and repeated this twenty times. Then on the last run, the throw was executed with more speed and as much precision as possible.

There were a lot of components to a good throw, including interception of the opponent's attack; achieving the correct and best angle; disrupting balance; establishing a fulcrum with a foot, leg, hip, or shoulder; generating power through speed and torsion; and then the actual throw, followed by a pin, pressure point, or finishing strike. The goal, according to the sensei, was to do every single technique at least ten thousand times to truly master them. As there were hundreds of techniques in jujutsu, Dana did not expect to become a master anytime soon.

However, the orderly, mechanical, and practical approach to these exercises steadied her. Nothing was mystical in jujutsu. It was all physics and physiology, cause and effect, logic and technique. She was far from the best student in the class, but she learned very quickly, and she loved deconstructing each move to understand how they worked. Leverage points, angles of mass displacement, velocity, and balance. It was machinelike in the best of ways, and as the class wore on, it pulled her back from the strange and formless places her mind had gone.

When they had completed these drills, Sensei Miyu ordered everyone to sit cross-legged around the edges of the large mat-covered area in the center of the room.

"I know this is not anyone's favorite drill," said the sensei, "but *randori* is important to the development of reliable self-defense."

A few of the students groaned, and Dana had to suppress her own trepidation. *Randori* was freestyle practice, where one person acted as attacker and the other had to defend, but without knowing which attack was coming. Dana didn't mind playing the role of *uke*, the attacker, even though it meant getting kicked, thrown, locked, or pinned. It was all controlled, though. What she didn't like was being off her game when she was *tori*, the defender, because she was supposed to be the one kicking, throwing, locking, and pinning. She did pretty well against students of her own skill level, but things never worked out when she was paired with Saturo. She had never once successfully defended against his lightning-fast attacks. And Saturo was uncompromising. He never cut anyone a break. His philosophy was simply, "If you don't want to get knocked down, be a better fighter."

Easy to say, but since he was a black belt, Saturo was the demon they all feared.

"Dana, Saturo," said Sensei Miyu, "you may lead us off."

Saturo smiled. Dana's heart sank.

They walked to the center of the mat and bowed to each other. Dana, being the junior of the two, was first *uke*, and she came in with a series of strikes, attempted grabs, and kicks. Each time Saturo seemed to turn into a blur, and then she was flying through the air and thudding to the mat. Over and over and over again.

She was hardly sure which techniques he used on her. All she saw was his smiling face, the winces on the faces of the other students, and then the mat coming up to greet her at thirty miles an hour.

"*Mate!*" called Sensei Miyu. *Stop.* "Change."

Dana climbed to her feet, bowed to the sensei, bowed again to Saturo, and settled into a receptive combat stance, feet wide, knees bent, weight shifted onto the balls of her feet, her hands open and raised, palms turned slightly outward. She was *tori* now and it was her job to be in control of the encounter and defeat any attack. Saturo, playing the role of *uke,* began circling, much as he had done when they did the knife drill. He loved to circle, and it worked to confuse his opponents and make it difficult to ever predict the exact moment or angle of his attack. When he moved in at her, he was even faster, if that was possible, snapping a kick to within a half inch of her knee or heart or nose, or slashing an open-handed blow toward her with the speed of a whip.

He attacked five times and scored five times.

A sixth.

A seventh.

Dana was starting to panic. Her head was still not right from her mind trip, and she was a little nauseated, as if this fight was happening on the deck of a ship out in choppy waters. She staggered backward a few times, tripped and fell on her butt once, and nearly walked into a back-fist punch. Instead of easing up on her, Saturo seemed to go faster, not trying to hurt her but definitely pushing her out onto the edge of her ability, trying to show her how vulnerable she was. He did not let her stop, never gave her a chance to catch her breath, cut her no breaks at all. She wanted to run, to hide, to cry.

And then something happened.

Suddenly the whole world seemed to shift, to skew around in the wrong direction. Instead of seeing Saturo rushing at her with a powerful round-house kick, she saw herself standing in the path of the kick. It was like she stepped into Saturo's mind for a moment and saw what he saw, even thought what he thought.

Scare the red clean off that dumb girl's hair.

That was the thought in Saturo's mind as he launched the kick, but somehow the kick was wrong. It abruptly slowed down so that it moved through the air as sluggishly as if he were kicking while standing chin-deep in water. It still moved, and Dana knew that it was all some kind of bizarre perceptual shift, and yet she was inside the bubble of slowed time.

Then she was back in her own body and the kick was coming toward her. Still slowly, still moving as if time belonged to her and she had it to spare. Anger surged up in her chest and then flashed out through her arms and legs, burning like jet engines. She launched herself forward, stepping inside the arc of that kick, closing to a distance that nullified the power of the attack; and at the same time her hands moved, striking him in the thigh, in the stomach, in the face. She saw blood fly like small rubies, she saw his eyes go wide with shock and pain. Far away there was a sound, the distorted cry of command and warning as Sensei Miyu ordered her to stop.

And then, with the abruptness of an explosion, real time caught up with her. *Bang.* All at once.

Saturo fell backward, his hands clamped over his nose, a cry torn from his throat as he fell hard and fell badly. Sensei Miyu grabbed Dana's shoulder and hauled her backward, spinning her, shoving her away from the fallen Saturo. Yelling at her. Furious. Scared, too.

Dana staggered a few feet away and barely caught herself at the edge of the mat. She turned to see Sensei kneeling over Saturo, speaking to him with forced calm, pulling his hands away so she could examine the damage.

Even from fifteen feet away it was clear to Dana, and to everyone else, that Saturo's nose was badly broken. There was blood everywhere, and he had tears in his eyes.

Dana said, "Oh God, I'm sorry."

She took a step forward, but Sensei hissed at her. *"Sit down."*

Everyone was looking at her. Shocked eyes, open mouths. Doubt and worry and even some contempt.

"I'm sorry," Dana said again. She bowed to Saturo, repeating her apology over and over again.

Finally, Saturo struggled to sit up. Blood streamed down his chin and onto his chest, staining his white *gi* with dark red. He looked at her with eyes that were filled with pain.

But he said, "Okay."

Just that.

She bowed again.

He nodded. It was the best he could do.

She turned and ran into the changing room, changed as fast as she could, and then hurried out of the dojo before they could see her cry.

"Dana," called Sensei, "wait. . . ."

She didn't wait. She ran.

CHAPTER 53

Hale Residence
8:47 P.M.

"Jeez," said Ethan when he opened the door, "you look awful."

Dana pushed past him and went into the house.

"Your uncle's not coming back, is he? He's not going to leave early 'cause he's sick?"

"No, we're good," said Ethan, closing the door.

Dana glanced at him. "Lock it."

"What? Why? He has a key."

"No. Just . . . just lock it, okay?"

Ethan did it, then paused and also turned the dead bolt.

"Thanks," she said, greatly relieved.

She followed him into the kitchen, where he poured them each a glass of chocolate milk from a half-gallon jug. He handed her one. "My aunt Louise always said that chocolate was the first line of defense against any case of the heebie-jeebies, and you look like you've got them in spades."

He smiled and then searched her eyes. His smile turned into a frown. "You're high," he said.

"No, I'm not," snapped Dana. "I never do that stuff." She saw the doubt on his face.

"Then what's wrong?" he asked. "Are you sick? Your color sucks, and your eyes are weird. All red and bloodshot, and your pupils are huge."

"How many times do I have to say it?" growled Dana. "I. Am. Not. High."

"Okay, okay, don't bite my head off. I'm a friend, remember?"

Dana turned away and looked out the kitchen window at the black night. "It's been a really bad day, okay?"

"No," he said, "it's not okay. You need to tell me what's going on."

He led her to the small office and they sat down on the overstuffed chairs, balancing their glasses on their knees. Ethan closed the door to that room, too, and for the first time all day, Dana felt like she was safe. Or at least as safe as possible.

Ethan wore a black T-shirt and jeans, and it somehow made him look older. Stronger. More solid, which mattered because the rest of the day seemed to have been made up of different levels of trippy transparencies. Nothing until now seemed quite real.

Dana sipped her chocolate milk, then set the glass down and held out her hand. After only a tiny hesitation, Ethan took her hand, held it. His fingers were warm and real.

She told him everything that had happened. It took a long time, and he never let go of her hand.

CHAPTER 54

Sycamore Street
8:59 P.M.

A lone figure stood, hands in pockets, in the utter blackness under the heavy boughs of a maple tree.

The street was empty except for a yellow dog that walked a crooked path from front lawn to front lawn, pausing every now and then to pee as if replying to messages left by friends. When the dog reached the maple tree, he froze, then backed away slowly, growling. The figure under the tree said nothing, did not move, merely waited for the dog to turn and run away.

Overhead, the clouds were rolling in, blotting out the stars, intensifying the darkness.

There were lights on inside each of the houses along Sycamore Street. From a few came the tinny sounds of muffled television. At one house, the one directly across from the big maple, a light burned in the window of a side room on the first floor. It was that window that the figure stood and watched with dark, intense eyes. He could see the silhouettes of two teenagers— a tall boy and a short girl.

When a cold wind blew down from the storm clouds, the figure shivered but did not move away. He barely moved at all, except for the slow clenching and unclenching of the folded knife in his pocket.

CHAPTER 55

Hale Residence
9:35 P.M.

Her curfew was up by the time Dana was finished with her story, and she and Ethan sat in silence for almost five minutes, each of them absorbed in the details. While he was still thinking, Dana went into the kitchen to phone home and apologize for being late, but it was Melissa who answered.

"Hey, nice of you to call to tell us you're not dead."

"Don't joke. It's been a very, very weird day. I'll tell you about it when I get home."

"Where are you now?" asked Melissa.

"Ethan's, and—"

"Ooooooh. Nice."

"It's not like that, Missy, and you know it," said Dana.

"Sadly, I do. It's tough being the sister of Dana the Pure Light of Virtue."

"Oh, shut up and cover for me, Missy. Tell Mom I'm still at the dojo or something."

"This late?"

"Tell her it's some kind of ancient samurai thing and I'll be home by ten. No, ten thirty. Tell her Sensei will drop me off."

Melissa snorted. "Oh, yeah, that sounds plausible."

"Come on, I already covered for you."

"Yeah, yeah, okay," said Melissa.

"You're the best."

Melissa paused. "Be careful, Dana," she said. "And I'm not talking about Ethan."

"I know," said Dana, and hung up.

When she went back, Ethan had Uncle Frank's case files out, and Dana could see that the folder was thicker than it had been before. She watched as Ethan made his sketch of the rubber bands and then carefully removed each one. He brought the folder over to the couch.

"Todd's stuff is in there?" she asked, sitting down next to him.

"Yes. It's pretty nasty, too," said Ethan.

"After today," she said, "I can handle anything."

It was a big honking lie and they both knew it, but they were each smart enough not to mention it.

Dana opened the folder and looked at what had been done to Todd Harris.

It was as bad as Dana imagined it would be. And it was strange. When his car supposedly crashed, he had been thrown through the windshield, but the collar of his heavy jacket had caught on a broken piece of the crumpled hood. In the crime scene photos, the smashed car was perched on a pair of rocks at the bottom of a steep hill, and Todd hung suspended, his toes inches above the ground. It was grotesque and looked like pictures Dana had seen of criminals hanging from a gallows.

She closed her eyes for a moment as the room took a spin. The dizziness from earlier was still with her, and seeing this kind of horror did not help.

"You okay?" asked Ethan.

"No," she said.

"Me neither."

There were a lot of photos in Todd's file. Because the car had rolled down the hill, the crime scene investigators had needed to photograph every piece of debris. She flipped through more than eighty pictures, going fast through the ones that showed a fragment of a red taillight lens or a blown-out piece of tire. Then she stopped at one that showed the ground below Todd's feet. The photoflash had caught the gleaming surfaces of a bunch of pocket change that lay scattered among the torn weeds. The photographer had taken three photos of the coins. Dana paused there, caught by the image without knowing why. An accompanying note gave an inventory of the coins. Fifteen nickels, eleven dimes, three quarters, and one silver dollar.

"What is it?" asked Ethan, leaning over to see what pictures held her interest.

"Nothing, I guess." She replaced the photos and went through the rest of the folder. She almost closed the cover, then stopped, frowned, and went back to the photos of evidence and debris found at the scene. She bent and examined one picture in particular, and her blood turned instantly to ice. "Ethan! Look at this."

He leaned closer. "What?"

She handed him the photo, which showed bits of broken glass, a few metal splinters, part of an orange brake light lens, and several coins scattered across a stretch of stony ground below where the body had been hanging. "See what they found on the ground below his feet?"

"What?"

"The *coins*," she said, tapping the picture.

It took Ethan a moment. "Sure, some change that fell out of his pocket."

"No," she insisted. "I think those coins were placed there."

"What? Why?"

"Count them."

"Okay. Fifteen nickels, eleven dimes, three quarters, and one silver dollar." Ethan did some quick math. "Three dollars and sixty cents?

Three-six? Are you going to tell me that it's a Bible reference? Chapter and verse, something like that?"

"No," she said. "Fifteen, eleven, three, and one. Add that up."

He did. "Thirty coins."

Dana shook her head. "No," she said. "Thirty pieces of silver."

He stared at her. "What . . . ?"

"How did Judas die?" she asked.

Ethan took the diagram of Todd Harris's injuries and ran his finger across the line that had been drawn across the throat. "Judas 'went and hanged himself,'" he murmured, repeating a biblical quote, one of the few that had ever stuck in his head. "Oh, man . . ."

"It all fits," Dana said, slapping the file closed. Ethan took it from her, added it to the big folder, replaced the rubber bands, and locked it in the drawer.

They sat together, and this time Ethan took her hand in his. His smile was gentle and he curled his fingers around hers. There are times to talk and times to say nothing. This was a time to let silence wrap itself around them. They were behind locked doors, safe inside, together, and all the storms and darkness were outside.

When she finally got up to go, he said, "I should walk you home."

"No," Dana said quickly. "It's not far. I'm okay."

"No one's okay."

The image of Saturo sprawled on the dojo floor with a broken nose filled her mind. Remembering that didn't fill her with pride. It made her feel like an animal. But a tough one, at least.

"Really," she said, "I can take care of myself. Besides, if I come strolling up with a guy, my dad will kill both of us."

"But he'll be cool if you walk home alone?"

"I'll tell him I got dropped off at the corner," she said. "Really, I'm good."

At the door, Ethan said, "What do we do with all this? With those visions, with the file? I mean, we both think that somebody's out there pretending to be an angel and killing people. We know it, but we can't prove anything. So what do we do?"

Dana leaned her shoulder against the door frame. She was still holding Ethan's hand, and she looked down at it, at the way their fingers intertwined. It felt good. Safe. And something more than that. The moment stalled, though, because Dana felt like she should say something and, clearly, so did Ethan. Neither of them seemed to know what, though.

Ethan nodded. "What about what that lady Corinda said? What do you think about that?"

"I don't know what to think. I mean, I can't believe I know anyone who would do something like this."

"They'd have to know some things," he said. "They'd have to know the religious stuff. They'd have to know about cars. It can't be easy to fake all those accidents so well the cops think they *are* accidents."

"And he has to know about anatomy."

"Why?" asked Ethan. Then he said, "Oh, right. To be able to make the other injuries look like they happened in accidents."

"He's smart," she said.

"He's an animal."

"Sure," said Dana, "but animals can be smart."

Ethan looked past her out into the night. "Sure you won't let me walk home with you?"

She smiled. "I'm sure."

Then, without thinking about it, she stood on tiptoes and kissed him. Neither of them expected it to happen, but it happened anyway. Dana suddenly realized what she was doing and immediately backed away, shocked, embarrassed beyond words, her hand rising to hide her mouth.

"Ethan, I'm . . . I mean I—" she began, but before she could get anything else out, he bent forward and kissed her.

One-millionth of Dana's mind tried to make her back away. The rest of her leaned in. She was no expert on the subject of kissing, but she was pretty sure this was a very good one, and it lasted a good, long while.

When they finally stepped back, they grinned at each other as if the world were a happy place and they weren't dealing with murder, conspiracies, and horror.

"Well," said Dana breathlessly, "I guess there's that."

"Um, yeah," he said.

They stood there, awkward and uncertain. Then they kissed again. And again. Afterward, Ethan looked dazed and glassy-eyed. That made her laugh. It also made her feel warm inside.

"Bye," she said, and then she was gone into the night. When she looked back from halfway down the block, Ethan was standing exactly where she'd left him. That made her smile, too.

CHAPTER 56

The porch light was on, and she moved toward it like a lost ship drawn to a lighthouse beacon.

The day had gone from frightening to surreal to broken, and Dana didn't quite know who she was. Or *what* she was. After leaving Ethan's, she had been happy for almost three blocks, but then the dizziness came back, and with it came her doubts and all the various fears that seemed to define her life here in Craiger. Those fears brought with them a strange, huge, complicated depression that settled heavily on her shoulders and made each step as difficult as if she were wading through mud. All the happiness leaked away.

Nothing about her seemed to fit right anymore. Ever since they'd moved here from San Diego, Dana felt like she was losing the connection with her own identity. She used to be an orderly person. Good in school, always on time, didn't run with the wild crowd, went to church. Prayed. All of that.

Now she was having psycho dreams, hunting a mass murderer, going on mind trips, and beating the crap out of people.

Was this still her? Still Dana Katherine Scully?

Or was Sunlight right, and she was transforming into someone and some*thing* else? If so . . . what?

The porch light was rich and warm and safe-looking. Then she paused when she saw a figure sitting there.

"Dad . . . ," she murmured.

She stood a hundred feet away, in a pool of shadows beneath a big tree across from the old church, watching her father. Dad was a big man. Blocky and hard, with a bullet head on a bull neck. He looked as tough as he was. But now she saw him in an unguarded moment. Dad was sitting on the porch swing, head bent as he read a book. Not being tough. Not being Captain William Scully of the United States Navy. Not being anything except a middle-aged man relaxing on a spring evening. Wearing a soft flannel shirt. The red-and-black one that he liked so much. It was old and worn, and Dana knew every place where it had been patched and stitched, and she knew that Dad wouldn't let Mom throw it out. Not that shirt. It was familiar, and he loved wearing it when he wanted to step out of the skin of his job and responsibilities. He was wearing that shirt in so many of Dana's best memories. Family camping trips. The day Dad taught her how to ride a bicycle, and when he'd taken her to the ice cream shop at the big old hotel in Coronado after she'd broken her arm falling out of a tree. He'd been wearing it the day they brought Charlie home from the hospital as a tiny baby. He'd worn it the first night they'd started reading *Moby-Dick* together when Dana was nine.

That shirt.

Dad.

She stood there and buried her face in her hands and started to cry.

"Dana . . . ?" said a voice. Dad. She looked through her fingers and saw him come down off the porch. "Dana, is that you?" he growled. "Melissa said you were out studying, but you're seriously pushing it, young lady. It's after ten. What could you be thinking? With everything that's happening in town, I think we need to talk about your judgment and common sense."

She wanted to run away right then. Instead Dana broke and ran toward him, racing the rest of the way to her house, and her dad came down the steps and jogged forward, arms out, to gather her in. He hesitated for a fragment of a moment, and then he pulled her to him and held her close in those strong arms, kissing her hair as she clung to him, sobbing uncontrollably.

"Daddy . . . oh, *Daddy.*"

William Scully held his daughter firmly as if he were the anchor that held her to the world. Stopped scolding and did not ask her what was wrong. He did not pollute the moment with questions. They would come later. Instead he held her and whispered her special, secret name.

"Starbuck," he said, and there was the thickness of tears in his voice, too.

Later they sat together on the porch swing. She had her sweater on and lay with her head against his chest. Silence was a friend to both of them, and they welcomed it.

It was only when it was getting late that her father spoke.

"You know you can tell me anything," he said gently.

She said nothing.

"Is it a boy?"

"What? No."

"School?"

"No."

He was quiet for a moment. "Dana, is it the kids who have been getting themselves killed?" When she did not answer that, her father sighed, deep and heavy. "I know it was hard on you when that teacher died back in San Diego."

Dana pushed away the memory. "That was sad, but this—" *This is different.*

"I won't let anything happen to you," he said.

"I know."

In the yard a lonely cricket chirped. Suddenly a second one chimed in. They pulsed out of sync and then gradually fell into harmony. It was nice. It screwed one of the loose bolts back into place on the machinery of the world.

"Ahab?" she said.

"What is it, Starbuck?"

"I know it's late, but can we read for a little? We haven't done that in a long time."

She felt a spasm in his chest, as if the request hurt him somehow. But he said, "Sure. Go get it. It's on the coffee table."

She went inside and brought out the old leather-bound copy of *Moby-Dick*. Dad put on his reading glasses and opened the book to the place where they'd left off long ago. It wasn't their first time through the book. They knew the story by heart, but that wasn't why they came back to it. It was the thing that connected them, and Dana sometimes wondered if the book was as much a lifeline to him as it was to her. There was a sadness in her father she'd never understood, and she suspected that his coldness was as much a defense mechanism as it was part of his being a professional military man. She knew for sure that a heart beat inside his bearlike chest.

She wanted to find some way to truly unlock him. She wondered if he was different at sea. She liked to think that he yearned to be riding the waves, chasing whales, navigating by the stars—and that his gruffness was from being trapped on land, and not from being trapped on dry land with his family. But she never asked, because she might find out the truth, and that would hurt too much, because sometimes the truth doesn't set you free.

They read the book and the crickets sang to each other in the grass, and for a while, at least, the shadows kept their distance.

CHAPTER 57

Craiger, Maryland
11:03 P.M.

The angel thought about Agent Gerlach and his masters in the Syndicate. He thought about what they wanted of him, what they needed from him, and what they thought about him.

They thought he was a madman, that he was out of control, that he was becoming a danger to their plans. They were working to save the world. Maybe some of them actually believed it. Gerlach seemed to. But they were going about it the wrong way. The Craiger Initiative was good, and it might even give them the weapon they needed.

Maybe, but the angel did not believe it. Oh, he believed that what he was doing for them would create weapons, even incredibly powerful ones, but the enemy they all fought was so very much more powerful. No army of psychic children could hope to oppose it. No, the angel believed that the Syndicate was going to lose the whole planet.

He, on the other hand, would not. He had a different idea about how to fight the future.

With the *grigori* and their children, the *nephilim*.

How could any fleet of invaders hope to win against a host of angels and giants?

He had tried to explain this to Gerlach, but the conversation had gone nowhere. The angel could see the doubt, the mockery, the fear in the agent's eyes.

The angel pitied him.

He pitied everyone who failed in his or her faith. When the painting on the wall was complete, when it changed from blood and hair and grease and sweat into a portal, then the faithless would burn in the same fires as the enemies of this world.

CHAPTER 58

Scully Residence

11:43 P.M.

The house was still and even the crickets outside had fallen silent.

Sleep seemed impossible. Dana lit the special incense Sunlight had given her and tried meditating, but failed. She tried yoga, and failed at that, too. Finally she crawled into bed and lay staring at the ceiling, trying to force her brain to shift from emotional reaction to logical analysis. There was a line from a Sherlock Holmes story she'd read once that really seemed to fit, and she spoke it aloud so that the sound of the words would reinforce the truth of the observation. It was from the short novel *The Sign of Four*.

"When you have eliminated the impossible, whatever remains, however improbable, must be the truth."

Absolutely, she thought. *But what is the truth?*

She tried to recatalog the facts as she knew them, updating a mental file as detached and precise as Uncle Frank's case files.

Point One: There have been six deaths of teenagers in Craiger, Maryland.

Point Two: All those deaths *appear* to have happened because of car accidents.

Point Three: None of the victims had been drinking.

Point Four: Five of them had something in their blood called 5-HT2A receptor agonists. Since Uncle Frank did not yet have the toxicology results for Todd Harris, Dana didn't know if he also had that stuff in his blood, but it was likely.

Point Five: She was having dreams about the death of Maisie Bell. Was she really some kind of psychic sensitive as Corinda and Sunlight seemed to think she was? If so, why her?

Point Six: Corinda and Sunlight both told her that her "gifts" could be fine-tuned. Was that true? If so, was that a good thing for her or bad? Could she live with even more visions in her head? She doubted it. Even the thought made her want to throw up.

Point Seven: Sunlight and Corinda both said that the killer was somehow projecting an image of a dark angel to hide his true identity. So who was he?

Point Eight: Maisie said something about a Red Age. What was a Red Age? Was she mixed up in a religious cult? The wounds seemed to shout that as the truth, but how to find out for sure?

Point Nine: The angel was male.

Dana thought about that. He was male in her dreams, and he was male in the parts of the visions viewed by Corinda and Sunlight. Did that mean he actually *was* male? Or was she imposing that on the angel because of the degree of violence? Could a woman have committed those crimes? Maybe. A strong woman. Alternately, could the angel be a "them" rather than a "him"? Could there be more than one person doing this? Not separately, but working together. It wasn't out of the question. After all, she saw a documentary once about two guys who worked together to commit murders back in the 1920s. Leopold and Loeb. That same special talked about other pairs of murderers. She fished for the names. Ian Brady and Myra Hindley, the child murderers from England in the sixties. And Charles Starkweather and Caril Ann Fugate, who went on a killing spree in the fifties. So, sure, it was possible. Did she believe that was what was happening here? Maybe, but the argument was one of pure practicality. Arranging the car crashes and making sure the victims' injuries were in keeping with an accident seemed like something that would take planning, muscle, and effort. Could a single person keep doing that? Especially in such a short period of time? Dana found it hard to believe.

Point Ten: Corinda said that the killer was someone Dana knew. What did that mean? Was it someone she'd met casually? Someone at school? Someone from another place here in Craiger? Since moving here, she'd met a lot of people, from the mailman to the teachers at school, but did any of them strike her as being a murderous psychopath?

No, she thought. *Not one.*

She continued listing points, but soon she found that they were becoming thin, with her forcing logic on pure supposition—something her dad once said was a poor way to manage strategic thinking.

So, without more facts to consider, she asked herself questions, even though she knew they did not yet have answers. Asking the questions was important, though; her gut told her as much. Those questions would give her a direction, give her focus.

Question: Why would someone want to kill them?

Question: What did the victims have in common besides being teenagers here in Craiger?

Question: Was this all drug-related?

Question: If this was a cult, was it a religious cult? (Was the Red Age some kind of religious reference? To the crucifix or to the blood of martyrs?)

Question: Who was the angel?

The incense was every bit as calming as Sunlight had promised. Soothing, making her feel safe and drowsy. She hovered on the edge of sleep.

Question: Am I just losing my mind?

"No," she said, saying it out loud so that it, too, would be real. "No. I'm not imagining it. This is happening. This is real. The truth is out there. I'm going to find it."

She believed that, but at the same time she knew she had to make a decision about how to react, and about what to believe. The psychic stuff was scary and weird and confusing, and maybe it was true. She certainly couldn't dismiss it out of hand, because too many of the things from her visions showed up in the case files. So, okay, ESP was real.

"So what?" she asked the night. There was nowhere to go with that stuff. She could not prove anything that she'd seen.

Dana thought about that for a long time. She did not want to be the girl who had visions. No way. Not now and not ever. Nothing that was as scary and disturbing as those visions could be the right thing for her.

Which left what other option?

Ethan. He was all about the science. Collecting hard evidence and analyzing it. Was that her path?

Maybe. But not exactly.

It was closer, though. It felt like a safer place to stand.

Much safer.

She got up and crept out into the hall, listened for noise, heard nothing. Then she lifted the receiver of the phone and dialed Ethan's number. It rang eight times before he answered, and it was clear she had pulled him out of deep sleep.

"Hello . . . ?"

"It's me," she said, keeping her voice low.

"Are you all right?" he asked, the sleep vanishing from his tone.

"Yes," she said quickly. "Listen . . . I want to go see Sunlight and Corinda sometime tomorrow. Will you come with me?"

He took a long time to answer. "Is that what you really want?"

"Yes," she said.

"Then, okay."

"Thank you," said Dana. "Really . . . thank you. I know you don't think it will help, but I really want you there. Is it too much to ask?"

"Dana . . . look, you can ask for anything and I'll do it." He paused. "And I hope that doesn't sound corny."

"No," said Dana. "It's nice."

The house creaked as if shifting in its sleep.

"I'll see you tomorrow," she said.

"Okay," said Ethan. "Sweet dreams."

It was the sweetest thing he could have said, and she clung to it like a talisman. She took those words to bed with her and lay with them, smiling, there on the edge of sleep. Then she put her hands together and said a quick prayer. She asked for guidance. She asked for protection. As her eyes drifted shut, Dana fell off the edge down into the well of sleep.

CHAPTER 59

"*. . . The truth is out there. I'm going to find it.*"

Agent Gerlach sat beside Danny, watching the Scully girl on the TV monitor. Gerlach reached out and touched the rewind button, stopped it, and then pressed play.

"*The truth is out there. I'm going to find it.*"

Danny cut him a nervous look.

"Yeah," said Gerlach, replying to the unspoken question. "That's going to be a problem for us."

CHAPTER 60

Dana felt a presence in the room with her, and it pulled her up out of a deep dream in which she stood on a tiny island with a man she did not know, surrounded by mist and darkness. Somewhere out in the darkness, something big and heavy and wrong moved through the waters.

And then she was awake, sitting up all at once, jolted back to the world and the present and the darkness of her room. Lightning flashed outside and revealed a figure standing at the foot of her bed. The shadows of the tree branches outside painted the figure with stark, jagged lines of black and white. Dana recoiled, a scream rising to her lips, but she caught it, held it, kept it inside.

When she spoke, it was a whisper.

"Gran . . . ?"

Her grandmother stood there, dressed in a pale nightdress, gray hair hanging loose, eyes completely black in the bad light.

"The angel is looking for you," said Gran.

"What?"

"He has all his thoughts bent on you," said Gran. "His mind is a furnace."

"Gran, how do you know about that?"

Lightning flashed again and again, but there was no accompanying thunder. The world was oddly silent.

"Listen to me, girl," said Gran. "There are webs and webs, layers upon layers, and you need to be very careful. Keep looking, but know that the truth is all around you, too. It is there to be seen, to be known. It's not enough to open your eyes. . . . You have to turn and look around. The truth might be standing right behind you."

"I don't understand."

There was another flash of lightning, and this time there was a monstrous explosion of thunder that shook the world and made Dana cry out. It was all so loud, so bright, that she turned away from it, covering her head with her arms.

When she looked again, Gran was gone. The room was empty, the door closed and locked. Outside, the storm clouds had thinned and parted, and the moon shone clear and bright through the April trees.

CHAPTER 61

The Observation Room
2:08 A.M.

"Agent Gerlach!" cried Danny, and the fear in the young man's voice snapped Gerlach from a doze. He jerked awake and launched himself from where he'd been sprawled on a threadbare couch.

"What's wrong?"

"I think we're in trouble." Danny pointed to one of the screens.

On screen number eleven, a thin olive-skinned girl was thrashing in her bed with such intense ferocity that they could hear mattress springs snapping like loud guitar strings. The whole bed was bouncing, lifting the front and back legs as if strong hands were raising and smashing them back down. Gerlach could hear the pounding of fists and the desperate cries of the girl's parents, but the dresser slid across the floor and wedged itself immovably against the door. The bedside lamp flashed on and off like a strobe, and steam rose from the screaming girl's open mouth.

"What's he *doing* to her?" demanded Danny.

Gerlach wiped cold sweat from his face. "Turning up the amplification," he said, echoing the order from the First Elder.

"He's going to kill her."

Gerlach said nothing.

Suddenly the girl was flung from the bed with incredible force. She crashed to the floor, twisting like a worm on summer-hot pavement. Then she shot to her feet, crouched for a moment like a wild animal, eyes mad and feral as she looked around, clearly seeing nothing she recognized. Then, with a howl like a wild dog, the girl ran toward the window, crashed through the curtains and glass, and vanished into the night. After an appalling moment, there was the soft, awful noise of her body striking the unforgiving lawn two stories below.

"Ah . . . geez," said Danny. "She looks pretty bad."

Gerlach cursed under his breath and then reached for the phone, dialed a number, and waited through three rings. "Sheriff," he said, "you're going to get an emergency call in a few minutes. No . . . no one's dead this time. This is going to be a couple of broken bones and maybe some head trauma. Maria Sanchez, age eleven. She'll be irrational. Make sure you put a deputy on her who knows how to keep his mouth shut. A specialist will be at the hospital within four hours. He'll have all the right papers. I need you to make sure he is afforded every courtesy and that no one gets in his way. He'll oversee her treatment. That's right. Thank you, Sheriff. As always, you can expect an envelope in the glove compartment of your car."

Gerlach set the phone down and let out a long, tired sigh. Danny gave him a hopeful smile.

"Hey," said the younger agent, "at least he didn't kill this one."

Gerlach unwrapped a stick of gum. "Day's young, kid."

CHAPTER 62

School the next day was a drudge and a blur. Dana was sure she did not actually learn anything. She was called to the nurse between classes for her test. The nurse's face was wooden as she tied a rubber tourniquet around Dana's arm, swabbed, with alcohol, jabbed, with a needle, and drew off a glass vial of blood. Five volunteer nurses worked with her. Six students at a time. Rinse, repeat. And all of it in a ghastly silence. Afterward, she looked for Ethan and finally found him in the lunchroom with the rest of the science club. Dana and Ethan told the others about the latest developments.

When they were done, Tisa Johnson swiveled her praying mantis head from Ethan to Dana and back again as she said, "I've been reading about ESP. The Soviets have been doing a lot of research about psychic spies. My aunt Sallie works for our government. Something in the Department of Defense, and we're going over to her house on Saturday. I'm going to see what she knows."

The others said they were also looking into it, but none of them had anything specific.

"We're going to see the psychics at Beyond Beyond," said Ethan.

Tisa nodded, but Sylvia rolled her eyes. "There's real research and then there's airy-fairy stuff."

"It's what we have," said Ethan. "Besides, Dana says they're pretty sharp."

"Worth a try," said Jerry, blinking his big frog eyes.

So Dana and Ethan found themselves at her usual table at Beyond Beyond half an hour after their last class. Sunlight sat across from them, stirring his tea, eyes hooded, lips pursed, saying nothing. He had listened to everything Dana and Ethan had to say, occasionally interrupting to ask clarifying questions, and then lapsed into a long and thoughtful silence.

Ethan was like a stone statue next to her, but Dana couldn't help but fidget. Around them, the usual hustle and bustle of the store continued, as if the world hadn't turned darker and stranger. Behind the partition, Dana could hear Corinda ringing up café customers, chatting with them, occasionally laughing. As if life were normal. Dana reached under the table and took Ethan's hand, squeezing it, giving comfort as well as holding on for dear life.

Finally Sunlight leaned back and folded his hands on the tabletop. "This is bad."

Dana and Ethan said nothing.

"I caught glimpses of this yesterday, Dana," continued Sunlight. "And I can see why you built this theory."

"It's not just a theory," she began, but he raised a single finger to silence her.

"Oh, I believe you," he said. "It all fits. As ugly and bizarre as it is, everything fits."

"I don't know whether to be relieved or cry," admitted Dana.

"What you should be," said Sunlight, "is very, very careful, because I believe this is bigger than you think."

"What?" asked Ethan. "Bigger than six teens getting killed by some kind of religious psychopath?"

"Yes." Sunlight glanced around, then lowered his voice. "If these murders were this well orchestrated, then how likely is it the angel is acting alone?"

"That's what I thought," said Dana. "Maybe there's two of them. Like Leopold and Loeb."

"Anything's possible," said Sunlight. "It could also be one extraordinary person and some lesser persons assisting him."

"Assisting?" asked Ethan. "Who would do that?"

"A charismatic person can often exert control over others. Ask Charles Manson. And I will not be surprised at all to discover that's what we have here."

Ethan looked unconvinced. "Is this a guess or did this theory come to you in some kind of vision?"

"*Ethan*," said Dana under her breath.

Sunlight smiled and waved it away. "It's perfectly fine if you don't believe it. I've been dealing with that kind of reaction my whole life. People who don't possess psychic qualities find it very hard to accept that these qualities exist in anyone. It's understandable. There's fear, of course, and a lack of understanding. There's some jealousy, too. Not only in you, Ethan, but in anyone who is outside of the psychic experience. It's a natural reaction. However, let me ask you this: When Dana told you that she saw Maisie Bell in the school locker room, did you believe her?"

Dana turned to watch Ethan's face, and she saw a rush of different expressions come and go. His eyes briefly met hers, then slid away. That hurt, because she saw the doubt, saw his struggle to believe, understood how it was all at odds with the pure science he loved so much. She still held on to his hand, but now his fingers were icy.

Finally Ethan said, "I want to believe."

It was exactly the same thing Dana had said to her sister a few days ago. *I want to believe.* It took some of the pain out of the moment, but it was a long, long way from saying *I believe.*

"That's something," said Sunlight, reaching out to salvage the moment. "It's a sign of an open mind and, perhaps, of an open heart."

Ethan cleared his throat. "I don't believe in much," he said. "This is all about someone trying to imitate religious murders, but I don't believe in God or anything."

"I could say something trite like, 'God doesn't require your belief,'" said Sunlight, "but that's beside the point. Someone *is* doing this, and that person *does* believe. It doesn't change how we view it, nor does it limit us from attempting a proper response."

Ethan thought about that, and nodded.

"I don't even believe all of it," admitted Dana. "I've always had to wrestle with this stuff. I mean, I go to church and I believe in God, but there are a lot of things I don't know if I believe. And stuff I'm not sure I *can* believe, and a bunch of stuff I don't want to believe in."

"That's the sign of a healthy mind and an even healthier intellect, Dana," said Sunlight. "And it's part of your personal evolution, your transition into a higher state of understanding. You are just now catching glimpses of what you will become."

Ethan looked down into his glass of root beer and made no comment.

Dana said, "What do we do now?"

"No," said Sunlight. "Before we talk about that, we have to go back to what I started to say. About being careful."

"We are being careful."

"No," he said, "you're not. You're looking at your own visions as if they are pictures in a TV screen. That's not how it works. Maybe it does when you have visions of ordinary people, but not when you are making deep contact with another psychic."

"What do you mean?"

"Have you ever heard of the German philosopher Friedrich Nietzsche?"

"I heard his name before," she said.

"He is often quoted by writers, politicians, and others. A quote from him applies very much to your visions, and it should stand as a strict warning for you. For anyone with psychic qualities. It is this: 'When you gaze long into an abyss, the abyss also gazes into you.' Do you understand what that implies?"

Dana felt her facial muscles turn to ice. "God . . ."

"Wait, what does it mean?" demanded Ethan.

"It means, son," said Sunlight, "that as much as Dana has been coming to know and understand the angel, the angel has likewise been learning about her."

"Oh no!" gasped Dana.

"Oh yes. And because it's very clear to me that the angel is a far more powerful psychic, it is very likely he knows quite a lot about you, Dana. And maybe about you, too, Ethan. He probably knows who you are, your names, where you go to school, and possibly even where you live. I would not be at all surprised if he wasn't already planning on how he will come after you. And make no mistake; he will *have* to come after you, because you are now a clear danger to him."

The whole store seemed to fall into a crushing silence. All Dana could hear were the artillery bursts of her heartbeat.

Sunlight still wore his smile, though. "Now that I have scared the life out of you," he said, "let me tell you how we can fix this."

"*Can* we?" croaked Ethan. "Isn't it already too late?"

"There is another expression, one I particularly like," said Sunlight. "'Where there's life, there's hope.'"

"What can we do?" pleaded Dana.

"You? For now, nothing. Go home, stay home. Talk to no one about this. As for me, I'm very well known in Craiger. I've been on TV and talk shows. Everyone knows what I am, or at least they think they do. They know enough to accept that I am a well-known psychic." Sunlight shrugged. "I've even helped the sheriff's department once or twice with missing persons cases. In each case the bodies of the missing children were found. The families were able to get some closure. I tell you this because it means that I have a certain relationship with the sheriff's department, and with the state police. Perhaps I can have a quiet word with them about this."

"Would you?"

Sunlight sat back and pursed his lips. "I need to think about how best to do it. This has to be done in such a way as to keep both of you completely out of it."

Ethan nodded.

"Oh, please," said Dana.

"For now, though," said Sunlight, "you two need to stop looking into this. No more peeks at Uncle Frank's case files. No more talking about it to anyone. Dana, if you have another vision, you come and tell me. I want you both out of it."

"What about the angel?" asked Ethan. "If you're right and he knows about her, how do we keep Dana safe?"

Sunlight nodded. "That's a good question. Dana, you need to start being careful. No more walking home alone at night. No more jujutsu classes. No more late visits here. No going out after dark at all. Not alone. Can you do that?"

Without meaning to, Dana cut a look at Ethan. "I . . ."

"Dana?" Sunlight said in a warning tone. "You're a smart girl. *Be* smart. And Ethan, be a gentleman. If Dana wants to see you, then go visit her at her house. Don't ever let her walk home in the dark alone again."

Ethan paled. "Yes, sir."

Sunlight nodded and reached out one hand to each of them. They hesitated, then took his hands. His skin was very hot.

"We'll get through this," said Sunlight. "I promise. Let me handle everything."

A shadow fell across the table, and Corinda was there. "Oh, hey! I didn't see you all here. I've been so busy you just snuck right past me. Is everything okay, Dana?"

"Yes," said Dana, giving Sunlight's hand a final squeeze. "Maybe it is."

PART THREE

THE
RED AGE

The treachery of demons is nothing
compared to the betrayal of an angel.
—Brenna Yovanoff

CHAPTER 63

Ethan and Dana stood on the street, holding hands, both of them trembling. They seemed to vibrate at a hundred different frequencies.

"That was . . . ," began Ethan, but he paused, uncertain how to finish.

"Weird?" suggested Dana.

"More than that. Different, strange, scary, bizarre. I may run out of adjectives."

"Sunlight's a little hard to take, I guess," she said.

"A little?" Ethan shook his head. "His plan is out there. Can't wait to tell the guys in the science club about this."

"Are you making fun of him?" Dana demanded.

"No. It's just that if all this new age stuff is real, then it has to be part of science. Tisa, Jerry, and Sylvia all seem to think there's something to ESP and all this. I have to admit that I still don't know where I stand. I trust you, Dana, but this is still hard for me to wrap my mind around. I want to talk to the science club guys some more. Maybe we can figure out a way to tie it all back to something we can . . . I don't know . . . measure? Study? Understand?"

Dana said nothing for a minute. "Either way," she said, "I feel better having Sunlight on our side."

Ethan nodded. "We can use all the help we can get."

They began walking. He lived closer to Main Street, and her house was more or less in a straight line three-quarters of a mile past his and two blocks over. The sun was tumbling toward the west, seeming to drag the day's warmth with it. The wind smelled of seawater. The trees on either side of the street were crowded with noisy birds. Crows and grackles seemed to dominate the chatter, their black wings glistening, their black eyes always alert and watchful.

"So, what now?" asked Ethan after they'd walked a few blocks. "We just pretend that we're not involved at all?"

"That's what Sunlight said."

"Can we?"

"Can't we?" countered Dana.

Ethan made a face. "No, I mean *how* can we? We're part of this. It's ours."

She stopped and faced him. "This isn't about taking credit, Ethan."

"I didn't mean that."

"Then what did you mean?"

He took too long in answering, and Dana gaped at him. "Are you serious? You *want* the credit for figuring this out?" she demanded. "That's it, isn't it? This is all about you wanting to be a forensic scientist. You want to break the big case."

"No," he said, but there was not enough emphasis in his voice. "We figured this out together."

"'We'?" she fired back. "I seem to remember it being *my* theory about the religious stuff that helped us figure it out."

Ethan scowled. "So, then *you* want to take the credit for it. You can't get all high and mighty with me and say that this is all about me wanting to be a forensic scientist when you're acting like you're the great detective, figuring it all out."

"I *did* figure it out," she yelled.

"Only because I showed you the case files, Dana. Let's not forget that I took a heck of a risk with that."

"Like I'm not taking risks every time I close my eyes," said Dana. "Like I'm not taking risks walking out the door in the morning."

"I never said you weren't."

"Oh," she said, "but you're taking a bigger risk, is that it?"

"I never said that, either," protested Ethan, his voice rising with hers. The birds scolded them from the trees, but neither of them noticed or cared. "I just want to know why we should be completely cut out of this."

"Because we'd get grounded until we're eighty," she snapped. "You said that yourself. Besides, do you think anyone would ever trust you with evidence if you were the guy who stole case files from your own uncle?"

"Hey, I didn't steal anything. I put it all back exactly as I found it."

"Like that will make a difference when you apply for a job."

"And I suppose your dad's not going to ground you?" said Ethan. "From what I heard, he's pretty harsh."

"Don't you dare talk about my dad."

"I'm just saying—"

"No. You don't talk about him. Or anyone in my family. You don't know him or us or anything."

"Dana," said Ethan, trying to step back from the moment, "I didn't mean anything."

She spun around and marched away.

"Whoa!" he yelled, starting after her. "You're not supposed to go anywhere alone."

When he caught up to her, she whirled on him and jabbed him hard in the chest with her index finger. "Back off! I don't need you to protect me,

Ethan. I can take very good care of myself, thank you very much."

"You're just a girl and—" he began, and then bit down on the rest.

Dana got up in his face, as much as her height would allow. She glowered up at him. "I'm just a girl and *what?*"

"No . . . no," he stammered. "I didn't mean . . ."

"Yes, you did," she said. She stepped back, and it was like stepping off a cliff. "Yes, you did," she repeated.

Then she turned and walked away.

CHAPTER 64

Her route took her past the school.

It was quiet there, the windows dark, the parking lot empty, everything bathed in the orange glow of sodium-vapor streetlights. Dana walked past, then stopped and went to the side of the building, to where bleachers rose above the soccer field. She climbed to the fifth row, which was exactly as far as her energy would let her climb, and then she sat down hard and stared into the middle of nowhere.

She wanted to scream. That would probably feel good, but there wasn't really a place in a town this small where someone could just let loose. She was too scared and mad to cry. So she sat with jaws clamped and fists balled.

Everything in her life felt weird and complicated and in a collision, and now this mess with Ethan. That really hurt, because she actually cared for Ethan, and now he'd done this. Now he'd shown that he was no different from any other boy, any other man. She was a girl and that meant she was less. That was what he tried not to say; but it was what came out. The world wasn't built for girls or women. It was built by men who did not want to share. Not the power, not the money, not the advantage, not anything. It made her so mad. After all, this was 1979. Shouldn't all this have been solved by now?

"*¿Qué pasa, mai?*"

She lifted her face from her hands and looked down to see Angelo standing at the foot of the bleachers. He was dressed in his janitor clothes, a blue sweat rag tied around his forehead.

"Go away," she said.

"No," he said, "I don't think I will."

"Look, I just want to be alone, okay?"

"Okay," he said, but he didn't move.

"Did you hear me?"

"Sure," said Angelo, "I heard. But you're sitting here all alone in the dark, looking like you want to strangle someone."

"It's none of your business."

He placed a foot on the bottom bleacher and rested his crossed forearms on it, looking up at her. His forearms and hands were very tanned, except for some small pink scars and a paler band where he usually wore a wristwatch. "Maybe not, *chica*, but I'm here anyway. So are you. If there's something wrong, maybe I can help."

"You can't."

He smiled. "How do you know? I'm a good listener."

"You're a guy," she said.

"Last time I checked, *sí*."

"Then no thanks."

"Ah," he said. He straightened and climbed the steps. When she tensed, he shifted to sit well apart from her. "Not trying to make problems, *chica*. I see you at Beyond Beyond all the time. You've been talking with *La Bruja* a lot."

"Who?"

"Corinda. The witch."

"She's not a witch."

"I know, I know. She's a psychic. I work there. I get it." Even so, he shook his head. "She thinks she knows everything, but she don't know much. Not the way she says. She's a—"

"She's my friend."

Angelo inhaled through his nose, then exhaled slowly. "Okay. Got it. Keep my opinions to myself. What do I know, anyway? I'm just a wetback working two jobs for crap wages. Who am I?"

"Don't say that."

"Say what?"

"That word."

"Wetback?" Angelo snorted. "Ain't the worst thing I've been called. Everybody's got a different name for me. Lazy, spic, greaser, illegal alien, take your pick."

"I never say anything like that," said Dana.

He nodded and measured out half a smile. "You're more polite than most."

"I'm not prejudiced."

"Everyone is," he said. "Not everyone admits it to themselves."

"That's not true."

"You told me to buzz off 'cause I'm a guy."

"That's different," she said.

"Is it? Why are guys on your hate list today?"

Dana didn't answer. A black car passed slowly by, and they both turned to look at it.

"Lot of those cats around," said Angelo.

"Who?"

"Men," he said, grinning.

"Be serious."

"Men in black," he expanded. "Scary guys in black suits driving black cars."

"They're probably undercover narcs."

"No," he said. "They ain't."

"Then what are they?"

He shrugged. "*No lo sé.* But they're around a lot lately."

She wiped her nose and crumpled the tissue. "You changed the subject."

He shrugged again. "Wasn't a good subject. We were talking about you hating on guys, and I'm a guy. I can't see how I'd come out on top of that conversation."

"Why do you care?"

Angelo tugged at a loose thread on the knee of his work pants. Dana watched the muscles in his hand and forearm flex under the brown skin. She thought about his scars. Saturo had scars like that, but not the same ones. And not on his . . .

Hand.

Suddenly Dana could hear Corinda's voice echoing in her head.

I see a knife. It flashes silver. It clicks. Not a . . . hunting knife. Smaller. Something that folds. I see a silver knife in a strong hand. I see scars. On the knuckle of the . . . ring finger. On the side of the hand. An old injury. He . . . hurt it . . . fixing a car. A wrench slipped. Sharp metal. Last year? Yes.

"Angelo . . . ?" Dana said in a small, tight voice.

"*Sí?*"

"Those scars on your hand. On the knuckle of your ring finger. How'd you get them?"

He grunted in surprise and looked at his hand. "Those? They're nothing. I was fixing a friend's car last year and a wrench slipped. Cut it on some metal. You wouldn't believe how bad small cuts can bleed. I cut my arm, too, see?" He pushed his sleeve up to show a much longer scar. It must have been very bad, and it cut straight through a small, round tattoo, bisecting it.

Dana stared.

It was a tattoo of an eclipse.

"Where did you get that?" she asked, her voice hollow.

Angelo glanced at the tattoo and quickly pushed down his sleeve. "I got it before I had the accident at the shop. Better than a year ago. What's it matter?"

Dana stood up. "I just remembered," she said. "I have to be home right now."

"Hey," he said, also rising. "Wait. . . . What did I say?"

"No. It's fine," she said as she snatched up her backpack and held it in front of her. "I have to go right now. My dad's expecting me. I'm late."

She ran down the steps and across the field and out onto the sidewalk, throwing terrified glances over her shoulder.

Angelo stood on the bleacher. He looked down at his hand and then at her. Did he frown? Or did his eyes flare with sudden understanding? Dana could not tell.

She ran as fast as she could.

CHAPTER 65

The Observation Room
5:41 P.M.

"She knows."

Agent Gerlach turned to face the angel. "What do you mean, she *knows*? Knows what?"

"She's seen my face," said the angel.

They stood in the hall outside the sacristy of the old church. Through the open doorway, Gerlach could see the strange painting the angel had been working on for the past month. It was disgusting. Not in its shape—since it seemed to be random smears with no attempt at presenting a specific form— but because of the media used. Blood, sweat, tears, and hair. He'd been briefed about how certain kinds of individuals liked to collect trophies.

Sick stuff, he thought. Killing was one thing, and maybe having some fun during a kill provided a certain kind of entertainment. Gerlach didn't indulge in that sort of thing, but he understood it. He'd killed people before in ways that provided different kinds of satisfaction. Not like this, though. This crossed a line. This was perverse.

If it was up to Gerlach, he'd put two in the back of the angel's head and bury the body where it would never be found. Neat and tidy.

It was not, however, his call to make. The First Elder and the top guys in the Syndicate called the shots, and they wanted the angel to deliver. If that meant allowing the psychopath some latitude in how he got his jollies, then it wasn't up to Gerlach to jerk his leash.

On the other hand, freedom of action was earned.

"Whoa, wait a minute, sport," growled Gerlach. "I thought you said that they could only see your dream-face. Now you're telling me you let her see your *real* face?"

Doubt, a rare thing, flickered across the angel's face.

The agent took a step toward the killer. "A lot of things could come crashing down if we have to remove her from the equation. You understand what I'm saying?"

The angel said nothing.

Gerlach cupped a hand around his ear. "Sorry, didn't quite hear that."

"I understand everything about what is happening and about to happen," said the angel. "I understand what will happen when the portal opens."

Gerlach brushed past him and walked into the sacristy and stopped in front of the painting. He took a couple of pieces of gum from a pack and chewed them for a long, silent minute. The angel came and stood with him.

"You don't believe it, do you?" he asked the agent.

Gerlach chewed.

"You don't know what I am," continued the angel. "Do you?"

Without turning, the agent said, "You're a monster."

The angel laughed out loud. "We're *all* monsters. You're every bit the fiend that I am. Maybe you're worse. You're the actual boogeyman."

Agent Gerlach chewed his gum and studied the image of the *grigori*, or whatever this madman believed it to be, and did not reply.

CHAPTER 66

Dana felt lost even though she was walking home.

Home did not feel like it was going to offer her anything but a room she could hide in and a door she could lock.

Angelo.

Angelo?

Could he be the monster?

The scars on Angelo's hand matched what Corinda had said. Did that mean he was the angel?

Could he be a monster?

She had no idea how to answer that kind of question, so she tried to catalog what she knew about Angelo. He had a knife—that much was certain. A folding knife with a blade that locked into place that she'd seen him open with an expert flick, and then use to open boxes at Beyond Beyond. He knew cars, too, and worked part-time at an auto body shop repairing damage. *Accident* damage. He worked at both high schools, too, which meant that he could have known every single one of the victims.

And his name was Angelo.

Spanish for "angel."

It all fit.

All the pieces of the puzzle fell into place. Almost all. She did not understand why he was doing all this. She couldn't understand why anyone would.

She didn't understand how he could visit her in dreams. Did he have psychic qualities, too? Sunlight thought so. He'd said that the angel was powerful.

Did that mean he had looked into Dana's mind back there on the bleachers? Did he know that she knew?

"Oh God," she murmured, and cut a terrified glance over her shoulder. And saw him.

Him.

Angelo was a block behind her, dressed in his work clothes but with a hood-sweater on, the hood pulled up to try to hide his face. She knew it was him, though. His hands were in his pockets. Was he gripping the knife, ready to pull it out? Ready to . . .

"No!" she cried, and then she spun around and ran flat out.

"Wait," yelled Angelo. "I want to talk to you."

Dana bolted. Her house was still six long blocks away and around the corner. It seemed like it was ten miles. Too far. Forever far away. Her backpack thumped against her spine with every step, but she didn't want to waste the two seconds it would take to shrug it off.

She did not know anyone on this block, and all the houses looked dark and quiet. Angelo quickened his pace from a walk to a trot.

Dana dug in and ran for all she was worth. Behind her she could hear the *slap-slap-slap* of Angel's work shoes.

Run-run-run! she screamed inside her head.

The footsteps were gaining, but she did not dare take another look.

Dana cut left through the front yard of a big A-frame house, zigzagged around a pair of fallen bikes, leaped over a soccer ball, jagged left again and raced down the alley between that house and the neighbor's fence, twisted between swings on a new-looking play set, flung open a small gate, ran through it and into the backyard of the house across the shared driveway. A small dog began barking furiously at her, but she ignored it. Then a much larger dog, a husky, lunged at her and would have taken a nasty bite had it not jerked at the end of its chain. The snapping teeth missed her thigh by less than five inches. Dana left that yard at an even higher speed and tore through two more yards before taking another alley back to the street, and then screamed and jumped sideways as a car appeared out of nowhere, tires screeching, horn blaring. The driver, an old man in a checkered suit, stamped on the brakes and skidded the car to a smoking stop ten inches from her. He leaned out the window and yelled at her.

"Help," she begged. "He's after me!"

The driver was surprised, angry, and confused. He turned around to look where Dana was pointing.

The street was empty.

There was no sign of Angelo at all. Nothing.

"Very funny," snarled the old man. "Why don't you go home and grow up?"

He put his car into gear and hit the gas so hard he left five feet of smoking rubber behind him.

Dana stood there, panting, running with sweat, eyes wide and mouth opening and closing like a beached trout. She saw a cracked tree branch hanging low from the willow a dozen feet away, so she hurried over, jumped and caught it, and tore the branch free. It was still green and must have broken during one of the recent storms. Dana stripped off the dying leaves and hefted the stick. It was about twenty inches long and as thick and tapered as a pool cue. The broken end was jagged, but the green wood wasn't sharp enough to use as a knife. Even so, she was sure that if Angelo came after her, knife or not, she was going to do some damage. She'd used wooden swords and staffs in jujutsu, and having a weapon made her feel safer.

Only about 10 percent safer, but if that was all the day was offering, she'd take it.

Clutching her weapon, she began edging toward her street. The sun was dipping behind the trees now, and shadows rolled like a dark tide toward her. Home was still a few blocks away. Dana stopped on the corner and faced back the way she'd come.

"Don't," she said aloud.

Maybe Angelo would hear it. Maybe he wouldn't. Either way, saying it gave her some strength. A little, and she'd take that, too.

She turned and ran down the middle of the street toward her house.

CHAPTER 67

The night was not done with her, though.

Dana was still two blocks from home when she saw a girl walk across the street fifty yards ahead. The girl looked familiar. She was black, pretty, and slender. Her hoop earrings bounced as she walked, and the glow from the streetlamp gleamed on the metal of a pendant hung on a silver chain. The girl wore a school team jacket but not in FSK's blue and white colors. It took Dana a moment to recognize the jacket, and in doing so she realized who this girl was.

"No . . . ," breathed Dana as she jolted to a stop. "No . . . that's impossible."

The colors on that jacket were the green and yellow of a school right over the county line. Oak Valley High. The girl wearing it was Connie Lucas.

Dana was sure of it, even though the only time she had ever seen Connie's face was on a stack of photographs taken at the place where she died.

Fear rooted Dana to the spot, but the name rose to her lips as a question. "Connie . . . ?"

The girl paused, glanced over at Dana, and smiled. It was such a small, sad, knowing smile that it broke Dana's heart.

Then, without saying a word, Connie Lucas walked across the street, onto the pavement, and up the short run of flagstones that led to a wooden front porch of a house where no lights shone. Was it her house? No, it couldn't be. If Connie lived here in Craiger, she'd have gone to FSK. She had to live on the other side of the county line. So whose house was this? Dana had no idea, but Connie walked right in without hesitation, and it was then that Dana noticed the door had been standing open. She quickened her pace and stopped in the street, the stick still clutched in her fist. The door stood open, and inside there was only a black nothing.

"Connie?" she called again.

Silence.

Dana stood there, trying to remember if she had gone home to bed and if this could possibly be a dream. Or was she still hallucinating back in the Chrysalis Room? What was real? Was anything at all real, or had her mind simply broken into so many pieces that none of them would ever fit together again?

And . . . how could she be sure of any answer she might come up with? Now or ever? It was terrifying. It was being lost at sea so long that land itself was becoming more of a fantasy than a memory.

Dana took a few uncertain steps toward the yard but was still unable to see inside. The house remained dark. Had that actually *been* Connie Lucas? If not, why hadn't the girl who lived here turned on the lights?

Turn around and get out of here, said a voice in her head. Her logical self. *This is wrong. Stay out of it.*

Dana moved halfway up the flagstone path. "Connie, is everything okay?"

Run. Angelo could be in there.

Dana shook her head as if arguing with her better judgment. Angelo couldn't have gotten this far ahead of her. No way. Besides, she had her stick, and it wasn't like she was going to actually go in there.

That was what she told herself as she lifted a foot to step onto the bottom riser of the porch.

You didn't even know this girl.

She hadn't known Maisie, either, but she had dreamed about her and then spoken to her. Dana went up the three steps very slowly.

"Connie? What's going on? Are you trying to tell me something?"

She was on the porch now. At the open door.

There was a breeze from inside. Cold and humid, like the rush of air from a meat locker. It smelled, too. Like meat. Not living flesh, but something older, lifeless. Preserved.

Those thoughts banged around inside her head, breaking furniture, tearing at her courage.

Run before he sees you.

The inner voice was begging now, and Dana heard it as clearly as if a twin stood beside her and whispered in her ear. She knew that she absolutely should turn and go. There was no sense to what she was doing. None. No logic, no plan, no advantage. It was wrong from every direction. She was totally aware of that. And yet her traitor feet kept moving her forward. It was like the way she felt when she was walking inside a dream. There was the logic of the dreaming mind witnessing and recording the actions, but the body moved of its own will or as if according to some preset choreography learned way down on the subconscious level.

And for a moment Dana wondered if, in fact, she was dreaming. Was all of this real? Was any of it? Had she even gone to Beyond Beyond with Ethan? Or met Angelo at the soccer field? Or been chased? Was any of that likely in her actual life? Maybe all this was nothing more than some kind of extended dream, a nightmare. They said that dreams were actually very short even if they felt real. Was everything about the angel, Maisie, Corinda, all of it just a complex fantasy playing out as she slept through a spring storm in her own bed?

The floor beneath her feet felt too soft, as if she did not stand on it with all her weight. It wasn't quite the same as when she had astrally projected with Sunlight, but it wasn't real, either. She almost floated. When she took a breath, the meat-locker stink carried with it the same incense smell of the Chrysalis Room.

Which was when Dana decided that she was not at home dreaming.

This was still part of her spiritual trip with Sunlight.

It jolted her, but at the same time it steadied her. Both in equal measure. All this was part of that same out-of-body experience.

"Sunlight?" she murmured, and her voice echoed as if she'd shouted in a vast, empty stadium. "Help me."

"He can't help you," said a voice. It was a male voice, and it was right behind her. Dana screamed and jumped, twisting around as she landed, dropping her backpack and bringing up her hands, ready to fight.

It was not Angelo who stood behind her. It was an Asian boy, and beside him was a brown-haired girl with hazel eyes. Like Connie, they both wore Oak Valley High jackets.

Like Connie, these were teens who Dana had met only through photographs.

Jeffrey Watanabe and Jennifer Hoffer.

Dead teenagers.

Standing right behind her.

Dana heard the soft scuff of a shoe and she whirled again, and now she saw other ghosts. Connie stood by the far wall, and there were two boys with her. Chuck Riley and Todd Harris.

And then someone walked out of the adjoining room. Another girl.

Maisie.

Dana was surrounded by the dead.

CHAPTER 68

313 Sandpiper Lane
6:09 P.M.

They stood there, staring at her, their eyes filled with shadows, their mouths smiling with sadness.

"No," said Dana breathlessly. "Please . . . no . . ."

Connie raised her hand and touched the pendant she wore. It was a black onyx disk surrounded by twisting red-gold flames. The sign of a total eclipse. Maisie wore the same pendant. Jennifer wore earrings with the same symbol.

Chuck, Jeffrey, and Todd all removed their jackets and pushed up their sleeves to show tattoos on their upper arms.

The eclipse.

Every single one of them.

"I see it," said Dana. "What . . . what does it mean?"

"The Red Age is coming."

Maisie said it. Then everyone else said it at the same time. All of them, speaking in a perfect chorus.

"I don't know what that means," cried Dana.

Maisie raised her arms out to her sides the way she had in the locker room. Instantly, bright red blood began to flow from her head, side, wrists, and ankles.

"He will rise," she said, speaking solo this time. "He will rise and the world will fall."

"Who?"

"They think they control him," said Maisie.

"He thinks he controls himself," said Connie.

"There is a darkness greater even than the angel," said Jeffrey.

"And it will consume him even as he consumes the world," said Chuck.

Their voices were those of teenagers, but their words and phrasing were not. It was like some perverse litany in a nightmare church.

Then Connie pointed to Dana. "He is coming for you, Dana."

Dana stumbled backward and nearly fell. "W-what?"

"He is coming for you," said Todd, "and we will make you his."

"His voice," said Jennifer.

"His accomplice," said Jeffrey.

"His apostle," said all of them.

Dana looked around for a way out, but the door seemed to have melted out of sight, becoming nothing more than a door-shaped smear on the wall. The window was fading, too, but there was still some light spilling in from the streetlamp.

"He will take others," said Connie.

"The boy will die soon," said Chuck.

"The girl will die first," said Jeffrey.

"Then you will join us in the world of shadows," said all the ghosts at once.

There was a narrow opening between Connie and Chuck, and she broke and ran for it, determined to fling herself through the living room window. She dived and crashed through in a spray of glass, but the sound of it breaking was not like glass at all. It broke with a sound like dozens of wind chimes—bars and bells and hollow bamboo—all jangling as if blown by a gust of cold wind. Dana tucked and rolled as she hit the porch, but then she felt her body suddenly lift and fly out over the rail as if someone had caught her and flung her away. She landed in the grass, thumping down with a teeth-rattling jolt, rolling, tumbling, and finally coming to rest in a sprawl of pain and fireworks.

She groaned and tried to get up, needing to run away from this place.

But her body felt broken, and Dana collapsed to the ground.

The front door was a door again.

The window was unbroken.

The night seemed to stop holding its breath. Crickets began chirping—tentatively, carefully—and in the trees there were the scuffle of bird feet and the soft caw of a nervous crow.

She sat up very, very slowly and looked at her arms and legs, expecting them to be slashed to ribbons from the window glass.

Nothing. There was no blood, no pain. Nothing. Her clothes were not torn or bloody. There was nothing wrong. Her mind felt like a fragile teapot on the edge of a table that crashed and shattered.

Then she saw the stick she had planned to use as a weapon against Angelo. A twenty-inch piece of green wood, thick at one end and thin at the other, standing against one of the slats of the porch rail. Her backpack sat next to it, all the snaps snapped and zippers zipped.

Who had put that stuff there?

Dana said, "What?"

But the night held its secrets and did not answer. She looked once more at the house. The house number was clear: 313, and this was Sandpiper Lane.

Who lived here?

Was this Maisie's house?

Dana picked up the stick and turned in a full circle. The yard was empty, the street was empty. She snatched up the pack, shrugged into it, took a firm grip on her stick, and ran all the way home. When she got there, she went upstairs and locked herself in her room.

CHAPTER 69

When someone knocked on her door, Dana did not answer. Not at first. She sat on the corner of her bed farthest from the door, a letter opener clutched in her fist, knees drawn up. She'd been that way for the last half hour.

Another knock.

And then, "Hey, let me in."

Melissa.

Dana got up very slowly and crept across the room. There was a quarter-inch gap on the hinge side of the door from where it had been hung wrong, and she peered through it, saw red hair, and leaned her head against the frame for a moment, exhaling a ball of pent-up air. Then she put the letter opener down, opened the door, and pulled Melissa into the room.

"Ow! What's with you?" cried Melissa, pulling her arm free and rubbing it. "I've barely seen you for two days and now you all but rip my arm out of its socket. What gives?"

Dana closed and locked the door, then wedged a chair under the doorknob. Melissa watched this and then studied Dana. A deep frown of concern etched itself onto Melissa's face.

"Okay," she said, "what happened? What's going on?"

"Too much," said Dana, and retreated to her corner of the bed.

Melissa came and sat down. "Tell me what happened."

Dana went through it all, giving her sister every detail she could remember. The wounds of the apostles, Corinda's warning, taking Ethan to meet Sunlight, the science club, Angelo chasing her, the ghosts. All of it.

"Okay," said Melissa, "I am officially creeped out."

"Tell me about it. They said, 'The boy will die soon,' 'The girl will die first,' and then I was going to die."

"Yeah, well, if he comes after you, sis," said Melissa with a steely glint in her eye, "he's going to come up against a couple of red-haired witches, and the Scully girls don't take prisoners."

Dana nodded and tried to smile, but she did not feel as confident as Melissa sounded. "Okay . . . but which girl and which boy?"

"Ethan, maybe?" said Melissa, and Dana nearly had a heart attack.

"What if you're right?" she cried. "Maybe the angel somehow knows Ethan's working on this with me and is coming after us!"

"Will he freak out if you tell him what you told me about what happened in that house?"

"Probably. Who wouldn't . . . though I don't think he really believes much in this kind of thing."

"That's his problem. His uncle's a detective with the sheriff's department, right? Even if he doesn't believe, it's still worth warning him. Maybe his uncle can arrange police protection." Melissa pursed her lips thoughtfully. "So who's the girl? I don't think it's me, because they'd have said, 'He'll come for your sister,' right?" She glanced at Dana. "Was this a real house or a dream house?"

"Real enough, I guess. The address was 313 Sandpiper Lane."

Melissa stiffened. "I think I . . ."

She stopped, jumped to her feet, pulled the chair out of the way, and went out into the hallway phone. She made a call, and Dana came and listened.

"Dave?" asked Melissa when the call was answered. "Put your sister on. No, this is serious. Good. Oh, hey, Eileen . . . Do you know Karen Allenby? Yeah, Maisie's cousin. You do? Good. Do they live on Sandpiper? What's the actual address? That's what I thought. Okay, what's her phone number?" She snapped her fingers for Dana, who ran and fetched a notepad and pen. Melissa took it and scribbled down a number. "Thanks," she said, and hung up. Dana tried to ask a question, but Melissa made another call. It was answered on the fourth ring. "Hello, Mrs. Allenby? This is Melissa Scully from school. Is Karen there? What? Oh yes, I'm so sorry about your niece. . . . Yes, we all liked her. No, I don't believe the sheriff's department is right, either. Maisie wasn't the kind of girl to do drugs. She was a great girl. You're welcome. Okay, I'll wait."

"What are you doing?" whispered Dana.

Melissa covered the mouthpiece. "Karen Allenby is Maisie's cousin, remember? She's the girl you met in school, the one you told me about. That's Karen. That's who lives in that house. I think those ghosts were trying to warn you that Karen is the next victim. Her mom just told me she was in the living room watching TV. Oh, wait." She uncovered the mouthpiece. "Hey, Karen, it's Melissa. Scully. Yes, from math class. Right. Look, this is going to sound pretty weird, but you know my sister, Dana, right? Uh-huh. The crazy one. Exactly. You know how she thought she saw Maisie in the locker room? Right, you talked to her about it. Well, Dana was walking home tonight and had kind of a weird vibe about you, and she thought she saw someone in your yard. Turned out to be nothing, but maybe you ought to, like, keep an eye out."

There was a pause while she listened. Then she scowled. "Yes, I'm being serious. Dana gets vibes. What's so weird about that? You seemed to believe her at school. . . . Hey, look, watch your mouth, okay? That's my sister. Dana just wanted to help. You don't want it, then that's on you. Excuse the heck out of me for trying to keep you alive. Yeah, well, you too."

Melissa slammed the phone down and said a few very ugly words with great emphasis. Then she shrugged and laughed.

"Some people get in their own way, you know?"

Dana said, "She didn't believe you?"

"I don't know. Karen's a bit weird, too. I see her at Beyond Beyond sometimes. She takes yoga and some of Sunlight's classes, and—hey—she even hangs around with Angelo sometimes." She stared at the phone. "You think I should have told her about him? His tattoo and all?"

"I—"

Melissa picked up the phone and made another call. When Karen came back on the line, Melissa said, "Hey, listen, I'm sorry, I didn't mean to freak you out. But with everything going on and . . . Yeah, so we're cool? Good. I wanted to bring up two more things. Don't hang up until I tell you, okay? Yes? Good." Melissa explained about Angelo being creepy and chasing Dana, and about the eclipse tattoo that Angelo had and how that tied into the jewelry or tattoo on each of the victims. Melissa suddenly winced and held the phone away from her ear.

"What happened?" asked Dana.

"She hung up on me. Very loudly. Probably broke the phone slamming it down like that."

They went back into Dana's room and sat on the floor with their backs against the bed. The chair was back in place against the door. Melissa shifted around and studied Dana's face.

"What . . . ?" asked Dana.

"Shame about Ethan," said Melissa. "Never spotted him for being a sexist jerk."

Dana felt her chest tighten. She was so mad at Ethan, but at the same time she wanted to talk to him. She didn't want to talk to Melissa about it, though, so she changed the subject. "What if what I saw was a vision of what's going to happen? Maybe not tonight, but sometime soon. If the angel is going after Karen next and she won't listen, don't I have a responsibility to do something more, no matter what happens to Ethan or me?"

They sat there, listening to the wind blow through the trees outside.

"Man, I don't even know what to say about that," said Melissa.

"We have to do *something*," insisted Dana.

Downstairs they heard the front door slam the way it always did when Dad came home.

Melissa smiled. "I think we call in the big guns."

CHAPTER 70

They sat at the kitchen table with both of their parents. Charlie was out in the yard chasing the sprites and fairies Gran had told him were hiding out there. The TV was on in the living room, but no one watching.

Mom made tea and laid out some cookies. No one touched anything except Dad, who slowly ate his way through a dozen fig bars while he listened. He did not interrupt once, which Dana took as a good sign.

Melissa said very little, except to agree with what Dana said.

As Dana laid it out, though, she downplayed the visions and emphasized all the hard evidence.

First she went through her dream of Maisie and the strange encounter in the locker room, and what appeared to be the wounds of Jesus. From there she went through the case files and detailed the wounds of the apostles and how they were cited on the autopsy reports, but how those injuries were hidden among the greater damage inflicted by car accidents. She produced the photocopies she'd made at the library and pointed out the matching wounds.

Then she showed them a sketch of the eclipse symbol that was noted in the autopsy reports and collected evidence logs.

Her parents sat as still and expressionless as the big stone heads on Easter Island. When Dana cut a look at Melissa, her sister gave her a weak but encouraging smile.

Dana plunged on and went over the toxicology reports next, and the fact that it disproved the thought that any of the victims were driving drunk but also showed something in their blood. A substance she hadn't figured out yet.

No reaction from anyone at the table.

She told them about Sunlight, though she skirted around the astral projection part. She said that he was considering talking to the sheriff but hadn't done it yet. Dana insisted that they couldn't wait, that something had to be done now.

No reaction.

Dana circled back to the eclipse symbol as a way of laying out the case against Angelo Luz. She told them about the scars on his hand that Corinda had seen in her vision, and how they matched the scars on Angelo's hand.

She told them about being chased. That was the first time her mother reacted at all. Mom began to reach across the table to take Dana's hand, but Dad stopped her with a curt flick of his hand. Mom withdrew her hand, and Dana could see her shutting down, dropping the blinds over the hurt in her eyes.

By the time she was done, Dana had told more than she wanted to. She laid her soul bare, and as she did so, it occurred to her how weird it sounded. Being fifteen did not help.

When she was finished, Mom looked at the two sisters and then at Dad. She had not said a single word the whole time.

Dad finished chewing the last bite of his fig bar, washed it down with a long drink of cold tea, set the cup down very carefully and precisely, and then folded his hands together atop the dining room table.

"Well," he said calmly, "that is quite a tale."

The kitchen was so quiet they could hear Charlie asking Gran a question about tree sprites and canned laughter from a TV sitcom.

"We need to call the sheriff's department tonight," said Melissa. "We can't let another minute go by."

"Right," agreed Dana. "Something bad could happen to Ethan or Karen."

"Something bad could happen to *Dana*," said Melissa, and that made Mom's eyes twitch.

"And we need to get them to arrest Angelo."

"Enough," said Dad, his voice very soft.

"But we—" began Dana, but suddenly Dad rose up and slapped his palm down on the table so hard it was like a shotgun blast. Everyone recoiled, the teacups danced, and one spilled.

"*I said enough!*" roared Dad. His face, which had been placid, blazed a fiery red and he stood there, his whole body trembling.

"Bill," began Mom, but he shot her a look so intense and withering that she flinched as if he'd raised his hand to her.

Dad pointed his finger at the girls, first Dana and then Melissa, stabbing the air with it. "I have had enough of this nonsense. Who do you two think you are? Who do you think *I* am? You come here and tell me all this? You talk about breaking into someone's desk and reading confidential papers? You lie about seeing dead girls? You do who knows what with hippies and perverts at that store? You try to get me to believe that some boy is stalking you? What exactly do you take me for? Is this how it is with kids today? You think you're so smart, so *hip*, that anyone over a certain age is a fool who will believe any batch of lies you try to sell. How dare you? Both of you . . . how *dare* you? Where's your common sense? Where's any sense at all? And where is your decency and respect?"

The words struck Dana and Melissa like a barrage of cannon fire, driving them back into their seats, stinging their skin, hurting like actual blows.

It took so much courage for Dana to speak. Her voice seemed lost, frightened away, leaving only mute silence. And yet she fought to defend herself.

"You have to believe us, Daddy," she said.

"I don't *have* to believe anything you say, Dana. I'm outraged. I'm shocked at both of you."

"Bill," said Mom, standing, "you're scaring them."

He wheeled on her. "Scaring *them*? I'm terrified *for* them. I should be able to trust my own children, and then they go and do this? To my own face? In my own house? I'm humiliated."

"Dad, please," began Melissa, but he growled at her.

"I expect this kind of nonsense from you, Melissa. You've never had your feet on the ground since you were born."

Melissa sagged back, tears welling from her eyes, and Dana knew that he could not have hurt her more if he'd shot her through the heart. But then Dad turned his venom on her.

"And you, Dana," he said, his face darkening from red to purple, "I had hopes for you. You, at least, tried to act right. To do your schoolwork, to be sensible. And now this? You're even worse."

"Dad—"

"Who do you even think you are? Investigating a crime? You're not a trained investigator. There are highly trained and important *men* whose job it is to catch criminals, and they don't need help from little girls."

There was so much in that statement that hurt her, diminished her, deflated her.

"I'm ashamed of you, Dana," said Dad, turning away. "I'm ashamed of both of you."

The silence that fell was a crushing weight. Mom sat there, bullied to silence as she was so often, tears filling her eyes but staying there as if not daring to fall. Melissa wept openly, her body shaking as if she were being hit with a series of electric shocks. Dana did not know how to think or feel, and there did not seem to be enough air in the room.

"You're both grounded," said Dad. "God only knows for how long. I'd lock you in your rooms if I could. And you can say good-bye to your friends in school and at that stupid astrology shop. No phones, no TV, no radio, no visitors. No boys. And as of Monday you'll both be seeing Dr. Kingston for psychiatric evaluations. Maybe this is some kind of hysteria brought on by the deaths. Maybe there's a pill for it, I don't know."

He stopped and turned sharply to see Gran standing in the doorway. She wore a small, cold smile, and all the glassiness was gone from her eyes.

"You're yelling, Billy," she said.

"Mom," said Dad, lowering his voice, "this is a private matter. Go back and watch TV."

"I know what this is, Billy. It's your own ghosts come to haunt you."

Dad's face drained of color and he wheeled on his wife. "You tell your mother to go sit down. *Right now.*"

Instead Gran turned to Melissa and Dana. "You should come and watch the TV. Someone you know is saying things you should hear."

Before anyone could ask what that meant, Dana heard the sound of someone speaking, using the tone and meter people did when they were being interviewed. The voice was very familiar.

"... these were murders and not accidents," said Corinda Howell. "Those dead children spoke to me in visions."

Dana bolted from the table. Melissa hesitated for half a second, then followed, edging around Dad and Gran. On the big console TV in the living room, Corinda stood in front of Beyond Beyond wreathed by a dozen news microphones and the words BREAKING NEWS pasted across the bottom of the screen. She had makeup on and a beautiful batik dress and lots of turquoise jewelry.

"It was Maisie Bell who spoke to me first," said Corinda. "She came to me in a dream and said that she had been murdered."

The questions kept coming in, and Corinda answered them, detailing how she began having visions of the murders and saw the face of the killer in her mind.

"At first he disguised himself," explained Corinda, "projecting an image of one of the Watcher angels, a *grigori*, and then as a *nephilim*, the offspring of an angel who married a human woman in ancient Canaan. Then I understood right away that these projections were part of his delusions, that this was how he *saw* himself. Psychotics are like that, you know. Over time, though, I was able to break through his defenses and pull off the mask and see his true face. That's when I knew that I had to come straight to the sheriff's department in order to prevent this madman from doing more harm to the beautiful children of our community."

"She's doing it," whispered Melissa, grabbing Dana's hand, "she's taking the fall for you . . . for all of it."

"And that led me to consider other ways in which the killer's religious mania could have manifested in his crimes," continued Corinda. "Maisie Bell had appeared in a vision to a girl at her school, and it was immediately clear to me that she had received the wounds of Jesus, that the killer had tried to simulate stigmata. I made the intuitive leap to the other deaths, and I told the sheriff's department to look for wounds that correspond with the deaths of the apostles, specifically James the Greater, James the Less, Saint Peter, Doubting Thomas, and even Judas."

The image cut away to the news anchor in the studio.

"We'll have more from Corinda Howell, owner of Beyond Beyond on

Route 302A, which is Main Street in Craiger. Miss Howell is a professional psychic who reached out to authorities today to help them investigate the case of the string of tragic deaths of teenagers. And this just in," said the anchor, turning to accept a sheet of crisp paper. "Sources within the Craiger sheriff's department have issued an arrest warrant for Angelo Luz, a nineteen-year-old Latino male. Luz is wanted in connection with the deaths of those six teenagers."

"Oh my God . . . ," whispered Dana.

CHAPTER 71

Melissa crept into Dana's room after midnight. She closed the door and came into Dana's bed and under the blankets with her, pulling them all the way over their heads the way they had when both of them were little girls. The rest of the house was dead quiet now that Dad had stopped yelling, and he had yelled a lot and for a long, long time. Eventually, he had exiled the sisters to their rooms and there were growled promises of consequences to come. Mom tried to intervene, but that turned into a more private war behind their bedroom door, and the muffled thunder of it filled the house for nearly forty minutes.

Now Dana and Melissa lay with their heads on the same pillow, faces inches apart, talking quietly in the dark.

"Why did she do it?" asked Dana. "Why would Corinda do this?"

"Do what?" said Melissa.

"Lie like that."

Melissa shook her head. "Is that really how you see it? 'Cause I don't. I think what she did was smart and brave."

Dana propped herself up on one elbow. "Brave? Smart? *How?*"

"She took as much of this off you as possible."

"Right, she made it all about her. Sunlight was going to go to the sheriff. She must have stolen the idea from him."

"That's ridiculous. And what does it matter *who* told the cops? That's exactly what we wanted to happen," insisted Melissa. "How does it matter to you who actually talked to the sheriff? You don't *own* all this, Dana. This is the real world. Sunlight would have done it the same way, which means he'd have left you out of it, too."

"Sunlight would have done it without TV reporters and being the center of attention. The way Corinda did it was cheap. It was all 'look at me.' It was all about her taking credit for everything."

"Credit? What's that supposed to mean?"

"Corinda made it look like *she* was the one solving this case," said Dana, thumping her mattress with a fist.

"Well, excuse me. Since when are you a cop? Hate to break it to you, sis, but you're fifteen. You're not police, you're not FBI, you're not Sherlock Holmes."

"But I figured a lot of this out."

"Right, and who would believe *you* if you went to the cops? No one. What would happen, though, is everyone would be looking at you as the weird girl who sees dead people. And you know who else would be looking? The killer."

"Angelo already knows I know. He chased me, remember?"

"Sure, but he doesn't know what *else* you know. Corinda's letting herself be the target instead of you. Just like Sunlight would have done. Or maybe she's smarter because she didn't wait to have a quiet word with the sheriff. She came right out and said it to everyone. That takes the whole spotlight off you. Why can't you get that? Corinda did it to *protect* you."

"I think she did it to make herself look better."

Now Melissa propped herself up, too. "You're really damaged, Dana. Corinda would never do something like that. She's bigger than that. She's all about helping people."

"Is she?"

"Of course she is. And she has incredible gifts. You've seen them first-hand. She can look into your head and read the truth. I mean, look at every-thing she knew about this whole thing. She knew about your visions, about what happened at school, about the case files, about all of it."

"She didn't know about what happened at Karen's house. I mean . . . when I had that vision that I was in there with everyone who was murdered. Corinda never mentioned any of that on the news," said Dana, "and it bugs me."

Melissa looked at her as if she were crazy. "Bugs you *how*?"

"I . . . don't know, but if she's everything she claims to be, then why didn't she know about that?"

"No one knows everything, Dana. But Corinda knew a lot of it. She knew about Angelo."

Dana sagged back down. "I guess."

They lay together in silence, listening to the two crickets singing in the grass.

"The whole Angelo thing is so freaky scary," said Melissa after a while, "to think that we *know* a killer. That we've talked with him."

"I know," said Dana. "Even now, though, it's hard to believe this is all him."

"Why? From what I heard, he gets into fights a lot, and he has that knife. He *chased* you, Dana. And he has those scars on his hand that Corinda saw in her vision. And the eclipse tattoo."

"I know, I know, but in my dreams the angel doesn't talk like Angelo. He's like a college teacher or something. Really precise, and he knows so much."

"Not everything in visions is exactly the way it is in the real world," said Melissa.

"More of Corinda's wisdom?"

"Yes, and don't be rude about her. I still think she did the right thing, and maybe that's why you're not in juvie right now. Or in a mental hospital."

"Thanks," Dana said bitterly. "This is all so wrong. Corinda should never have taken credit—"

Melissa made a sound of disgust and stood up. "What's *with* you? What's with this 'taking credit' crap? You have your head so far up your own butt that you can't tell when someone is going way out on a limb to help you. Corinda's the best, and you're being a real snot about her."

Dana stood up, too. "Why are you defending her, Missy?"

"Because my crazy sister keeps attacking her," snarled Melissa. Before Dana could reply, Melissa jabbed her finger toward her. "You think you're so special, Dana, because *you* have visions and *you* have gifts, and now that someone else has those same gifts—and better ones—all you want to do is cut her down. If I had those same gifts, I wouldn't be acting all jealous and nasty. I'd use them to help people like Corinda's doing. God! Sometimes I can't believe we're even related."

And with that she stormed out.

CHAPTER 72

Dad was up and out before Dana came into the empty kitchen. She had no appetite for anything and poured a cup of tea.

Then she saw two things left for her on the table.

The first was a note in her father's strong, precise hand.

Come straight home after school.

She sighed and looked at the newspaper atop which the note had been placed. There was a picture and a headline, and it froze her into a block of ice.

The headline read:

PSYCHIC WARNING LEADS TO
ARREST IN TEEN MURDERS

The photo showed two sheriff's detectives, a white man and a black woman, flanking a cuffed and bleeding Angelo Luz. The woman was identified as Nora Simpson, and her partner was Frank Hale. *Uncle Frank!*

Melissa came in, saw that Dana was there, and turned around without saying a word.

Dana sat down hard on a chair and read the article. It quoted Corinda extensively and then gave the lurid details of the manhunt and capture of Angelo. It was clear from the photos that Angelo had not given up easily. His eyebrow was torn and blood ran down his face. Even though the picture was black and white, Dana could imagine the color with perfect clarity.

She tried to make sense of why she was so angry that Corinda had been the one to take all this to the police when Sunlight was going to do the same thing. Was it only because Corinda did it in such a showy way? What if Melissa was right and Corinda's grandstanding had simply been a play to draw all possible attention away from Dana in order to protect her? She didn't know. However, Dana felt that there was more to it, and not being able to figure that out might be driving her crazy.

"What am I missing?" she asked the empty kitchen. Whatever it was felt important, but she simply did not know where to look for an answer. The clock ticked loudly and the world seemed to lean away from the security of its hinges.

CHAPTER 73

Going to school was a bad idea.

Dana knew that as soon as she got within a block of the big building. Everyone stared at her. No one said a word to her, but several times she saw girls leaning close to each other to say something she couldn't hear. She heard the laughter, though. They all know she was the "girl at school" Corinda mentioned on the news.

Deputy Driscoll, the school narcotics officer, gave her a long, cold look that was filled with suspicion. No, it was more than that. He looked at her with the kind of contempt someone like him would have for the kind of person he arrested.

In homeroom the teacher did not look at her at all, not even during roll call. No one sat next to her.

There was a word she had read once. *Pariah.* It was used to describe an outcast, and that was how she felt, and yet she didn't really understand why. None of this was her fault. She hadn't done anything wrong.

Because they have to hate someone, she told herself. *And it's easy to hate a freak.*

Why did she feel guilty, though?

Near the end of homeroom, the door opened, and the narc beckoned to the teacher. They both cut looks at Dana. She saw the teacher stiffen and then nod.

"Miss Scully," said the teacher. "Please step into the hall."

Every pair of eyes in the room snapped toward her. A few nodded as if whatever was happening made sense with how they had this all figured out. A few smiled at her as she gathered up her backpack and walked down the rows of desks. None of the smiles were encouraging, none were nice.

In the hallway, the narc took her backpack from her, pulling it roughly from her shoulders. "Principal's office," he said. "Now."

The teacher went inside the room and closed the door.

"What's going on?" asked Dana.

"Best thing you can do, little miss," said the officer, "is keep your mouth shut."

He walked beside her to the office, and Dana immediately realized that a bad morning had gotten worse. Dad was there, his face as red as it was last night. Mr. Sternholtz stood behind his desk, his face cold and hard. The school nurse was there, too, and the two detectives whose faces she'd seen in the paper, Nora Simpson and Frank Hale. She flinched, terrified of what she'd see in Uncle Frank's eyes. Did he know about Ethan and the case folder? Was that what this was about? Her blood turned to icy slush.

"Dad," began Dana, taking a step toward him, but her father actually stepped back from her.

"Sit down, Dana," he ordered.

She collapsed onto a chair, crushed and terrified.

Detective Hale was on her left. He was a tall, thin man dressed in a navy-blue sports coat over tan pants and with a boring blue-and-tan-striped tie. Anyone could tell he was related to Ethan because he had the same wiry build, the same intelligent eyes. However, Frank's eyes had a hardness to them, and a sadness, as if his job had made him look at too many bad things and he had reached some kind of personal limit on horror and pain.

On her other side was Nora Simpson, who wore a green tailored suit over a cream blouse. Low-heeled, practical shoes. She was a few years younger than Uncle Frank, and there was some of the same sadness, but it had not yet filled her to the top. There were still traces of optimism in her expression.

"Miss Scully," said Detective Hale, "the blood test conducted by the school nurse has been processed and my partner and I obtained the results."

"Um . . . okay?"

"Your blood contains trace elements of a controlled substance called Helios 5, which is the trademarked name for a synthetic version of a 5-HT2A receptor agonist. It's an experimental hallucinogen developed for the treatment of schizophrenia. It has been showing up on the street under the name Eclipse."

Dana stared into the absolute silence of the moment. This was the same compound she and Ethan had seen in the files. How did she have the same drug in her system as the dead students?

"Because the amount of the drug found in your blood is minimal," continued Uncle Frank, "it is not clear whether you have recently begun using it or not. We would need to do more medical tests to determine the extent of your addiction."

"No," she said. "That's impossible."

"The test is very precise, Dana," said Detective Simpson. "The court will likely have an independent lab run it as well."

"No," she insisted. "That is not possible."

"Dana," said her father softly. "The best thing you can do for yourself now is to come clean. Tell these detectives everything. How you got it. How much you took. Who gave it to you. Everything."

"But, Dad, I never took anything."

"Don't lie to me," he said, and she could hear in his voice how heartbroken he was. "You have to tell the truth."

"I don't do drugs," insisted Dana. "You *know* that. I would never do anything like that."

"Who gave you the Eclipse?" asked Simpson.

"No, you don't understand, the whole eclipse thing is part of my—my dreams. The pendant Maisie had, the tattoo . . ." She blurted it all out, everything she knew about the sign of the eclipse. "It's *his* symbol. The angel's. If the other victims had it in their blood work, then he gave it to them."

Principal Sternholtz said, "This is what I was telling you about, Detectives. She thinks she's having 'visions.' It's the talk of the school."

Uncle Frank nodded but did not pursue that. Instead he latched onto something Dana had said. "What makes you think that the victims had Eclipse in their blood?"

"I . . . ," she began, and realized that she was dangerously close to outing Ethan. Even though she was mad at him, she knew this would destroy him. She took a breath and said, "Everyone's saying that they had taken drugs. I just assumed it was the same thing."

"Stop it," pleaded her father. "Stop lying and tell them the truth."

"We'll help you if you agree to help us," said Frank Hale. "We can take an anonymous statement. You're a minor and if you have information that can help us, then you need to tell us. Even though you don't have enough of the drug in your system to justify arrest, if you know the parties responsible for providing Eclipse to students here at FSK, then you need to speak up. If you're involved but decide to help us, the district attorney can make a deal. Immunity from prosecution. We have a lot of latitude at this point, Dana, but only if you help us."

Dana pounded her fists on the tops of her thighs. It hurt, but it also fueled her rising anger. "Look, are you all deaf? How many ways can I say this? I. Don't. Do. Drugs. Ever. If there's something in my blood, then I don't know how it got there. Check the school cafeteria. Check the water in the town reservoir. Check our coffeepot at home. How would I know where it came from? All I know is that I have never gotten high and I never will and this is all bull—"

"*Enough!*" roared her father. He stood up. "Dana, this nonsense has gone on long enough. I expected better of you." There was such a weight of disappointment and anger in his voice that it pummeled Dana until she slumped and turned her head away.

"Dad, I'm sorry, but I really need you to believe me."

"Believe you? Dana, you've done nothing but lie to me. To everyone."

"Captain Scully," said Sternholtz crisply, "as much as it pains me to do it, I see no other option but to suspend Dana pending a full review of this matter."

It was very clear that he was not pained at all. He was the only person here who seemed to be enjoying himself.

After everything else that had happened in the last few minutes, being suspended should have been minor. And yet it smashed into her.

"No . . . ," she began, but didn't know what else to say or how to react.

"Dana," said her dad, "you are going to go home and go to your room and stay there. Be thankful there wasn't enough of that stuff in your system for these detectives to arrest you. I'd take you myself, but I had to leave an important meeting to come here for this. I have to go back to the base. Go home. Give me your word you'll at least do that."

"Dad . . ."

"Please, Starbuck," he said, and his deep voice broke. "Please."

Dana reached for her father's hand, but her father stepped back. Stepped away from her. Stood out of reach. Stood ten thousand miles away in that cramped office.

"Go home," he said.

She was a crushed thing, a stepped-on bug. She was nothing.

The principal sat primly behind his desk, fingers laced, a smile almost showing itself on his mouth. The detectives wore their cop faces, which showed nothing. The nurse dabbed at tears in her own eyes.

Dana's face burned hot as the sun, but the room was cold. So this was how it would be. She walked from the room and took care to slam the door behind her on the way out as hard as she could.

CHAPTER 74

Dana got halfway home before her anger faded and a great sadness replaced it. The birds in the trees fell silent and shadows covered the sun as if it, too, were ashamed to look at her. As if it, too, had abandoned her.

She stopped at a corner and stood for a few moments, trying to make sense of things, trying to pinpoint the exact moment when everything had fallen apart.

Had it really started when they moved here to Craiger?

All her logical analysis crashed together in her thoughts. The case files, her mental catalog, what she knew and what she'd experienced. Corinda and Angelo.

She did not want to go home. That was going to be too much like showing up for prison on the first day of a life sentence. Dad hated her now—she was sure of that. Melissa was in trouble, too.

On the other hand, running away was not really an option. It sometimes *felt* like a plan, but there was no way to make it work. She didn't have money. She was a minor. She was a *girl*. She had no place to run to. There was no one who would risk taking her in. And Dad would find her. The cops would find her.

Maybe the angel would find her.

And that was a weird thought, because Angelo had been arrested.

Did that mean her visions would stop? After all, how could iron bars stop him from stepping into her dreams? Would he haunt her? Would he target her and try to destroy her? Or more correctly, destroy what was left of her life?

The street corner was empty, and no one stepped out from behind a tree to offer her answers or solutions.

"Ethan," she said aloud, surprising herself by speaking his name. And then she said, "Sunlight."

They were still out there. Sure, Ethan had been a jerk, but he was a friend. Maybe more than that. Would he help her? No, she decided, he probably wouldn't. His uncle Frank was the one who was heading up this investigation. Asking Ethan for help would be cruel and unfair. It would force him to make decisions that could only do him damage.

Which left Sunlight.

Dana turned and faced the direction that would take her to Main Street. She thought about going there, but then realized that Corinda would be there, and probably a lot of reporters. Even so, Sunlight was smart, and he was the most powerful psychic around. If anyone could help, he could. And maybe he would.

Thinking about how lost she was turned some of her fear and heartbreak back into anger. This wasn't fair. None of it was fair. She hadn't asked for any of this.

And it made no sense. Everyone lately had been asking her if she was getting high, that her eyes looked weird. She'd seen it in the mirror, too, but assumed it was from everything she'd been through. After all, she really did not take drugs. Just the thought of taking something that would take away some control of her thoughts and actions was both frightening and disgusting. She liked being in control. That was why she did not think she would ever want to do more of the astral projection she'd done with Sunlight. She imagined that was what being high might be like, and she wanted no part of it.

That did not explain the blood test. It didn't explain Eclipse.

How did she get that drug in her system? Seriously, how was it even possible? She demanded her mind to make sense of it. She went over everything she had eaten or drunk in the last few days. The only things she could not say for sure could not have been tampered with were the food at school and the stuff she ate at Beyond Beyond. She started walking again, not heading in any particular direction beyond "not home."

If it was the food at school, that could account for some of the victims having it in their system. But if it was cafeteria food, wouldn't everyone have been exposed? How could someone target specific students? Angelo worked there, but not in the cafeteria. On the other hand, the school janitors went everywhere, and they had keys to every door.

If it had been at Beyond Beyond, then it would make more sense. Angelo worked there, too, and it would have been pretty easy to tamper with a tea bag or a scone. Melissa hadn't been drugged, as far as Dana knew. She only drank coffee. So did that mean it *was* the tea?

The tea.

Yes. She had tea every time she went to Beyond Beyond. Every single time.

Dana felt a flush of excitement. Could she get into the place and get some of the tea bags? If Uncle Frank had them, he could do some kind of tests.

Her pace quickened, and she began to walk more definitively in the direction of Corinda's store.

CHAPTER 75

"There she is," said Danny.

He was Gerlach's driver today because the usual guy had called in sick again. So had the new guy. It was becoming a thing with anyone who spent a lot of time with the red-haired agent. Danny understood it. No one was sick. They were just afraid of Gerlach. The rumors among the lower-level agents was that Gerlach could sometimes get inside their heads. Danny knew it firsthand, and though it creeped him out, he could roll with it. Maybe if the other agents were there to watch the monitors and see what the angel was doing, they wouldn't be as freaked about Gerlach.

"I see her," murmured Agent Gerlach. He had his hat on, the brim pulled low so that it rested on his small, powerful binoculars.

"What's the call? Do we pick her up?"

"I haven't decided yet."

"Don't we have to, though? She can ID our boy."

Gerlach watched Dana Scully stride away from Francis Scott Key Regional High. He sat chewing his gum, saying nothing.

"She's moving," said Danny.

"I see that."

"She's not going home, though."

"I can see that, too," agreed Agent Gerlach.

"I thought that was the plan. She goes home and we take her."

Gerlach shook his head. "That was a possibly contingency. There are a lot of ways this thing could still go."

They watched Dana walk away.

"I could put a bullet in her from here," said Danny, reaching back to pat the sniper rifle in its case on the backseat. "One shot and we close the book on her."

"Maybe," said Gerlach. "That's another contingency."

"So . . . what are we supposed to do?"

"We follow her and see what she's up to."

Danny started the car. "Say, boss . . . what do we do about Angelo Luz?"

Gerlach gave that a few moments' thought. "That's a whole different problem," he said.

"Do we, um, have contingencies for that?"

The red-haired agent smiled. "We always have contingencies, kid."

The black sedan drifted along a block and half behind Dana Scully, moving silent as a shadow.

CHAPTER 76

Beyond Beyond
9:13 A.M.

"Dana," said Corinda, a bright smile blossoming on her face as she looked up from the counter. "I'm surprised to see you this early. Don't you have school today?"

Dana marched up to the counter and slapped both her hands down on it, making Corinda jump. There were only a handful of customers in the place, each dressed for yoga and heading toward the back, with their rubber mats rolled up under their arms. They glanced at Dana, clearly reading the fury and tension in the taut lines of her posture. Dana ignored them and leaned forward and nearly spat her reply at Corinda. "I got *suspended*."

"Suspended? Why?"

"You're the great psychic. I thought you'd already know."

Corinda's smile leaked away. "Okay, you're clearly upset. Your aura is crackling with negative energy."

"My aura's fine," snapped Dana. "My life's falling apart and it's your fault."

"Mine?" Corinda looked truly surprised. "How is it my fault that you got into trouble at school?"

"How? *How?*"

"Stop yelling."

"You went to the cops. You were all over TV. Your face is in the papers. I think you know."

Corinda hustled out from behind the counter, took her by the arm, and half led, half pulled her to the table on the other side of the screen. "You need to sit and calm down, Dana."

"Why? Because you don't want people to know what kind of egotistical jerk you are?"

"No, because this is a sacred place of spirit and there is a yoga class starting. Show some respect."

Dana lowered her voice but not her intensity. She sat with her back to the partition but leaned across the table to hiss at Corinda. "Sunlight was going to talk to the sheriff."

"I know."

"So why did you?"

"Because he was thinking about it and I didn't think we could afford to wait any longer. I did try to find him, though, but he was out. I waited as long as I could, and then I drove over to the sheriff's office."

"You made this all about you," said Dana. "You made this all about the great and powerful psychic Corinda Howell."

Corinda's eyes narrowed. "What exactly would you have had me do? Tell everyone that a fifteen-year-old girl was seeing angels and devils? That the dead were talking to you?"

"It's the truth."

"Sorry to break it to you, sweetie, but the truth isn't always the best thing. If I'd told the absolute truth, they'd have put you in the spotlight. What chance would you *ever* have for a normal life? They already think I'm weird. I'm the strange lady who runs that weirdo store in town and does tarot card readings and talks to the spirit world. That's me and that's who I am already. If people think I'm some kind of nut, it won't exactly be a news flash. But, Dana, you're new here in town. You're still a kid. I know what it's like to be strange in school. I was mocked and made fun of my whole life. I never had a chance for a normal life. Never. You still do. I can make it so that the thing that happened to you in the locker room was because of your exposure to me. I can sell that and people will buy it. The focus won't be on you, and after a while people won't even care about that. Not even the kids at school. The story is already so much bigger than your vision of Maisie that you aren't even mentioned in the papers. You're mad at me because I'm taking credit for it? Sure. Be mad, that's okay. And later on when you're able to make friends at school and meet guys and go to proms and have a regular life, maybe you'll take your ego out of high gear and realize that what I did was done out of empathy and compassion for you."

Dana sat there, stunned into silence.

Corinda reached across and took her hands. "I'm your friend, sweetheart. I always will be. I care enough about you that I can deal with you being mad and even hating me at the moment. It won't change how I feel, and it won't drive me away."

Dana was too confused by the rush of conflicting emotions in her heart and head to say anything. Corinda patted her hands and then went off to fetch tea and a muffin for her.

She set them down and then had to go off to ring someone up.

Dana stared at the little carrier of tea bags, and as she did so her fear and anger returned. Quieter now, though. She picked up one of the kind that she usually drank. The small paper label read SOOTHE. She sniffed it, then glanced around to make sure no one was looking as she quickly stuffed it into her backpack. There were three other Soothe tea bags, and she took a second one, stripped off the little paper tag, stashed the bag with the other one she'd taken, then took a plain tea bag of a common commercial brand, removed the tag, crumpled the SOOTHE tag around the string, then dunked the bag into her cup. She pushed the tea carrier away.

CHAPTER 77

Dana was about to get up to leave when she saw Sunlight come out of his Chrysalis Room. He wore baggy black pants like a modern dancer might wear, and a blue velour shirt embroidered with spinning planets and suns. He spotted her and came over quickly and slid onto the opposite bench seat. His handsome face was creased with concern.

"I hate to crib a line from the movies," he said, "but I sense a disturbance in your Force."

"You could say that."

"Is it because of the news story?"

"Kind of. How come you let Corinda take all the credit? I wanted you to talk to the sheriff."

Sunlight smiled. "She feeds on attention, Dana. I don't."

"But—"

"Give her some credit. She kept you out of it."

"Oh, yeah, I'm *so* out of it." She told him about the blood test and being suspended.

His smile did not waver. "Don't worry about it, little sister," he said. "I have every confidence that this is all going to work out. You'll be fine. I still intend to have my conversation with the sheriff, and I know Mr. Sternholtz as well. I can have a quiet word with him."

"You know him?"

"It's a small town, Dana, and I pay a lot of taxes. That gives me a forum for—shall we say—frank discussions."

"Oh. Well . . . that's . . ."

He shook his head. "Be calm, Dana. This terrible matter is coming to a close and you'll be fine."

"But what about Angelo?"

"Ah, poor Angelo." Sunlight shook his head. "I am seldom wrong about a person, but I was wrong about him. We all were."

"How?" she asked. "If you and Corinda have all these super psychic powers, how did you not know it was him?"

"Remember I told you that the angel had powerful qualities, too? This is what I meant. He clearly possesses the ability to block psychic perception. That's a great gift, and it's so sad that he used it for the wrong purposes."

She shook her head slowly. "I know that he's the angel, but I still can't believe it."

"That is the nature of charismatic personalities, Dana. They can convince you that they are angels or saints or people who can and should be trusted. Cult leaders and politicians have used the power of charisma for thousands of years. A psychic with control over his own charisma is to be greatly feared. I can only imagine what will happen during his trial. He is no doubt powerful enough to influence the minds of the prosecutor, the jury, and even the judge. Our legal system is not structured to cope with a person like him."

"What are you saying? That he'll get released?"

"It's possible. Which is why you need to continue developing your own qualities. I can teach you techniques of psychic defense."

She sipped her tea but didn't answer.

"This must all hurt you very badly," Sunlight said gently. "I don't need to be psychic to see the pain in your eyes. You liked Angelo, abrasive as he was."

"I liked a killer, great. At least until he chased me down the street. That says so much about me."

"You showed compassion and kindness to someone who had lived a hard life. Take that part of it and own it. It speaks to your character, Dana. Being fooled and lied to speaks to his."

She nodded. "Thanks."

"I expect I won't be seeing you for a while," said Sunlight.

"You're right, because I got suspended."

"But a suspension won't last forever, and even your father won't actually keep you grounded until you're old enough to retire."

"He'll try."

"He won't," Sunlight assured her. "Now . . . listen to me. I am going to help you figure this out. You're one of *mine* now. You belong to my spirit family, and we protect our own. I may not be as dangerous as Angelo Luz, but I have my moments. I have my qualities. And there is nothing I won't do to protect my family."

"I . . . don't know how to even . . ."

He shook his head. "You're dangerously close to blowing some important fuses, Dana. Here's what you need to do. Go home. Let your parents yell at you. Nod and look contrite and promise to be a good girl. Tell them whatever they need to hear so that they stop lashing out at you. Play the game their way and let them win this round. Then, when things cool down, they'll reward you for being a nice, obedient daughter who has clearly learned her lessons, and they'll lift their restrictions on you. So will the school. And then you'll come back here and we'll get to work. I'll teach you everything I can to make you as powerful as you can possibly be, and I believe that you possess incredible potential. Together we'll apply our qualities to what is going on in this town. If Angelo really is the angel, then we will get the proof that will make it impossible, even for him, to manipulate his way to freedom. We'll figure out who is selling Eclipse in Craiger and we will shut them down. As we *become* the most powerful versions of ourselves, we'll show everyone what people like us are capable of. Not just reading palms and telling fortunes, but being actual forces for good in a troubled world. That's what I offer, Dana." He held out his hand. "How does that sound?"

"It sounds . . . amazing."

She took his hand and shook it, and for the first time the clouds that had gathered in her life seemed to split open and let clean, clear sunlight spill down.

"Be strong and be patient," he advised. Sunlight gave her hand a final pump, and then he slid out of the booth and walked out of the store.

Dana watched him go, feeling her heart swell with admiration for him. He was like her mentor, sure, but more than that. Much more. Why hadn't her own father offered her that kind of love, trust, and support?

Her thoughts were interrupted by Corinda's voice speaking to a customer on the other side of the partition.

"Yes, I'm happy to help the sheriff's department in any way I can."

Dana half turned in her seat to listen. The customer was gushing about how wonderful it was that Corinda was using her gifts to help the town. Corinda was eating it up.

Then something occurred to Dana, and it made her blood run cold. She could *hear* everything that was said at the café register. The partition was, after all, nothing more than a piece of colored canvas over a wooden frame. And if she could hear Corinda have a conversation, what could Corinda hear from the booth behind her?

Dana thought back to the times she and Melissa had been here, and everything they'd talked about. Dana's visions, the angel, seeing Maisie in dreams and at school, the reaction of the teachers and other students . . .

Pretty much everything.

Every.

Single.

Thing.

Before she knew it, Dana was out of her booth. She all but pushed the customer away from the register and pointed an accusing finger at Corinda.

"You lied!" she yelled.

"What? Lower your voice," demanded Corinda.

"You're a fraud," cried Dana, her voice rising. "You're not a psychic, and you didn't *see* anything. You're a fake and a liar."

"Dana, I asked you to lower your voice."

People in the store were looking, eyes wide, gaping at the outburst, appalled at the scene Dana was making. But Dana did not care. She wanted to crawl over the counter and punch Corinda.

"You *heard* me and Melissa talking. That's how you know so much. You're about as psychic as a dead rat. God! How could I ever believe in someone like you? You snoop and eavesdrop, and then you pretend it's all stuff that came to you in *your* visions. What a joke! You're a slimy, backstabbing, egotistical—"

"*Shut up!*" roared Corinda with such force that it shocked Dana to silence. "Shut your mouth right now and get out of my store. Get out. No, don't say another word. Out. *Out!*"

She came around the counter and pushed Dana toward the side door. Corinda was tall and strong and filled with furious anger.

"You're a stupid girl who doesn't know what she's talking about. Go on. Get out of here and never come back."

And then Dana was on the sidewalk, watching Corinda pull the door shut. She watched through the big picture window as the customers inside the store came hurrying over to offer comfort to Corinda and throw hateful glares out at Dana.

CHAPTER 78

And so Dana headed home.

Home.

It should have been a beacon of hope promising an oasis of calm and of acceptance. As if. She trudged along the street, dragging behind her the wreckage of too many things. Despite Sunlight's encouraging words, Dana had to think about everything that had happened at Beyond Beyond.

That she was right about Corinda being a phony seemed beyond question. Everything that Corinda had said on TV and to her in their "sessions" could have come from things Dana said at the store. Maybe there were some things from Dana's session in the Chrysalis Room, but at this point Dana wouldn't have put it past Corinda to have bugged Sunlight's room. Maybe that was her whole thing—stealing information and insights from the people who trusted her. She was always gossiping in the store. Was that how she picked out details about the regular customers?

Every fiber of Dana's being screamed *yes*.

It saddened her as much as it made her angry. She'd trusted Corinda, and she'd trusted Corinda's abilities as a true psychic. Now so much was a lie.

Not all of it, whispered her inner voice. *Sunlight is real. Believe in him.*

She did, but even that felt fragile as spun glass.

Halfway home Dana saw a figure running toward her. Even from three blocks away she knew that run, knew that wild, curly, bouncing ponytail.

"Missy," murmured Dana, and there was a catch in her throat. She broke into a run to meet her sister, knowing that somehow they'd both cut through whatever tangle of knots had snared them last night. But as they closed on each other, Dana could see that there was something wrong. Melissa wasn't smiling. This wasn't going to be a happy reunion. She was scowling. Her face was twisted into a mask of pure anger and resentment.

"What's *wrong* with you?" cried Melissa from half a block away.

Dana skidded to a stop. "What are you . . . ?"

"She called Mom and she was crying on the phone, Dana," said Melissa with real heat as she slowed to a walk. "How could you do that to her? How could you say those things?"

"Corinda called home?" asked Dana, shocked by the news.

"Of course she did. Corinda cares about you. She's worried that you're going to do something stupid."

"Like what? Tell everyone that she's a phony and a liar?"

"No, she's afraid you're going to fly to pieces and maybe hurt yourself."

The two sisters stood facing each other, both of them flushed and angry, fists balled, eyes bright.

"She's a liar," Dana repeated.

"And you're an idiot. You had no right to say those horrible things to her in front of all her customers. She was so upset, and Mom had to calm her down. It's awful. I never thought you could be this mean."

"You're going to take her word over—"

"Over yours? Yeah, I guess I am. Who wouldn't? I heard about your drug test, Dana. I can't believe you didn't tell me. After all this, who would believe anything you say?" Melissa pointed toward home. "You should be lucky Mom took that call and not Dad. You were supposed to come home right from school. Mom called the office, and they pulled me out of class to go look for you. You'll be lucky if your suspension doesn't turn into you getting completely kicked out. Mom wants me to bring you home if I have to tie you up and carry you."

Dana opened her mouth.

"I don't want to hear it," snapped Melissa. "Mom said she won't tell Dad if you come home right now."

And there it was. No options, no way out. And no allies, even in her own sister.

Melissa turned and began heading home, fists still balled, shoulders rigid with anger. Dana followed like a prisoner going to the guillotine.

CHAPTER 79

Mom cried a lot. She asked the same questions everyone else had asked her. Dana repeated the same answers, but now it was like she was repeating lines in a script. Mom sent her to her room. No calls, no anything.

Later, though, there was a knock on the door, and when Dana opened it, she found a tray of food on the floor and heard Mom's footsteps on the stairs, retreating quickly so she didn't have to engage. It was horrible.

Dana slammed the door on the tray and sat on her bed all day and into the evening. Dad came home but did not come upstairs. Charlie played alone with toy spaceships in the front yard below Dana's window. Melissa turned on her stereo and played very loud, very tragic music.

When Dana heard the front door creak open, she listened and heard Mom and Dad on the porch, talking quietly. Mom sobbed every once in a while.

That was the opportunity Dana was waiting for. She opened her door very quietly and crept into the hall. Melissa's music was loud enough to provide good cover while Dana lifted the phone receiver and dialed a number.

Ethan answered on the sixth ring.

"I need to talk with you," said Dana.

"Yeah, I figured you'd call with everything that's going on," he said. "But it's going to have to be quick, because Uncle Frank just went to the store. He'll be back any minute."

"Ethan, I . . ."

"No, let me talk first," said Ethan. "First, I'm really sorry about what happened. I didn't say things right."

"It's okay," she said.

"No," said Ethan, "it's not. I don't know how to talk to girls, and I really like you. I'm sorry I hurt you."

She cleared her throat. "I like you, too, Ethan, and it *is* okay."

"Thanks. Look, I just hope you know this isn't your fault."

"No, it's Corinda's fault."

"Huh?" he said.

"Screwing up what we were doing. She heard me talking to Melissa, and that's where she got all the stuff to say."

"Dana, I'm not talking about that. I'm talking about what happened tonight. I thought that was why you called."

"What do you mean? I'm confused. I . . . I was afraid and . . . wanted to make sure you were okay and to see if your uncle came down on you. So . . . are you okay?"

"Me?" Ethan said. "Wait, you didn't call about Karen?"

"No, why should I? Karen's safe now. Angelo's in jail and—"

"Dana, don't you even watch the news?"

"What are you talking about?"

"It's all they're talking about. They just broke the story an hour ago. They found Karen Allenby in the school soccer field. Dana . . . she's been murdered."

CHAPTER 80

Dana slammed the phone down and ran to Melissa's door. She knocked but there was no answer, so she tried the knob, and the door opened. Melissa was on her bed with her feet propped up on the wall, ankles crossed. She turned her head with a great show of uninterest.

"Go away," Melissa said.

"Listen to me," barked Dana. "Someone just killed Karen Allenby."

Melissa swung her legs over and stood up, eyes wide. *"What?"*

"It's true, it's on the news. Ethan told me."

"How? Wait, you called him?"

"Yes, I called him. So what? Karen's *dead*. Don't you understand what that means?"

"I—"

Dana grabbed Melissa by the upper arms. "If Angelo's in jail, then he couldn't have done it. It means Corinda was lying. It means this is Corinda's fault. She got the cops to arrest Angelo instead of looking for the real killer. God, how could I be so stupid? I should have done something about this."

Melissa looked as dazed as if she had been hit by a stun gun. "Was it another car accident?"

"No," said Dana. "She was stabbed on the soccer field."

The horror of that—both the way Karen was killed and *where* she was killed—sucked all the air out of the room.

"We have to call Corinda," gasped Melissa. "Maybe Angelo had an accomplice and she can find out who it is. She'll help us and—"

"Gah, you're useless," growled Dana.

She shoved Melissa back onto the bed, spun on her heel, and ran from the room. She was halfway down the stairs when she realized that her parents were still on the porch. Then a figure stepped out of the shadows of the den. Gran. Smiling a strange and distant smile.

"You used to like to ride your bike, Margaret dear," asked Gran. "Why don't you ride your bike anymore?"

Dana blinked. "Bike? Great idea. Thanks, Gran."

She kissed her grandmother and took a step toward the backyard, but the old woman caught her arm and held her with surprising strength.

"Be careful, Dana Katherine Scully. So many people love you. So many people need you. Even some you haven't met yet."

"What?"

The clutching hand lost its strength and Gran gave her an empty smile. "You always loved your bike."

She let go and wandered back into the darkened den. Dana wanted to ask her what she meant, but there wasn't time, so she headed out the back door, grabbed a heavy hood-sweater off a peg by the door, took her bike from where it stood against the shed, and walked it quickly through the gate and down the back alley. She mounted it when she reached the cross street, and then she bore down and flew into the night.

It took no time at all to reach Main Street, and she cut right and raced in and out of traffic. It was after nine and there were only a few cars. She saw the sign for Beyond Beyond ahead of her. The window lights were off, and her heart sank, but as she skidded to a stop, Dana saw Corinda inside, standing beneath a single light, totaling the front register. Dana dropped her bike in the middle of the pavement and jerked open the door.

"Sorry, we're closed," said Corinda without looking up.

"Believe me," said Dana, "I'm not here to have my aura read."

Corinda looked up. "What are *you* doing here?"

"That's what I'm here to ask you," Dana fired back. "Did you hear the news?"

"What news? Did you go to the TV people to say that it's all you and that I'm nothing but a fraud? Isn't that the story you're telling people?"

"I want to punch you right now. *No.* I mean the news about Karen Allenby."

Corinda sighed impatiently. "What about her?"

Dana leaned on the counter and shouted it in Corinda's face. "*Karen's dead!* Someone killed her, and it wasn't Angelo Luz, because he's in jail thanks to you."

"No . . . ," said Corinda in a tiny voice. "No, that's impossible."

"Why? Because you're this big, infallible psychic? Because you're Corinda Howell and you can't be wrong? Well, guess what? All that psychic stuff is pure crap, and you know it. You're nothing. No, I'm wrong about that. You're responsible for Karen. Because of you, the cops stopped looking for who really killed everyone, and now Karen's dead and it's *on you.*"

"No, no, I told them what I knew. . . . This is wrong. It can't be true."

"What made you so sure it was Angelo anyway?"

"All the signs point to him, Dana."

"Signs? *Signs?* How about facts? How about evidence?"

"Belief does not require proof," said Corinda sagely, "not in the presence of true intuition."

"Are you out of your mind?"

"You don't understand. . . ."

"Understand what? You're saying you don't really have proof that Angelo is the killer? You told the police he was. You somehow convinced them."

"And what did he do? He ran away. I think that's proof enough."

"No it's not!" roared Dana. "All you do is lie and make excuses and hurt people, Corinda. What's wrong with you? Are you hiding something else? Is that it?" Dana pounded her fist on the counter. "Is that what this is all about? Are *you* the one who's helping the killer? Or are you the one selling that stupid Eclipse stuff? Is that what you put in my tea so I'd freak out? What did Angelo do to you? Did he know you were dealing drugs out of here and you lied about him to get him out of the way? I'll bet that's it."

"No, no, no, no, no, *no!*" babbled Corinda.

"Are you dealing drugs out of here? Did you slip me some Eclipse?"

"Don't be absurd."

"I'm serious as a heart attack, Corinda. They found it in my blood, and now I'm wondering if you used it to spike my tea."

"I would never do something like that, Dana, I swear," said Corinda, backing away so that her shoulders hit the partition hard enough to knock it from its hooks. It crashed down to the floor, exposing the booth behind it. Dana thought it was a great statement about how Corinda managed her whole psychic con game.

"I took some of those tea bags today," announced Dana, "and I'm going to turn them over to the cops. Then they'll come here and arrest you and lock you away forever."

"I never gave you drugs. God, I would never do something like that. You're only a kid."

"So was Karen. So were Maisie, Todd, Jeffrey, Chuck, and the others. We were all kids and you tore us apart. Maybe you didn't hold the knife, but it's all your fault. And you tried to blame poor Angelo."

"Angelo's a monster," snapped Corinda. "He's always sneaking around. Always listening at doors and sticking his nose where it doesn't belong. He knew every single one of the kids who died. Did you know that? No, I bet you didn't. They all came here for classes, and I saw Angelo talking to each and every one of them, one time or another. That's how he targeted them. He was using this store—*my* sacred space—to select his victims. If anyone slipped you Eclipse here, it was him. He *has* to be the one who did this."

"He's in *jail*."

Suddenly, the store lights went out and the whole place was plunged into darkness. Dana and Corinda both screamed.

Then there was a sound behind them, and a figure stepped out of the darkness in the back of the store, his face lit by weak light that slanted in through the windows. He was broad and muscular, and his clothes were streaked with blood.

"Angelo . . . ?" whispered Corinda as she stepped out from behind the counter.

Angelo took another step forward, and now the light glittered off the sharp knife he held in one bloody fist.

CHAPTER 81

Beyond Beyond
9:19 P.M.

"Corinda, run!" screamed Dana, and shoved the taller woman toward the front door.

"Don't," ordered Angelo.

Dana whipped a heavy glass tip jar off the counter and flung it at Angelo, catching him on the cheek. The glass exploded and he reeled away, throwing a hand up to shield his eyes. Corinda cringed back against the wall. Dana was caught in a moment of terrible indecision, and it rooted her to the spot.

Angelo was here, which meant he'd broken out of jail.

Karen was dead.

Angelo was covered in blood, and he had a knife.

Dana felt like the world's greatest fool, but instead of crippling her with self-hate, her fury welled up and focused like a laser on the monster who had destroyed her entire life.

She knew that she could not possibly hope to beat him.

It was stupid.

That thought flashed through her mind as she charged Angelo. He was still off balance, and she slammed into him with both hands outstretched, sending him crashing into a table of crystals. He hit the table and went over it, falling hard with a dozen wickedly sharp pieces of rutilated quartz crunching down on him. The silver knife went spinning off toward the back of the store. Dana jumped over the table and tried to land on his stomach with both feet, hoping to knock the wind out of Angelo, but he twisted away. Her feet thumped onto the floor beside him and one of her heels crunched down on Angelo's left hand. He cried out in pain and lashed out with his shin, sweeping her legs from under her, and she went down hard on her butt. Pain shot from her tailbone all the way up through her head, and she pitched sideways. Angelo climbed clumsily to his feet, bleeding from a score of cuts on his face and body.

"Stop it," he yelled, but then he staggered as Corinda stepped out of nowhere and hit him across the lower back with a big Australian didgeridoo that was longer and heavier than a baseball bat. She swung it awkwardly but with great force, and Angelo went flying into another table and fell with copies of astrology books scattering around him.

Dana reached for something to throw, but the table closest to her was full of little knickknacks and tribal fertility statues, most of them weighing less than half a pound. Even so, she began hurling them as fast as she could as once more Angelo fought his way back to his feet.

Despite being bashed and cut, he came up quickly and began slapping the figurines out of the air with one hand.

"Will. You. Stop. It," he said, punctuating each word with a hard slap.

"I got him," yelled Corinda, and she swung the didgeridoo again, but this time Angelo was ready. He stepped into the swing, caught the instrument with the same hand he had been using to deflect the figurines, and tore it from Corinda's grip. Angelo snarled and flung the thing halfway across the store, where it crashed through a mass of wind chimes.

Dana dived for one of the bigger chunks of quartz, but Angelo beat her to it and kicked it out of the way as deftly as a soccer goalie thwarting a shot.

"*STOP!*" he roared, with such force that it froze them all. He stood there, panting, shaking his head. "This isn't what you think."

"You killed them all," said Dana. "You're a monster."

He stared at her with a look that was nothing like what she expected. Instead of triumph or hate or contempt, Angelo's face crumpled into a mask of pain. Of grief. Tears glittered in the corners of his eyes.

"No," he said. "I never killed anyone."

"You killed Karen Allenby," said Dana.

He looked startled. "Karen's dead?"

"Don't play innocent. You killed her. That's her blood all over you. You broke out of jail and killed her."

"You're *loco, chica*. I broke out of jail to kill someone, but not Karen. No way. She was one of the nice ones. I'd never hurt her. I busted out of jail because no one believes me, and if I couldn't set things straight, they'd put me in the electric chair."

"You're a liar and a psychopath," said Corinda.

"You call me a liar? *Eso es gracioso*," he said. "That's really funny coming from you."

"Really?" sneered Dana. "You're a psycho, Angelo. You would have killed me last night if I hadn't outrun you."

"Outrun me? You really are *loco*," laughed Angelo. "After you freaked out at the school, I followed you to try to explain. I lost you for a moment, and then I saw you lying on the grass outside that house. I watched from across the street until you got up. I followed you every step of the way to make sure no one hurt you. You think *I* wanted to hurt you? If that's what you think, then you're nuts."

"Don't even try," warned Dana, hefting a sharp piece of quartz. "I found out that was Karen's house. Is that why you picked her, because you saw me in her yard?"

"That was Karen's house?" he said, seeming to be surprised. "I . . . didn't know that."

"Don't lie. You had that knife and you're covered with her blood."

"Her blood?" Angelo looked at his clothes and then at his right shoulder. He tried to raise that hand, but it only twitched, and Dana realized that during the entire fight, Angelo had only used his left hand. He licked his lips. "I . . ."

Then his legs suddenly buckled and he fell hard on his kneecaps.

Corinda took that moment to grab another didgeridoo, and she raised it to swing at his head, but Dana yelled, "*No!*"

Angelo sagged down and lay on his back. Dana crept toward him.

"Don't," warned Corinda. "It's a trick."

But Dana inched forward. There was just enough light coming through the window for her to see the hole torn in the shoulder of Angelo's orange jail jumpsuit. Blood, black as oil in that light, pumped weakly from the skin beneath. She bent close and saw what it was. She understood what it was.

Angelo had been shot.

She looked at him and he nodded. "Didn't get away . . . clean. Guards . . . Didn't get an artery . . . I think. But . . . it hurts." He tried to smile. "You two crazy ladies didn't help."

Dana knelt beside him, but she kept the chunk of quartz ready in case she had to smash him. "You said you broke out to set things straight. . . . What did you mean?"

"I mean this . . . wasn't me. . . . ," he said, his voice weaker than it had been a moment ago. "The newspeople . . . they interviewed a cop . . . and he said that they were looking to . . . connect the murders to . . . that drug."

"What drug?" asked Dana. "You mean Eclipse?"

He nodded weakly. "Eclipse was . . . never supposed to be out on the streets," he said. He was starting to breathe strangely, and blood was pooling under him. If the bullet wound had been bad before, then the fight had made it worse. "It was only for . . . helping people. That's why . . . it's given only . . . to people like . . . us . . ."

"What? What do you mean? What people?"

Angelo's eyes were becoming glassy, but he looked at her, and into her. "People . . . like you . . . and me. *Personas con cualidades, chica.*" He coughed, and blood flecked his lips. "You just . . . sit with it and . . . let it in. Ride the . . . smoke . . . so easy. That's what he . . . promised. No . . . addiction . . . no bad high . . . nothing illegal . . . you just let the visions . . . come . . ."

And that was when it all made sense to Dana. She stared at him as the pieces of the puzzle lifted from the wrong shape and fell back into place with perfect, cruel clarity. Then she turned slowly toward Corinda. The tall woman lowered the didgeridoo.

"The incense . . . ?" murmured Dana.

Corinda chewed her lip for a moment, looking worried, looking like she wanted to run. "It's supposed to help bring out psychic qualities," she said.

"Oh my God," breathed Dana. "It's not the tea. I've been breathing it ever since I started coming here for yoga, haven't I? For *weeks*. You've been getting me high for weeks. Why would you do this?"

"She didn't," said a voice. "The incense was only for special students."

Dana whipped around as a man walked slowly toward them from the back of the store. He wore loose black pants and a blue velour shirt embroidered with spinning suns and planets. He bent and picked up Angelo's knife.

"A good blade." He tossed it aside and drew another from under the hem of his shirt. "But I prefer my own," said Sunlight.

CHAPTER 82

Beyond Beyond
9:36 P.M.

And the world, which had been hanging on its last, twisted hinge, broke off and fell.

Dana stared in horror.

Corinda covered her mouth with a hand, as if trying to hold back the kind of scream that would tear her apart. On the floor, Angelo tried to rise, his body twitching and shuddering, but then he collapsed back and lay still, arms and legs spread wide.

Standing at the edge of the shadows, Sunlight looked from one to the other and then back at Dana. "And now, my girl, do you understand?"

Dana said nothing.

"Are you ready, Dana, to help me wash this world clean of sin and weakness and impurity?"

Her lips moved, and Dana heard herself echo the words. "Wash it clean? How?"

"With blood, of course," said Sunlight, taking a few small steps forward. "That is always the way. Blood is the life. No, let me be more precise: blood is the pathway to life. We are all born in blood, are we not? Born in blood and pain, screaming our way into this world. This is no different. The Red Age is upon us, and we sacred few will usher it in. We will be the midwives for the birth of a better world to come."

"You're—you're—"

"The word you're fumbling for is 'prophet,'" he said. "And every prophet must be mad by the standards of the ordinary world, for they see a different world that is beyond the vision of the sheep. For thousands of years, people like us—yes, *us*—have been hunted and stoned and crucified and burned because we see a larger world than the rest of the human herd can ever see. And in each age of the world, when a prophet comes to preach of a better world to come, he is killed. His own blood is spilled as a sacrifice to stupidity and fear and closed-mindedness. The Christ of your faith was beaten and whipped and nailed to a tree for speaking of a better world to come. There have been many others. That ends here, with me, with us, tonight."

"No," said Dana, but she was almost hypnotized by his words. Sunlight spoke gently, quietly, without hysteria or force. He spoke reasonably, as if they both shared this place and this destiny. Dana felt herself hanging on his words.

"Don't listen to him, Dana," warned Corinda, but her voice sounded like it was a million miles away. Faint and meaningless.

"I told you about people with qualities, Dana," continued Sunlight, stepping closer still. "I had my flock, my apostles. You've seen them here, coming and going from my psychic enrichment sessions. They were among the strongest of those like you. Like us. Each had special gifts. Each was in the process of *becoming* something else, of breaking free of the shell of *was* and emerging into the state of *will be*. Do you understand?"

Dana felt herself nod.

"I selected each and guided them, cultivated them like the rare flowers they were. And when they were strong enough, I introduced them to the secrets of the Red Age. But"—and here Sunlight looked genuinely sad—"not everyone is suited to higher concepts. Not everyone has the courage, the depth of compassion, or the vision to do what is necessary to save the world from itself."

"And you killed them?"

"Of course I did. I released them from their weakness and sent them flying into the ether toward a next and hopefully better incarnation, where more of their *nephilim* heritage will shine forth. Their deaths fueled the doorway that will open us to the Red Age."

"Oh my God . . . ," whimpered Corinda. The didgeridoo dropped from her hand and clattered to the floor. No one even noticed.

"The Eclipse was wasted on them," said Sunlight. "It's so rare, so difficult to obtain, to refine. The chemistry is boggling, but the effects are sublime. For the ordinary ones, the sheep, it's a cheap high that lasts a few hours and goes away without side effects. No addiction, no tissue deterioration. Ah, but for those with qualities, there is a completely different chemical reaction. It sinks deep and lives in the blood. It *sings* in the blood. And it turns on all the lights until the mind blazes like the rays of the sun shining out from the occluding moon. A light that cannot be hidden. How lovely, how beautiful."

He took another step and now stood a few feet from Dana.

"You've felt it, haven't you, my girl? Your mind had been closed and now it's open. Gloriously, wonderfully open. Burn one stick a day, every day, and soon your qualities will blossom at an exponential rate. Dana, you could become as powerful as me. You could share the power with me. You could help me save the world, transform it, *rule it*."

"Yes," she murmured, and now it was she who took a step toward him. The small crucifix that hung beneath her blouse seemed to suddenly grow hot against her skin.

Sunlight smiled at her, and there was so much love in his eyes. Like a father's love was supposed to be. Like any love should be. Completely accepting, completely open. Allowing her to be who she was. Encouraging her to become whatever she wanted to be.

"You are my angel," he said as he brushed a strand of red hair from her cheek. "And together we will give birth to the age of angels and giants. Together we will bathe this world in blood."

"Yes," said Dana. "Blood."

And then she hit him with the fist-sized chunk of quartz as hard as she could.

The chunk of crystal smashed into his cheek, ripping the skin, cracking the bone, sending Sunlight reeling, the smile disintegrating from his screaming mouth.

Dana chased him, swinging the stone with savage force as one long, inarticulate scream tore itself from deep in her chest. Sunlight staggered and went down to one knee, throwing an arm up to fend off her attack. She struck his arm, battering it aside, and hit him again and again, striking shoulder, head, chin, chest. He twisted around and stabbed at her, and Dana felt a line, hot as lava, open up across her ribs. She screamed even louder and tried to smash at the knife hand.

Sunlight was hurt, but he was fast.

Very fast.

He ducked under her next swing and punched Dana in the stomach with his left hand and then tried to drive the knife into her chest. But Dana flung herself backward and down, trying to back-roll like she had been taught in jujutsu, flubbed it, rolled like a flat tire, and crashed into a table filled with charms and jewelry, which rained down on her. Sunlight staggered to his feet and started toward her, but then jerked to a stop. He looked down in surprise to see Angelo, more than half-dead, clutching his ankle with one bloody hand.

Sunlight gave him a contemptuous sneer. "You could have been one of us, too, boy. Such power. Such potential. Such a waste." He raised his other foot and stamped down on the bullet-torn shoulder. Angelo began to howl but then abruptly collapsed back. Unconscious or dead, Dana could not tell.

So she threw the chunk of quartz at Sunlight and hit him squarely between the shoulders. It sent the man catapulting forward, crashing into another pair of display tables, where he collapsed with books and more crystals hammering him into the floor.

But again he rose, sweeping the debris away with a furious backhand swipe.

"Enough!" he roared. His face was a mass of blood, and one eye was beginning to puff shut. He rose into a crouch, the knife in his hand, the edge gleaming with silver fire. "I gave you a great gift, girl, and I took a terrible risk to do it. I should hand you over to the men who run this little science project of a town. You think I'm a monster? They're so much worse." He grinned with bloody teeth. "You have no idea what's in store for you. Or . . . what would have been in store for you. You'll never find out. I will send you screaming into the darkness."

He slashed at her with the knife, and Dana felt the tip draw a burning line—hot as flame—across her stomach. She stumbled backward several steps. The pain was incredibly intense, and for a moment she stared down through torn cloth at the blood that welled from a long cut.

"God . . . ," she murmured. Half a statement of shock, half a prayer.

Sunlight laughed and raised the knife and advanced on her, slashing at her throat.

"No!" screamed Corinda, and she snatched up a small table and flung it at Sunlight, craft jewelry and all. The table caught Sunlight on the side of the head and knocked him down. Then she grabbed Dana's wrist.

"Let's go," she yelled, and pulled her toward the door. Dana resisted at first, wanting to finish this, but Sunlight was already getting up. Could nothing stop the man? What *was* he?

He bared his teeth like a wolf and began moving toward them.

Dana and Corinda ran, leaping over fallen tables as they fought to reach the door. Dana had no idea how seriously she was hurt, but she could still move. She was still alive.

Despite everything, Corinda pushed Dana out first and turned to block Sunlight's way. The knife flashed, and she went down with a cry as sharp and high as a seagull's. But even as she fell, she wrapped her arms around Sunlight's waist to try to slow him down.

"Run . . . ," she wheezed. "Dana . . . *run*."

Dana ran.

Her heart was broken, but she ran.

She wanted to stand and fight, to beat this man, to crush him. To kill him. But she did not think he could be beaten.

And so she ran. She felt blood running down under her clothes.

She heard him running behind her.

Fast. Despite everything, so fast.

Catching up before she was even halfway across the street. In the windows of the darkened store on the other side, she could see the reflection of her own body running and the man behind her, so close, reaching out with one hand to grab, holding a bloody knife with the other.

Suddenly, headlights dazzled her and there was a car. Right there. Horn blaring. The engine roaring but no sound of squealing brakes. The car was accelerating toward her.

She heard the awful crunch.

But it was not her body that was lifted and flung through the air. Dana staggered, tumbled, fell. She sprawled in the street, inches from the far curb, and turned, her whole body a mass of pain, and saw Sunlight strike the parked cars on the far side. Saw the car that hit him finally brake, skid and crash into one of the parked cars.

She knew that car.

It made no sense, but she knew it.

She heard doors open, and figures silhouetted against the headlights. A slim figure coming from the driver's side, a bulky figure emerging from the passenger side. A smaller figure coming out of the backseat.

They ran toward her.

"Dana!" cried Melissa.

"Oh my God," cried Mom.

"No, no, no," moaned Dad as they surrounded her, gathered her in, held her safe.

In the doorway across the street stood Corinda, one hand clamped to her bleeding side. On the ground, sprawled like a scarecrow, was Sunlight. His fingers opened and closed, opened and closed. Still alive.

But he wasn't getting up.

Then there was a new sound. A wail. And lights. Red and blue. People. More faces. She looked up and saw Uncle Frank and Detective Simpson. She saw other deputies. She saw people. Far above the street, she saw lightning flash in the sky, painting the edges of the storm clouds with white fire.

Mom held her close and Dad bent to kiss her head, and Melissa held her hand.

CHAPTER 83

She lay bundled in blankets on the couch, day after day.

She had stitches in her knee and stitches across her abdomen, and three stitches in her hairline. She had no idea where those came from. It didn't matter.

Dana did not have to go to school. School came to her. Mr. Sternholtz and the nurse stopped by. They brought flowers. They apologized. She said very little to them, and they went away.

Uncle Frank Hale came by with his partner. The detectives told her that they found Eclipse in the incense. They had testimony from Angelo Luz and Corinda Howell. No one believed Dana had willingly taken drugs. She didn't say much to them, and they went away.

The school sent a psychologist. The hospital sent one, too. They told her that her visions were not visions at all, but merely the result of the Eclipse drug. At first Dana protested and argued, but with each day it became easier to believe that it had been just that. She had been drugged, and nothing she saw, dreamed, or remembered could be trusted. There were so many lies and betrayals wrapped up with Sunlight and Corinda and Eclipse that Dana wished she could carve it all out of her head.

The psychologists seemed happy with her newfound perspective. They smiled at her. And eventually they stopped coming around.

Corinda was in the hospital, but she was also on the news. On every channel and in the papers. Somehow she had become the one who had taken down a madman who called himself Sunlight.

Angelo was on the news, too. A tiny, passing reference about charges being dropped. No one interviewed him. He was in the hospital and would be for weeks, and the doctors weren't sure he was going to pull through. Blood loss, shock, and severe trauma had pushed him all the way to the edge. That hurt Dana. She prayed for him every night, clutching her gold cross.

Ethan came over and sat with her every day after school. He brought her flowers and chocolate and books. They held hands and they didn't say much. There would be time for that, though.

"What's your verdict?" he asked one afternoon.

"About what?"

"All that psychic stuff. ESP, becoming, all of that. Everyone in the science club's been hammering on me to ask you what you really think. Now, I mean. After all this. Does any of it make sense to you?"

"It's a trust thing," she said after giving it some long, serious thought.

"Trust?" asked Ethan. "What do you mean?"

"Everyone lied to me about it. It was all . . ." She stopped and shook her head. "I can't even think about it now without feeling sick. I *trusted* them. I opened my heart to them, and they just made a fool out of me."

"Yeah, but where's that leave you? Aren't you supposed to have ESP?"

"Who knows? I was being drugged the whole time. If so, I want to shut it off. It's not like it's done anything good for me. Everyone I know got hurt by it." She shook her head again.

"Are you saying none of it was real?" asked Ethan. "Your visions were accurate."

She took her time with that. "I . . . don't know. There are some parts that I guess I can't explain. The visions I had before we moved here. And how I saw Maisie so clearly, with such detail. If Eclipse made me see visions, then why did I see her? How could a drug make me know so much about her? I mean, what was that? What if it was just the power of suggestion, picking up details from Bible stories and the news?"

"Tisa insists that ESP is real," said Ethan, "and she's a pretty hard sell for anything weird or spooky. She thinks it's a part of science that we just haven't figured out how to measure or test yet."

"Maybe. If so, then I'll wait until we *can* measure it. Until then, I can't trust it."

"Then what do you trust, Dana?" he asked.

"Science," she said. "This whole thing came down to that. Chemistry, psychology, forensic science. That's all it really is, and if that's what it is, then I can deal with it. So . . . yeah, science. I like science. I can trust science."

"So does that mean you want to be a forensic scientist, too?"

She thought about Angelo, hovering on the edge of death in the hospital. She touched her crucifix. "Angelo could still die," she said. "I wish I could help him. When he was there bleeding, I blanked. I should have applied a compress. I could have done something, but I didn't."

She sat quietly for a moment. "I held a garter snake once while it died in my hands." Ethan raised his eyebrows but didn't press. "I won't ever let that happen again," she vowed. "If I can help someone like that, I want to." She thought about it and shook her head. "No, you can keep forensic science, Ethan. It's cool and all, but it's too far away from people."

"Which leaves you doing what?"

"I don't know," she said, shrugging. "Maybe medicine."

After he left, Melissa came and sat down on the end of the couch farthest from Dana. They looked at each other, and it took a long time before either of them spoke. Melissa wore a new strand of crystals around her neck, one Dana had never seen before. A recent purchase or a gift? In either case, Dana knew where it had come from.

"You're wrong about her," said Melissa.

"About Corinda?" Dana snorted and shook her head. "Oh, come on, Missy, you can't sit there and tell me you still believe in her."

"Of *course* I do. She saved your life, Dana."

"She lied about everything."

Melissa shook her head. "She told the truth every time."

"She lied about Angelo."

"She's human," snapped Melissa. "Anyone can make a mistake. Besides, it was Sunlight blocking her from seeing the whole truth."

"So what is it?" demanded Dana. "Did she make a mistake or was it Sunlight?"

"Both. Corinda is doing everything she can to help you, to help everyone in this town. If it wasn't for her, you'd be dead, and the killings would never stop. Did you ever think about that?"

Dana stared at her. "I . . . I don't even know how to respond to that."

"That's because you know I'm right."

Dana turned away and stared at the wall. "No, that's not what I know."

Melissa said nothing. When Dana glanced over a few minutes later, her sister was gone. She hadn't heard her slip away.

She felt it, though.

The family moved through the crisis like people recovering from a hurricane or a tornado. They found their way back to routines. Dad spent a lot of time at work. Mom and Charlie drifted back into their quiet inner lives. Gran was Gran.

Melissa was there, but there was something different about her. Or maybe it was about how they were together. Melissa still believed in Corinda, in her powers, in her insights. Dana did not.

What she believed was that Sunlight was a madman. Corinda was a liar.

And Dana could feel her heart change. It did not actually break, but it went cold. She felt that happen. The world went colder, too. It shrank from the larger world into something that made more sense, even if it was an uglier thing.

She thought a lot about God and the devil. About good and evil. All of her life Dana had accepted "evil" as a part of the world without stopping to consider what it actually was. Or what it meant. Now she had no choice but to look at it as more than a Sunday school concept, as something alive in the world. In her world.

She had seen evil. She'd looked into its eyes.

She did not, however, understand it. Was evil something the devil put into the hearts and minds of human beings? That would be the easy answer.

It wasn't answer enough, though. Not for her. Not anymore.

Dana wondered if evil was something humans had invented. That was horrible, but it also seemed to make more logical sense to her. It meant that people, good and bad, had to be responsible for who they were and for what they did.

Sunlight was evil. She was sure about that.

Why, though? Was he sick? Was he damaged from some kind of abuse? That was what the newspapers were saying. The reporters went on and on about it, talking about "nature" and "nurture." About what his own biology was responsible for and about what the influences in his life did to shape him. If that was true, then did that make him evil or sick?

But . . . what if it wasn't true? There were plenty of people who suffered abuse. Only a tiny fraction of them ever hurt someone else. It wasn't an excuse that made sense to Dana. It wasn't logical.

Nature? Nurture?

That wasn't a definition of evil. And as she thought about it deep into one lonely night, she realized that for any of this to make sense, for *Sunlight* to make sense, there must be a third option.

Nature.

Nurture.

And choice.

That, she thought, was what evil was.

It made sense. It fit logic, it squared with science. But it also scared her so badly she stayed awake all night. Dana knew that, like all truths, now that she knew it, she could not un-know it.

For some people, evil was a choice.

EPILOGUE

-1-

County Road 63
Near the Craiger City Line
April 10, 11:11 P.M.

The deputy driving the patrol car killed the siren as soon as he crossed the city limits but left the blue-and-red flashing lights on as he drove into the country. He and his partner sat in tense silence.

The night was immense, with mountains of clouds revealed in flashes of lightning from the coming storm. Wind shear tore and shaped the clouds, so the front wall of the storm looked like towering cliffs that rose thousands of feet above Craiger. Lightning inside the clouds revealed cracks and veins, as if the whole sky could split apart and collapse onto the town.

There was no traffic this far out. The driver clicked on the high beams as he searched for the unpaved side road that led to a quarry that had been abandoned in the sixties.

Up ahead, a pair of headlights clicked on and off, on and off.

The deputy pulled to a stop thirty feet away, tires crunching on old gravel and twists of dead vine. The cars sat there for half a minute with nothing moving except the flashers. Then the doors of the black sedan opened. The gleaming, highly polished paint job of the car was as intensely black as the suits of the two men who got out. The men walked slowly over to the sheriff's department car. One of the men twirled his finger to indicate that they should lower a window. The driver did.

"Let's do this," said the shorter of the two men in black suits. His red hair looked almost black in the wash of red-blue lights.

The deputies exchanged a look but did not move. Agent Gerlach reached into his inner pocket and withdrew an envelope. He pretended to give it to the driver, pulled it back, chuckled, and then handed it over.

"Don't be a smart-ass about this," said the deputy behind the wheel. "We're earning this."

"Sure," said Gerlach.

The cops both peered into the envelope, and the second deputy used his thumb to riffle the sheaf of fifty-dollar bills. There were a lot of them. They nodded to each other, and the deputy riding shotgun put the envelope of money in the glove compartment. They both got out. The second deputy drew his service revolver while his partner jerked up the handle to open the back door. He reached in and yanked the prisoner out. Sunlight fell heavily to the ground, groaning in pain. His face was smeared with blood, his eyes puffed shut, one ear nearly torn off. He rolled up onto his knees and spat blood into the dirt. There were small fragments of tooth in that mess. His hands were securely cuffed behind his back.

"He looks like crap," said Danny, who was the driver of the black sedan.

"Guess he messed with the wrong little girl," laughed one deputy.

"I guess so," agreed Gerlach. They were all laughing when Malcolm Gerlach drew his automatic and shot both deputies. Twice in the body and once in the head. Six quick, precise, efficient shots.

His driver looked away briefly, took a breath, nodded to himself, and pulled Sunlight to his feet. The killer stood there, swaying, only half-conscious.

Gerlach walked around to the passenger side of the patrol car, leaned in, thumbed open the glove box, and removed the envelope of money. He peeled off one fifty and squatted down, then tucked it partly under the leg of one of the cops. He let two others blow into the bushes, then walked over and pushed them more securely into the branches of some roadside brush.

"Why'd you do that?" asked his partner.

"It'll confuse things," said Gerlach. "The bills are from a bank job in Reno four years ago. No arrests were made. They'll drive themselves nuts trying to connect that to this."

Sunlight watched all this, his puffy eyes shrewd, his body tensed for whatever was going to happen next.

"So, what's your plan for me?" he asked, his voice thick with pain and missing teeth. "Will they find me on the road, killed while trying to escape?"

Gerlach and Danny exchanged a look, and then they cracked up laughing. It was a short laugh. Brutal. Then Gerlach fished a handcuff key out of his pocket and unlocked Sunlight's cuffs.

"People have invested a lot of money in you, sport," said Gerlach. "Just 'cause you screwed this up doesn't mean you're done working for the Man. The project has to go on."

"I want—"

"No," said Gerlach. "This isn't a conversation. Get in the car. There's a plane waiting."

Sunlight studied Gerlach for a long time. Then he gave a single nod, turned, and walked toward the waiting sedan. Danny stood with Gerlach in the gap between the two dead sheriff's deputies. The road was on a hill, and far below they could see the small lights of Craiger with the towering clouds rising above it. The humid air distorted the image so that the whole town seemed to tremble in awful anticipation.

"So what's our next move?" asked Danny. "Do we try to find a new angle with the Scully girl?"

"No. Dana Scully's a dead end," said Gerlach.

"Her dad'll be happy."

The red-haired agent chewed his gum for a moment before answering. "We're not in the business of making Bill Scully happy, kid. He does what he's told because he knows what will happen if he doesn't."

Danny nodded. "What do we do about Sunlight's painting at the church? Some creative arson or . . . ?"

"Nah. Those two drivers who keep calling in sick? Put them on it. Scrape the walls, dispose of all the evidence. Wipe it all down."

"With all that blood and stuff? They'll hate it."

"Kind of the point."

Danny grinned and nodded again. They looked at the lights of the little town.

"Okay," he asked. "So what do we do now?"

"Now," said Gerlach, "we go to Plan B."

-2-

Scully Residence
April 16, 2:26 A.M.

It had been ten days since the fight at Beyond Beyond. The doctor at the hospital had called to say that Angelo Luz was out of danger.

Dana fell asleep a little past two in the morning. Mom and Dad had said that she could stay home from school for as long as she wanted. That was good, because all she wanted to do was sleep.

And she did sleep.

Soundly, deeply, and for the first time since the Scullys had moved to Craiger, without dreams.

No dreams, no visions, no nightmares.

She smiled as she slept.

-3-

FBI Headquarters
Washington, DC
April 16, 11:48 P.M.

Special Agent Delbert Albritton looked up as his office door opened. People rarely came down to this remote corner of the building, and usually only because they had lost their way or had bad directions. He couldn't remember the last time someone came to see him. And never this late. It was why Albritton preferred to burn the midnight oil.

The man who entered his office was tall and wore a plain gray suit and quiet tie. He wore no name badge, but Albritton knew who he was. He'd heard stories about this man, and some of those stories scared him more than the cases Albritton investigated in his underfunded, one-man division.

"Can I help you, sir?" asked Albritton.

The tall man glanced down at the folder that had landed on Albritton's desk less than an hour ago. The folder lay open to show photocopies of official reports from the Craiger sheriff's department, and surveillance photos of several dozen people, including a pretty girl with red hair. The man considered the contents; then he reached down, slid a fingernail under the edge of the folder, and closed it.

"What are you doing?" asked Albritton.

The man gave him a small, cold smile. "This case is closed. There's no need for any further action."

"But I just got it."

The tall man fished in his jacket pocket for a pack of Morley cigarettes, shook one out, clicked on the flame from a steel lighter, and took a long drag.

"Excuse me," said Albritton, "they don't let us smoke down here. The ventilation is bad."

The man exhaled blue smoke. "We can get the ventilation fixed, agent."

He glanced down at the closed folder.

"Be seeing you around."

And he left, leaking smoke from his nostrils like a dragon. Ⓧ

DON'T MISS
FOX MULDER'S STORY

ACKNOWLEDGMENTS

Thanks to Chris Carter, Gillian Anderson, and *The X-Files* team. Thanks to Josh Izzo at Fox for helping me navigate the minefields. Special thanks to my editor/publisher, Erin Stein, and my fellow *X-Files* chronicler, Kami Garcia. Thanks to Ted Adams of IDW Publishing for first inviting me in to play in the world of aliens, monsters, and conspiracies. Thanks to Ashleigh Ammari for Japanese translations.

SMITH | HOWELL
HOUSER | FENOGLIO
THE X FILES™
ORIGINS
THE HIGHLY ANTICIPATED GRAPHIC NOVEL FEATURING THE BEGINNINGS OF THE ICONIC AGENTS LANDS THIS FEBRUARY!
IDW
WWW.IDWPUBLISHING.COM
Full Color • 140 pages • $19.99
The X Files ™ & © 2017 Twentieth Century Fox Film Corporation. All Rights Reserved.
COMIC SHOP LOCATOR SERVICE
COMICS
888-COMIC-BOOK
comicshoplocator.com

Trust

No

One